TASK LYST

a novel

BY SCOTT HYLBERT

TURNER PUBLISHING COMPANY

Turner Publishing Company
Nashville, Tennessee

www.turnerpublishing.com

Task Lyst

Cover design: Kenny Holcomb
Book design: Tim Holtz

Library of Congress Cataloging-in-Publication Data

Names: Hylbert, Scott, author.
Title: Task lyst : a novel / by Scott Hylbert.
Description: Nashville, TN : Turner Publishing Company, 2019. |
Identifiers: LCCN 2018049262 (print) | LCCN 2018051821 (ebook) | ISBN 9781684423187 (ebook) | ISBN 9781684423163 (pbk.) | ISBN 9781684423170 (hardcover)
Classification: LCC PS3608.Y545 (ebook) | LCC PS3608.Y545 T37 2019 (print) |
DDC 813/.6–dc23
LC record available at https://lccn.loc.gov/2018049262

9781684423163 paperback
9781684423170 hardcover
9781684423187 eBook

Printed in the United States of America

To Ashley, Henry and Annie

CHAPTER 1

A MEDINA IS A GREAT PLACE TO GET LOST. *Particularly in the blue pearl of Chefchaouen, located in the gem of Africa that is Morocco. For one American and three other travelers who'd met only days before on a beach in Barcelona, it provided a sanctuary from the madness outside the old walls, which, while exotic and charming, had become exhausting in a short time. Notorious for being awash in blue hues, the residential and commercial structures lined tight, mazelike alleys that snaked up and around the quaint, hilly town on the base of two peaks of the Rif Mountains. Chefchaouen got its name from these twin peaks, which resemble two horns of a goat. It was a tranquil destination to escape from the manic grind of main-street tourism, not typical of where most visitors to Morocco would venture, unless they wished to experience a slower-paced, small-city setting and maybe to hike the mountainous terrain—or if they held a deep, scholarly obsession with the Rolling Stones.*

The terraced hotel, or pension, was quiet and mostly vacant and offered a view of the vastness of Morocco's topography: rugged mountains giving way in some distance to beachy coast, and a sun setting beyond in the direction of America. An occasional whiff of hashish permeated the open air. It was dusk, and an orange glow danced against a stark blue sky just as Henri Matisse would have seen it. Echoes of evening prayers hypnotized the foreigners who felt, at last, that they'd truly vacated their programmed realities. The floor was cool to bare feet, warmed by area rugs positioned around the rooms.

Yes, negotiating the legendary market, known as a souk, in Fez had been hectic—shopkeepers offering tea and conversation with unbridled enthusiasm. The American repudiated relentless come-ons from individuals offering to serve as guides until it finally was evident that a guide was necessary, if only to cease the never-ending offers. So much for rugged individualism. The travelers weren't ready to buy rugs and trinkets. Somewhere near here, Keith Richards had rescued

Anita Pallenberg from his bandmate Brian Jones' abusive clutches in a 1967 road trip that combined betrayal, romantic love, and chivalry for the modern age. Chefchaouen hadn't changed a whole lot since then, but the world outside had. In fact, it had lost Brian, founder of the Rolling Stones and a victim of his own ambition. He had lost himself on that trip, if not before. Abandoned by his better angel, his old lady, his bandmates, his creation. Left to listen to the millennia-old pipes of Pan, alone in Joujouka.

CHAPTER 2

ALICE SEEGAR PORED OVER THE FINANCIALS OF TASK LYST, a start-up company seeking a second round of venture funding. She twirled a red ink pen with the fingers on her left hand. It was up to her, as a senior associate, to decide whether or not to recommend the investment to the partners at Blue Hill Capital, a prominent Silicon Valley venture capital firm.

"An online exchange," the company described itself. "A secure, open-market app for swapping services." Examples included lawn mowing, dog sitting, and odd jobs. But where was the revenue? She wrote a memo explaining Task Lyst as the latest arrival to the increasingly saturated gig economy. It was like several other tech companies she'd reviewed exploiting the side-hustle craze with the same dubious upside. Her impulse conclusion? Pass.

Yet Alice was reticent. The crowdfunding deal that had imploded after a year of due diligence still haunted her, and she needed a sure thing to justify her seat and keep her on the track toward partner. She considered options. Opening a yoga studio was a nonstarter, incompatible with her graduate school loans. The music business had shrunk since her early dalliance with it. No, she was in the big sandbox and would need to survive somehow. Her third-floor window looked westward over Interstate 280 toward Portola Valley. It would be good to get a trail run in before dark, she thought. She placed the pen over her ear and under strands of ginger-blonde hair that maintained just enough body to avoid being called thin. In her reflection on the idle computer screen, she searched for any sign of aging or imperfection amid freckles and minimal makeup that most envied as wholesome, girl-next-door looks. Her style was more or less the same as it had been during her undergraduate days at a leafy liberal arts college some called "the Harvard of the Midwest," but now, with much of her thirties in the rearview, she was becoming increasingly conscious of the biological clock ticking as she journeyed deeper into her professional career. An instant message popped up on her screen.

"You sure? Nothing there? Gordie was gushing over this at the board meeting last week." The instant message was from Larry Chang, a pal from Stanford Business School and a newly knighted principal at Blue Hill. Larry, who sat on the firm's advisory board, was enjoying a hot streak. Alice thought Larry was an upbeat guy, sharp, but a little reckless when it came to scrutinizing numbers. Still, it seemed to be working out for him.

"But what does he know (lol!)" Larry added.

"He" was John Gordon, or "Gordie," the firm's founding partner and one of the Valley's venture capital legends who'd made early bets on several dot-coms, including Google and PayPal. Alice couldn't figure out why he'd be interested in something she saw as very small potatoes.

She replied, "I don't see it. The revenue model isn't scalable, no barrier to entry, existing competition."

Larry answered, "Your call. I'm out tmw. Golfing Pebble with clients and then some me time in Big Sur, meditation and yurt camping."

"You spend more time recharging than charging." She liked to razz Larry about his idiosyncratic lifestyle choices.

"You should try it sometime. A microdose with that Pacific Ocean view will unveil all the mysteries of a tricky business plan. Plus all the influencers are hanging out down there. I ran into the Chief Technical Officer of Tesla naked in the hot springs at Esalen last time."

"Jealous, enjoy," she typed.

Alice made it through traffic with enough time to run the six-mile Portola Valley loop. She stretched her athletic frame and warmed up to a new indie playlist that her sister had shared with her. She wore black running tights and a cream zippered top. Conditions were mostly sunny with a little breeze and fog coming over the hill from the Pacific with pace. The Task Lyst deal preoccupied her as she got up to speed. *What am I missing? What does the management profile look like? What is the user experience?* It occurred to her that she hadn't even looked at the user interface being beta tested. *Probably ought to in case Gordie asks about it at our lunch meeting next week.*

Next morning was Friday and Alice worked from home. She rose early for Bikram Yoga and, upon returning, logged into her email with a tall chai latte she'd bought en route. She sorted her email by subject and located the beta test user login she'd received from the Task Lyst demo she sat in on two weeks prior. The credentials worked, and she created a profile. "Post a Task?" or "Fulfill a Service?" were the two options. She hit the service button. The profile asked multiple-choice questions, some silly, some straightforward, some prying . . . she was a little annoyed, recognizing some as questions aimed at testing IQ and logic as well as a few fitting standardized criminal profiling. She hit submit and was shown a list of available tasks offered to her with corresponding rewards. They included (1) tutoring kids prepping for college admissions tests, (2) an au pair position in Atherton, and (3) playing tour director for visiting trade officials from China—the latter of which paid handsomely: $5,000 for the approved candidate. Interesting. Five thousand for a long weekend? She considered what a few extra bucks could do for her. Her comfortable six-figure income had to cover her house note, grad school loan, expenses to keep up appearances, car lease, personal trainer, yoga, wardrobe, juicing. Her year-end bonus covered the deficit her lifestyle generated. She remembered her prestigious standing with the firm and thought it unlikely they'd approve of her moonlighting for spending money. Still, she could investigate a little, in the name of research. Method acting, learn the biz firsthand. *What does Tour Director entail?* she wondered.

CHAPTER 3

ELLIOTT TEMPLE PARKED HIS VESPA SCOOTER next to the bicycle rack in front of the Faustian Bar on Ashbury Street. He carried his helmet with him inside. It was dark, and he removed his sunglasses to orient himself. Burning incense blanketed decades of tobacco smoke as Elliott recognized a duet of Nancy Sinatra and Lee Hazlewood holding court from the jukebox. On the wall by the bathrooms, next to all the racks of free papers and flyers, he was to look for a certain show poster that would contain the instructions he needed to carry out his task and get the dough he needed to make rent this month. Easy enough, there it was: the Pit Dragons record release party. He freed it from the thumbtacks, glanced around, and headed for a booth in the corner.

Elliott had been making a name for himself since arriving in San Francisco seven years prior, writing songs and touring regionally with his rock 'n' roll combo. His latest project, the Golden Mean, was closer than ever to the mercurial sound that haunted his dreams. These were *his* songs, *he* was the front man, and he had players that believed in the vision. Critical validation was imminent and commercial reward would follow. It was just a matter of staying the course. For financial sustenance Elliott had been hustling set production work for television and film and chasing other short-term paychecks that he funneled straight into his art. He had learned to fly without a safety net in the pursuit of lofty goals. Reward requires risk, so why not double down?

Elliott placed his helmet on the table and ran his hands through his shaggy, light-brown hair that still had remnants of a temporary black dye experiment. He wore a vintage motorcycle jacket with a racing stripe down one side and tattered, flared jeans held together by an assortment of pop culture patches and velvet fabric. He was more fit than his image led on. He sat down and studied the poster; the address of the fictitiously named club was the information he needed. The other clue was "Playing their hit single—'Smashing Car Windows'" along with an image of a Porsche 911. Elliott grimaced. He hated the idea of busting up someone's pimp ride. He contemplated passing on the task. But, according to the rules of Task Lyst, you only get one pass. Plus he needed the dough yesterday. It was clear enough. Go over in the tiny hours of morning, take a crowbar to the windshield, and get the fuck out. Within twelve hours the money would appear in his account, untraceable and tax optional. Previous jobs had included an innocuous three-day dog-sitting gig and spying on a housewife for four hours while she dropped her kid off at preschool, did some Pilates, and had coffee with her church pastor, downing a fifth of vodka along the way. Elliott was beginning to enjoy the assignments, or the variety at least. It was all done through the Task Lyst platform on his computer and smartphone using an alias. All very secretive, but it made sense in his mind. He didn't have a gamer-geek background but had read enough dystopian novels to believe in the fantastic. For this latest job he'd need to find a new level of nerve. This was crossing a line into illegal activity with real consequences. But the pay was a game changer. He accepted the task and put it off until later that evening after band rehearsal. A couple of beers into the evening, he grabbed a nightcap with his bass player, Salami.

"You wouldn't happen to have a tire iron in your truck, would you?" Elliott said.

"Why, you have a flat tire? You don't even have a car."

"The scooter. I need to swap out the back wheel, and I think the lug nut is car sized."

"We can check. You need it tonight?"

"Yeah, I'll give it back tomorrow."

"What time is bus call tomorrow?"

"We load in at four in Chico so leave at noon, to be safe."

"We gonna make enough to cover?"

"If we're lucky."

Elliott grabbed the tire iron from Salami's 1979 Ford pickup, said goodbye, and turned the corner toward his scooter. It was after midnight, and an ocean breeze made him glad he'd wrapped a Liverpool Football Club scarf snug around his neck. He plugged the address into his navigation app and revved the throttle.

CHAPTER 4

TIM MIDDLETON SWITCHED CARS WITH HIS WIFE, SANDRA. He needed to take the minivan this morning since it was their turn for carpool. He'd drive the neighbor kids and his two youngest to Mountain View Middle School while Sandra took the leased 328i to drop off fifteen-year-old Harry at Bellarmine Prep. Tim reminded her to fill it with super premium—"It won't run on regular!" She'd return home to shower and head to her office while Tim stopped at Peet's Coffee for some motivation. He had an hour to kill before the hardware store opened. He'd been up late into the night optimizing the gimbal on his drone camera. Tim's latest hobby was shooting high-definition video from his remote-controlled drone. He had worked for two years on his landscape photography and had now taken to the skies. Unfortunately, the gimbal wasn't cooperating, and he couldn't get real-time video to feed back into his goggles. Tim scoured the online forums to exchange best practices with geeks around the globe, early adopters to this latest grown-up toy.

He fidgeted with his facial hair as he stood waiting for his coffee order amid a weekday morning mix of Silicon Valley caricatures. There were ultra-lean cyclists refueling after a ride up the ridge, MILFs in yoga gear, some of whom may actually have practiced yoga. Consultants, entrepreneurs, software execs working remote . . . Tim's restless mind speculated on each of their net worths. His was a dialect of exits, iterations, escape velocities, pivots, and liquidity events. It was his tendency to measure himself not by height, as that weighed heavily against him, but in the subtleties of extreme upward mobility. Held highest among these was home zip code. He was a few neighborhoods away from where he wanted to be.

• • •

Tim paid the clerk at Los Altos Hardware seven dollars and change for the hardware to rig the gimbal. He pulled the minivan onto Page Mill Road in the direction of Foothills Park. Within the hour Tim was flying the drone, a pizza box sized–white quadcopter, hundreds of feet above redwood trees on the ridge separating Silicon Valley from the Pacific Ocean. The goggles allowed him to follow what the GoPro camera was recording. Virtual piloting! Even better than the Flight Control video game he'd mastered. Tim sent the drone a quarter mile north along the tree line, slowed to a hover above a vast residential property, and took a few stills, testing the resolution. His landscape shots from an aerial perspective would wow his friends on Facebook. The employment applications for such expertise flooded his brain. Apple, Google . . . he could get back into product work.

Tim panicked for a second, realizing he'd lost sight of his machine. He tried to pick it out of the tree line, the sky . . . the last resort was the recall button. He hit it. In theory this meant the drone would return on a beeline to the GPS coordinates from where it had started. Tim hadn't practiced this part and wondered if he'd see the thing again. He considered the worst-case scenario: finding the address of the house he was filming and asking to look around for his drone. Suddenly it appeared. A nervous smile returned to his face; the thing was working exactly according to specs.

Tim raced home to download the footage. Some of it he'd already seen in real time, but now he'd be able to zoom in and out, drop it into Final Cut Pro, and mess with it. His cell rang.

"Hi, honey, what's up?" he said.

"Are you picking up Harry? Did you forget about his orthopedic appointment?"

"Heading over there now," he said, trying to cover his tracks.

"It started ten minutes ago. He's been waiting in the school office."

"We'll need to reschedule, then. I'm late getting out of a webinar."

"Tim, don't b.s. me. Is it another online film course? Or is it Photoshop this time?" She was trying to act pissed, but it was like being mad at an eight-year-old.

"Okay, I forgot, but wait till you see the shit I'm doing."

"Can't wait. Bye!"

Tim had it good, and he knew it. Sandra kept navigating the early retirement buyouts and the downsizing happening at Intel to keep the family flush. The fruits of his own heyday were all but dried up, and he was relying on his folks' estate planning distributions to keep fueling the coffers. Tim still talked reverently about his eBanc days. He'd made some money on options and bonuses that had put him in the highest tax bracket for a small handful of years. He wore that status on his sleeve but was insecure about what he'd accomplished lately, which amounted to expensive hobbies, chauffeuring the kids around, and staying heavily medicated on Zoloft, Adderall, medicinal cannabis, and Cialis. His life was a frenzy of spinning wheels and a decade-long midlife crisis. The new Bimmer was meant to help; so were the online New York Film Academy classes and the thousands spent on top-shelf gear. He piled on so many distractions and wore so many masks that he had wasted countless opportunities dropped in his lap. Tim connected the GoPro to the computer in his studio off the den and fiddled with a Nikon DSLR while he waited. It reminded him of the music video project he was working on with a friend: he was two weeks behind on delivering some new edits. He put his camera back on the desk. The progress bar pinged and he opened the file in Final Cut Pro.

CHAPTER 5

ALICE REVISITED THE TASK LYST INTERFACE that night over a glass of malbec. Okay, a couple of glasses. She sat back on her white leather sofa, feet propped on the ottoman and a fleece blanket covering her legs. Bluegrass music played from the ceiling speakers, gently filling the media room with David Grisman's mandolin, as her fingers engaged the computer keyboard on her lap. *Friday night and I'm working from home,* she reminded herself. She shouldn't have moved out of the city she loved. Her first two years out of Stanford were glorious, but the commute down to her new job in the Valley got to her. She felt old now—not alone, just old compared to the younger staffers who shared tales around the water cooler of weekend concerts, courtship, and misadventure. Most of her contemporaries were coupled off for Napa weekends or were changing diapers or, worse, had moved back home to the flyover states. She logged in, returning to the page where she'd left off: available options. She clicked on the terms and conditions, knowing what to look for: privacy policies, length of terms, ownership of data. The level of sophistication intrigued her. It was legal heavy, with a tone trending toward trepidation. She felt comfortable enough to proceed to the next step, figuring she hadn't compromised any rights yet. The process took her through some clever ebbs and flows—from silly and fun to bizarre and invasive. The wine was making her playful, and she edged further into the site. She strongly suspected manipulation and was almost combative, daring it to get the best of her. She started to regret having okayed the "this app is asking to verify your location" question. She'd done the same thing a thousand times trying out new phone apps and internet services. Subtly, she felt it pulling her in, like the Centrum of Amsterdam had when she had driven through the Netherlands that time high as a kite. She'd been there road managing a band while working for Sony Records, taking a turn at the wheel of the touring van. She wasn't one to cede control, and the band had spiked her cigarette while she was supposed to be babysitting them. Somehow she'd negotiated the white-knuckle trip by finding her inner calm—and the loading dock to the Melkweg concert hall. Since then she'd been comfortable operating with risk.

Now her thoughts turned to a small stash of cannabis oil in the cupboard next to the coffee beans. It was acceptable now, particularly for medicinal purposes, and everyone had a buyer's card. She partook occasionally, as it relaxed her. She preferred the higher CBD to lower THC ratio in tincture form—just a couple of drops in her red wine to help her find the Zen. It was common practice with the other progressive yogis in the Valley as an evolved form of meditation. She kept to wine for now, returning her attention to the site. On a whim, she "applied" for the tour director task. Rules stated that if she was accepted, she'd have to carry out the task or risk a low site rating, which would jeopardize future opportunities. If that was the worst thing that could happen, she reasoned, big freaking deal. This was, after all, only due diligence.

Lying in bed the next morning, Alice fidgeted with her phone. "Call me about Task Lyst when you can," Alice voice texted Larry Chang. She hit cancel and started over.

"Need to ask you about Monday's meeting . . ." Again, she canceled out the message. She meditated on it for thirty seconds. She was thinking of buying time on her assessment of the investment opportunity and needed his counsel on the best approach. Larry was the kind of guy she could talk turkey to, using Valley speak but also gut reaction. She didn't want to show up Monday and get caught off guard by Gordie. Recalling the poor cellular reception down in Big Sur, she opted out of bothering Larry. *No better way to ruin your buzz sculpture than to have a coworker getting all neurotic on you for nothing while you're getting right with the universe.*

Alice felt a mild rush when she heard simultaneous alerts on her cell phone, tablet, and laptop. It was a notification from Task Lyst and instructed her to call a number right away for further details.

"Hello, please enter your validation code." She thought a second. Looked at the email message and saw a seven-digit alpha-numeric sequence. She entered it on the phone's keypad.

"Thank you. Please hold while we connect."

"Miss Seegar?"

"Yes, speaking?"

"Paul Patel, from Event Logistics. I understand you'll be helping us today and tomorrow with the Chinese trade ambassadors?"

She paused and grew less comfortable. "I'm actually not sure, there may have been a mix up. I . . ."

"Are you Alice Seegar? I was told you'll be working in hospitality for us. I've got a car headed for you now. You should be receiving a dossier shortly with details. I appreciate you helping on such short notice." She opened the email and scanned to confirm. He was right.

"Miss Seegar, again, thank you for signing on with us. I think you'll find the experience stimulating and lucrative. Good luck."

CHAPTER 6

ELLIOTT CHECKED HIS ACCOUNT BALANCE when he woke the next morning and was surprised to see it funded from last night's task. *Man, that was quick. How the hell do they confirm it so fast? Good for me,* he thought.

A text came. "Yo, we bringing backline or just guitars and amps?" It was from Salami. "Oh, and bring my tire iron, make sure you clean the blood off it."

Elliott read it a second time. *He's just kidding, but wtf?* he thought. "Will do, c ya noon, signed Dr. Jekyll," he joked back. "And just guitar amps, we are using house backline."

Coffee would be necessary to go any further into the day, so he walked half a block to Cafe Trieste. A familiar face would usually hook him up with whatever he wanted for the price of a tip. He got a triple cafe cortado and a gluten-free date scone and read the critics' picks in that week's free newsweekly. He was glad to see a couple of friends get some ink for shows that weekend. The *Fishwrap* was his barometer. He still believed in print media. Social was too democratic; traditional media acted as a filter that separated the pretenders from the contenders. That's how his ex-publicist used to put it. She was great and he missed her. *A true Svengali. And now she's working for dot-coms making a mint. Following the money. Smart folks are following the money. And I'm toiling away at rock 'n' roll, which nobody gives a fuck about anymore.* He stirred the espresso and milk into a froth and sipped. He was into cortados now, less milk, less volume, more bang. Efficiency was everything these days. His band used to be five but now operated as a trio: lean and mean, no fat. He'd considered dropping to a duo, just guitar and drums, but drew the line on three. *Rock has to have more than two or you lose someone to blame shit on. Ah, the evil of three.* He laughed aloud at his internal monologue.

After the evening's show, a light rain kept the windshield wipers busy on Interstate 5 South back to San Francisco. The show had gone well enough, but the group decided to brave the drive back from Chico rather than spend money on accommodations. The totals were $389 at the gate, $125 in merchandise, minus $100 in fuel, minus $50 each for their pal Gator running sound and lights and Kyla handling the merchandise table. After paying their booking agent her 10 percent cut, the trio could pocket roughly $75 each. That's with no per diem. Elliott ate and drank strictly from what was provided in the green room so he incurred no expenses. He compared that to what he'd made the night before on his secret adventure with the sports car. He should be depressed but he wasn't. *Cynical* was the word he was looking for. Art and commerce were dead; service was where the money was. He could make serious money and play rock 'n' roll as well. But "to live outside the law, you must be honest," as Bob Dylan said. He'd always liked that line. He'd need to be careful about this whole business of Task Lyst. One slipup and it's curtains. He'd pay his rent tomorrow and restock the band's merchandise inventory. Then he'd pick up some steaks and grill the bastards. Forget being a vegetarian this week.

CHAPTER 7

TIM ZOOMED IN ON THE RESIDENCE HE HAD BEEN SHOOTING during his test flight. *Holy freaking shit, you can see some chick cooking in the kitchen. No, she's juicing; that's a blender, frozen fruit. Banana. Some kind of protein powder. No way. This is insane. I'm spying on silicone-breasted babes in Silicon Valley.* He laughed about not feeling bad. He also knew that the window of opportunity for this type of know-how would close pretty quick. Online forum chatter and common sense anticipated some kind of FAA restrictions on the private use of drones in public areas. There was a rapidly developing line in the sand regarding the morality and ethics of drone use, both on the international stage in places like Afghanistan and Syria, and on the domestic front in private and institutional formats. Tim felt energized by being part of the forefront of the technology, an early adopter. But mostly he thought of it in terms of applications for concerts, sporting events like skiing and surfing, and the geeky tech world that immersed itself in it. He tweeted part of the test flight, just enough to show off his skillful navigation and nerdy enthusiasm. He was pleased with the amount of "likes" and comments the post generated. Perhaps someone had a need for his know-how.

CHAPTER 8

WITHIN THIRTY MINUTES ALICE HAD FUSED TOGETHER A FUN but professional outfit and was locking the front door to go off on this ridiculous adventure. She couldn't believe she was following through on it and questioned her grip on sanity. The fact that she'd kept her professional identity somewhat vague when registering with the app comforted her, as if she were going undercover or acting on stage. Monday morning and this would be nothing more than a holiday weekend. A diesel sport utility vehicle idled in her driveway, the driver waiting to open a passenger door. She exchanged nods with the driver, whom she assumed was hired livery, not some accomplice that she could chat up for details. He handed her a folder once she sat down inside the vehicle.

CHAPTER 9

ELLIOTT LOGGED BACK INTO HIS TASK LYST PROFILE to see his status upgraded to Centurion level. He had started out as Pawn and had become Knight when he'd completed his second job. There was no visible listing for the hierarchy; mystery shrouded what level came next. He liked having some cash reserves for the first time in a while, and the prospect of stockpiling more appealed to him—hopefully something quick and easy, aboveboard. He decided he was ready for his next assignment. This one seemed ideal. Pick up a suitcase from San Francisco International Airport, Air Nippon flight 136, arriving at 9:00 a.m. He was to deliver the suitcase to the Mark Hopkins Hotel. He'd use the band van.

Traffic southbound on the 101 was backed up, so he took 280 around Daly City, only to find congestion there too. His phone said 8:39 and he was worried about arriving late. What scenario could play out: it would just keep going around the carousel. Elliott looked for alternate routes, surface streets, some faster way to get the ten miles to SFO. He scanned the radio dial for traffic updates. "We've got a sig alert on both sides of 280, cleaning up from an earlier accident." It was 9:16 when he finally got to short-term parking at the international terminal. And 9:27, once he finally arrived at the terminal. He checked the monitor to confirm the flight info. Confirmed. He looked around, waited a minute or two before inquiring at the baggage counter. It was 9:33.

"Hi there, yes, I'm looking for my suitcase. Silver Samsonite, name is Itochu."

The clerk continued typing on the keyboard, focused on the screen.

"Is it one of those?" Elliott scanned the grouping of bags just outside the door.

"Do you see a silver Samsonite?" The clerk looked up. He was Latino, clean-cut, slight build. He grinned. "You tell me."

Elliott gave him stink eye. "Look, bro, I don't see it out here. Is there somewhere else it might be?"

"Let's check it out, sir. What's the name again?"

"Itochu. I-t-o-c-h-u."

The clerk looked up at Elliott. "Do you have your baggage claim ticket or boarding pass?"

Elliott impulsively felt around his pockets, stalling while he contemplated a plan B. "I don't, must have left them on the plane."

"Can I see your ID?"

Elliott, sensing defeat, took a straightforward route. "Hey, man, I don't have a baggage claim ticket because I am picking this up for someone and delivering it. The company I work for can confirm this if you'll just locate the . . . bag."

"I'm sorry, sir. It's against policy to release bags to unauthorized personnel. And if it's not here, I'm afraid it's either been picked up already or it didn't make the flight from Tokyo."

Elliott shook his head and formed an ironic smile.

"Can I help the next person?" said the clerk.

Elliott retreated out of the baggage office and looked around for a sign of some sort. He saw a woman pulling a similar bag out the sliding exit doors but figured what are the chances. What to do? He pulled up the confirmation email. It didn't provide a contact for questions or concerns. He'd botched this one and was afraid he had zero recourse for straightening it out.

He logged in at home, marking the task as incomplete, a button he'd never previously hit. He waited nervously for a response. "Case Review in process" appeared when he refreshed his browser. The money obviously wouldn't get transferred over, a fact that sank Elliott into a sour mood. Now his account was "temporarily frozen," with no sign of when or if he'd be able to work. He wished he hadn't lived lavishly, counting on today's payday, for the past five days.

CHAPTER 10

TIM HAD PUT A CALL IN TO HIS FORMER EBANC BOSS, Mitch Levy, who was now entrepreneur-in-residence at Stanford Business School. They'd been talking about grabbing a bite soon, and Tim, with a new sense of urgency, initiated a lunch.

"How's Sandra and the kids?" Mitch asked.

"All is well, busy, you know. Soccer games, play dates, and private tutors."

"Tell me about it. I go up to Carneros once a month just to treat myself to a little sanity. So how's the consulting going? You doing product work?"

"Actually, more creative projects: soundtracks, video editing, B2B stuff. Maybe something Yahoo would be interested in. I've got a quadcopter drone with a GoPro mount for video and stills and it's insanely cool."

Mitch finished a forkful of three-beet salad. "That shit scares me. I was riding Pacific Coast Highway near Half Moon Bay, and one of those buzzed me. I nearly bought the farm about five hundred feet above the water. Some motherfucker."

Tim imagined for a second being responsible for such an act.

"No question, there are some potentially nefarious applications. What I'm interested in is entertainment, events, mapping, news. This is the very forefront of drone technology, and I'm right there with it."

"You should talk to the guys at Blue Hill Capital. They're backing all the techie gaming crap—robots, virtual reality helmets, web currency. You know Alice Seegar, used to work for me at Sony. She's over there."

CHAPTER 11

ALICE OPENED THE ENVELOPE AND A CELL PHONE DROPPED OUT. A light-green sticky note instructed her to activate the phone by calling a number, which she did. A voice prompt confirmed her authorization. By the time she'd read the itinerary, bios, and protocol sheet, the SUV had pulled up to the international terminal at SFO. This was an unscheduled stop. A text appeared on her phone. "Ms. Seegar, please retrieve from baggage claim silver Samsonite suitcase, name Itochu, one of visiting emissaries left behind upon arrival." It was 9:25 and she found the suitcase at baggage claim. It was medium sized, fairly heavy, but on rollers. She located the name on the tag to match the one in the email. She used the restroom and made her way back to the idling vehicle.

En route to the city she caught up on some personal emails: mom checking in, some LinkedIn notifications, meditation moment of the day, Kate Spade spring/summer collection. Bart Stevens's fortieth birthday invite.

CHAPTER 12

ELLIOTT CHECKED HIS PROFILE AGAIN LATER IN THE DAY. To his surprise, no mention appeared of the snafu. But his "new user mulligan" was grayed out. He took this to mean he could no longer pass on a job, should a task not jibe with his schedule for some reason or another. He understood the logic but felt spooked by the arbitrary nature of the ruling. What, was he on probation? A little hand slap? Two minutes in the sin bin? Curiosity called on him to run a job search to see what was available. Only one came up: valet parking for an event in Piedmont, eight dollars per hour plus tips, four-hour commitment. Elliott made a middle-finger salute to the page, aware of its meaning. He'd been demoted back to the bottom to prove himself again. Screw this shit. He stewed in his anger, then realized it could be merely a short-term test, to gauge his commitment. He'd do the time.

CHAPTER 13

TIM DID IN FACT KNOW ALICE. His wife, Sandra, socialized with her on occasion. They did barre class together, or maybe it was book club. Tim looked up Alice's profiles on all the requisite channels. He replied to one of her tweets about the latest mountain lion sighting in the trails up on the ridge. Tim got on her social media radar, then moved in with a casual reach-out by email. Tim put a note in his phone calendar to follow up with her if she didn't reply by Tuesday. He'd propose a morning coffee meet-up somewhere close to Blue Hill Capital in Silicon Valley.

Tim had his running gear on but missed his window between shuttling kids around, scanning online GoPro forums, and emailing Alice. All of these Saturday activities meant Tim didn't get any downtime to think about how overcommitted he was for a guy without a job. He took an edible cannabis cookie out of its wrapper and devoured it like it was a Power Bar—his modus operandi for watching his oldest's travel soccer games.

CHAPTER 14

THE MARK HOPKINS ON NOB HILL WAS ONE OF THE OLDEST and most exclusive hotels in San Francisco, founded by its namesake in the years following the gold rush. Alice's driver pulled into the entrance while valets and bellhops bounced into action, opening doors. She followed the bellhop into the lobby to the reservations desk. A smartly dressed clerk greeted her with a professional smile.

"Good morning, Miss, checking in?"

"I'm meeting the NeuTech party, who I believe are already here."

The clerk nodded. "Very well. I can ring the guests."

Alice stepped aside from the desk and took in the interior. She hadn't been there since a fundraiser for the governor a few years ago. The marble floor, chandeliers, incredibly high ceilings; she hadn't recalled the peach-colored wallpaper. She didn't know how she felt about all the old-school opulence.

"Ms. Seegar?" The clerk motioned her toward a young woman of Chinese descent walking over from the high archway leading out of the lobby, her heels echoing off the marble floor and reverberating across the entrance area. She wore a white crossover top draped across her shoulders and identically colored bell-bottom slacks—sexy, cute, and stylish. She led with an outreached hand, her professional smile following right behind.

"You must be Alice. I'm Iris Chen," she said. Her accent was more Northern California than China, and her manners were devoid of any foreign protocol.

"Yes, hi . . . Iris?" The two shook hands and made eye contact.

"Any trouble at the airport at all?"

"None at all. Here's the suitcase. I hope they've survived without it."

"Oh, I think they have. Thank you for doing this. So, you should have the itinerary. We're getting ready to go to a luncheon concert at the symphony hall. The ten emissaries will travel over separately in pairs. You'll be assigned to Wanquan Cho and Charles Zeng. A translator will be with you most of the time."

Alice raised an eyebrow. Escorting middle-aged Asian business leaders around wasn't exactly her usual pay grade. Iris's expression betrayed sympathy but also a sense of fait accompli. She clarified: "Relax. We are only the day escorts. A separate team takes over for the dinner engagements. With your education and professional background, you'll be able to provide some insight into these gentlemen's outlook on trade, culture, politics."

"Wait, escort?"

Iris smiled again. "We wouldn't ask you to perform anything out of your comfort zone. You'll simply fill out a questionnaire before you leave today and tomorrow. That's it."

Alice was skeptical. But she was also professional. She figured she'd wing it until something made her decide otherwise.

CHAPTER 15

ELLIOTT TOOK HOME SIXTY-FOUR DOLLARS IN TIPS, along with whatever crap wage he earned. It wasn't very rock 'n' roll, running back and forth for cars, holding doors open for blue bloods, accepting a couple of singles, repeating, "Thanks a lot, I appreciate it." He thought seriously about splitting with a Maserati but returned it to its owner against his darker impulses. On his way home he stopped for a bourbon at Chestnut Grill, where his former drummer tended bar.

"Pappy Van Winkle twelve year, and don't give me that 'we don't have any more' bullshit. I know you keep a reserve for when Joe Montana comes in."

"I might have some twelve year, if you've got twenty-eight dollars."

"Put it on my tab."

"Ha. Tab. Tell you what, first one's on the house."

"My man, I owe ya."

The aproned bartender used a step stool to locate the bottle on an upper shelf and reached for a tumbler. "You guys been out on the road at all?" He measured out two ounces of some of the rarest Kentucky bourbon available.

"We just did a one-off up in Chico. Making a southern run this weekend: San Luis Obispo, LA, San Diego. How about you, getting out at all?"

"Eh, here and there. Subbed on a country starlet's radio tour. Paid my mortgage for a couple of months; nice tour bus, drum tech, caught up on my reading. Now back to mixing drinks. Neat?"

"Just one cube, to open it up a bit. Drag a lemon peel around the rim," he said. The glass arrived in front of Elliott. He watched the ice settle into the amber liquid, sending a beautiful color spectrum rotating through the ornate glass. The glass was heavy, felt substantial, and he savored the ritual. He admired the bourbon up close, then checked the body. The swirling elixir created a rattling sound, like the wind chime in the late afternoon on his grandparents' patio when he was a kid: dreamy, reassuring, and secure. The first taste revealed an oaky, caramel nose and sweet, smooth finish. It was decidedly less spicy than the Pappy Rye. Elliott recalled the days when the stuff was readily available at an affordable price. Before the latest bourbon craze. Before fifteen-dollar hamburgers. Back when people actually bought records and the radio played decent music. He raised the glass again. Before the internet disrupted commerce and obliterated any semblance of mystery a band could exploit. He didn't care anymore. Might as well get a straight job and live like an inlander, to quote Bear in the classic surfing film *Big Wednesday*. He would ride the north swell—the great swell—and find redemption as he pulled into a truck-size barrel, daylight barely creeping in from the shoulder. He'd make it through the green room or crash and burn. Better to paddle big than to fade away. Neil Young might have said that if he surfed. But Neil didn't surf. Probably the only knock against Neil was that he didn't surf. Jerry Garcia didn't either, but he got into scuba late in life. Keith Richards climbed coconut trees, but not very well, evidently. Elliott wanted to chill on a beach between tours. Write songs, record, play 'em, tour, relax for a minute, rinse, repeat. And then when someone would ask him, "You still playing, Elliott?" he would answer, "Only when it's necessary." Just like Matt Fucking Johnson. Only playing because it's good to go out and play with your friends.

Elliott took another hit of the bourbon. He was aware of the contradictions. One minute fed up and the next fired up! All it took was a small bit of stoke to flip the switch. Life was returning to his spirit. A new tune, a new recording, bringing the house down with a crowd favorite. Was it wrong? If the cap fits, let him wear it . . . ah, Robert Nesta Marley . . . wisdom! True words, dat! His bartender pal chatted up a couple down the bar while mixing Manhattans, leaving Elliott alone to enjoy his fix.

CHAPTER 16

TIM SLID THE FOLDED CHAIR OUT OF ITS COVER. He positioned it on the sideline of the soccer field with comfortable separation from the center line, where the critical mass of parents would assemble. He set up a tripod and began to fiddle with his lenses. It was a passive-aggressive move as much as anything, giving him license to enjoy his chill and not engage the crazy moms and dads screaming at the officials. Some of them sucked on lollipops to contain their passion. *Silly,* he thought. But the metaphor was apt. For him, a couple of grams of White Widow baked into a space cake worked more than fine, as long as he had his cameras to keep his ADD mind occupied. He'd limit his interactions to brief, manageable dialogue at halftime and use the camera to run interference. But first he'd have to trade banter with Trip Lerner, his sideline nemesis, a guy worth upwards of a quarter billion whom Tim had known from his early days working in San Francisco. Trip had dated Tim's wife, Sandra, briefly. It was years ago, when the two were among the hordes who came to Tim's gigs back in the glory days. "Bad" Trip is how Tim referred to him now, as their encounters usually ruined his emotional disposition for days. A combination of causes factored into this dynamic, least of which was Trip's son's status as the team's leading scorer. The real source of enmity was Trip's rumored veto of a deal Tim had quarterbacked a few years prior. Had the acquisition gone through, eBanc would have absorbed patents to an online payment technology that proved critical to PayPal's success. Trip, the CEO of the target start-up, defied popular sentiment and held out for a legendary payday. It was the elephant in the room whenever the two got together, much more so in Tim's mind than Trip's. In fact, the latter likely wasn't aware of the former's involvement in the landmark "what if." Trip was more occupied with driving a Maserati GranTurismo to soccer matches, chartering private jets to exotic destinations across the globe, and competing in triathlons that he featured in his bio page on the Redwood Capital website. Tim braced himself.

"Tim-ah-tay-ho, que pasa, amigo?"

"Hey." The two fist-bumped. Tim was five inches shorter than Trip, which exacerbated his feeling the Billy Joel to Trip's Sting. The nemesis wore a lightweight muted-black fleece vest over a fitted gray T-shirt that exposed his 7 percent body fat. His jeans were dark indigo with a perfect fade worth every bit of the $395 price tag. On his feet were the latest model Brooks running shoes, a serious runners' brand, the neon yellow logo his outfit's only sign of color. An alpha intensity in his eyes penetrated Tim, who looked away for fear of the wrath of Horus.

"How's Harry's shoulder? He going to give it a go today?" Tim's son was recovering from a contusion sustained in a recent game. He was the new starting goalie since the previous kid had left the club. Many thousands of dollars of private training hung in the balance. A sophomore in high school, fifteen-year-old Harry needed to make a strong impression this club season if college soccer was going to be an option. Stanford, Cal, and UCLA were the targets.

"He's better. We've had him doing PT over at Elite Sports Medicine, and Dr. Haeligarian gave him the green light. I guess we'll find out here shortly."

"I've got another guy you should take him to, worked on my rotator cuff. It's always good to get a second opinion." Tim bit his lip. It was typical of Trip to assume that they hadn't already gotten a second opinion. Or that "his guy" would have a better opinion. The two were joined by another parent, and the conversation turned to her recent meditation retreat at some Mayan ruins in Mexico. Trip apparently was an expert in that subject as well. Tim tried to tune them out, or faked it at least, turning his attention back to which oversized lens to use on a Canon 1D X.

CHAPTER 17

THE LUNCHEON AT FLEUR DE LIS WAS FORMAL AND STIFF. Alice made small talk—with the help of interpreters—and established that Mr. Zeng was a major shareholder in the Chinese Google. He seemed more interested in talking about real estate: Pacific Heights, Stinson Beach, and Napa Valley especially. A photographer worked the event, snapping photos of the visiting emissaries enjoying California cuisine paired with top wines from the region. Reluctantly, Alice offered her cordial, professional pose when she couldn't otherwise escape the lens. She'd have to provide some explanation if the photo appeared in the *Nob Hill Gazette,* the *Business Journal,* or worse, *San Francisco Examiner.* This nagged at her, but she was pretty good at deflecting inquiries on her social and private life. She excused herself, needing a bathroom break.

En route to the restroom, she checked her phone for messages. A text reminder of an upcoming hair appointment, another LinkedIn notification via email, and a voicemail from an unknown number were the highlights. She played the message while walking through the plush hallway to the powder room. Task Lyst customer service requested she contact them as soon as possible. She hit the call back button and stepped inside the vacant restroom.

"Task Lyst, this is Lenore."

"Hi, my name is Alice Seegar. I'm returning someone's call."

"Ms. Seegar, yes. Thanks for calling back. I apologize for this intrusion. Our system made an error in assigning you to this task. Basically, your profile was mistaken for someone else's."

"I'm not sure I understand."

"It's simply a case of misunderstanding. The client requires someone of a different skill set and is prepared to compensate you for your time and inconvenience."

"So, I'm done, in other words?"

"More or less, yes. If you don't mind excusing yourself at the luncheon, your client contact—Iris, I believe it is—will arrange for your dismissal. Thanks for your understanding on this."

Alice experienced a combination of disbelief and embarrassment. She was being fired. It was all a strange and silly experience, yet stung just the same. She felt like demanding more of an explanation but struggled to articulate the reply.

Lenore from Task Lyst continued, "If you have any further questions, please feel free to include them in your task completion summary, which you'll be sent shortly. Again, thank you for your understanding, Ms. Seegar. Bye now."

Alice sat in the stall, looking at her phone. It was the strangest thing, she thought. Somehow, in some way, she'd been manipulated. She could sense this wasn't all on the level.

CHAPTER 18

ELLIOTT MADE IT SAFELY BACK TO HIS PLACE, riding through the early morning hours. He squeezed in between two parked cars, jolted the scooter on its kickstand, and took stock of the dense, wet fog enveloping the city. A foghorn sounded, which Elliott rarely noticed anymore after all the years of living there, the soundtrack of the city that its sleepwalking, street-hustling inhabitants took for granted. Unique features that once fascinated had become sidenotes to a struggle to find a sustainable spot amid the gilded landscape of trust funds and masters of the universe pushing the cost of living way out of reach of artists like him. A recent cover story in the alt-weekly posed the question, "Has Our City Jumped the Shark?" Elliott pinpointed it to when Bill Graham died and then—for sure—when Jerry Garcia passed. The technology revolution and the music renaissance shared the same mother, but Cain was killing Brother Abel, he was sure of it. Elliott wasn't sure if it was murder, cannibalism, or Darwinism.

He went inside, placed his helmet on a shelf by the door with his keys, and checked the fridge for a nightcap. He used the counter's edge to pry open a Cerveza Pacifico, leaving the cap to bounce across the kitchen floor. A to-do list on the counter reminded him rent was due. He took the beer into his bedroom, reached for a pair of Sony studio headphones, and pushed play on the compact disc player. He reclined into a beanbag and enjoyed the latest mix of a recent recording. "Cutting Glass (with Diamonds)" came through the headphones, filling Elliott's head with an arena-anthem chorus and layered guitars. He easily imagined his band performing the song at Coachella, Bonnaroo, or Glastonbury. He played the song multiple times with equal effect. Once his ears were ringing, he checked his social media accounts. Twitter showed some modest progress on new followers and a direct message from a fan to "come play the Netherlands!" Facebook was more of the same but even more lame. His streaming media dashboard showed steady plays for the week on Spotify, three downloads on iTunes, and five direct purchases from the website. Another ten bucks, yippee.

Finally, he checked Task Lyst to see if his valet job had been uploaded. It had, which meant he could run a query on new opportunities. A compelling result showed up, which read: "Performance Studios seeks immediate help: flexible hours, entertainers welcome, and Task Lyst Preferred Users only. Contact 7712mpshto@gmail.com using the email you have on file. Reference: GRETCHEN." Elliott, finding the intrigue amusing, complied. An immediate autoreply message appeared: "Stand by for instructions."

CHAPTER 19

THE SOCCER GAME ENDED IN A ONE-TO-ONE TIE. Harry played well in the net, stopping a penalty with his outstretched glove. And Trip's superstar kid was held scoreless. Tim, the proud dad, treated his son to In-N-Out Burger, and they chatted about the game while waiting in the drive-through.

"I got some good shots of you. The lighting was a bit too overhead, but I'm using new filters that are super cool. I wish they'd let me fly the drone over the game; imagine the footage I'd get."

"Dad, you can't play soccer with the sound of giant, prehistoric insects hissing overhead."

"I bet you could, once you got used to it." Tim started thinking again about his burgeoning expertise and how to apply it. He could shoot recruiting videos for elite soccer players angling for top colleges. The aerial perspective would showcase their skills in a unique way. Or he could film games for area clubs. Or San Jose's professional soccer team, the Earthquakes. He could broker a deal with ESPN to cover West Coast games. "Dad, Dad. DAD!" Harry nudged his dad out of the daydream as a courtesy honk from a hungry patron blurted from behind.

Once they got home Tim took his double-double wrapped in lettuce instead of bun into his office studio to read the drone forums. There was chatter online about entities paying for aerial photography expertise: a rancher who hired a drone operator to film his property in preparation for a sale, law enforcement up in Humboldt County using them to search for illegal pot farms, and one guy who made a few bucks collecting footage of a surf contest at Mavericks in Half Moon Bay. Tim thought that sounded like a great idea, taking the drone to the beach and getting some surfing footage before sunset. He told Sandra he'd be back in a couple of hours, taking his remaining half burger with him.

CHAPTER 20

ELLIOTT SPENT SUNDAY EVENING WONDERING what the status was with his next task. He felt like he had been left hanging, and the week ahead loomed with slim prospects for him to make any money. His bandmates would be busy with their day gigs while he would keep kicking the ball forward with club owners, concert promoters, and other music shysters. It took money to send out promo kits, print handbills, replenish merchandise inventory . . . he needed his side hustle.

He logged into Task Lyst but found no developments beyond the cryptic "stand by" instruction. He browsed around and found himself in a user chat group discussing cryptocurrency. A user named Claybourne300 advocated receiving payments in Bitcoin, which Elliott didn't know much about. The thread discussed the blockchain and Ethereum as if they were common knowledge. Elliott understood PayPal and the newer payment form, Venmo, but this crypto stuff seemed very "dark web" to him. He lost several hours educating himself on Bitcoin and Task Lyst's support of these alternate pay methods. Might be worth exploring, he told himself.

CHAPTER 21

ALICE PLAYED THROUGH THE SEQUENCE OF EVENTS on the way home. The short notice could be written off to logistical challenges faced by any events-planning operation: replacing someone who fell sick or thinning the herd once the event got under way. Or was it something she had said? Or didn't say?

She needed a dose of intense physical punishment to recalibrate. At home, she changed into her running gear, devoured an energy bar, swigged a bottle of electrolyte water, and hit the trail with abandon. She was annoyed at the numerous mountain bikers she'd have to avoid at this time of day, which inspired her to run harder. She needed to get to the three-mile mark for the endorphins to start killing the pain. That was where the magic happened. Ideas flowed; the floodgates opened. *Fuck you Iris Chen and your goddamned emissaries. What about the suitcase? Who does that? Pays $5,000 for two hours, work and then sends you packing.*

Back at her car, stretching after the run, she fielded a couple of emails, including one from Tim Middleton, her friend Sandra's husband. She replied.

"Tim, how are you? Sure, I'd love to hear what you're up to. My weekend got crazy, volunteered for this last-minute nightmare thing, anyway—long story. Catch up for coffee midweek? Love to Sandra."

Monday, at the associates' lunch, Gordie asked about the Task Lyst deal. He'd seen the memo she'd sent on Thursday and wanted to vet her analysis.

"Seegar, you've gone cold on Task Lyst?"

She quickly swallowed a forkful of salad she'd just shoveled in. "Actually, yes and no. I spent some time on it over the weekend, and it's interesting, but, I dunno, something doesn't add up. I'd like to dig deeper this week if we can stall them."

"What, the numbers? The model? They are trying to close this next round by end of Q2."

"I know. I can give you a definitive in seven days. I'm clearing my calendar this week to focus on it. The UI is more complex than at first glance."

"Sounds like you had a hell of a weekend," Larry Chang said.

"Not all of us get to stargaze in a yurt camp. I actually worked," she said. Larry laughed with her. He liked the banter.

"Someone's got to do it."

"What, work?" Gordie added.

Larry dug in. "I get my best meditating done during deep tissue massages, Tai Chi, and Big Sur hikes. We really ought to open an office down there."

CHAPTER 22

IT WAS WEDNESDAY AND TIM ARRIVED FIRST. He placed his sunglasses and keys on a table where he could see them from his place in line at the counter. He texted Alice, asking for her order, and in the process confirming their meeting at Peet's Coffee on Los Altos Boulevard. She was on her way and requested a green tea latte with almond milk. Tim went with his default tall coffee with skim milk, along with two bottled waters. It was the normal, bustling, post-morning rush hour scene: work-from-homes, just-worked-outs, and just-dropped-kids-off-at-school types. She found him and they caught up briefly on domestic life in the Valley.

"Our mutual former colleague Mitch Levy mentioned that you guys are hot on companies in the virtual reality and gaming space," Tim said. "I've been dabbling a bit in product consulting, particularly as it relates to GoPro photography and aerial drone piloting. You could say I've been geeking out."

"Fun! I bet your boys are enjoying that."

"Totally. I'm a kid at heart, what can I say? Have you ever tried one?"

"I've seen people running with those cameras but never used one personally. We missed out on the GoPro dog and pony show. I'm surprised Gordie didn't see that one coming, what with all his ultra marathoning and whatnot."

"Well, the drone takes it to a whole new level. I can view the footage in real time with monitor goggles. The gimbal allows me to pivot the camera angle, absorb flight turbulence, zoom in—ridiculous stuff."

"What are you trying to do with it? I'm guessing something more than aggravate your neighbors."

"Ha! Right, I think they are starting to take notice. No doubt. I'm looking for an 'in' with any projects or start-ups that have a use for this: Google Maps, Electronic Arts sports, SpaceX, spying on Larry Ellison's tiki party blowout. Know of any doors I should be knocking on?"

"That's funny; you could make some serious money as a paparazzo."

"Sadly, it had occurred to me."

Alice added, "I can see Sandra explaining to the kids that Daddy's black eye was the result of spying on Sean Penn's backyard sunbathing." After a pause, it came to her. "Have you ever heard of Task Lyst?"

"Umm, vaguely. Is it a babysitting site?"

"I've been looking at their prospectus. I actually demoed their beta user interface this past weekend—very weird and long story. But they have this sort of Craigslist, Backpage-type service marketplace where you can find quick, one-off jobs or recruit people for them. I tried it out with mixed results. You might find some leads."

"Interesting. I'll have to check it out. Are you guys making a play? Feel free to plead the fifth if I'm prying."

Alice watched Tim reach for his paper cup full of caffeine and sip it. She admired the life Tim and Sandra had: a happy marriage, full house of kids, careers. Sandra always seemed so together and balanced. They were a few years older than Alice and had long crossed that border where post-college career hunting pivots into the natural progression of settling down with someone to build a shared life. She felt safe with Tim, unencumbered by sexual tension or some hidden agenda. She'd spent many evenings socializing at parties where his band had held court. It was an incestuous scene where people were hooking up with their roommates and their best friends' exes. Tim's band was a centerpiece to it. He felt like family. Like a brother she'd never had. They were on the same team. "Well. We're all looking for the next big thing, right? Gordie likes something about the space."

CHAPTER 23

THE SUSPENSE ENDED FOR ELLIOTT TUESDAY NIGHT when a Task Lyst alert sounded on his smartphone. He clicked on the notification and opened the application to accept the next task. It was code-named GRETCHEN and was identified by the same Performance Studios logo from several nights before. Upon hitting the "Accept" button a message appeared: "Southwest corner of Judah and Great Hwy 0600." He knew the spot, having picked up the Judah line bus at the beach there. The 0600 could mean the time, 6:00 a.m., he presumed. It was nearly two now. He groaned, lamenting the lack of sleep and cold early-morning scooter ride out to the beach from the Inner Sunset. Options: *Don't* go—no more jobs? *Do* go—could be a good paycheck. Could lead to even better paychecks. Rent was due. He set three alarms: his phone, Casio watch, and a clock radio that had been in the apartment before he took over the lease. Elliott fought the urge to skip his wake-up call after dreaming through the first two alarms. The third, an old-fashioned automobile horn on his phone at maximum decibels, killed his snooze. He powered through his grogginess, thankful that he wasn't too hungover. Early rises weren't part of his routine. He made it out to Ocean Beach on time and parked his ride a hundred yards away from the southwest corner of Judah and Great Highway. Fog blanketed the dawn, with just a hint of light visible over the twin peaks of the city. A lone jogger ran by in the bike lane, stopping at the light pole positioned on the target corner to stretch. As Elliott neared the runner—within twenty yards—the figure resumed its course, continuing southward. Elliott approached the pole and noticed a key left sitting at its base. A handbill pasted about face-high promoted a mime performance in the Tenderloin. To be certain, he loitered around for a few minutes, checking for alternate clues. A public restroom loomed close, but the door was still locked. He studied the windows of houses nearest the corner but saw nothing suspicious. Elliott picked up the key and removed the handbill, careful to keep it in one piece so as not to lose any detail. A block away was a coffee house where he could warm up, wake up, and look closer at his material. A few surfers chatted outside the Sunset Cafe, steaming to-go cups in hand, wetsuits draped over boards waiting to be used.

Elliott ordered a Keith Moon: two shots of espresso in an extra large coffee with cane sugar and sweetened condensed milk. A curly redhead with a double nose ring approved the order. She looked vaguely familiar to Elliott, like maybe a musician he had crossed paths with, or a groupie he'd tried to bed. He wasn't sure, and she didn't seem to be either. It was déjà vu being out this way, getting up predawn, recalling early-morning surf sessions, seeing a grunge girl from a previous decade. He needed to start surfing again. His preferred seat, the burgundy stuffed armchair, was vacant, so he sunk into it. It was a furnishing that, allegedly, had once resided in the Grateful Dead's house at 710 Ashbury Street. A crowdfunding campaign had been waged to get it reupholstered. Duct tape held it together in the meantime. The smell of roasted coffee beans comforted him as he tested the temperature of his drink. Six twenty a.m. wasn't so bad. Quiet, peaceful. He took the key out of his pocket. A Chinese symbol stared back at him on the stainless steel key ring, and the key itself looked ordinary. It was most likely not a vehicle. Door? Gate? Safe? Not a safe. *But how would I know if it was a safe? Am I an expert on locks all of a sudden?* More intrigue. The heck was he getting himself into? He checked out the handbill. Mime Troupe, Mr. Grey's Picture Show Theatre. British spelling. There were never accidents in this cat-and-mouse business. Going to the address would be the obvious next step. His phone map showed it to be on Turk Street near Hyde. He'd head over there to scope it out once the coffee kicked in and the morning rush hour subsided.

Elliott stood up from the Grateful Dead chair and got up to retrieve his scooter to head toward the Tenderloin district. With a little luck, he'd beat the congestion across town. He walked himself through the information so far. Location, check. Time, not clear. Purpose, unknown. He liked the challenge and mystery of it all. "They" seemed to be testing him. This wasn't likely another valet job. He was getting a taste of something richer for sure.

Elliott parked near the intersection of Turk and Hyde—the Tenderloin district in all its decadent glory. Here, homeless panhandlers and gay errand boys mixed with theatergoers alongside strip clubs, peep shows, massage parlors, and hip, new boutique hotels. A fight for the soul of the city waged here as much as anywhere. The old-fashioned opulence of Nob Hill, the ethnicity of Chinatown, and the melting pot of Polk Gulch weaved together here just blocks from city hall. The Tenderloin served as a major crossroads of the city: raw, savage, governed by Darwinian principles. The aesthetic charm of other neighborhoods—the Castro, Russian Hill, the Mission—was lacking here. Rather, a vortex swallowing the identities of San Francisco's diversity held court. It preyed on those who wandered too close. This is where souls were lost. Bodies were buried elsewhere, but the death spiral started here. Yet it had a strong heartbeat and offered pleasures unavailable outside its small wedge on the map. It was the theater district and red-light district; high brow and low. Equal opportunity offender.

Elliott was no stranger to "the Loin." He'd rehearsed at a facility where bands rented rooms by the month and gigged occasionally at the Great American Music Hall, a Gilded Age relic that ranked high on any list of the best places to see live music. There used to be a gringo taco joint called Oaxaca. It was where, over margaritas, Elliott had formed his first San Francisco band with some pals from Boulder. They'd had a solid, three-year run, headlining venues for the post-college set. Oaxaca had promising tortas but it, too, folded.

Elliott explored the block and saw no sign of a theatre, a Mime Troupe, or a Mr. Grey. The multitude of street hustlers were nonaggressive, but lacked the charm and focus one might find in the same population in a third world country. They were selling black-market handbags and watches. A small gap in the crowd opened at the entrance of the Hyde-Turk Market, so he walked in for a peek. Elliot went unnoticed amid the excitement. The shop clerk was exchanging banter with two hippies about moving out of the doorway. An old man was slowly and deliberately counting out coins for his purchase. Elliott pulled a soda out of the cooler and made his way toward the counter. The shopkeeper addressed him with a Middle Eastern accent.

"That is it? Eighty-five cents please."

Elliott paid for the Coke and asked the clerk if he knew of a Mr. Grey's Picture Show Theatre. The man shook his head, passing Elliott his fifteen cents in change.

"No. I'm not of knowing." Then, to his loiterers, "Gott Dammick, out of doorway, or I call vice."

One of them engaged Elliott directly in the doorway: "Achmed the Terrible, man . . . fascist establishment, shipping all his profits overseas. It is written—"

Elliott slid by him while the guy's sidekick whispered, "Doses." Elliott gestured no thanks and jaywalked to the other side of Turk. He noticed a bland commercial building standing out among three Victorians. The structure towered over the vacant parking lot on the corner; on its upper wall was painted "Storage Units. Monthly Rentals. Lowest Rates!" He fingered the key in his pocket and continued to the building. At a locked gate, he pressed the button for entry. He was buzzed in and greeted by an older woman sitting at a desk behind a window.

"Can I help you?"

"I hope so. I want to make sure I have the right key for my locker. I get them all mixed up." He showed her the key. She raised the reading glasses off her nose and leaned toward him.

"Um hmm, that's one of ours."

"Good, that's what I thought." He looked around the window. "What are the hours again?"

"We open at 9 and close at 10." She chewed her gum and maintained a gaze on him, waiting for him to let her return to her reading.

"Right. Okay, thanks. I'll come back."

"No problem."

Although, there actually was a problem, he decided, stepping back out on the sidewalk. Slim chance he'd find the right locker in a place bound to have a hundred. There must be more information he was overlooking. The Chinese symbol. Google was vague, making it out to be a sign for either happiness, death, or opium poppies. He figured he should narrow it down to avoid any mistakes. And if it did turn out to be something along the lines of opium, he could figure out an exit strategy should things get heavy and dark. He hummed the melody to "Happiness Is a Warm Gun."

CHAPTER 24

AFTER HIS MEETING WITH ALICE, Tim sat at his computer workstation and researched Task Lyst. He spent the better part of the afternoon looking at the website and studying the landscape of online service marketplaces. He might not have given it a second thought if it hadn't been for Blue Hill's interest. His predilection for product management threatened to squeeze out his original intent of finding work projects for his drone hobby. To him, the user interface was clunky but the concept clever. These dual interests kept him preoccupied with Task Lyst, and he nearly forgot to pick up his younger two kids from school. Tim sent an introductory email to Task Lyst pitching his latent product management consulting services. He could help with the user interface and mobile application development, among other things. For a negotiable fee, flexible hours, and an equity stake, this was the sort of opportunity Tim salivated over. He'd be back in the tech game.

"How'd your coffee with Alice go?" Sandra sat down on the love seat in Tim's office, a mug of green tea in hand. She was in her comfy clothes: sweats and a hoodie, the combo she favored between the hours of work and bed, perfect for chauffeuring or for those working-out-of-the-house days her employer generously granted, like today.

"It was okay. Nothing game changing, but a few leads to follow up on. I helped her vet a deal she's working on. She says hello."

"Cool. I think I'll see her at book club this week, if I go. I haven't read the book."

"Do you guys ever read the book?"

"No."

"Hey, what's the rest of your day look like?"

"I have a conference call here shortly and then I don't know. Why?"

"I might need some help collecting the kids. I have a project I want to pursue and I should jump right into it."

"Another photo thing?"

"No, well . . . maybe kinda. I just need a few hours this time."

"I suppose. Can I at least make my pedi at six o'clock and you pick up dinner?"

"Thanks, honey." Sandra was supportive of his "me time," encouraging him to find himself on these little outings. Within the recent six months he'd driven to Death Valley, Joshua Tree, Yosemite, and San Luis Obispo to take photos for his portfolio. She felt Tim needed the outlet from all his domestic duties since his last job had ended three years prior. They were financially okay for the time being, but eventually the buffer would erode, and they'd be facing substantial tuition bills. The irony was that it was fiscally wiser for him not to work since the nanny salary was exorbitant. He'd have to be near his previous income level to make it worthwhile. Best-case scenario was him picking up short-term projects he could squeeze into the ten o'clock to three o'clock time frame. He'd strung together a few; a video he scored for the Intel annual shareholders' meeting netted him $3,500, and he got another $2,500 for a MacWorld product demo, helping him build his reel for some unclear endgame.

CHAPTER 25

ELLIOTT DROPPED IN ON FREDDY FU, a quasi-spiritual guru to the musician crowd. Freddy had played bass in the eighties punk-metal band Sacrament and later in Miss Pearl's Night Tremors, who featured on some early Lollapalooza tours. He was a surfer and owned popular body art studios in the Lower Haight-Ashbury and Outer Richmond neighborhoods. His Chinese-American roots extended back to the mid-nineteenth-century laborers who immigrated to California to lay the tracks of the Central Pacific Railroad. Over subsequent generations his family had thrived in Chinatown and throughout the city in various ventures, including real estate, Chinese medicine, import and export, and local government. Freddy was an enigma who'd strayed from the Chinese-American culture as a youth but re-embraced its traditions as he grew older. An iconoclast—musician, entrepreneur, Zen Buddhist, and black belt.

"Freddy, been too long, brother."

Freddy was working on a female client's left shoulder, a fire-breathing dragon's head on a stallion's torso. He looked up slightly to acknowledge his visitor. "Elliott, the man with the plan. How's rock 'n' roll treating you?" He continued his work on the tattoo.

"It's a disease without a cure. I'm terminal."

Freddy chuckled. "One day at a time, right? Keep feeding it and it gets bigger, never to be satiated."

"I don't know about bigger," Elliott said. He sat down on a chair and picked up a magazine from the table in front of him.

Freddy said, "You still with Veronica, the singer girl? I remember you two had something going."

"Naw, she moved to Portland a couple of years ago."

Freddy took a break from the ink, grabbed a towel and stood, stretching his core in a Tai Chi pose.

"It's a young man's game, even this." His trademark ponytail was long gone and he wore his hair close cropped, but the stinger and beard remained, forming a point just beneath his chin.

"How's the Tongue holding up?" Freddy said, referring to a Rolling Stones logo Elliott had tattooed onto his ankle.

"Ha! You remember." Elliott pulled down his wool sock to show off the ink. Freddy inspected it.

"Dude, we should touch it up. On the house. Lifetime guarantee."

"Aw, thanks, I might take you up on that sometime. And maybe get John Lennon on the other one."

"I've done 'Imagine' a couple of times." He hummed the tune in falsetto, eyes closed.

"That would be cool." The two grinned at each other like old friends. Freddy offered him a water.

"I've got to finish up the dragon lady in a minute. What else you got going?"

Elliott removed the key fob from his pocket and handed it to Freddy.

"Any idea what that symbol means? I've tried looking it up online but can't really narrow it down. Thought you might be able to help."

Freddy gave it the once-over, looking closely. He walked over to a shelf and pulled a reference book down. He compared it to a few symbols, turning a couple of pages, forward and back.

"Medicine. Or doctor." He returned the book and brought the key fob back over to Elliott.

"Interesting—so like a universal symbol or something? Not an organization or anything specific?"

Freddy paused. "You running some kind of PI scheme or something?" he laughed. "My man E, the private dick." Elliott laughed with him.

"I just found it, thought it would be helpful to, you know, find the owner."

"Yeah. Maybe a doctor?" Freddy said. "A female doctor." He winked and laughed some more.

"Hey, thanks, man. I'll let you get back." They hugged it out.

"Let me know when you want to touch that up," he said, pointing down. "Take care of yourself. And don't get too curious," he said, emphasizing the *too*. "You remember what happened to the cat."

CHAPTER 26

ALICE SORTED HER INBOX FOR THE EMAIL NOTIFICATION about the payment. She logged into her account to confirm the receipt of five thousand dollars with the option of transferring it to a bank account (subject to fees), Venmo, PayPal, or through a third-party exchange, Bitcoin. She read through the terms and conditions on the tax implications and determined she'd have to report it as contracted work, to be safe. The company, Task Lyst, assumed no liability, as it was merely facilitating an introduction to two parties conducting a transaction, if in fact there was one. She debated disclosing the money to the partners at Blue Hill and considered what conflicts of interest it posed. If it were a check, she could avoid cashing it. Conversely, it was sitting in her account. She could donate it. Her phone vibrated; it was Larry Chang.

"Hey," she said.

"Guess who I just ran into."

"Huey Lewis?"

"Bigger, richer," he said.

"Your ego?"

"Nice, I like that. Vijay Praharashi. He uses Task Lyst for personal assistant stuff: rides for his kids, shopping. Evidently it's all the rage for college kids wanting to make extra cash. We gotta get in on this."

"I'm surprised Vijay doesn't have full-time staff to help, with the kind of money he's made in tech."

"He's interviewing nannies, and it's a great resource for that. Where are you with due diligence?"

"I understand the marketplace appeal, but the numbers are gray. They don't touch the transaction money, so it seems like they're leaving it all on the table. Tax and liability might be the sticking point."

"Are they charging to post jobs? Or for end users?"

"Not for end users, not sure about posting. I'm working on that."

"If you want me to copilot this with you, I'm available. Don't take it the wrong way. I just feel an opportunity here."

"I can appreciate that. I'll have a definitive recommendation on Monday and I'll call if I need to bounce anything off you."

"Beautiful. Ciao!"

"Bye."

Alice ran her fingers through her hair, starting above her eyes, pressing on her skull, and ending up down the back of her neck. She looked straight up at the ceiling, stretching her throat muscles, one of her methods for finding her equilibrium. The fan above her rotated, circulating the air from two open windows. She watched the blades follow each other around at a steady and calming pace. The hum was gentle and soothing, a white noise that masked the sound of the nearby interstate. Her 1930s bungalow had great natural light, and the plentiful houseplants and garden added to the sensory potpourri. Twenty minutes passed as she lost herself in the moment, meditating on nothingness. The earthly world slipped away as she relaxed her mind to an almost unconscious state. A notification alert from her phone broke the spell. Her thoughts returned to the call with Larry. He was right. But she couldn't reconcile it with everything she'd learned at business school. It was like stepping off campus into a casino. Rolling the dice on whichever color was hot at the moment, black or red. Her intuition was being put to the test. Maybe more empirical knowledge would do the trick.

She made a salad of local field greens with almonds, apples, and avocado and paired it with a glass of sauvignon blanc from an opened bottle in her refrigerator. She read through her mail, browsed a Patagonia catalogue, and played some ambient new-age music on Pandora. Her neighbor came by to talk for a few minutes about going out of town. She said she'd be happy to grab his mail for three days. He was off to Seattle on business and might stay the week but wasn't sure. He sold enterprise business software for Oracle and was recently divorced. Worked hard, played hard. They flirted a bit here and there, had shared two bottles of Silver Oak on his porch one time, but fought primordial urges that might ruin their neighborly dynamic. Alice inferred that he liked the distraction she provided after years in a tired relationship. And then a new girlfriend materialized, which paralleled her own brief entanglement with the yoga class guy who turned out to be a drip.

Half a glass in, she pulled up the Task Lyst site to explore the "services offered" side of the marketplace. It offered a rudimentary demo on examples of tasks you could post: household, office, length of term, budget, target demo. As she proceeded through the setup, pull-downs offered variations on how to customize the task or service. She was impressed by the level of depth the platform offered. Her imagination was stoked. With $5,000 of the house's money to play with, why not really test the sucker out. Alice posted jobs for laundry retrieval, grocery shopping, a ride to the airport (the following week she was heading to Denver to see her sister), and pruning the overgrown palm tree that was stealing too much light on the south side of her house. She priced the jobs generously based on averages the interface displayed. Thinking of her friend Tim, she placed one under the category of photography/video, with a vague description about landscapes and thrill seeking, figuring he might be lurking around the site for similar opportunities.

The interface offered suggestions and best practices for how to consummate the transactions. On the user forums, the mysterious Bitcoin payment system was strongly endorsed for its decentralized, peer-to-peer format. Users could avoid the traditional banking system and government tax authorities. PayPal was supported but seemed archaic to early adopters interested in the upside of cryptocurrencies. Many of the tasks could be handled face-to-face, like basic domestic services: lawn care, handyman work, errands. Others, it was noted, could be undertaken without the parties meeting. These included dropping laundry off, messenger service, and other errands. The latter options included fields to enter descriptions on how to accomplish said task. Alice posted one for delivering bagels and pizza—the best outside New York City—to her Monday morning office meeting with Gordie and the gang. She'd present her findings and use the delivery as a real-life example of the service in action. Gordie would eat it up.

Alice topped off her glass and tuned in her favorite Pandora station. "Junk Bond Trader" pulsated through the ceiling speakers.

CHAPTER 27

TIM UPDATED HIS CV AND DOCTORED A PHOTO OF HIMSELF giving a simple slide presentation to a conference room of fifteen salespeople at his most recent consulting job. He dropped the image—in which he was standing up facing the audience, gesturing behind himself at a screen—onto a larger one of Steve Jobs unveiling a new product at MacWorld. Now he appeared to be speaking to hundreds of people at a product-launch conference. He changed the stage's color scheme and added his own PowerPoint slide. In it, he was wearing a button-up shirt with sleeves slightly rolled up and a wireless mic on the open collar. His expensive selvedge denim jeans atop perfectly relic'd black motorcycle boots gave the impression of hipster tech veteran, one foot in the creative department and the other in a C-level executive suite. He added some color to his skin tone and manipulated the pixels to boost his height-to-weight ratio. He uploaded the finished product as his LinkedIn profile shot and, via a mutual friend, requested to connect with the hiring manager at Task Lyst.

Tim refreshed the login page for Task Lyst and searched around for available jobs matching his profile. He found one requiring use of a drone, and applied. The description was straightforward and right in his wheelhouse. Plus it paid $750. He could monetize his hobby while educating himself on this new tech play.

CHAPTER 28

ELLIOTT RETURNED TO THE STORAGE FACILITY once it had opened for the day. With no locker or door number on the key, he'd ask the gatekeeper. The same woman worked the desk, but with a heightened sense of urgency: checking folks in, taking calls, helping tenants, scaring off itinerants trying to gain access to the restroom. She buzzed him in and he thanked her, displaying his key before heading back through the hallway. The first-floor hallway was flanked by rows of spaces approximately six feet by six feet, full of furniture, moving boxes stacked high, bicycles, and junk, all bounded by seven-foot-tall chain-link fence. Further down were ten presumably larger, more private spaces behind pull-down garage doors numbered eleven through twenty. At the end of the hall was a freight elevator that led to identical layouts on floors two, three, and four. Artificial light from sporadic light bulbs, many of which were bare, lit the inside of the facility. The walls were marked up, banged, and scraped with several patched-up areas of primer awaiting fresh paint. The smell of urine wafted through the hall thanks to a restroom marked "Storage Tenants Only." Latin pop music played from a radio as he passed by one of the visible spaces. Inside it, a guy in a tank top stacked some brown cardboard moving boxes. Elliott returned to the front desk.

"Pardon, ma'am. I can't seem to recall which room I'm in. Last name is Gray."

He made the assumption it was a closed room rather than one of the visible spaces. Other than that, he didn't have much to go on. She looked through a binder in front of her. There wasn't a computer screen on the desk. She scanned the page with her finger until it stopped. She looked up.

"Three fifteen. Are you part of that mime troupe?"

"Yes ma'am." He went with it. She picked up a ringing phone and Elliott took his leave, returning to the hallway in search of room 315. He called the freight elevator and waited for it to return to the first level. The metal gate was cool as he pulled it open to enter. An inspection sheet verified that it was safe for use as of July two years ago, signed someone illegible. He pressed the three button and a mechanical noise—a deep clicking of gears which reverberated through the shaft—signaled the journey's beginning. *Next time, the stairs,* he thought.

The key fit the padlock at room 315 and he lifted the overhead garage-style door. He had some hours to kill until band rehearsal and hoped he could get whatever waited for him accomplished in the meantime. Light from a small external window overlooking Turk Street illuminated the confines. There was a wardrobe box with the top half opened to reveal a few mime suits hanging inside. A solitary metal folding chair sat under a table with a decrepit vanity mirror leaning against the wall. Several round bulbs framed the mirror along each side. Taped on it, a photocopy of a typewritten note gave instructions on applying mime makeup. Along the opposing wall were scores of identical four-inch square brown boxes addressed to mostly Asian names with San Francisco zip codes.

Elliott snooped around the storage space. He flipped the switch for the fluorescent ceiling lights and pulled down the overhead door. He studied the layout, covering it on foot and looking for clues as to why he was there and what he was into. The space was spartan except for the stacked boxes with shipping labels, the wardrobe, and the vanity mirror and chair. Elliott didn't have any experience as a mime. He picked up one of the boxes. It was neither heavy nor light; whatever was inside moved a little when gently shaken. The surface was smooth cardboard, not meant for all-weather shipping. The pre-printed laminate label included no return address and no postage. On the floor was a large black canvas duffel bag, empty and folded up. He inferred that it was meant to transport the boxes. Was he supposed to dress up like a mime and deliver packages? Odd. No, ridiculous. He considered bailing out. Then thought of the money. It would take him the better part of a day to get them dropped off, for which he'd be able to cover rent and then some. But he might miss band rehearsal. *Best not to ask questions,* he thought. *What you don't know can't hurt you.* He loaded as many of the little boxes as possible, approximately fifteen, into the duffel bag. He'd have to come back at least once to get the rest. Peeking inside the wardrobe, he counted four mime costumes. One for each size possibility, at first glance. He pulled one from the middle—a medium—and held it up to his body. "Yep, ridiculous," he said aloud. And then, recalling a favorite movie line, "Mime is money."

Elliott changed into the horizontal-striped, long-sleeve black-and-white shirt and then the black suspendered britches. Two white gloves fell out of the black bowler hat that was propped on the wardrobe. The instructions on the mirror included very basic detail: white face, black eye shadow, red or black lips, optional eyebrow or mustache. He was familiar with applying his own makeup from his rock 'n' roll performances and occasional theater cameos over the years. A few minutes in he started to look like Alice Cooper. *Hey, I'm good,* he thought. *Maybe next time I'll go with Ace Frehley.* He posed in the mirror, trying out some mime moves. He executed a feeble invisible box, then attempted walking in the wind. Pulling a rope was decidedly easier. The duffel was bulky but not particularly heavy. He threw his clothes in with the boxes and hung the bag over his shoulder, clutching the leather handle with two hands. After shutting the storage space he made his exit. It was a trick bungeeing the bag onto his scooter, but he'd had similarly obtuse items on there in the past, including guitars and amplifiers. He thought about borrowing the band's van again. But it was out of commission until the timing belt got replaced. After their run up to Chico State, the thing had barely limped back into town before going offline. It wouldn't be fixed until the mechanic could get to it later that week.

Elliott started with the closest addresses, guessing those were the obvious Chinatown locations on Stockton, Powell, and Kearny Streets.

The time he'd spent in this neighborhood was either for late-night eats at Sam Wo's, a favorite of the Beat generation, or for dim sum on Sundays at Golden Harvest. Now he was delivering odd packages there dressed as a mime. The first place was above a storefront for Tai Fung Trading. He parked the scooter on the sidewalk and rang a bell. It was business as usual on Grant Avenue. Not crazy like the weekends, when tourists crowded the narrow sidewalks and shops displayed their produce, trinkets, and imported foodstuffs. But alive still, with nary an English word audible, and multiple dialects of Mandarin, Wu, and Cantonese blending together. It was just as well that he was here to speak the international language of mime. A voice answered through the intercom. Elliott wasn't sure how to speak mime through the line so he resorted to English.

"Delivery? I have a package for . . . Huang Tran?" No reply. But he waited. A door latch was unfastened up the stairs, the chain dangled off its resting place, and someone rambled down the steps. An elderly Chinese gentleman greeted him at the gated door, squinting at the sunlight. Elliott pointed at himself, then the package, then the man, who returned a confused, if slightly amused, look. He tried again, this time by pointing at the name on the label, believing the man would at least recognize his Anglicized name. The old man nodded in the affirmative and opened the gate to receive the package. With no fanfare he started back up the steps as Elliott mimed a thumbs up.

CHAPTER 29

ALICE RECEIVED EMAIL NOTIFICATION that one of her task offers had an interested party. In time, she fielded inquiries on each of the five tasks she had set up. Impressed with the turnaround, she reviewed the activity, updating her entries with approvals, follow-up questions, and procedures. She instructed the laundry valet to pick up and drop off, providing addresses and times. She elected to keep identities anonymous, selecting code names for herself and her hires. She would be "Beatrix," named after the former Dutch queen. The launderer, "Omar," would pick up dry cleaning on Friday morning at Sunbeam Cleaners in Mountain View and drop it off at her side door inside the small white picket fence under the awning. The grocery errand would be at Chef's Market in Los Altos, where she opened up an account tied to her debit card. She provided a list to "Arlene" of items she needed for hosting her book club Sunday evening. The groceries would be delivered in a store-supplied cooler at her side door on Friday afternoon. The palm tree trimmer would be "Gilligan," and she'd meet him in person Saturday morning at the house. A person with the username Buckeye69 was interested in her drone camera gig.

CHAPTER 30

JOHN GORDON SAT AT THE HEAD OF THE TABLE in a glass-walled corner conference room looking out at the hills of Portola Valley. It was a sunny, late Thursday morning, and he nursed a room-temperature bottled water while a venture lead summarized the latest fiscal quarter. Gordie's starched light-blue shirt, tieless and open to the second button, matched the cool blue eyes that monitored the body language of the speaker, Teddy Goldsmith, who had worked his way up the firm's hierarchy from junior analyst to recently made partner. "Thanks, Ted, we look forward to seeing those numbers continue on that trajectory. Alice, do you want to tell us a little about Task Lyst? Are we going to move on this one or pass?"

"Thanks, John. And everyone, for the opportunity to vet this one." She touched an icon on her laptop and pulled up a slide presentation that projected onto a large wall-mounted monitor at one end of the conference room. She rose from her chair and clutched a clicker. She wore a wide-lapeled Armani pantsuit that recalled Lauren Hutton's 1970s feminist elegance. Her hair had a waviness to it, courtesy of the extra-body product she had used that morning. The scent she wore, "citrus and fresh," was meant to exude energy and sophistication according to her style consultant—not dreamy and exotic like her "date" fragrance. The first slide was a stock image of two eager individuals shaking hands. With deliberation, she circled the conference room table to narrate.

"Task Lyst is about supply and demand and trading goods and services. It is a combination of eBay, Amazon, Craigslist, and Angie's List. It's one of many new start-ups serving the emerging gig economy. What makes it unique is its superior user interface and nearly real-time action horizon." She advanced to the next slide, which displayed some dollar figures and tables. "They are a lean start-up, doing about a million in sales—"

"Monthly?" Ted said.

She glared at him. "Yearly. Very scalable, though. As, or *if,* they gain traction, they'll be in escape velocity in no time." Alice checked her audience for cues. "They started with a hyperlocal focus, which gives the platform a competitive advantage over some larger players. As we've seen recently with Uber, Airbnb, and others, you conquer a couple of key beta markets and ride the momentum into a national, then international, launch. They're seeing month-to-month user growth of 500 percent, and it's been live since October."

"How many users are they up to?" Larry said, throwing her a softball.

"Eleven thousand active in the Bay Area. They're ready to turn on the spigot in Seattle, Austin, and Nashville."

The next slide showed an avatar for Alice in a moment of panic, eyes wide and mouth open, as if realizing she'd forgotten something important. She stood next to the image.

"Yesterday, I had a moment of panic. I had too much on my plate and needed desperately to off-load some of my to-dos. I logged in and found people willing to . . ." She clicked to the next slide. ". . . shop for my groceries, pick up my dry cleaning, trim an overgrown palm tree, *and* . . ." She looked at her watch, then up through the glass window to the reception area, where a college-aged young man waited for her signal. ". . . and bring us a quick snack to get us through the rest of the meeting," she said, as heads turned.

The courier carried a gluten-free vegan pizza, another regular pepperoni, a bag of bagels, several pieces of fresh fruit, energy bars, and two large bottles of Pellegrino sparkling water. He placed it on the table to a combination of raised eyebrows and welcoming enthusiasm. Gordie accommodated the diversion, even smiled for a moment. She knew that her clean-living, "body is my temple" boss wouldn't indulge in a non-planned snack.

"Oh, and for you." She tossed Gordie a pack of sugar-free Trident gum—his singular vice—which won her more laughs. An assistant brought in disposable plates, and a few helped themselves to the food.

"So," she paused. "Does this make it a good investment for Blue Hill Capital?" She advanced the slide. All eyes focused on her, despite a few chewing mouths.

"Yes, a five-million-dollar infusion for ten percent puts their valuation at fifty million. They could have a market cap of half a billion the second it goes global."

Ted forced down another bite of pepperoni. "What's the management team look like?"

"Head programmer flamed out at Facebook but led the team at Task Lyst that developed the mobile app. CEO is a young Swiss kid, Pierre Henry. Kind of brash, bright, ambitious. Intellectual background. They're mostly kids wearing hoodies," Alice said.

Ted continued. "How's their burn rate?"

"If they weren't bleeding cash I don't think they'd be out looking for money," Alice replied.

Gordie piped in. "What makes you think they'll give ten percent for five mil? If I were them, I'd go all in or bust. They're seeing deals go down for three billion for a company with ten employees! Probably holding out for Google or Facebook."

Alice clicked to the next slide, which presented three scenarios for the future of Task Lyst.

"Dominic 'Taz' Tarasenko, the CTO, hates Zuckerberg. And I don't think Google has them on its radar. It's just a cute little community tool at this point, with no clear technology angle."

"Any patents?" Larry said.

"That's the million-dollar question. They've disclosed some applications, but I don't know the specifics. We'll need to make some sense of them."

"Who else is looking at Task Lyst?" Ultracompetitive by nature, half the game for Gordie was being first on the scene to secure bragging rights.

She answered, "They were making the rounds before activity on the site took off. Their initial angel is Gwendell Percy who—"

"The musician?" Ted was still wolfing pizza.

"He calls himself a technologist now. He's been making the rounds with them to other accredited investors, calls this the new frontier, micro economies or something," she said, still looking at Gordie.

Gordie seemed amused. "Ah, tribalism. Percy spoke about this at the Grove last year." Gordie was referring to his Bohemian Grove escapades, a perk that came along with riches and influence in the Bay Area. "We're evidently moving away from globalization and back to smaller, independent states based on ethnicity, tribes, and shared interests."

"Scary nut-ball stuff," Ted said, and slugged some water to wash down his grub.

"Depends which side you're on," Gordie said. "Look at Ukraine, Syria, Sudan. . . . People want to break free of outside influence. California could go five or six different ways, let alone three. Everyone fighting over precious, limited resources like water."

"That sounds libertarian. They get to you, too?" Larry said.

Gordie chuckled. As senior managing partner, he enjoyed some reverence from his staff but also appreciated free thinking, second guessing, and good old-fashioned locker-room smack talk. "Everyone's got their price."

Alice said, "Task Lyst does seem to be building a cult following. It bypasses a lot of the traditional conduits of business, like banks and lawyers. The transactions happen outside of the money supply, through Venmo and cryptocurrencies like Bitcoin and Ethereum. The hackers and gamers love it."

Cynthia Varden, who hadn't spoken yet, added, "Great, let's go back to the barter system. Better yet, pure social Darwinism." Cynthia was general counsel and senior partner. A veteran of both tech and liberal politics, she often played the foil to the testosterone-fueled risk-taking that powered much of the office.

"If I can get thirty percent returns and a major liquidity event, I don't care what they're preaching," Ted said.

Gordie ignored Ted. "Gwendell Percy is a capitalist in hippy's clothing. He's looking to make a buck out of this thing . . . before he loses his shirt." A pause filled the air. Gordie was leaning back in his chair, cross-legged. His right fingers stroked an imaginary beard, one that reappeared whenever he left on his extreme vacations, only to disappear soon after he landed at SFO. Alice clicked to the next slide and let it marinate in the silence. Larry poured some water into a glass and added a lemon wedge.

Gordie sat forward. "Cynthia, let's put a pro forma together and take it to our investors in the El Dorado Fund. Alice, can you bring them in this week?"

CHAPTER 31

TIM ACCEPTED AND DELIVERED ON HIS FIRST TASK of filming and editing a five-minute video of coastal footage set to original music with rights clearance. He deployed his drone and GoPro camera for much of the material and synced it up to an ambient soundtrack featuring guitar work drenched in heavy reverb. He Dropboxed the file to "Beatrix" ahead of deadline. The $750 that showed up in his account cemented Task Lyst as his new obsession. Tim was offered additional jobs from the same provider, and his enthusiasm for the platform continued to mount. He began scouring the site for new challenges and thinking of ways to offload some of his own responsibilities. The next Adderall-fueled morning, he cold-called the Task Lyst office to follow up on his job inquiries from the previous week.

Tim was anxious while on hold, awaiting Pierre Henry to pick up the call. His professional tenure in Silicon Valley had once earned him direct-line relationships with many in the start-up world, but now he felt more like a groveling job seeker.

"Hello, it's Pierre," the voice said, almost monotone. The call had connected with his cell phone judging from the background noise.

"Pierre, this is Tim Middleton. I sent you an introductory note early this month and wanted to follow up with you about a consulting opportunity I can provide for Task Lyst. I'm an active user and veteran product guy with several successful exits and think I can add some value to the great work you guys are doing."

Pierre sounded a little distracted, as if he were holding his cell phone with his chin on his shoulder. "One moment please." The distraction continued.

"Sure, take your time." The sound of Pierre at the ticket counter relaxed Tim. He gained the momentum he'd lacked going into the call. He made out small details of Pierre's activities—gaining potentially valuable insight—and concentrated to pick up more. Something about business class and upgrading on United flight 753 to New York. Pierre spoke fluent English, with an impatient continental accent—French or Swiss, Tim suspected. The counter conversation wrapped up.

"Hello? Sorry about that."

"No problem at all; sounds like you're traveling."

"Your name again, please?"

"Tim, Tim Middleton. I sent you—"

"Okay, Tim. You're the guy from eBanc?"

"That's me."

"Product manager. You like working with technical and marketing?"

"I'm part geek and part alpha."

Pierre chuckled. "Better you than me, my friend. Why don't you set up a meeting late this week. I'm away for two days, but my office can schedule something for us. I know we need help with a project, so we'll see what happens, yeah?"

"Terrific. I'll call now and look forward to meeting."

"Thank you, Tom. Have a nice day."

"Uh, that's Tim. And you too, Pierre. I appreciate the chat. Safe travels."

CHAPTER 32

ON FRIDAY MORNING BLUE HILL CAPITAL WELCOMED PIERRE HENRY, Taz Tarasenko, and Gwendell Percy into the office for a breakfast meeting with the intent of exploring an investment stake in their growing start-up. Alice, who had orchestrated the gathering, met them in the lobby. She strode toward the trio at a brisk pace, her heels echoing off the marble floor, calling attention to the combo of khaki skirt and black oxford shirt that straddled the line between professional and sexy. She reached her hand toward Pierre, introducing herself.

"Pierre Henry, I'm Alice Seegar. It's a pleasure to meet you."

"Ah, Alice. The pleasure is mine." He spoke with a sophistication that matched his clean appearance, both of which surprised her. He wore a fitted light-gray Paul Smith suit, blue shirt with no tie, and Prada sneakers. It was natural for him to recognize an attractive woman with a compliment that might run counter to American office politics, but he let his body language do it for him.

She turned toward Taz, the chief technical officer at Task Lyst. "Dominic, welcome to Blue Hill Capital. We appreciate you guys coming by this morning."

He extended his hand to meet hers. "No problem." He came in standard head engineer attire of zip-up hoodie, jeans, and skateboard shoes.

Hanging back was Gwendell, careful not to put himself before the talent. He was bearlike. He wore a Mao coat over his blousy shirt, with a peace sign necklace featuring prominently. His shoes were New Balance running shoes, worn for cushiony comfort rather than performance. His facial hair was passing salt and pepper and approaching Santa Claus, yet trimmed and maintained. His wristwatch was futuristic, like a prototype for martian expeditions. She approached him. "And I saw you play a set at Telluride Summer Fest at least a decade ago. It's such a thrill to meet you in person, Mr. Percy."

"Please, call me Gwendell. Well, as they say, if you remember it, you weren't there." He received her with a two-handed handshake as a symbol of his distaste for convention. She led the three up a staircase, which wrapped around a sculpture that dominated the lobby. Gesturing toward the mythological lion-fish statue, Gwendell asked, "Does Merlion spray water?"

"I think it did before they brought it here from Singapore," she said.

They reached the second floor and proceeded to a coffee kiosk operated by an in-house barista who stood by cheerfully awaiting orders.

"Anyone need refueling?" she said. They all decided it was a good idea, if only to give the charming barista something to occupy her time. They admired the original artwork on display on the foyer walls while they waited for their drinks. Alice thought the trio made strange bedfellows: middle-aged hippy guru, elegant European intellectual, and classic coder geek. *There must be a good story here. We'll start with that.*

They took their drinks down to a conference room near Gordie's corner office, where Cynthia joined them. Cynthia had studied at the Sorbonne in Paris and engaged Pierre in some chitchat in French while the others spectated.

CHAPTER 33

TIM HAD SET A MEETING FOR FRIDAY LATE MORNING with the product team at Task Lyst. He was told on arrival that Pierre and Taz were off-site but might be available for an introduction afterward. Tim was given a tour of the office, which was located south of Market in China Basin Landing next to the ballpark. It occupied three thousand square feet on the southeast corner of the third floor. The atmosphere was cramped, fast paced, and upbeat. Clusters of desks faced each other while small conference rooms enclosed in glass lined the perimeter. Transparency seemed to be a theme. Tim's first impression was that it was a lean, efficient machine primed for scalability, provided it had adequate financing.

Tim and his hosts sat down at a table in one of the glass-walled spaces. Remnants from an earlier meeting remained on a dry-erase board, flow charts and timelines bleeding over one another. Tim noticed an organizational hierarchy with groups of four "monads" assigned to subgroups under the title "market makers." Somebody had doodled a Janus-faced character looking in opposite directions. One was sedate and normal looking; the other had a wild, crazed disposition. *Not bad,* he thought.

The head of product, Rajneesh Mani, went on about the company in broad, vague terms, providing a sort of overview from a product perspective. "There are no other players in the gig economy space that have the programming talent we have," he said, and looked over at a colleague.

A guy sitting on the edge of the table said in the Queen's English, "Which is where someone with your skill set fits in. Our market-making strategy has been successful and we need to expand it, create sellables, monetize the rollout. Raj here has been begging us to scale up his team." He had introduced himself earlier as Clay Crookham. He wore a shirt and tie under a tweed vest, cuffed jeans, and distressed, lace-up ankle boots. His beard was neatly trimmed and he wore thick-framed glasses and cocoa hair in an Afro. He spoke at an urgent pace, with confidence and efficiency, very direct. Tim took note of the cricket bat in his hands. It looked well used, either his or maybe some famous player's, and Clay clutched it tightly as he spoke, rotating it, gripping it as if getting ready for a turn at the plate. He continued. "You played this role at eBanc?"

Tim replied, "I did. I oversaw the active trader platform and was responsible for capturing thirty percent market share of the day trading—"

"By users or volume?"

"Users and volume. But we were after the whales more than the minnows."

"Win over the opinion leaders and the others will follow."

"Precisely."

"What kinds of projects have you been doing lately?"

"Mostly creative. I've been really into photography, digital stills and video. Lately I've been focused on drone technology. I've got the late model Quadcopter, which has been fascinating."

They chatted about the pros and cons of public use of drones and speculated on recent news accounts of some big tech players creating commercial applications involving drones. Many offered anecdotal evidence to support their positions: being stalked by one while hiking, being distracted while driving, and having one land on a soccer field where their brother's kid was playing. Clay was particularly interested, claiming that the technology would support an entire new infrastructure for operations and maintenance, managing flight paths and streamlining the delivery of goods and services.

"The market potential is there, and I think the demand will win out before the government agencies place too many restrictions on who and how they are used. It's basically a footrace for first mover advantage."

Sensing the momentum in his favor, Tim reached into his pocket and pulled out a thumb drive.

"You want to see a quick demo?" Tim pointed to a laptop on the table and assisted in getting the video projected onto a screen positioned at one end of the room. "This is a project I finished this week for a client." He pushed play. It was footage Tim had taken for a real estate office, pitching their knowledge of the high-end residential market in the Bay Area to big spenders overseas. Through the Task Lyst platform he had been paid $1,000 for the three-minute video, which started in Marin County with GoPro footage of the Golden Gate Bridge from the headlands. A great view of San Francisco was captured along with the East Bay in the distance to the east and the Pacific to the west. A voice-over said, "Unparalleled beauty in the highest growth economic market on the planet." Tim had used Philip Glass's "Metamorphosis" as the soundtrack. The soaring aerial shots of the opening scene cut to images of neighborhoods in Pacific Heights, waterfront views from Tiburon, estates in Atherton, and, his magnum opus, a coastal shot of Carmel's Pebble Beach, which culminated in the camera hovering over a foursome putting at the infamous eighth hole. Laughter spread as one of the golfers nearly jumped out of his skin at the presence of the unidentified flying object above him—a subtlety Tim had included for fun, which was not lost on the viewers.

"Poor bloke about had a heart attack," Clay said. "Probably some billionaire thinking someone was putting a hit on him."

Tim jumped in. "These things have a really wicked sound, like a prehistoric wasp."

"At least you know it's coming. Imagine it in silent mode. Whoever develops that generation is going to really be on to something," Raj said.

CHAPTER 34

ELLIOTT SPENT FRIDAY DELIVERING MORE PACKAGES, taking a break for lunch before noon at El Farolito deep in the Mission District. The girl at the counter reminded him with her smile that he was wearing a mime costume. Breaking out of character, he ordered in Spanish, "Carne asada torta, por favor, y un agua fresca."

He sat down by the window and thumbed through the *Fishwrap* that was left on the table. Latin folk music filled the taqueria, and traffic noise from nearby Mission Street crept in through the open front door.

The cover story was titled *Is Tech the New Rock 'n' Roll? Reports from the Cultural Divide.* Elliott had long subscribed to the idea that the money-grab culture of Bay Area technology was pricing out the artists who made the city dynamic and vibrant. Google and Facebook busses shuttling their employees from the city down to the peninsula created an "us versus them" divide matched by the disparity in income each side represented. Many saw the power being centered too much in one place, violating the tenets of sixties idealism to which Elliott subscribed. The predator fish in technology were swallowing up all the minnows, absorbing them into their master plans for monopolistic domination. He viewed anyone joining the conformity as a sellout, reminiscent of the squares who didn't tune in and drop out during the Woodstock generation. The tech revolution, accelerated by rebels like Steve Jobs and Bill Gates, true disrupters, had become corrupted by power, shareholder pressure, and groupthink. Costs of living had skyrocketed, chasing blue-collar residents from their homes. An ocean of pimple-faced programming geeks and newly minted ivy-league MBAs held the future in balance. Music no longer presided over the party, having been displaced by a new gold rush with silicon as the currency.

Elliott was being victimized by this vortex—or was allowing himself to be. Whatever revolutionary voice he had wasn't being heard, which in some way appealed to him. Perhaps he enjoyed a martyr complex, thrived on having a clear enemy to oppose. Maybe this cycle was entering a phase similar to the one the Beats howled about, amid McCarthyism and the complacency of the postwar fifties, stoking the antiwar and civil rights protests that followed. His outlook was framed by a comfortable, suburban upbringing with every opportunity for success. Yet he harbored some hidden conscience that directed him toward short-term fulfillment, steering him away from stable, long-term options. He had skipped his college graduation ceremony and headed straight for the Colorado mountains, following, not leading, classmates there. His plans were of the romantic variety: skiing, freight training, backpacking Europe, and finding some elusive inner peace. He was buying some time, as if he hadn't already bought four years' worth. He half-heartedly joined the middle of the road on occasion, only to be run back onto the shoulder or into the ditch, bailed out by a call home for reinforcements. It made him wince to think about the indignity of failing to pay back debts incurred along the way. His checkered past was littered with small, seemingly minor transgressions that still gnawed at him, justified in the pursuit of art—forward: root, hog, or die. He took the last bite of his torta and closed the newspaper.

CHAPTER 35

GORDIE JOINED THE GROUP AS THE SMALL TALK STARTED.

After Alice made introductions she caught him up. "Pierre was telling the story of how Task Lyst came to be."

"I have a background in neuroscience and came from Lausanne to Stanford to work on my doctorate. I developed an idea for an experiment, which would become the foundation for the company," Pierre said. "Essentially, it can be explained as 'tit for tat.' It is the basis for how we cooperate as humans, to keep us from killing each other."

"Treat thy neighbor kindly until they try to screw you," Gordie said.

"More or less. Generally, one aggressive action is exchanged for another, and then a détente," Pierre said.

Gwendell added, "Nature's balancing act: our genes want to survive by reproducing and snuffing out competition, but our competition wishes the same on us. A stasis develops: we watch each other, sleeping with one eye open."

"Sounds like a cynical outlook on life," Alice said.

"Unfortunately, it's reality. The late, great ecologist Lyall Watson explained genes as following three principles: they inform us to be kind to our kin, to be nasty to our neighbors, and to cheat whenever necessary," Pierre said.

"So how did you get from that to this?"

"To the company? I found Taz through our mutual appreciation of international sport, rugby for me and what you call soccer for Taz. We happened upon each other through mutual friends at a pub in the Lower Haight."

Taz, who had been quiet until now, joined the discussion. "I'm a football nut. Originally from Ukraine. Chelsea is my club team." He spoke with an Eastern European accent, very matter-of-factly, with a quiet confidence.

Pierre continued. "I needed empirical evidence for my theories, so I hired Taz to program my experiment. We set up an online exchange to barter for services. The question was: How far can someone be pushed over his or her self-stated line of morality? You show someone a carrot and keep pulling it further away. Before long, the experiment turned into the thriving marketplace that it is now. Thank God."

"An accidental tourist of sorts," Gordie said.

"I suppose, yes," Pierre replied. "I was an idealist who grew up to be a capitalist. A bridge not so far. And here we are."

Gordie nodded. "Welcome to our world."

Gwendell sensed their curiosity about his role in the company and offered some preemptive context. "We met at a conference the Freedom Forum was hosting. I was moderating a panel on Business 2.0 internet ethics, and Pierre raised some objections to the conclusions I was drawing. A coffee turned into Pernod and the rest is history. The Future Foundation, on which I sit as chairman of the board, led their first round of funding, and now we're out looking for round two."

Alice glanced at Gordie and quickly at Cynthia, taking the cue to proceed. "It's a great story. So you've created something productive with evidence of supply and demand and scalable growth. We've looked carefully at the interface and competitive landscape and feel a well-capitalized second round could give you the escape velocity to claim the space. We'd like to partner with you on this new phase of your growth."

Pierre looked over at Gwendell and Taz, and then back at Alice. "We are ready to see your term sheet."

Alice nodded at Cynthia, who divided a stack of documents into six sets and handed them out. "Please have a seat, and we'll walk you through our proposal," she said, pointing them toward the conference room table.

CHAPTER 36

TIM SENT AN IMMEDIATE FOLLOW-UP EMAIL thanking the Task Lyst group for the meeting. He felt it had gone well. He'd nailed his presentation and was certain they'd established a strong rapport during the two-hour visit. Tim visualized working on the market-making team, heading up a division, and finessing the technical team into actionable items for the marketing department to deploy. He was ready to get going. Within an hour of sending his follow-up email he received a reply. "Dear Tim, It was a pleasure getting to know you this morning. You have an impressive skill set and terrific ideas we see as compatible with Task Lyst initiatives. We'd like to schedule a follow-up meeting to talk specifically about a new project we are launching. Do you have time over the weekend?"

CHAPTER 37

AFTER RETURNING TO THE STORAGE UNIT and filling the duffel bag with more packages, Elliott revved his scooter up the winding road toward Twin Peaks. The iPhone GPS placed his next delivery near the location that had the highest elevation in San Francisco. From Portola Drive he looked down toward Noe Valley. It reminded him to restock his EP records at Monster Records before his next show. That seemed to be the local store that moved his product best. He dug that neighborhood, nestled into a little pocket of the city, hidden and cool.

He found the address and parked a few houses down from it. It was an orderly, clean neighborhood of postwar bungalows, not the rows of Victorians that marked much of San Francisco. This was almost bedroom community territory: cops and middle-class Asian families. He removed his helmet. He was still pretty high up, and the sun penetrated the dissipating fog just enough to warrant sunglasses. The street was quiet. He grabbed the parcel and made his way toward the house. A woman watered a flower box underneath a window that flanked the front door.

She looked midfiftyish, her graying hair in a ponytail underneath a wide-brimmed gardening hat she might have been using to hide from the sun. She snuck back into her house from the tidy porch when she saw the mimed, sunglassed pedestrian approach. Elliott double-checked the address before ringing the door chime. The sound reminded him of handbells, the kind worn by white-gloved players at a Presbyterian church service, a rich, warm tenor slow to attack followed by deep sustain. Jasmine scent and a sweetness he couldn't quite place permeated the entrance. The address on the box said "Xiang Xi."

A younger woman answered, maybe twenty years old. She opened the door enough to be heard. "Yes?"

He displayed the package, with the address showing.

In perfect English she responded, "Are you a mime messenger?"

"How did you guess?"

The older woman called out to her in her native tongue, Mandarin he assumed, and the young woman answered in English. She opened the door further to accept the parcel, which she inspected with a slight frown. "Mimes aren't supposed to talk."

Elliott exaggerated a shrug, contorting his face, and then placed his right index finger to his mouth, the universal sign for "shh, don't tell anyone." Her mouth didn't smile but her eyes did. He wondered if she knew what was in the package. She seemed annoyed by it. The awkward silence was broken by another call from inside and she thanked him and closed the door. He nodded and took his leave.

CHAPTER 38

CYNTHIA LAID OUT A PROPOSAL FOR THE DEAL: five million dollars for 10 percent, valuing the company at fifty million dollars. Blue Hill would receive two seats on the board and get favorable terms on future financing rounds and equity buyouts. Current management would remain in place.

The Task Lyst principals listened, nodding occasionally, wearing their best poker faces. Pierre took notes. Cynthia spoke for nearly five minutes before pausing, turning the floor over to Gordie.

"Thanks, Cynthia. So, this is the cash infusion that will lock up the service exchange space. You guys are positioned to own the market. But it's got to be scaled up now, buoyed by experienced advisors. Perfected locally, launched nationally, then globally."

Cynthia let Gordie's comments marinate. "Still, there's tremendous risk. Money is getting tighter in the banking sector, and some major players could provide formidable competition."

Pierre looked up from his note-taking. He set his pen down on the document and made eye contact with his audience.

"Your valuation is low. We could sell in nine months for a billion dollars if, as you say, a national launch goes well. That would mean twenty-five million active users generating five hundred million impressions and a hundred million in transactional gross revenue."

"That's a stretch. You're at five hundred and forty thousand users now," Cynthia said.

"We're only in beta—" Taz said, before being cut off by Gwendell.

"Look, this proposal is a great starting point. If I can speak for all of us, there's something here that is new, which will benefit how we exchange services. It will disrupt the current landscape in a substantial way, a sea change—"

Pierre cleared his throat, then raised his voice a few decibels. "Five million is five percent. Simple math. Tomorrow it might be two and a half. Or it could be five percent of a much greater number."

Alice did not like the direction the meeting was heading. Egos were being inserted into the equation, which rarely ended well. Pierre was asserting his alpha male intellect over the bean-counting, narcissistic vulture capitalists.

She extended an olive branch. "If the valuation isn't accurate, I'm sure we are amenable to another, closer look at the books. I think we can all agree on the shared opportunity here." Alice said it with some desperation not lost on the others. It was a noble and necessary move, tolerated by both parties. She was sweating through her blouse, she was sure of it.

Gordie further diffused the tension. "I'm hosting a Memorial Day party this Monday out on the bay. I'd love to have you all as my guests. Purely social. We can get to know each other better and go from there." Gordie was well known for his aquatic interests. His passion for sailing included both racing and pleasure cruising, the latter bolstered by his recent purchase of a luxury yacht out of auction from an imprisoned Russian oligarch.

CHAPTER 39

TIM CALLED ALICE TO TOUCH BASE ABOUT HIS MEETING. He wanted to get her intel on where Task Lyst was sitting in terms of seed capital. It was with some certainty he felt she'd divulge at least a little insight into whether it was an opportunity with some upside. Alice was among the hordes he'd cast his spell on playing "Fooled Around and Fell in Love" back in the day. And besides, it was her idea that he look into the company.

"I met with that company you mentioned, and something may come of it."

"Task Lyst? That's interesting. We presented our offer to them today."

"Really. How'd it go?"

"It's still in play. I probably shouldn't say a whole lot."

"Well, they need a product manager for a new rollout, and we have a follow-up meeting off-site to massage the concept a bit. I'm optimistic. I'd like to meet the CEO and CTO, though."

"Oh! I might be able to help with that. Gordie invited them out on his boat Monday. Maybe you and Sandra could make it . . . I'm sure I can add you to my RSVP. It's another of his Electric Kool-Aid Cocktail events."

"Ha! I've only heard about them. Nearly played a gig at one back in the day."

Tim saw no problem spending Memorial Day aboard a sailboat. He was anxious to close the deal on the Task Lyst opportunity, so he made plans to meet for coffee on Saturday with the manager in charge of the project, Raj.

"Tim, good to see you again. Did you order anything?" Raj said.

"Not yet, I just grabbed this table. Let me get this." Tim motioned to get up from his chair but was waved off by his prospective new boss who took his order for a tall coffee with skim milk and cup of ice water. Tim dressed down, it being a more casual follow-up chat to the earlier formal interview. His faded black T-shirt, jeans, and sandals combo was textbook weekend meeting material. The two exchanged small talk about their Friday night activities. Raj complained of a hangover from attending an EDM show in the city, with the disclaimer that "I had a friend in town from grad school." Tim's domestic highlight was a youth lacrosse game, so he spiced it up a bit with references to a power nap, a quick 10k, and juicing.

Raj got right to it. He produced a document for Tim to sign. It was the familiar nondisclosure agreement, making the discussion confidential.

"Tim, we've got a project code-named "Gray DeLorean." It's an experiment to see if we can capture some of the Backpage.com-type business. Are you familiar with Backpage.com?"

Tim thought a moment. "Yeah, the smut ads that used to be in the *Fishwrap* . . ."

"They make a mint on the personals. We think we can disrupt that space, pull the market into Task Lyst. We think you can lead the initiative, what with your history in product management." Raj took a pull from his coffee and readjusted his posture. He looked around the immediate space, a habit he'd developed during off-site meetings, knowing you are likely only a table away from someone else in the Valley working with or against you. He noticed only one suspicious patron against the front window, headphones on and working on an iPad. But headphones were a common decoy for eavesdroppers. Give the impression you aren't listening, then fill in the gaps: who, what, why . . . and sell the info to ValleyWag.com, the Page Six of Silicon Valley.

"This sounds compelling. Would this be a contract job, full time . . . start date?"

"Need you on it yesterday. You'll be an independent contractor. Your official role will be "Outside Consultant," sitting in on occasional market-making meetings and offering some competitive analysis. In reality you'll be dedicated to "GD," working with a coder and designer. You'll be the only one aware of our mission."

Tim sat back. Raj broke eye contact by digging out another document for Tim. It was a formal offer sheet. He turned it around and placed it in front of Tim, first making sure the suspicious patron wasn't watching. Tim leaned forward over the table. It was more than fair, a combination of retainer, performance bonuses, and revenue share.

"What kind of equity can I expect?"

"Five thousand share blocks, based on three benchmarks."

Tim looked for leverage points, but they both knew this was an ideal and generous opportunity.

"Raj, this looks pretty good. I can give you an answer tonight, once I talk it over with my wife. We'll have to make a few quick domestic adjustments if I take this on."

"Fully understand. You can call my cell phone anytime, or text. I think you're a great fit for this, and I hope to be working with you on it." Raj extended his hand across the table, scooping up an Audi key fob in the other. Tim took the cue that the meeting was adjourned, and they returned to small talk as they got up and headed for the door.

CHAPTER 40

MONDAY AT 9:00 A.M. GORDIE LIFTED ANCHOR from a marina on the peninsula and set sail north. The routine was to make stops in Tiburon, Sausalito, and out under the Golden Gate Bridge, depending on wind and wave height. They were picking up some folks along the way and forming a flotilla inside Richardson Bay where it was calmer. Alice was part of the first boarding, and she brought along Tim and Sandra, who had left their kids at home for a day with their grandparents. Gordie barked orders to his crewmen and put Tim to work unpacking a sail as they idled out of the slip. Tim was not an experienced sailor but a quick enough study and welcomed the participation. Sandra intended to do less sailing and more socializing and sported a wide-brimmed straw hat and white linen cover-up. Gordie's wife, Eva, hosted the women on the party deck, while the Gordon boys served as able crewmates. A chef was assisted by two servers who offered mimosas to the group. The sixty-foot yacht was newly named. Having taken it over from the son of a Russian oligarch, Gordie took the opportunity to select his own name rather than translate the old one, "Chelski," to English. It was now dubbed the *Snark II* after Jack London's famous globetrotter. Gordie came over to help Tim finish preparing the sail.

"Alice mentioned you were with eBanc. That was one we let get away."

"Well, I rode it for as long as I could. It was a great experience, good times."

"What are you involved in now? You're also a musician, right?"

"Jack of many trades, master of jack diddly . . . for the moment at least. I'm starting to get back into consulting, product stuff mainly."

"Have you done much sailing?"

"Nope, just around here, nothing competitive or anything. I'm impressed you are actually sailing this thing. It's not just a pleasure cruiser like most of them." Tim ducked underneath the line as Gordie moved the sailcloth to the other side.

"Wait till we get out into the open bay. It really cooks!"

Tim thought Gordie looked straight out of Central Casting for a Viagra commercial—wavy salt-and-pepper hair, tanned complexion, and muted floral-print, short-sleeve, button-up shirt, untucked over tan all-weather shorts and canvas Sperry Top-Siders with no socks—only he was more fit, with low body fat and shaved legs revealing calf muscles toned from cycling.

"You do any racing on this sloop?" Tim immediately regretted making the assumption it was a sloop and not a cutter, brig, or schooner.

"Technically it's a ketch, since it has two masts. A sloop has just one." Gordie answered a cell phone call.

On the main deck Alice and Sandra caught up on life. Alice was dressed to sail, having grown up navigating Hobie Cats in the Long Island Sound. But she kept Sandra company with four other wives and girlfriends of Silicon Valley masters of the universe. Eva, wife number two for Gordie, instructed the servers on where the serving trays and composite "glass"ware were stored.

Sandra said, "We owe you big time for hooking him up with Task Lyst. He's going to be helping them out a bit, consulting. He's excited about getting back into something. *I'm* excited about him getting back into something."

"I'm so glad. They are lucky to have him. A couple of the principals should be joining us later up in Tiburon."

CHAPTER 41

ELLIOTT CALLED IT A DAY. It was too hectic to get over to Telegraph Hill with Friday rush hour, so he decided to finish first thing tomorrow and parked in front of his flat. He had three more deliveries in his duffel and could drop them off before an eleven o'clock Saturday breakfast meeting with his booking agent at the Labyrinth Agency. He changed out of his mime costume and opened a can of Olympia, a delicious reward for a couple of days of hard miming. He put on the first side of Luna's *Penthouse* and started a bath. In it he'd finish reading the weekly he'd started at lunch. As he slid open the bag's zipper, his curiosity returned about the contents in the box. He had come up with a few theories over the course of the day. Some themes materialized. But he wasn't sure he wanted to know. Ignorance is bliss. What if it wasn't legal? He was pretty sure he knew the answer to the question. On some level, it was fishy. But fishy was better than outright wrong, and the money was good enough . . . too good, actually, to blow it by bringing the conscience into it. On the other hand, maybe he was just being paranoid. It could just be some old-world method at play for avoiding taxes, flying under the radar, getting things to people outside of the mainstream capital structure. Fuck it, sounded good to him. Irreverence was okay in his book; screw the system. He made a list of debts and bills coming due and thought about what to do with his imminent surplus.

He could have used a gig like this a few years back when he needed to sell off a trove of musical instruments for some quick cash, a decision he now regretted. His band at that time had disintegrated, and, acting on impulse, he made plans to follow a girl to New York, where she was enrolling in graduate school. On the eve of Elliott's departure from San Francisco, a guy answered his classified ad and arrived with an intoxicating wad of greenbacks. The buyer took the advertised '79 Fender Stratocaster for asking price and the Roland JC-120 amplifier for another $800.

"What else you got?" he said.

Elliott held the $1,600 cash in his hands, contemplating what another grand or two could add to his freedom.

"I've got a couple more things, but they're not really for sale." He was hesitant, but the buyer knew vulnerable when he smelled it.

"Well, I'm stocking up, so if you have anything, I'd be happy to look at it."

Elliott scratched the back of his head and looked out over the bay toward Marin County. If he was truly springing free, he ought to just lighten the load and start fresh. He'd miss this view, but he was antsy, feeling played out. His debutante old lady was pulling him just enough that it was worth uprooting for a new adventure. Without the band, it seemed logical. Elliott wanted to be the poet, or to star in someone else's epic poem. He wasn't sure if he wanted to be Kerouac or Moriarty. But he was sure he didn't want to be a towel boy at the fancy downtown athletic club where he'd spent his first year in town working. He recalled his last day on the job when some capital markets guy, heading up to the roof sun deck, asked Elliott to apply sunscreen to his back. It seemed innocent enough, help a guy out, it being part of the job description and all. He'd only signed up to check people in at the garage entrance for shit pay while strumming a hidden guitar. It was great to have access to squash courts and free weights, and some okay folks worked there. But he grew tired of the captains and queens of the universe who paid a shiny nickel to keep themselves beautiful. Faced with the task of applying lotion to another dude's back, Elliott no longer accepted the trade-off.

"Even pedals. I'll look at any stomp boxes, effects, microphones . . ."

"Gimme a sec." Elliott returned to the living room with his 1968 Italian-made Vox. It was in its original gray coffin case with a roach burn they all speculated was from the early seventies. It was Elliott's signature axe during his late teens playing beach parties and all ages cafes. It was unfathomable that he'd be without it.

"Ooh, nice man. Mind if I try it?" the buyer said. He picked it up and looked down the neck for any warpage. He made the rudimentary finger positions for an E chord and strummed twice. That appeared to be about all he knew.

"I'll give you five hundge for it."

"It's not really for sale." Elliott replied before the figure registered with him. It wasn't worth any more in dollars. But quick math took him up to $2,100 if he accepted. Some impulse not governed by his rationale self-answered, "I've got a matching Vox amp, a Berkeley II on the original stand." He went to fetch it.

"Hmm, Solid State, right? Better if it were tube. Let me see. Everything works on it? Reverb? Tremolo? I can do nine hundred for both. That taps me out." Elliott, blinded by the wad of greenbacks, relented.

Any surplus, he reasoned, should go toward cutting a new single. An A and B side of some new material. He'd do it right and get something shop-able and slick. Any money beyond that would go toward touring behind it, and stopping in LA to pitch music supervisors. But the move to New York ended up lasting only three weeks, and with his band dissolved, he ended up back at square one.

Two weeks went by, and Elliott fell into a routine of delivering the identical little boxes that kept mysteriously appearing in the storage unit. His latest theory had him delivering homeopathic medicines, herbs, and Chinese remedies to law-abiding folks outside of the mainstream of corporate medicine. He'd almost forgotten any suspicions he'd had. He abided by the mime suit, thinking the anonymity couldn't hurt. He didn't want to upset the system, one that seemed to be flowing money. And like clockwork, his account balance grew. Elliott had by now switched to taking his payouts in cryptocurrencies via a third-party exchange. His initial foray of $2,000 for four Bitcoins increased 20 percent in value literally overnight. He doubled down on his next few payouts, seeing his Bitcoin holdings cross the $15,000 mark. With bills to pay, he had to convert some into cash. He found a smattering of online retailers that accepted the mysterious new currency, but these didn't include his big-ticket expenses: rent, student loan, and walking around money. Otherwise, he had to navigate the murky waters of Bitcoin exchanges. The market's volatility made trading out of Bitcoin for dollars somewhat challenging. He took a hit the first few times, watching the value shoot up after swapping out. But he made a killing when the value shot up 1,000 percent on a historic three-day run. After reading stories of hackers making off with millions, he took out some profits and stashed them away in a Wells Fargo ninety-day certificate of deposit to hedge against a major correction. Ongoing, he would adopt a 50/25/25 split: half out in dollars, one quarter staying in Bitcoin, and the remaining quarter into a Wells Fargo cash account. He was comfortable riding out the roller coaster of market sways considering the tax advantages of hiding the paper trail.

CHAPTER 42

GORDIE ENDED HIS CELL PHONE CALL. "Thanks, Tim, you look like you're gettin' the hang of it. I think we're good for now—let's see what the rest of the party is up to." Gordie shimmied his way between a railing and the bow, leading the two toward the main deck.

"My pleasure. It's great to be on board," Tim said. "How far have you traveled on this baby?"

"I've had this one since the beginning of the year. Sailed her down to Catalina, and planning a Hawaii trip next. Eventually I, we, plan to live on it for a year or two, once the kids are out of the nest."

"Nice. Like Jack London," Tim said. Gordie turned around, sizing him up again.

"You a Jack London guy?"

"Well, a little, I guess. I know he sailed the world on a boat called the *Snark*, although I seem to recall it didn't end well."

Gordie grinned, patting him on the back. "My man Tim knows his stuff; impressive. I play Jack in a little play we do occasionally up in the Grove. He was a regular, you know. A true and original Bay Area bohemian."

"I haven't been to the Bohemian Grove, but I'll take your word for it," Tim said.

Gordie answered, "We'll have to get you up there sometime." He sent Tim up the stairs to the main deck, first patting his shoulders for a second like a football coach would a young player's.

Alice was holding a Diet Coke, listening to Sandra recount a recent visit to Solage in Napa Valley. Balancing a high-pressure job in the

Valley with three active kids required rejuvenating treatments and other indulgences.

"Tim and I were married there and try to get back at least once a year on our anniversary. It's heaven."

"So true. I've been a few times." Alice indeed had been twice, once with Mr. Wrong and once with Mr. Could-Have-Been. She was anxious to change subjects, but Sandra pressed her.

"So what's going on in your love life? Any new prospects?"

"Not much and not really. I think I aged out of the meat market scene. But I seem to attract every middle-aged married man experiencing a midlife crisis."

"Yikes."

"I know. Rich and bored, looking for a distraction. No thanks."

"What about Tinder or Bumble? Have you tried those sites?"

"I'm more of an online Scrabble gal. Word games with strangers. No risk of a bad date."

Tim joined the conversation.

"You learning how to sail this thing?" Sandra said, kissing his forehead as she playfully pulled him toward her with her free hand, the other holding her glass.

"I'm ready for the regatta."

The *Snark II* coasted into port at Sam's Cafe in Tiburon a little before 11:00 a.m. Gordie anchored a hundred yards from the marina and sent a dinghy to load the next wave of guests. The cove at Tiburon was protected from the strong ocean breeze coming through the Golden Gate, making for a pleasant pit stop. Scores of conversations blending with the percussive clamor of silverware could be heard above the restaurant's music system. Pierre and Gwendell were settling their tab at a patio table among the revelers while a party of three hovered, ready to pounce on the next available table. Pierre reached for his wallet in a tote bag hanging off the back of his chair. Gwendell took it all in behind sunglasses that had giant lenses that wrapped around his face. They featured a prototype mechanism that allowed him to read electronic messages.

"Looks like our ride is here," Gwendell said, glimpsing the *Snark II*'s mast beyond the marina.

"Boys and their toys, my grand-mere used to say," Pierre said, before looking down to sign the credit card receipt. He adjusted his sunglasses and tossed his napkin on the plate of fruit he had hardly touched. He threw back the remnants of his Bloody Mary, bit off the end of a celery stalk, and rose to greet the crew in the dinghy next to the dock.

Also joining them on board was one of Gordie's adrenaline-junkie pals, Ned Wolfe IV, who presented a case of vintners' reserve cabernet to the hosts as he climbed on board.

"I meant to send you one for the christening of this baby, but better late than never." Ned's bio usually listed him as "sportsman" and "angel" investor along with "scion to one of the oldest Napa Valley wineries." Gordie and Ned were connected through the Bohemian Club and shared a penchant for extreme skiing, destination surfing, and return on investment. Ned didn't make it through undergrad because he was sowing his oats on adventure instead. But what irked people the most was the ease at which he had turned a modest trust fund into stupid wealth. For two decades he'd been placing the right bets, rarely missing. By investing in early rounds of start-up tech companies, he'd built an empire of equity in the likes of Cisco Systems, Sun Microsystems, and Intuit. He held the largest individual position in the El Dorado Fund managed by Gordie and Blue Hill Capital.

Introductions were made and the crew prepped for open water. Pierre asked Ned about the wine, and they chatted at length about viniculture, hitting it off immediately.

CHAPTER 43

THE AMERICAN, WHOM THE OTHERS KNEW AS JEROME, *scribbled some thoughts into a well-traveled spiral-bound journal. They had settled into their accommodations, and there was a discussion about grabbing something to eat. The pace in Chefchaouen was lazy, dreamlike. Any sense of urgency whatsoever was left outside the medina, and group decisions seemed comically ambitious. Simon, the Aussie studying near London at The University of Kent, rolled a cigarette filled with loose-leaf tobacco and locally procured hashish. It was habit at this point, partaking on the hour to keep spirits high. Except for the duo from Cambridge. They were square about the kif. They had come along for the journey from Barcelona two days earlier, having overheard the middle-class bloke from Oz and the American talking about Morocco. On a lark, the pair asked if they could tag along, hoping for warmer December weather. But they kept to themselves. They shared a stiff, academic air that was lacking a sense of humor or inspiration. Still, they recognized the value in mixing with other nationalities and taking chances on their winter recess from university.*

The American, full of optimism and restless energy, was acting ringleader. He was slightly older and out in the real world. His fixation on Chefchaouen became a quixotic myth to the others. There was question as to its actual existence let alone relevance to students on break from studies. The Yank's magnetism offered a mysterious upside, however, one that they didn't want to take for granted. He seemed the West Coast type: suntanned, beachy hair, personable, and athletic. He embodied lightness, or lack of gravitas at least. This rubbed off on others, making him easy to follow. They could leave their caricatures for a brief time, rallying around this new curiosity. The Kentian grad student, Simon, identified with him right away on the Barcelona beach. Sharing a similar socioeconomic background, it was easier to be the extrovert and engage the Yank. The stiff Cambridgers could then follow.

The journey had taken them through Madrid to Gibraltar by train, then down to Tangier by ferry. Outside the station in Madrid, the Yank dazzled a pack of Spanish children when he joined them in playing football in the moonlit street. His technique and fitness were more than what would have been expected for an American playing the European game. Simon commended the American on his "brilliant footwork and playmaking, a bit of magic, really."

With busy Tangier and crazy Fez now in the rearview, it was on everyone's mind that they'd found their destination. What happens now? Breathe, take in the view, be in the moment. *The American took a break from his journaling, took a hit of Simon's spliff, and imagined being there in 1967.*

Out of earshot of the square duo, he said, "Simon, let's have a look around. I read about the Stones getting into some poppy tincture down here. I'm curious about it. I'd like to walk around and see if any of these shopkeepers are hip to it."

"You mean like opium? I suppose I'm interested. I'm not looking for a habit of course, but I wouldn't mind sussing it out. I'm on interlude, after all."

The four dressed to explore the medina. Shorts and sandals were augmented by fleece pullovers or the equivalent. A pleasant but cool night awaited them. The American and Simon paired off in search of tincture. The other two followed but soon drifted off to pursue their own curiosities.

"Any clue how we'll find our way back here? It all looks the same," Simon said.

"By design, I imagine. We'll just walk until we hear the accents of two upper-class Cambridge muppets." The American gave his best Cockney impression on the final words.

Simon loved it. "Hey, that's impressive. Very Dartford East End!"

They wound around and down, looking back up the fifty feet or so to their balcony in the pension, creating a mental image of where they were. As the tight-walled path in the labyrinth flattened out, they came to occasional merchant shops identifiable only by the counter and stools or Coca Cola signage. At one of these stalls Simon inquired, using makeshift sign language, about tea.

"Do you have any tea? Or could you point us in the right direction?" He pantomimed drinking tea, then pointed left and right.

The old man with the gray beard gestured for them to have a seat at the stools at his counter. They obliged. The floor was bare, just a dirt surface but well kept. The place was tidy, and the kitchen was merely a single-burner stove and two cabinets. The old man presented two canisters of loose-leaf tea, one that appeared to be a mix of tobacco and cannabis and the other smelling of mint.

"Do you make opium tea here?" Simon said. The American was impressed with the bravado of his friend, direct and on point.

"Poppies . . ." With two hands he created a bulb-like form and ran his fingers down a long imaginary stem.

The old man casually affirmed the question in his native tongue. "Khash-khash." Much was left to translation, but he stepped out from his place behind the counter and instructed the two to stay. He scurried off while the two glanced at each other.

Simon said, "You don't suppose he is going to get the police?"

"For what, asking for something unintelligible?"

"Right, we'll just deny it."

The old man returned after a long minute. He mumbled something they didn't understand and pulled a handful of light-brown, dry organic material from the cylindrical storage container. He put his fingertips to work breaking up the substance into smaller bits while a kettle of water simmered on the burner. The two watched. It certainly looked like poppies—the shape of the buds was unmistakable.

"Is there music around here?" Jerome said. He mimed a flute melody.

The old man looked up and took notice of the question before scooping up a cup of the organic material and dropping it into the kettle. He made eye contact again and said, "Brian Jones?"

"Yes," Simon said.

The American added, "The Pipes of Pan at Joujouka?"

The old man nodded his head and pointed somewhere toward where the sun had just set. His words were lost on the duo, but the message was clear.

"We can find them over there?" Simon said.

The man tended the boiling concoction, stirring the material around. He reached for a strainer hanging from a peg and two ceramic drinking cups.

Placing the strainer over the first cup, he poured the steaming liquid, catching various-sized plant matter on the metal screen. He repeated the step for the second cup and delivered the drinks to his patrons.

"Well, bottoms up, then. Tell me mum I love her." Simon sipped first. "It's not Bushmills, but not half bad either." He sipped again. The old man watched them. The cool evening had replaced the dusk in their short time at the shop. It was a pleasant sixty degrees, the air was still, and an unpolluted sky displayed Andromeda in full view. Evening prayers were tapering off. Remnants of the chants wafted over the walls of the medina, winding through the paths, blending together occasionally but each standing alone, distinct. Never a chorus or in unison. The exotic wails of the devout paying homage to Allah. Time slowed down considerably as the two made their way through their tea. The American wondered if he was feeling any effects from the elixir. Or maybe it was just the hashish from before. The relentless warm glow of a smooth, all-day buzz. No, it was pretty clear. Dried poppy bulbs and their long stems. Crushed up and boiled. It was Simon who suggested they settle up and move along. Both shook the old man's hand, bidding him adieu. The American cupped both hands around the old man's bony, wrinkled appendage and bowed slightly. The man handed Jerome a torn-out page from a map with a village circled on it. "Joujouka," he said, and Jerome nodded and repeated, "Joujouka."

Outside, Simon said, "I feel like we just met our guru. Keys to the city and all that. Brilliant."

"Keys to the door of perception . . . and whatnot."

CHAPTER 44

THE *SNARK II* SLIPPED OUT OF THE CALMER WATERS of Tiburon and back toward Alcatraz in the middle of the bay. The wind picked up considerably in just a quarter mile. Gordie was in captain's mode, steering the vessel and reading instruments. Ned Wolfe helped unwrap a sail and ducked under the mainsail boom. Sea spray came over the stern as he dropped below to the cabin lounge. Tim, Alice, and Sandra were there and greeted him.

"Ned, I'm Tim. We didn't meet formally earlier." Tim extended his hand and added, "And this is my wife, Sandra." Ned accepted his hand and then Sandra's. Alice and Ned acknowledged having met up on deck a few minutes prior. Ned stood an inch over six feet and appeared to be in active shape. His faded T-shirt showed off his naturally defined biceps and triceps shaped from a lifestyle rather than a gym. His pants were rolled up high above his bare ankles. His footwear was similar to Gordie's and seemed the right tool for the job. He unwrapped a weathered gray wind jacket from around his waist and tossed it on the chair. His eye contact with each of them displayed a warmth that balanced a strong sense of self-confidence.

"Who's up for a gluten-free, low-carb, locally sourced, electric snack?" Ned said, reaching into his daypack. "I've got some medicinal grow fields up in Mendocino, and I make a point to test the merchandise." He held up a ziplock bag of baked goods and flashed a Cheshire cat grin. He opened the bag and wolfed one portion and passed the bag to Tim. Inside were a half-dozen two-inch-square pieces that resembled energy bars. On the bag was a logo sticker that read "Day Glow Squares" in front of a pot leaf.

"Tempting," Tim said, inspecting the goods.

"My biochemists are patenting a quicker-acting recipe that metabolizes in half the usual time. Don't ask how they do it. I've set them up in a lab that would make Owsley Stanley jealous." He laughed. His eyes moved to the ladies. "What do you say, ladies? Want to make things interesting?"

"Sounds like you know what you're talking about," Alice said.

Ned answered, "I've had some experience. And with the new legislation, I didn't want to get left on the sidelines."

"I'd consider splitting one. I'm a lightweight when it comes to grass," Sandra said.

"I'm worried even that much would mess me up," Alice replied.

"I'll take one," Tim said as he plucked one out and gobbled it up. "I have a medical card, so technically it's doctor's orders."

"Doctor's orders . . . I like it. I'm very suspicious of any doctor who doesn't let nature nurture." He took the bag from Tim and split one square for Sandra and Alice. "Satisfaction or your money back!" he joked.

A voice came from above. "Ned, let's make a move. I want to make a run for the bridge before the wind blows out."

"Yes, Captain," he shouted back. He whispered to the others, "The ink's not dry on Gordie's captain's license, but I like to make him feel like he's in control. But I'll be the one sailing this thing once we get into the big stuff."

Tim positioned himself on the deck, and while awaiting shipmates' orders from the alphas, he reintroduced himself to Pierre, mentioning their brief phone conversation and his meeting two days prior with Raj about the consulting gig.

"Pierre, I don't know if you remember, but I'm the one who cold-called you about working in product at Task Lyst last week."

Pierre replied, "Oh yes, how are you?" He shook Tim's hand.

"Terrific. I didn't expect to hear back so fast, but I met with Raj and I'm starting this week on a UI project, sounds like it needs a quick turnaround."

"How are you connected to this . . . regatta?"

"I go way back with Alice. In fact, she—" He was cut off by Pierre.

"And Sandra's your wife?" He pointed to her.

"Indeed."

"She's a very pretty lady. And do you have kids?"

"Three. One pair and a joker."

"That's a lot of fun, I'm sure."

Tim cleared his throat and changed the subject to shoptalk. "And thank you for giving me the opportunity to help. I think it's a terrific product already, clearly the front-runner in the space."

Pierre's expression turned quizzical. "And which space is that?"

Tim thought for a split second. "A marketplace for services, an online exchange—"

Pierre smiled. "Is that what it is?"

Gwendell had returned and caught the tail end of the discussion, handing a bottled water to Pierre. In his rich baritone he said, "The creator likes to think of it more as a laboratory than a bazaar. A company can be as complex and adaptable as any individual, continually shaped by internal motives and external pressures. It is pure at birth and then becomes a reflection of the culture it permeates."

Pierre laughed. "It sounds so theoretical when you say it."

Tim laughed too. He was trying to stay above water with them.

Pierre added, "Tim, yes, Task Lyst is as you say it is. But we must be careful not to give it such a precise definition for fear of stasis, rendering it unable to compete in a fluid market. In the first dimension it could be a marketplace. In the second? The third? There are layers hidden to the naked eye to consider."

"In work as in life," Gwendell added.

"And in love," Pierre added, trying to keep a straight face. Gwendell belly laughed, and Tim felt his social skills swirl down a vortex of twisted logic and passive-aggressive humor.

Pierre continued, "To most people, the company is whatever they want it to be: an employer, an exchange, an investment, a—"

"A godsend, a white knight." Gwendell added.

Pierre nodded. "A scape goat, a cause célèbre, or a monster . . ."

The *Snark II* edged past Alcatraz Island to its north and set its sights on the Golden Gate Bridge. The sun was out in the middle of the bay, but fog rolled over the headlands to the bridge's north from the distant Pacific. Looking to the left, the fog blanketed the outer reaches of the city and dissipated as it approached the financial district toward the inner part of the bay. To the immediate north, sun and calmer waters placated pleasure cruisers and small watercraft in Richardson Bay near Sausalito.

Sandra looked over in the direction of the latter. "Aren't we heading over to Sausalito? Looks warmer there. I think I'll go below deck and borrow a wrap." The boat picked up speed in the channel and approached twenty-five knots. Wave height was increasing, making the ride bumpy and wet. A massive cargo ship loomed ahead, emerging part way out of the fog. Its periodic fog horn grew louder and joined a chorus of several others entering and exiting the bay.

Alice was tempted to join Sandra down below but felt cozy enough in her fleece jacket. She had learned to dress warmly on the water, in layers, and to expect both sun and fog along with wind and waves. The rhythm of the boat became hypnotic. The sun was still out and warm on her face despite a light spray of icy seawater threatening with each wave crest they hit. She recalled sailing the East Coast spots off Block Island and Martha's Vineyard as a kid. Dad and his new wife had enjoyed fabulous weekend excursions that differed from the ones to which she was accustomed before her parents' divorce. Memory snapshots of family trips from her earlier youth, when her family was still intact, seemed black and white, or sepia, but at the same time more holistic. It was a core family, and Alice was still naive about the sustainability of love and marriage. Upon further reflection there were cracks in the foundation, but at the time she led the life of the entitled oldest daughter of Mr. and Mrs. Waspy Privilege. Shit hit the fan in high school when the split was announced over dinner at the family home, where her father was rarely sleeping. He was commuting to New York, and the truth of his new life there wouldn't reveal itself for several months and wouldn't hit home for much longer thereafter. She had heard somewhere not to blame herself. Maybe in an afternoon special on ABC. She took the divorce the only way she knew how and built a steel wall in front of her to ward off anyone who broached the topic. Resentment was thrown on her mom and any other family members for whatever role they'd had in perpetuating the charade of family happiness. There was no scorecard for who won and lost, just a body count. Yes, there were rumors. It was post sexual revolution. Like many couples, her parents had married too young. Once her dad's new girlfriend entered the family mix, those sailing trips became painfully awkward. Alice pretended to play nice with the future stepmom, who offered no empathy or olive branch and was quick to reinforce her higher position in this newly forming hierarchy.

"I rescued a puppy out here in the channel once." Ned Wolfe had snuck up on Alice and broke her daydream. As she turned to face him, the boat topped a wave and sent her off balance. He caught her hand and steadied her.

She fixed some hair back behind her ears. "Did you say a puppy?"

"I did." Ned leaned against the starboard railing. "We were on a twenty-four footer, same heading we're on now. I look starboard and see this thing swimming. Struggling, it looked like. I'm thinking, 'Did we just sail past a dog?' But you know, we're going fifteen knots, and coming back around would have been a serious detour. But the lady I'm with, she sees it too. So yeah, we're doubling back. We take a couple passes before we find it. At first it looked like a seal, but it was dog paddling. So I take a beach towel and reach over and pull the little thing in, all wrapped in a towel. It's getting dark by now, and instead of meeting friends in Sausalito, we need to get this tired, wet puppy back to shore. So, the lady I'm with holds the puppy all wrapped up in towels, and I get us back to the slip in Belvedere. She's got this houseboat there, and we take the little feller in and dry it off, offer it some water. It's a mangy looking thing, real bizarre. And it's a little feisty. We think, well, maybe it's scared. Let's not mess too much with it. We lock it inside and I go and tie up the sailboat, batten down the hatches, while she walks to the dock shop for some dog food and to call the humane society. We're both back there in fifteen minutes, and first thing we see is her cat freaking out, climbing the screen door. It's got blood on it and my lady friend goes into panic mode. I grab her arm and keep her from entering. I'm like, 'Hold my beer.'"

"Ah, chivalrous," Alice said.

"Right, total dumb-ass move, had I known what a dingbat she was. So I take this antenna pole that's resting next to the door. Slowly I open the screen so the cat can get out. It flies out of there. Lady can't even grab it in time. Not sure she ever saw it again. Now I'm inside and looking for this beast. But you know, I've got this metal pole to defend myself. I inch my way into the cabin and peek down into the pantry. I see the dog down there so I close the pantry door, locking it in. We'll get the humane society over here, and they'll take it from here, right?"

"Sure," Alice agreed.

Ned nodded, waving a finger in front of her. "Humane society won't come until the morning. So we're stuck with this thing until then. By now I'm pretty irritated. Lady friend is bugging out about her cat. I'm plotting my escape, but she'll have none of me leaving. Not with the thing in the pantry. So what am I gonna do?"

Alice considered his predicament. She realized a warm pleasantness had come over her. She was captivated by the story and very much in the moment. A cannabis high had crept up on her. She had forgotten about it in the forty-five minutes since she'd eaten the energy bar. Suddenly she was very comfortable listening to this rambling story from a guy she had only just met. He was radiant in his storytelling, animated and funny. She imagined herself with him in that houseboat. "You're gonna stay with her until the morning."

Ned broke into a smile. "Right? It was a first date, if you want to even call it that. And I'm in like Flynn. I mean, that's what I was thinking, silver lining. We open a bottle of 1974 old vine zinfandel I had with me, and I do my best to comfort her. Usually I don't drink something this old without a decanter, but I make an exception. Don't get me wrong, I'll drink from the bottle, but this is a '74 for cryin' out loud. About an hour goes by and we're having a laugh. Bottle's long gone and we're drinking her grocery-store swill. Out of my left ear I'm hearing this sound coming from the pantry area. A few minutes pass and I'm curious. I tell lady friend, 'Wonder what Fido's getting into under there.' A continuous chipping sound, syncopated like. I get closer. It sounds like it's gnawing on something. I ask her, 'What's down there that might be getting eaten?' She thinks maybe some cereal or pancake mix. We get sidetracked and forget about Fido. Morning comes. Knock on the door. Humane society. She shows them in and points to the cabinet hatch. The guy has a dogcatcher contraption and a heavy glove in the other hand. He points a flashlight into the space and looks around. 'See anything, pal?' I ask.

"'Looks like you've got a pretty sizable leak. But I don't see a dog.'

"'Say what?' I peek in next to him. 'Holy shit!' There's water coming in from a soccer-ball-size hole right at the water line. There's water spilling in but not enough yet to conceal a dog. The hole is gnarly, with shards of fiberglass sticking out.

"'What did this dog look like?' the humane society guy asks. I explained where we got it and what it looked like, how it behaved.

"'Hmm. Let me make a quick call. Can I use your telephone?' He talked for a few minutes while we looked for a water pump and a patch kit. I expressed my concern that the patch kit wouldn't be enough and she'd be advised to call in professionals before she sank. The guy hung up and said, 'Well, from your description, that probably wasn't a dog.'

"Lady friend looked at me and then back at him. 'Well what the fuck was it, then?'

"'We've seen some cases similar to this before. They're all variations on the same thing though. Struggling small dog found swimming in shipping channel, rescued by thoughtful boater, brought back to land . . . fortunately this one doesn't end in injury or death, yet at least.'

"I give him the stink eye for a second and say, 'You want to be a little more specific, pal?'

"'What you caught out in the water and brought home was a Liberian cargo rat. Big as a small dog and meaner than a snake.' He lets it sink in. I just stare back at him. Lady friend got sick, I think. Physically ill." Alice spasmed as she imagined the horror that the "lady friend" had gone through. She felt herself grab Ned's forearm as if they were in a theater watching a horror film and the killer had just jumped out at the damsel in distress. He continued, "Dogcatcher said, 'They fall out of cargo ships, possibly thrown overboard by seamen. They're pretty good swimmers, and some make landfall at Angel Island; others ride the current over to Oakland and Emeryville. Biggest one we've come across was twenty-eight pounds and pregnant. It's actually living in a lab somewhere. No matter how recent you are on your rabies shot, I'd get checked out. No telling what foreign diseases they can bring with them.'"

Alice had so many questions, but her state did nothing for her articulation. All she could muster was, "That is so disturbing." She wanted to listen to Ned some more. She liked having him do the talking so she could veg out and let her senses fly their freak flag. The sun was starting its fall over the bridge in front of them. The fog seemed to have burned off somewhat. But the wind was stronger. It felt good on her face even with her eyes watering from behind her sunglasses. When she closed her eyes and opened them again, wide, a kaleidoscope of colors flashed in front of her. She repeated the trick several times. She was thirsty. Saltwater spray, wind, and sun was dehydrating her, and some water would be nice. But how would she get it? She might run into people and have to speak. It was safer here with Ned.

"How fucked up is that?" he said.

"That's fucked up," she replied.

"How about you? How's that edible treating you?" A boyish grin and eyes hidden behind sunglasses penetrated her self-awareness. "How about a water?"

"Yes," she blurted out. "Please." Ned reached for a cooler on deck and produced two plastic bottles of spring water, handing her one.

"You gonna be okay while I go check on Gordie?"

"Please." She waved him off, blushing at his forwardness. "I'm not *that* high."

"I am," Ned said, and he wandered off.

Alice scrutinized the white caps for signs of life and saw hallucinations of swimming rodents in all directions. She took a swig of water and shook her head free of the visions. Yes, she was feeling the effects of the pharmaceutical-grade cannabis coming on strong. There was a mantra she'd practiced the few times she'd been overserved psychoactive substances. "If you get confused just listen to the music play." It was a lyric that stayed with her from her first Grateful Dead show in high school. She'd been given something before the concert and struggled to deal with the crowd and intensity of the disorientation. When the band played "Franklin's Tower," it was as if Jerry Garcia was empathizing with her fragile mental state. The lyric wrapped around her like a quilt and she ceased to think heavy thoughts; instead, she began to feel the music's groove, reacting to it physically. She let it lead her in dance, and she escaped from herself and her ego. Only a few times since had she let go like that, each time deciding that it was healthy and good.

Alice opened her ears and heard different music. There were foghorns from container ships moving in and out of the bay ahead. A flock of seabirds crowed in the water a few meters off the stern, and their chatter increased as they took off back toward Alcatraz. The constant ruffled sound of wind on sail provided a soothing rhythm to the experience. Each sound was clearly audible in its own channel, which she could tune in and out at will. She adjusted her dial to the human voices around her and picked up the voices of Tim and Sandra.

"Well, nobody told me we'd be sailing out to Timbuktu," Sandra said.

"That would be hard, since it's not in the ocean," Tim replied.

She turned square toward him and glared. "Do you have to be a smart-ass?"

"Relax, I'm kidding. Here, take my pullover; I'm fine without it."

Sandra obliged and noticed Alice taking in the surroundings with a centered tranquility. "You look like you're having no fun at all."

"I'm zoning out. I think I ate too much cookie," Alice said.

"Me too, and I got cold all of a sudden," Sandra said. "Can't we go back to Tiburon?"

"I think Gordie has to burn off some testosterone first. Ned is going to help him do something stupid," Alice added.

"You guys seem to be hitting it off." Sandra reverted to her sorority gossip tone.

"Oh please, he's got an ego bigger than this boat. And he told me some disgusting story about a swimming rat."

"I don't know. He was digging you."

Tim wandered away from the women's conversation and made his way to where Gordie and Ned were discussing the approach to the openings under the bridge. There was the conservative "safe play" and the "ballsy" alternative. Locker-room jockeying had them both on opposing sides, with neither willing to back down. Tim enjoyed the camaraderie and opened a beer as Pierre and Gwendell looked on.

"Tim, Ned wants to go check the surf at Fort Point. I think he's just afraid to go out past the bridge," Gordie said.

"No, we sail past the break and then cut under the south span. I've done it a hundred times," Ned explained, using hand gestures.

"Which means you've done it once in a kayak."

"Hey, if you don't think she can handle it. I thought you said you bought a high-performance sailing vessel."

Gordie took the bait. "Fine. Take the wheel, Captain Cook. Let's see your chops."

Ned took control and shouted some orders to the crew. He changed course and headed across the shipping lanes toward the city with the intention of banking back out near the surf of Fort Point under the southern span. Without any scientific calculation, he aimed his crossing close on the stern of a tanker and approached the wake as the sails picked up speed.

"Might get a little bumpy," Ned said. The wind and sun glare intensified as they traversed the shipping channels with spray whipping onto the deck. Tim turned his cap around backwards and tight around his ears. He held on to a handle and fought the elements. This was good stuff. Yachting with captains of industry. Or, put another way, the capitalist elite. The guys who provide liquidity to the economic system, lubricating growth and expansion, powering the engine that drives the global market. The lubricators. Tim saw San Francisco's Pacific Heights slightly to the left. The mansions of Broadway on the hill stood out like trophies, some representing old money and others the property of newly minted twenty-something billionaires. Tim had lived under the shadow of those homes during his twenties and thirties while renting flats in Cow Hollow and the Marina District. He had slowly moved his way up the hill but not as a buyer. Once the kids came, squeezing a family of five into a rent-controlled two bedroom got increasingly difficult. The au pair was another three grand a month, and she'd take up a room. Tim liked to say "we punted" by exiting the city for a $1.4 million, 2,300-square-foot ranch house down the peninsula. Until that point, he deemed it a failure for anyone to move out of the epicenter of action. He'd witnessed friends upon friends bail out to the northern and eastern suburbs. Others fled the state to raise their families closer to kin in Pittsburgh and Denver. By "punting," they merely detoured onto the peninsula where the action was more professionally acute:

closer to work, better schools, more upside. And here he was with Ned and Gordie, racing a pretty badass toy across the bay with his past in the rearview.

The *Snark II* was on a heading to meet the tanker's wake on an angle. On a calmer day this wouldn't present as much a problem. However, wave heights were increasing the closer they got to the Golden Gate. The choice was to head straight across the advancing waves from the west and risk a sideswipe from the approaching wake or maintain course to traverse the channel. Ned committed to the latter and swung the wheel to the port side. One of Gordie's sons shouted a warning about something as he frantically adjusted the main sail. Then he approached Ned and Gordie, his voice raised over the sound of wind, sails flapping and spray coming over the deck.

"I think you want to straighten out; it's getting pretty high out there," he said.

Ned nodded. "You think? I'm going to go over this wake and then we'll pitch her back around." The wind was constant, and the boat continued to pick up speed as the crew started to untie the main sail to slow down. They approached the five-foot wake at a forty-five degree angle just as a wind gust broke a wave over the starboard front side. The sailboat rose up over the crest of what was now a rogue wave and lurched down hard to the left, breaking its forward momentum and plowing the bow under the surface. The strength of the wind on taut sails caused a terrific jolt that launched everyone from their footing. Tim, maintaining his left hand grip, lost his beer amid a rush of surf under his feet. He pulled himself back up and struggled to balance himself as the boat teetered on edge. Ned spun the wheel to get the rudder to reconnect with the water. He'd had plenty of experience blue water sailing to know what to do. The steering system was responsive enough for him to correct the heading, and they gradually turned back into the swells. The chaos lasted a long ten seconds until it appeared they'd live to tell the tale. Sails were adjusted and the survivors assessed fallout for lost purses, scrapes, and bruises. Ned released a loud "Woo-hoo," his natural response to a lively little detour. He was dripping wet and smiling. He lowered a hand to Gordie, who had lost his footing reaching for a throw ring, and helped him up while keeping his other hand on the wheel. They were straightened out now, facing due west, heading into the swells. The crew scrambled to get things back into order.

"What the fuck was that!?" Gordie slipped again but held on. "You nearly capsized us."

Ned responded, "She handled it pretty good. Wow, what a trip!"

"Gimme the fuckin' wheel." Gordie forcibly took the wheel from Ned. "Go check on everyone; you're banned from the bridge."

Ned obeyed the captain's orders and bellowed, "Is everyone accounted for? What's our casualty count, Gilligan?" He maintained his grin, only halfheartedly allowing the gravity of their near miss to ruin a good day's fun. Everyone but the crew huddled below deck for towels and respite from the wind. Alice helped Eva and the servers clean up the catering mess while one of Gordie's boys opened the first aid kit to treat Sandra's elbow. She had sustained a minor flesh wound that would require some cleaning and a wrap.

Ned poked his head below deck. "Everyone accounted for? Nobody wanted to swim?"

"I hope your case of wine survived, because I'm ready to start drinking it," Eva said.

"Good news is the *Snark II* is ready for the open ocean. She's a beaut," he said. Ned caught site of Sandra's arm being tended to. "Uh oh, what's the prognosis?"

Sandra waved him off with her good arm. "Oh, I'm fine. Just a scratch." She smiled back at him, more embarrassed than anything. Tim dabbed some hydrogen peroxide on the wound and caught the spillage with a cotton ball. The vessel continued its rhythmic lurching over each wave, but the immediate danger was averted. Ned apologized to Sandra after inspecting the damage himself. "I've got something for that, if it continues to bother you," he promised her.

• • •

The *Snark II* abandoned plans to exit the bay into open water due to wet clothes and dampened spirits. Instead, they limped into Sausalito and, in the warmth of the sun and drier climate, celebrated their adventure with cocktails at the Spinnaker. Pierre Henry ordered a round of Brandy Alexanders to kick things off. He gave a toast to their warming spirits.

"An ancient Roman said, 'If one does not know to which port one is sailing, no wind is favorable.' I think I felt that way a bit earlier." The group erupted in laughter and raised their glasses. He continued, "À votre santé!" They exchanged cheers and clinks and Gordie continued to rib Ned for nearly sinking his boat, which Ned took with humility and grace, admitting in his own toast: "I've brought dishonor to the once-proud Wolfe seafaring name. I beg of you all, and Poseidon, to forgive my careless transgression. Lady Sea must be respected!"

As dusk approached, Gordie made arrangements to dock the *Snark II* overnight in Sausalito to have everything looked over. A sedan service was dispatched to return the guests to their various pick-up points. Pierre Henry and Gwendell thanked Gordie and Eva for a memorable tour of the North Bay and returned to their vehicles in Belvedere. Tim and Sandra rode back with Gordie's group to the peninsula. Alice, on the pouty prodding of Ned, agreed to stay in Sausalito and watch the Memorial Day fireworks display.

"Have you had an eighty-four Opus One? Pairs well with fireworks," he said before nodding to the sommelier. It was just the two of them left. They clinked glasses. Alice had someone's fleece blanket wrapped over her shoulders as she stood against the railing on the deck of the restaurant. The view over Richardson Bay included Berkeley to the distant far left and San Francisco's Fisherman's Wharf and North Beach straight ahead. To the right was the Marina District and Millionaire's Row of mansions lurking above from Pacific Heights. It was now, of course, Billionaire's Row. Further right and out of view was the Presidio and Golden Gate Bridge. Nestled into the hillside of Marin County, Sausalito, in all its Mediterranean-like charm, offered a contrast to the white cityscape in front of them. Wooded, steep, and endowed with world-class vistas, the hamlet was known as a stomping ground for those seeking serenity and escape from the city's hustle and bustle but who were not quite ready for the picket fences of Mill Valley, Ross, and further up-county. Children were not allowed in Sausalito. At least it seemed that way. The town was for lovers, bachelors, and spinsters; poets and musicians; eccentric financiers, trust-funders, and houseboat hippies. A certain discretion existed there, collegial but private. Geographically it was close to the city, but its redwoods and topography kept it tucked away from too much exposure. Tourists could drive the main drag, coming over by ferry or Golden Gate Bridge. But much of the residential element was uphill on winding, narrow roads, with balconies and windows maintaining their suspicious glare.

"What do you say we take in the view a little higher up? I've got a place just up the hill," Ned said.

Alice was no longer cold and, in fact, radiant with wine, the remnants of edible grass, and now the potentially indecent proposal from a guy she'd only just met.

"Why does that not surprise me?" she answered.

"What, the place? Or the question?"

She smiled at his answer and studied his confident charm. She raised her glass and took in the bouquet. "The place."

"It's been in the family a while. My old man used to post up there during his little excursions away from domestic life in Napa. Before that, his mother went crazy there writing poetry and cursing her good fortune. It's got some ghosts, and the view is the best in Marin."

"I'm picturing nymphs walking the gardens, anxious for your eventual return."

"Maybe for my old man. You're giving me too much credit. There's a car in the garage, and I can drive you home."

They walked a few hundred yards before Ned ordered an Uber.

CHAPTER 45

SIX WEEKS INTO HIS NEW GIG AT TASK LYST, Tim had already led his team to several benchmarks, including sign-up volume, user retention, and revenue. Not only was the service taking a cut of the transactions, it was now charging a posting fee for tasks. Tim's clout with management grew, and he exercised an option to buy some private shares for a steal of a price. Within the month he'd been offered an extension and a restructured compensation plan to lock him in to the project while the company expanded his team. He added coders and product managers to handle volume, and by early next fiscal quarter had twenty direct reports. Meanwhile, the operation still existed in the shadows. So far as market analysts, investors, and even the majority of Task Lyst employees were concerned, the company was seeing its success from the continuation of what it had always been doing, "providing a marketplace for swapping basic everyday services that the general public needed to add efficiency to their busy everyday lives." These were the old standbys: babysitting, rides, odd domestic chores, tutoring . . . a portrait of domestic bliss. The new NPR radio underwriting spots and print branding campaign in the alt-weekly underscored the platonic nature of the message that Task Lyst was essentially "Mother's Little Helper."

Tim helped mastermind the integration of his division into the main site by introducing the "anonymous" setting, enabling users on both sides of a task to keep their identities hidden. This was marketed as a simple, safe, and secure method to limit interactions with strangers when such wasn't necessary. Tim used the example of auto detailing. The service could be performed in an office parking lot without the need for parties to meet face-to-face (perhaps a safety issue from the perspective of a female office worker). What became clear to many users, however, was the advantage of such an option for nefarious purposes. Pranks were an immediate favorite: kids hiring other kids to toilet paper houses, spray paint public areas, and perform light acts of vandalism associated with school football games, homecoming, and suburban revelry.

Tim's anonymous setting became the default choice for most transactions, even those not requiring it. The added layer of discretion made it easier to mask financial expenditures and income. Household help began receiving payment in Bitcoin to avoid the implications of failing to pay tax and insurance. Small businesses outsourced jobs to the Task Lyst platform, putting a number of vendors in limbo. They would be forced to join or risk losing the work. The effect snowballed along with the financial growth of the company.

Tim's Adderall consumption doubled, as did the cannabis to bring occasional sleep. He hadn't been to one of his kids' functions in weeks.

CHAPTER 46

ELLIOTT, IN THE VAN ON THE WAY TO A GIG IN SAN LUIS OBISPO, answered a call from an unidentified number.

"Elliott this is Quint O'Rourke with *San Francisco Fishwrap* newsweekly. I'm writing a story on the rising popularity of Task Lyst, and I understand you were an early adopter and financed your new record with funds you made from the service. Can you comment—"

"I'm sorry, who's this?"

"Quint O'Rourke. I'm a journalist for the *Fishwrap*."

"How—what makes you think this?"

"I'm working on a lifestyle piece about how Task Lyst is impacting life in San Francisco. Our music editor mentioned in a blog piece about your new record that you self-financed it working exclusively through Task Lyst. Sounds like a compelling narrative."

Elliott recalled the blog post and regretted flapping his gums. The financing method had made for good PR material at the time, framing him as an industrious individual and early adopter. Rather than begging family and friends for Kickstarter support, he was out hustling up the capital himself, paralleling the public's awareness of Task Lyst as the "next big thing in tech."

"I don't know, man, it really wasn't much of a thing. I used it a couple of times, parked some cars, you know . . ."

"Yeah, well, I'd love to chat with you about it. Can you meet at the Mad Dog in the Fog tavern this afternoon at two?"

Elliott thought for a second. "I've got something this afternoon. Let me call you when I free up some time."

"This evening, seven?"

"I gotta roll. Let me holler at you later in the week." Elliott ended the call. He was not comfortable with the association the reporter was making. He held a general distrust of journalists, music critics or otherwise. It was love/hate; he needed publicity as an ambitious musician but didn't always get the outcome he was looking for—like the review that compared a previous album of his to "sterile, eighties-era Jackson Browne but lacking the catchy hooks." Or when a caption under his picture identified him as "poor man's Jeff Tweedy." But nothing compared to the female Australian reporter who, unbeknownst to him, had taped their phone interview and quoted him bad-mouthing several contemporaries, costing him an opening slot on a national tour.

But here he had a deeper feeling of suspicion. He had his own questions about the legality of how he was buttering his bread. Yet he was cashing the checks. The legitimacy of Task Lyst made him feel like he was just punching a time clock and kept him from overscrutinizing his complicity. And the money. He thought about the stockpile he was accumulating—had accumulated! Maybe it was time to cut and run, take the profits.

Yes, Elliott resolved to scale back his activities and thought it wise to try to cover his tracks. He was hedging against the potentiality of trouble. True, the call from the journalist spooked him. But something else gnawed at him each time his Bitcoin balance grew. He rode his scooter over to the storage space to drop off the mime suit. Earlier, he had submitted an email opting out of the deal. He said he was no longer able to fulfill the task and would return all related items. He didn't receive a reply. Per usual, he parked his scooter out front and got buzzed in by the aloof woman working the front desk. He carried a duffel over his shoulder, empty of parcels but with the mime uniform inside. He had the door key hanging around his neck, attached to a backstage artist laminate he had been given at a recent music festival on Treasure Island.

He unlocked the door and slid inside, closing it behind him. Notably missing were any parcels he normally would have loaded into the duffel to deliver. His routine usually started with him counting the number of packages to give him an idea of how long and how many trips would be required. Not seeing any stacked against the wall was a stark change. Opposite the wall, on the vanity, sat a manila envelope, sealed. It was addressed to his Task Lyst username, Geronimo69. He hung up the mime costume inside the cardboard wardrobe and returned to the vanity. He took his time inspecting it. "Open" was handwritten with a black Sharpie. The envelope felt substantial, and things shifted inside when he moved it. He squeezed his index finger inside the edge of the flap, broke the seal across the top, and emptied the contents into his left hand. Photographs, 8½" × 11", twenty or so. He rotated the stack so they were right side up and flipped through them. He saw images of himself in various stages of coming and going to the storage space, changing into the mime uniform, and delivering the parcels. Several even appeared as overheads from a distance, so that street signs and landmarks were visible. Elliott sat down to collect his thoughts. He took the message as a threat, blackmail. It frustrated him to be unable to give a face to the messenger. Whomever he was engaged with in this power struggle had the advantage of being invisible, in the sense that he had no clue as to the look, sound of voice, or description of the perpetrators of this exchange. He was at their mercy. Elliott squirmed to find a way out, an angle. Should he close up the room and escape, never to return or make any mention of its secrets? Or was the message to keep calm and carry on with the task?

Elliott tucked the envelope into his jacket and left.

Late in August, the *Fishwrap* hit the street with a piece about the emerging popularity of Task Lyst titled, "Shadow Task: The Underworld of the New Service Economy." In it, the reporter related his first-person experience posting and carrying out a variety of tasks, some of which stretched the boundaries of the law. For some readers this was revelatory journalism, uncovering a hidden world of deeds and transactions lawless in structure. Others lamented the publicity, fearful that the secret was out. Specifically, the article followed an individual, for the purposes of the story referred to as "Mitch," as he made his rounds delivering parcels, which the article speculated were narcotics. The reporter was investigating the use of Task Lyst by a heroin syndicate operating out of a storage facility in San Francisco.

The story alarmed local government officials, especially the district attorney and chief of police. Pressure mounted to investigate and regulate the service. Apologists defended the platform as being merely soiled by a few bad apples. The company saw the publicity as both fortuitous and potentially damaging from a liability standpoint. A subpoena arrived at Task Lyst headquarters a week after the article hit the street. In it, the DA requested all records pertaining to a suspect accused of using the platform to arrange drug deals. The company referred the request to its downtown white-shoe law firm, who brought forth the requisite delay-and-stall tactics. From a readership and online traffic standpoint, the story was a blockbuster for the newspaper, and it fomented much public debate about the role and usefulness of a service like Task Lyst.

Elliott and his bandmates were headed to Colorado for a couple of gigs. On the plane, Elliott sat in a window seat. He had grabbed a copy of that day's *Fishwrap* and pulled it out of his bag to read. The image on the cover along with the headline sent his head spinning. He had a bad feeling about what awaited inside the piece.

The exposé punctuated the gravitas of Elliot's predicament. It was officially a legal matter and clearly a personal safety situation. Especially if *he* was this "Mitch." He looked up from the article and watched California's Central Valley rise up into the Sierra Nevada range below. The rugged landscape remained remarkably unmolested by the sprawl of the major California coastal cities. California's geographic diversity never ceased to amaze him. Last week the band was heading south of Salinas toward San Luis Obispo on a path of golden hills and hints of the agricultural flats to the east. The rugged coastline of Highway One, from Big Sur down to San Simeon and Morro Bay, was set off to the west, tucked away under fog, twisting along as two lanes. The monotony was broken up by eighteen-wheelers traveling the opposite direction, creating a movie projector–like series of celluloid frames. Now, he was looking down at majestic, snowcapped mountain peaks sandwiched in between the rich breadbasket to the west and vast, empty desert to the east. One could easily disappear down there. He wondered if he were living a fictional existence, too far-fetched to even share with his band brethren. Surely they'd howl at the idea of him being in serious trouble for wearing a mime costume while making scooter deliveries.

CHAPTER 47

GORDIE CALLED AN EMERGENCY MEETING Thursday evening for the Blue Hill board of directors, some key company partners, and their legal team, via video remote, at Anderson, Bloom, and Connolly. Damage control was the topic. Blue Hill was by now a major shareholder in Task Lyst, and their investment was at stake, not to mention the potential liability. Gordie took his spot at the head of the oval conference room table, dropping a sheaf of papers and files in front of him with a thud. He passed copies of the new *Fishwrap* both directions around the table and sat back in his chair. His physical appearance was especially lean, almost gaunt, as if he'd just returned from one of his ultras.

"We've got a problem at Task Lyst. As all of you know by now, this birdcage-liner of a newspaper dug up some dirt and is portraying the company as the mother of all evil," he said. Gordie looked at the cover again and held it up, pointing at it and slamming it back down on the table. "Aiding and abetting the distribution of Schedule I narcotics, racketeering, prostitution . . . what next?"

Silence followed his question.

Gordie continued. "We are holding a substantial chunk of a company flirting with catastrophe."

Larry Chang avoided the line of fire by studying the cover of the paper. Across from him, Ted Goldsmith stirred. "What's legal have to say about this?"

The answer came from the large video screen across the table from Gordie. A spectacled gentleman in a loosened coat and tie with an obvious five-o'clock shadow spoke.

"Hey everyone, this is Matthew Bloom. I'm not troubled by the activities if they aren't directly being promoted by the company. In other words, there is no liability as long as no agents at or of the company are promoting the platform directly for nefarious purposes. I've looked for statutes involving other online marketplace entities and can't find any cases where they are held liable for actions perpetrated via their service. On the other hand, if the opposite can be proven, if in fact Task Lyst has promoted its platform for use by actors engaging in criminal activities, I do see a criminal liability issue as well as, potentially, a litigious environment from a civil standpoint."

Cynthia leaned in. "Matthew, in the event there was or is a provable criminal collaboration, can it be isolated from the whole?"

The voice deadpanned. "Typically the company will pay legal costs for an employee to fall on the sword. They will isolate the rogue agents and thereby protect the greater organization."

Cynthia leaned back and looked over at her boss. Gordie's eyebrow was raised, and he appeared to be focusing his breathing with his hands locked under his chin. He stared into space for several seconds and then back at the screen.

"Matthew, as substantial stakeholders in Task Lyst, what level of risk does Blue Hill carry moving forward? Our round of funding has precipitated an extremely high-growth period for this company, and we've been publicly identified as such. I see a legal issue as well as the obvious public relations nightmare."

"If the company, Task Lyst, is viewed as a viable, thriving public utility, if the good outweighs the bad . . . the old "bad apple" adage . . . I see it surviving relatively unscathed. Of course this is assuming the company is not actually promoting these criminalities. Or, to be more specific, proven to be doing so."

Larry glanced at Alice. She had been quiet. It was her deal, and the turn of events wasn't how she would have drawn it up. Larry was a consistent sounding board for Alice. Not so much a mentor but a supportive and trusted colleague. He went to bat for her.

"Could this be an opportunity?" he said, looking around the table. All eyes turned to him, interest piqued. "There's no such thing as bad publicity, in the entertainment business at least. And that's where you came from, Alice." He let it sink in. "This could be spun to our, to Task Lyst's, advantage. It's obviously disrupting the whole black market. I bet they'll see an increase in volume from this. It'll catapult the company far and wide. You can't buy this kind of marketing!"

His grin was inspired by pure, unbridled capitalism, and Gordie was starting to like it. Here was a guy seeing the dollars and cents, the euros and yen, while others in the room were stuck on appearances and liability. "Be bold" was a constant John Gordon mantra.

"I like your spirit, Larry. But the liability could wipe out the company and our investment. Some things trump the financials," Gordie said.

Larry deftly waved his boss off, turning back to the screen. "Matthew, you guys got this. A little due diligence on the inside and I'm sure we'll find a lily-white organization top to bottom."

Alice spoke up. "I can dig a little. I've got a friend on the inside. A consultant. You've met him, Gordie. Tim from the boat, on Memorial Day. He took a contract gig there and has been working on the rollout."

CHAPTER 48

TIM GOT THE SPEEDOMETER UP TO THREE DIGITS in the small window of time in the two-exit distance between Los Altos and Palo Alto on the 280. This was a fabled stretch for letting the engine whine, where Highway Patrol officers rarely stalked their prey, and the road was hidden beneath the shadow of hills and redwoods. He turned onto the off ramp and downshifted toward his coffee appointment with Alice. It was Friday at 10:00 a.m., and he'd been working remote with the coding team fine-tuning the user interface. Alice had texted him the previous evening about getting together as soon as possible. She suggested a Starbucks near Stanford University. Tim found a spot under the building, parked, and made his way up the stairs and inside. He opted for a mineral water, having already blasted off the morning with a fifteen-milligram Adderall and a cold-press coffee.

Alice walked toward him carrying her iced chai. "How's it going?"

Tim shook his head up and down, swallowed a mouthful of water, and said, "Busy."

"That's good, right?" She glanced around and located an empty two-top over toward the merchandise shelves, motioning them toward it. "Hey, thanks for meeting me on such short notice. I need to catch up with you on . . . your project."

They settled into the chairs and she continued. "I've got an eleven o'clock so I'll jump right to it. You read the article in the *Fishwrap*, I assume."

"I read it online right when it hit."

"And?" She paused. "No concerns?"

"Not here. Should I?"

"Well, Blue Hill is looking at the legal implications. Gordie gets a little nervous when investments get bad PR."

"I don't see a problem. Task Lyst just provides a platform for people to trade services. What they use it for is beyond our reach." Tim's use of the word "our" didn't appear to go unnoticed. He could sense her taking note of the fact he was "all in" on this project, viewing it as more than just a short-term contract job.

Tim continued. "What is your general counsel saying?"

"Not much yet. There are some red flags but no panic. It's possible you're right, and it will only build the user numbers and transaction volumes."

Tim thought about his role in the organization. He believed what he said. But he knew there was a gray area for what he'd been contributing on the market-making side of things. He had planted a few comments on the user boards to encourage people to consider a broad array of applications for tasks. They could be traceable. He should have been more careful hiding his internet protocol address. Moving forward, he would engage rote security in his actions.

"Right. I mean, any company enjoying our type of growth is bound to encounter some collateral damage."

"Are Pierre Henry and his inner circle concerned about any of this?"

"They are likely paying high-priced lawyers to worry for them. The kind of money you guys threw at them, they can afford it." He reverted to "they."

Clear to both of them was the fact that Alice was running point on the Task Lyst deal. It was her baby. And the stakes were considerable. With her encouragement Blue Hill had, in fact, sunk a sizable investment into a company that was barreling down the tracks beyond their expectations. Venture capitalists adored high growth, but they also liked steady, by-the-book fundamentals, and this could be getting away from them.

"Can we keep in touch on this, Tim?"

"Of course. I'm basically just helping out on a small project. Way out in left field." He smiled.

"Good, I'll check back with you. This could be great for everyone, right? Who would have thought?"

"Absolutely."

CHAPTER 49

ELLIOTT ALWAYS LOOKED FORWARD TO GIGS IN COLORADO, particularly when wealthy patrons were willing to fly the group in and put them up in luxury accommodations. This would be the second annual appearance for the Golden Mean, Elliott's group, at the Telluride Film Festival. An acquaintance in tech was partners in a new vineyard in Napa, and they underwrote the Music in Film Stage at the fest. Elliott, Cameron, and Salami would drive a rental van from Denver with stops along the way in Nederland, Breckenridge, and Aspen, packing in a few extra shows for the trouble.

The Nederland gig netted them $683, including two T-shirt and four record sales, and a very potent nugget of hydroponic indica, which Salami discovered the hard way. He sat out the opening numbers of the second set due to "dehydration," stage parlance for too high to play. Elliott strummed some solo tunes before inviting a guest from the audience to fill in. She was in a Boulder-based group called Falling Rock and was better than Salami. Later, Elliott asked her how she came up with the name.

"Well, I moved here from Britain when I was young, and we were driving up the winding mountain roads and kept seeing signs for Falling Rock. So I asked my mum, 'Why are there so many places with the same name? Can't Americans think of more names for their towns?'

"She looked back at me quizzically. 'Whatchu mean, darling?'

"'I mean every place is called Falling Rock.'

"She and my dad had quite a laugh. My older brother still taunts me about it."

Elliott enjoyed a laugh too. "I thought it was a reference to Mick Jagger's solo career. Or rock music in general."

"Cynical much?" She posed it as a statement more than a question. They exchanged social handles and promised to stay in touch.

The Breckenridge show got canceled because of a double booking, so they routed straight to Aspen, taking the Independence Pass. Elliott had spent some time there but it had been a while. His ski-bum friends had mostly moved on, and many of the vibey old haunts, like Jake's Abbey, the Pub, and the Little Nell, had closed, replaced by fancy new retail and condo developments anchored by sushi joints and martini bars. En route, Elliott read a collection of short stories written by a notorious poet and lyricist who lived in the area. Elliott was intrigued by his background as a prizefighter, and neo-Luddite. Elliott admired his strict stance against allowing his art to be used for commerce. "No commercials for cowboy wordsmith" was how one music business insider described him. Elliott suggested they stop at Woody Creek Tavern on their way into town to see if the elusive mystic might be lurking around.

Aspen was a bust, musically. The Golden Mean took the stage in a basement venue that had recently transitioned into a country and western bar. Elliott squeezed in as many Neil Young and Eagles songs as he could, but the people wanted Garth and Miranda Lambert. They settled for Willie, Patsy, and Merle with most of the lyrics mumbled and jumbled. The take was $1,000 plus a chef's special and stocked cooler in the artist green room. Elliott sold a few records and gave away a shirt to a grandma who sang along the loudest. The promoter said they did okay once they agreed to ditch their original material.

Telluride, on the other hand, was great on all accounts. The group hung out with familiar faces and performed a guest slot at the Fly Me to the Moon Saloon, getting further acclimated for their advertised set on the outdoor Town Park stage. Elliott made time for a single-track mountain bike ride up the Wasatch Trail Loop, which he hadn't ridden since his first Telluride Bluegrass Festival a decade ago. He recalled the time concert promoter Bill Graham introduced a historic set with:

"Ladies and gentlemen, it's my pleasure and privilege to introduce this next act. There's nothing finer in the known universe, the Allman Brothers live in Telluride, Colorado!" Elliott recalled the "oneness" he felt with humankind as the rain clouds parted during Dickey Betts's guitar solo in "Blue Sky." Magic was alive and well in the world.

The Golden Mean channeled this mysterious current in their "golden hour" dusk slot to the wine-soaked film bacchanalians. They weaved in some classics from the previous nights' work and found great response for their own material, stretching out the jams, exploring the possibilities, listening to each other's playing and to the audience for their cues. The set crackled with energy, and Elliott felt they did Dickey and Bill justice.

CHAPTER 50

ALICE STEPPED INTO THE CORNER OFFICE where Gordie was engaged in a phone call on speakerphone. He motioned for her to just give him a minute to wrap up and switched over to his Bluetooth earbuds. She took a seat on the couch in his sitting area. Gordie didn't have a traditional desk, preferring to stand in front of an elevated platform for his two computer screens. He burned extra calories that way and kept his energy level up. His wearable tech device monitored an array of health data, including steps taken per day. His personal benchmark was twenty thousand, which was exactly twice the layperson's suggested goal. The contemporary-designed sitting area contained a firm leather sofa opposite two upholstered chairs imported from Scandinavia and a coffee table, all floating on a Persian area rug. Depending on the meeting, Gordie would take one of the chairs or ride a stationary road bike positioned at the head of the table facing out at the view of the ridgeline. It was not uncommon for him to manually check his pulse, blood pressure, and body fat index while conducting business with associates.

The workspace was well appointed yet sparse. Each item needed to answer to its inclusion in the room as if it were a subatomic particle responsible for its own role in maintaining the balance that established order. Every overdose of testosterone was tempered by an offering of Zen. The photo of Gordie's knife-edge ascent of Pyramid Peak complemented the photo portraying the tranquil setting of an Ayahuasca ceremony in the Peruvian Alps that sat next to it. A shelf displayed books by Thich Nhat Hanh, Nietzsche, and Ayn Rand. An incredibly rare magnum of Bordeaux stood next to a bottle of low-brow Cabo Wabo tequila, a gift from his mountain-biking pal Sammy Hagar. Alice noticed a platinum wedding band in solitary confinement on a tray meant for a key fob.

Gordie nodded along with his call, adding his two cents here and there. He reached for a room-temperature mineral water and two glasses and set them in front of Alice.

"Look, let me ask you something," he said to the invisible recipient. "The carryover from Q2—I, I realize that. What I'd like to know—Can I finish?" Gordie gestured and then flicked the pen he was fiddling with into the plant in the corner. "Capital gains are not our biggest worry here. I'm stepping into another meeting. I'll talk to you next week."

Gordie shook his head and released a sardonic chuckle and leaned over to pour himself and Alice glasses of water. "Taxes. We could be on the deck of the *Titanic* about to hit an iceberg and accountants would be looking for ways to minimize tax exposure."

He sat, leaned back, and balanced his ankle on a knee. Then he exhaled and reworked his face into a smile.

"So what did we find out from the inside about Task Lyst?" he said.

"I met with Tim, and he's business as usual. My sense is he's nose to the grindstone, just focused on growth and adding value. Without any skin in the game, I don't imagine he'll be concerned much with questions of liability and negative publicity."

"What is Tim doing there exactly?" Gordie was now sitting up in the seat, perfect posture, with one leg crossed over the other. Alice was aware of his active eyes studying her body language, impatient while she delivered her point. She could tell he liked the way she was dressed today. Her business-casual T-shirt under the blazer over jeans showcased her sex appeal but also her athleticism, and showed just the right amount of cleavage. Every woman in the firm knew of Gordie's affinity for leggy female staffers. There was water-cooler talk of misconduct lawsuits and office trysts, but surely times and habits had to have changed.

"Officially he's just a contractor. He works mostly remote and doesn't appear in any company listings with an extension or direct remote," she said.

"And he's a product guy? Maybe he's working on 'unofficial' projects," he said.

She paused before asking. "You mean, like a rogue unit?"

"Possibly. You said he's part of the market-making team. Wasn't he working with high-volume traders at eBanc? He's got experience building user-interface platforms. I bet he's aware of what's happening in the shadows over there."

"Interesting. He does seem pretty dug in." Alice had sensed Tim was rather aloof about his exposure and energized by his involvement. He hadn't seemed as lost or lacking focus as when they met initially on the topic of Task Lyst. She wondered if he'd be a reliable resource moving forward. Perhaps she'd lost him.

"Look, Alice, this has got the board asking all kinds of questions I don't like to answer. I've been on the phone with Pierre, lawyers, and now accountants trying to do damage control. Worst-case scenarios could be bad in this case. Real bad. Career-ending bad. Fortune-losing bad." Gordie got up to shut the office door. In this era of transparency, he still had an office with a door that closed. An element of discretion remained on his floor of the building, barely. It was known that the founding partner enjoyed some old-school perks and, perhaps, a few liberties.

"Is . . . is my job at risk here?"

"All of our jobs are at risk here. Fuck, this is DEFCON Three here." Gordie stood up and poured some more water. "Lots of eyeballs on us." He swished the water around his mouth and stared out the window.

"What's my next step here? I can follow up—"

"Post Ranch Inn," he said.

She waited for him to clarify. "Big Sur?"

He turned around to face her. "Meet me there tonight."

"What?" She tried to read his body language. It was an odd request. "I'm not following."

"I want to have an off-site meeting. I want you to be included."

"What exactly is the nature of this off-site?"

"Call it partner initiation." He moved toward her and hovered behind her.

"Gordie, are you feeling okay?"

"Okay, look. My spiritual advisor has me taking microdoses of LSD to get through what he calls my midlife crisis. Says I have success guilt, and regular introspection is bringing me back to a oneness with the world," Gordie said.

Alice fought the urge to laugh, but played it safe. "Well, I'm glad you're talking to someone. A lot of men are too macho to talk about their issues. What does this have to do with me?" Alice crossed her arms in front of her and moved her eyes toward the door.

"I don't know. Maybe I have feelings for you. That shouldn't surprise you."

She shook her head and got up to leave. "Gordie . . ."

He placed his hand on her forearm. "Alice, I'm not trying to complicate anything here. Just being honest."

"John, I'm a little uncomfortable with where this is leading."

He removed his hand from her arm and walked away. "I'm sorry, you're right. I don't know what the fuck is the matter with me anymore." He stood in front of her, looking for a response. Alice made sure her body language was succinct. She noticed the little boy in his eyes, pleading for someone to offer comfort. There was also a burned-out old man in the same eyes. One that was scared of a reckoning that might be right around the corner for a life spent taking more than giving. It was the first time Alice saw him as something less than a superman. He always seemed to embody success as defined in Silicon Valley terms. For all the material wealth, quixotic adventures, and mythic status among his peers, here was an underlying emptiness. The façade of Gordie as primal man succumbing to darkness. One that questioned all he'd accomplished as the bells of mortality ringed louder. His eyes, now devoid of light, continued to search Alice's for an answer.

"Gordie," she said. "Go home to your family."

Gordie folded his arms and looked to the floor. "All right, well, you can't blame an old guy for trying." He smiled and let out a one-syllable chuckle. "You know, things didn't used to be so complicated. You could leave work at home and home at work. Now we've got sensitivity training and trigger warnings. I interviewed a Berkeley graduate who requested to go by the pronoun 'they.' Said he/her/they didn't believe in traditional gender identification. I laughed. Next thing I know I've got a lawsuit on my hands for discrimination." Gordie took a couple of steps to the window and looked toward the ridgeline. "Our society suffers from disparate impact, Alice. Reproduction can't take place without opposite sexes. Survival of our species can't take place without reproduction. We're softening the edges and killing ourselves silently."

He turned to her. "Attraction is the most powerful force in the universe. Why are we trying to fight it?"

"Gordie, I don't know where to start. Like, you're married, you run a high profile company, you're rich beyond most people's wildest dreams. You're having an existential crisis. Buy a Ferrari or something."

"It's not enough. The game starts every morning, and only occasional sleep stops it at night. You get so wrapped up that . . . where does it end?" Gordie stopped himself, shaking his head side to side slowly.

"You're not yourself, Gordie."

He nodded his head at the rate of a struggling heartbeat. "I've become a mysterious stranger."

Alice was compelled to walk over and comfort him, but she thought it wiser to keep some distance. "I need to get going, Gordie. I can't go to Big Sur. I have a board meeting for the March of Dimes. I'm sorry. Are you going to be okay?"

Gordie whispered, "*Oppositus Maximus.*"

Alice said, "Sorry? I didn't catch that."

He turned. "*Oppositus Maximus.* It's Latin. Our collegiate secret society motto."

"Goodnight, Gordie."

"Night," he answered, and turned to look back out the window.

CHAPTER 51

ELLIOTT STRODE TOWARD THE AIRLINE TICKET COUNTER and cursed the lengthy queue that snaked around itself in a confusing helix. His bandmates were ahead of him in line since he had dropped them off at the curb before returning the rental van. It was twenty-five minutes until he was supposed to board his return flight from Denver to SFO and he wasn't yet to the security checkpoint. His felt the blood pulsing through his head keeping a steady time like in Poe's "The Tell-Tale Heart." Nausea from too little sleep and several post-gig beers added to the agony. Every thirty seconds or so he would kick his duffel bag of merchandise forward while hoisting his guitar and carry-on bag as the line inched along. Elliott avoided all eye contact for fear of getting sick among hundreds of bystanders.

The ticket agent was struggling to keep up with the onslaught of Sunday morning travelers. He flash read Elliott's identification and loaded his bag onto the scale. A hundred anxious outbounders monitored the transaction for any sign of inefficiency. Elliott snared the boarding pass and rushed toward security with reserved optimism about making his flight. Another queue. A middle-aged checkpoint lady named Klein scolded him for approaching her post before her instructions. Once she motioned to him he smiled, careful to avoid drawing the ire of TSA employees whose cooperation dictated his making the flight. She checked the boarding pass against his driver's license.

"How come this ticket says Elton but your ID says Elliott?"

He looked at the ticket. "I don't know. I must have messed up when I texted my travel agent. Autocorrect probably." She looked again at the two documents. And back at him. A troubled look appeared on her face.

"The names have to match. I'll need to call my supervisor over." She walked over to another TSA official in a blue coat and had a brief chat. They both returned to Elliott.

"You'll have to come with me while we verify this." She led him to a kiosk where she radioed another person with a description of the problem. After, she had Elliott complete a form to confirm his identity. He checked his watch, emphasizing the urgency. The airplane was due to take off in fifteen minutes.

"We'll try to straighten this out as soon as possible," she assured him. Five minutes passed as she recited his driver's license number repeatedly to various people on the other end of the line. She listened, answered questions, asked him for clarification on some information. He produced additional cards with his name: credit cards, an old student ID, a health card. They only seemed to confuse matters.

"Okay, copy that. Do I tell him he's been flagged?" She asked the latter question in a hushed tone, hand cupping the receiver. This alarmed him. He had the first inclination this would not be quickly resolved. A martyr complex started to build in him. He imagined being cuffed and manhandled by an advancing team of homeland security agents. Sure enough, she relayed to him there would be some officials joining them to help "clear things up."

A pair of fellow TSA personnel arrived, one putting on sanitary gloves. The more professional-looking agent explained that the name confusion required special attention. The other walked him to a staging area for a thorough pat down and careful inspection of his carry-on bag. Included was a test for explosives and everything short of a cavity search. This staging area was in public view, mere feet from the end of the x-ray scanning line. The activity wasn't lost on any of the scores of travelers passing by, each expressing sympathy or, alternately, scorn at him for being subject to the extra attention. The pat down was explained ahead of time in great detail. He declined the option of a private venue because it would probably take more time, resulting in him missing his flight for sure. Elliott also wanted to share the experience with the other travelers. His martyr complex took flight. He was almost sure he wasn't carrying any contraband. Once, previously, he'd been forced to turn over a compact fishing knife he'd forgotten about. But nothing came of that incident, not even a request for identification. A few months ago Elliott had some medicinal cannabis, one dose, in his sunglasses case. But he'd since dispatched with that. If anything remained it was unknown to him. His confrontational nature welcomed the inquisition, yet he remained calm and cooperative. The search yielded nothing, and the TSA officer thanked Elliott for the cooperation before reporting his lack of findings to his colleagues. The other remained in a long conversation on a telephone, occasionally nodding and offering comments. Elliott snapped a smartphone photo and shot a short video of the gathering. Two airport cops showed up and were briefed on the situation. Elliott remained a few feet away, technically in custody but free of restraints. A woman in her late thirties approached him, flashing a badge.

"Good morning, I'm Inspector Susan Heinrich with Homeland Security. How are you doing?"

"Okay. Is this a little overkill to call in Homeland Security?"

"Well, the name inconsistency triggered some other stuff, and we take these things very seriously."

"Other things? Care to elaborate?"

"Not at this time. Look, it's clear you have missed your flight. We are going to work through this systematically, and it's in your best interest to just bear with us. What's the nature of your travel?" She came across as sympathetic yet methodical. Elliott imagined her monitoring his body language and whether he answered her questions consistently. She asked him twice for his birthdate, interspersed with several other questions about his check-in process. She took notes on a reporter's notebook, playing the good cop role. An older mustachioed cop in uniform asked tougher questions and acted more suspicious. He likely didn't relate to the Oranje Holland soccer shirt or the shaggy haircut.

The officer's large stature made him a caricature of the donut-eating former beat cop who is relegated to a desk job.

"What's the nature of your travel today?"

"I'm heading home from a music gig."

"What's your final destination?"

By now resigned to missing his flight, Elliott let the question resonate. What was his final destination? He wasn't sure. How would Schopenhauer or Nietzsche answer? He considered a Manichaean response.

He cleared his throat. "For now, just San Francisco."

Elliott's phone buzzed. It was a text. The rest of the band were seated on the plane and wanted a status update. He told them he'd be catching a later flight and to grab his checked baggage.

A new woman vibrated over. "Sir, I'm Regina, customer relations with Frontier Airlines. I'm going to get you scheduled on the next flight if you want to come with me." His license and boarding pass were returned to him and, somewhat surprised, he followed Regina into the concourse to get rebooked.

CHAPTER 52

ALICE WROTE FIVE OR SIX TEXT MESSAGES, deleting each and starting again. Finally, she typed, "Tim, coffee catch-up today? Three? I'll come to you."

"Tied up now. Try for three thirty, the Starbucks on East Diablo?"

She agreed, curious of the request to meet at a spot different than their usual meeting place, and only half a mile away. She ran an errand before parking at the rendezvous point.

Tim pulled up. "Hey, get in. I've got your chai latte here."

She obliged, locking her car and entered Tim's BMW on the passenger side.

"Road trip?" she joked as he pulled out of the parking lot.

"A little extra security."

"Why?"

He adjusted the stereo volume up a few decibels. Alice noticed a pungent aroma of weed in the vehicle.

"Tim, I need an update. There is increasing concern over our exposure."

"Concern?" He turned the volume up yet again and pulled onto the freeway.

"There are whispers of shady things happening. Look, let's cut to the chase. Are you okay? Is there anything I need to know?"

Tim repositioned himself into a reclined slump as he drove. Alice looked for clues behind his aviator sunglasses. He was distant or maybe just high. She watched him trigger the right turn indicator and cross back toward the right lane as if to exit. He downshifted as the engine whined in their approach to the off-ramp. He took it aggressively, still silent, as if considering his options. They took a left and headed up the hill toward the skyline, winding around a half dozen turns before pulling into the parking lot of a roadside cafe.

"You hungry?" he asked her.

They took one of the five tables and Tim headed to the counter to order. It was an old hippie hangout popularized when the personal computer was but a glimmer in the eye of Steve Jobs and Stephen Wozniak. The walls reminded the patrons of how things had been and who had frequented the slow-paced pit stop over the years. Framed photos, unframed Polaroids, autographed dollar bills thumbtacked next to vintage football memorabilia. A small stage hosted intimate, rustic picking parties for locals and visiting singer-songwriters.

Tim returned with the tuna salad sandwich they were sharing. "The quick answer is everything is going great. But I don't think that's the context you're looking for."

"No."

"The story in the paper still has you worried."

"Well, yes. We've got a sizable stake tied up in the company. It's beyond the loss we are worried about. It's a liability. Gordie—"

"Gordie sent you here to get the lowdown?"

"Gordie's working his own angles. I think he's losing his mind on this one, but that's a whole other story. Look, at the end of the day, this is my deal. I will swim or sink with it."

"You're going to make a lot of money on this deal. You'll be swimming in it."

Alice paused, reading his body language. "I'm not interested in money if it comes at a higher cost."

Tim turned to face her. "We're talking about a disruptive service here. Of course it's going to ruffle some feathers. That's where the intrinsic value is."

"So, you're comfortable with all the legal aspects and . . . this is all a witch hunt?"

"It's nothing Craigslist and eBay haven't dealt with."

"You do understand, though, if this turns into another Silk Road, we're all facing heavy scrutiny at best."

"Alice, people will do what they're going to do regardless of platform. Task Lyst provides a marketplace for honest, hardworking folks to trade for services. Legal services."

"You sound like you're reading your own PR."

"It's the foundation for the company."

"You drank the Kool-Aid."

"You have to know what the product tastes like."

She ran out of clichés to barb him with and matched his smirk with one of her own. "If you say so." She took a bite out of the pickle from the basket.

CHAPTER 53

ELLIOTT WAS BACK IN HIS FLAT, staring at the ceiling from the mattress on the floor. The tin backsplash between the crown moldings was evidence of his rental's former Gilded Age glory. Sconces framed the fireplace against the wall, though it was no longer in service. When he had first moved to town, the Victorian architecture and interiors inspired him, making the city seem to transcend time. It was always a fascinating place, governed by geological tension, with earthquakes, dense fog, and the exchange of goods, services, and ideas from all over the globe. It had been that way before the 49ers, Jack London, Ken Kesey, Jerry Garcia, and Dirty Harry. And the debutantes and rich scions of East Coast fortunes. And princes, baronesses, hobos, poets, guitar slingers, and vampires. It was where opportunity and wanderlust met to live or die. Still was and would always be. San Francisco, the continuum: no absolutes. Always in flux, shifting, restless, shaking its agitators. Informed by danger and possibility. This was its main attraction.

Elliott listened to the N Judah as it stopped at the corner. People got off and loaded on. A car behind it honked. The bus didn't move. Instead there was the familiar routine of a bus driver exiting to the street with the long pole used to reset the connection to the electric line. It seemed to be a recurring problem at the stop in front of his flat. Added another minute to the route, which, he imagined, probably added up, compounded over the course of the driver's day and the day of all the riders. If it took sixteen minutes to get downtown, you planned accordingly. How agonizing to have to wait a minute or two extra, to see a green light go wasted. Such was life in the hustle under the shadow of financial district towers.

He reached over the edge of the mattress to his phone, which sat on the hardwood floor. It was 8:15 a.m. on Monday. The hassle at the airport the day before meant he'd gotten in after midnight, almost twelve hours after his scheduled touchdown. What did they mean he got flagged? He would have to call the number they gave him for airport security to find out. They still let him fly, he reasoned, so it couldn't be anything too heavy. Colorado, despite his "bummer in the summer" exit, was a productive and needed respite. He loved touring: each day heading toward a specific destination, culminating with an evening celebration and plenty of down time along the way to chill out, read, catch up on sleep, or look out the window. If only it were a month instead of half a week. It scratched his itch, but now he was back to the grind. Elliott looked for connections between the airport hassle and his Task Lyst woes. He imagined a grand conspiracy involving drug cartels, foreign intelligence services, and Silicon Valley. He was a pawn in their game. Or a prawn. A small cog in the wheels of injustice. His martyr complex did not mix well with Monday morning gloom.

Elliott prepared French-pressed coffee and called Freddy Fu's tattoo studio. He made an appointment with Freddy for eleven o'clock the next day to get his tattoo touched up but also to seek advice on the trouble he was in with the Task Lyst gang syndicate. He returned a text to one of his band members about meeting up later and logged onto Task Lyst to see what was up.

CHAPTER 54

IN SEPTEMBER TIM RECEIVED A STOCK BONUS of another five thousand options for his team's quarterly performance. Task Lyst revenue was up across the board but especially in his division. The company was expanding into new markets and exceeding all forecasts. Water-cooler talk of an initial public stock offering persisted. Everyone was going to get filthy rich.

Tim sat in his home office on a Tuesday evening plugging numbers into a spreadsheet. He'd been asked to forecast his division's financials for the following year and was considering a few different scenarios. A few members of his team were anxious to hire more help. Things were going well, but they felt overworked. Somewhere between ten and fifteen extra bodies would help scale up operations to meet the revenue goals. Tim liked the control he had over his team and worried about growing too fast. He didn't want a newly minted MBA to come in and challenge his leadership. Nor did he want an industry veteran to come between him and senior management. He'd seen this play before. It had cost him his eBanc gig, in fact.

His recommendation was to outsource the heavy lifting to a software outfit in Bulgaria. They were based in Sofia, and he knew them from a previous consulting project. The head guy, Aleksander Draganov, went to school in the States, near Philly. He was fluent in English, sharp and ambitious, if a little greasy. He wouldn't get caught up in the morality debate about which tasks were appropriate to facilitate. Tim convinced himself that he was merely facilitating the flow of services; the types of services offered were of no consequence to Task Lyst or himself as the product manager. The language barrier and time difference would add value to Tim's position as a buffer. If approved, it would be a win-win.

"Aleksander, can you hear me okay?"

"Call me Zander. Yes, I can hear you fine, Tim. I see you fine, as well." Zander's appearance on the computer monitor for the Skype call highlighted his two-day stubble and dark, unkempt hair. His pasty-pale face was puffy and bore the markings of a guy with large appetites. He wore a horizontally striped black-and-white shirt and made little effort to hide the clutter around him. A cigarette burned in an ashtray to his right. Dark eyes twitched inside wire eyeglass frames between his sniffles and coughs.

"Great. I'm getting a little delay, but it should be okay. So, how's it going on the ranking platform? Will it be ready to go live on schedule?"

"Of course. I've got my team working round the clock. Will be no problem."

"To be clear, this update will allow both sides of the transaction to grade each other. To add quality control, reward success, and punish failure. I think it's important to have accountability on both sides."

"Absolutely. You can give priority to those with high ratings."

"Precisely, Zander."

Tim finished with the videoconference and scrolled through the customer help desk emails. He liked to monitor what was happening on both sides of the transactions like a voyeur peeping in on a dressing room. He had access to all the logins from Taskmasters to Taskminders. He had been following the progress of one in particular that involved mime suits and delivery of little boxes. The Taskmaster had a username of Shogun75 and was driving heavy volume for its relatively short time on the platform. It was employing several Taskminders as delivery agents who were making pretty good money. Shogun75 was like a prized pupil for Tim. He made sure any help tickets were promptly dealt with to keep the volume rolling. He'd been troubled by one particular email request from a person opting out of a task. It was one of the deals using the new anonymous setting. Tim reviewed the file for some context. It was amazing how much access he had to information. It alarmed him to think about how much of his own activity was probably monitored by employees behind the scenes at Facebook and Yahoo. At eBanc, in the wild, wild west of the dot-com early days despite regulations and restrictions, he could log in and see balances and look for trading patterns he could personally benefit from. His own day-trading account benefited more than once from a big pop or a short sale. It was just part of the game. Membership has its privileges.

The Task Lyst backend revealed details of the tasks and interactions between parties. In this case, the Taskmaster was paying the Taskminder for services rendered on an ongoing basis. The generic service type was categorized as Errands. The Taskmaster was a high-volume customer on the site with a successful track record of transactions across a variety of categories, including Errands, Deliveries, Temporary Employment, and Day Labor. What these actually were made Tim curious. The site allowed for a certain amount of discretion. What happened between the two parties was their own contract. Both parties graded each other upon completion, so the system policed itself.

The end user in this case, Geronimo69, was requesting to opt out of the ongoing contract. There was no response from the Taskmaster, so Tim made a note to have Zander's coding team initiate a change to the system requiring the Taskmaster to answer the request within a short time frame, say twenty-four hours. Otherwise an alert would be sent out and a possible freeze placed on the account. It was important to keep things fluid and maintain customer satisfaction on both sides of the engine. Tim studied the scenario further. If the Taskminder wished to end the relationship with the Taskmaster, it would be helpful to know why. This would give closure to the deal and not leave any loose ends. Tim added this to his email to Zander. Tim was irked when he saw the dollar amounts on this deal. Why would the Taskminder stop working on a gig that was generating $1,500 per week? The Taskmaster would undoubtedly find another party to accept the task. And this Taskminder was a Gold Level user. Things were going so well, it seemed to Tim. He didn't like seeing momentum shift. It was his job to facilitate scalability, hockey-stick growth! Even the smallest defeat he took personally. He made a note to keep an eye on this customer account by setting up an alert for any and all activity generated by either party. Tim enjoyed this role as Svengali from his perch behind the curtain; conducting the symphony was the ultimate buzz.

CHAPTER 55

THE DAY AFTER THE FALL EQUINOX, news outlets reported a homicide in the Upper Market neighborhood. A popular gay rights activist, Baxter Morris, was bludgeoned to death while on his nightly walk with his French bulldog. Police were holding a nineteen-year-old male suspect based on witness descriptions and unnamed evidence. Within days Task Lyst was implicated in the crime as leaked information revealed that the suspect was allegedly fulfilling a task for hire. Indications were the suspect didn't know the victim and merely intended to "send a message." Instead, the man died of a brain hemorrhage, and the botched task became the poster child for Task Lyst's dark side.

Alice listened to a voicemail from Larry on her way home from early yoga. It was Friday and she had planned to work from home. The news coverage of the homicide was a major distraction for Blue Hill Capital. In the weeks since the *Fishwrap* article, damage control efforts had gained traction with aggressive marketing campaigns controlling the narrative. The net result was an uptick in user volume. Gordie was away on business but working the phone lines and email channels. Anderson, Bloom, and Connelly were making the rounds between city hall, the Task Lyst offices, and Blue Hill headquarters on the peninsula.

"Alice, hey, it's Larry. Just checking in on you. I think this is going to blow over. Task Lyst will play ball, make some cosmetic changes to appease the DA, and this little teenage fucker will plead out. I'm advising the company to hire High Seas Public Relations to spin all the positives and try to bury this as an isolated bad apple. Call me back when you get this. I'll be in all morning."

Alice wasn't so hopeful. Her upset stomach told her this was headed in a bad direction. She started imagining life after Blue Hill. Gordie's bizarre behavior in his office a few weeks ago: the sense of alarm, the indecent proposal. She was over it, whatever "it" was. She parked in front of The Juicery, ordered a Hillary—spinach, cucumber, lime, and ginger—and called Larry back as she waited.

"Alice, you got my message."

"Yes, although I'm not as optimistic."

"You worry too much. I've got Berarducci and Sloane from High Seas on the case—meeting with them for lunch. Join us if you want."

"I feel like you're putting out my fire."

"Nonsense. Just chipping in. We're all in this together. Task Lyst will be kissing babies from here on out."

"Gordie will be so thrilled."

"Don't worry about Gordie. You're going to be his little superstar in next year's annual report. The El Dorado investors will think you hung the moon when all's said and done."

Alice said she'd meet for lunch and hung up. The cashier stuck a straw in the Hillary and handed it to Alice, who took a seat by the window to check another couple of messages. One was from her mom reporting on her uncle's tumor biopsy. It was benign and he was going to be fine, thank God. The other was from Stuart somebody, assistant district attorney. He wanted to talk to Alice about her involvement with Task Lyst, if she could be so kind as to return his call at her earliest convenience.

CHAPTER 56

ELLIOTT WAS PARKED UNDER THE GOLDEN GATE BRIDGE on the south end of the span. He had a towel hanging around his waist and was changing into his five-millimeter wetsuit. It hadn't been worn in quite a while. He watched the waves lining up to the left of Fort Point as they wrapped around the rocks and inside the nearest bridge support. He recognized Freddy on the big left-hand shoulder soulfully carving turns and surfing the wave into the inside section. Freddy had touched up Elliott's tattoo a few week's prior but the shop was too bustling to comfortably discuss the Task Lyst problem. Elliott reached out again and Freddy texted him back about getting some afternoon waves. "You ought to meet me at the bridge," he'd said.

Elliott negotiated the rocks for his entry point into the water. His bare right foot—he couldn't find his booties—touched the icy water, sending a shock through his system. Surfing in the Bay Area required commitment. Water temperatures ranged from "cold as gin" to "frigid as fuck," as one might say under their breath when wading in. Sharks were of the great white variety, and the waves could get monstrous. Here at Fort Point, tourists could enjoy the under view of the Golden Gate Bridge while cheering on surfers from the nearby parking lot. Ocean freighters passed in and out of the bay just the other side of the support pier. Dense fog and frigid wind normally added to the fun. Elliott wasn't a die-hard surfer in these environs. The pounding winter surf at Ocean Beach was too intense, while the summer temps were rarely warm enough to warrant surfing the seasonally smaller waves. But when necessary he paddled out, to remind himself of where he lived and why he'd come in the first place. It was a cleansing ritual he required only slightly more often than a trip to the dentist.

A hedge-sized wall of white water crashed toward Elliott as he thrust himself over and away from the rocks. More shock to the system as he plunged into the sea. This time the water penetrated his wetsuit through the small tear by his neck and down through the collar. An ice-cream headache was offset by the survival instinct of needing to paddle out into the lineup through the coming onslaught of waves or risk ending up on the rocks. His heart rate increased as he focused on digging into each stroke, his hands cupped and chilled to the bone. He shook the hair out of his eyes without losing a beat. The first wave broke in front of him before he could make the shoulder. He duck dove, forcing the nose of his six-and-a-half-foot board under the curl. He shot out the back into an immediate paddle, anticipating an even bigger second wave—they usually came in threes. Sure enough, he had timed his entry poorly—just as the biggest set of the day was rolling through. This could mean panic city, but with relatively fresh arms, Elliott charged toward the wave, confident he could get under. He duck dove again. This time he wasn't as lucky and got trounced through the spin cycle, losing his grip on the board and getting pulled by its leash until the wave spat it out. Perilously close to the rocks, he got back on and paddled toward the next beating. He made it through to the other side and was relieved to see the bridge support and a freighter instead of another massive dark wall of water. Dog tired, he rubber-armed it toward the lineup to wait for the next set. Freddy caught up to him, having just rode one of the set waves.

"E-man, aloha. Pretty stout out here today, eh?"

"I got clobbered on the inside. I'm a little out of shape for this. But it seemed like a good idea at the time," Elliott said, still panting a bit.

"It's good for you and your rock 'n' roll lifestyle. Let's get some waves."

Elliott and Freddy traded off waves, occasionally dropping in together. It was a fun session once Elliott got into it. It made him wish he got out more. He was still a little wary of getting caught inside, so he kept a cautious eye on the horizon for a clean-up set. During lulls they spoke about life in the city.

"E-man, you ever figure out those symbols you asked me about?"

"I think you were right, something about medicine."

"Ah, that figures."

"In fact, I wanted to talk more about that with you. You and I go back a ways. I may have gotten mixed up in something a little heavy."

"Uh oh, what's up? You know I'll help anyway I can."

"I appreciate that. You been following the Task Lyst stuff in the news?"

"Yeah, the dead guy and all that? Poor sucker was just out walking his chow-chow, and POW! Messy stuff." Freddy went after a wave but didn't catch it. He drifted back over and sat up on his board. "So what's your involvement in this Task Lyst?"

"It started out pretty simple. Just collecting some extra bucks here and there parking cars, running errands. Until I started delivering packages with that symbol on it. I should have known better. My better angel told me it was something sketchy."

"And you think the medicine might mean trouble. Drugs?"

"Right. And I don't know the people I was working for. But they know me."

"How'd you hook up with this gig?"

"The website. I qualified for it and they were offering some good money—too good to be true, of course. I get paid in cryptocurrency, very under the table."

"Should I know what that is?"

"It's some new form of virtual currency. Dark web type stuff. But it's becoming more legit."

"World's getting crazier by the day." Freddy positioned himself for a nice overhead wave coming in off the point. With a couple of easy strokes he was dropping in next to the curl and bottom turning with his left hand trailing in the water. He was a goofy foot, like Elliott, so he was facing the wave with his right foot forward as it extended in front of him to the left. Elliott watched as Freddy bobbed along the wave as it passed behind him. The San Francisco skyline was visible in the frame beyond Crissy Field, the Marina District, and Nob Hill. Elliott turned to find a second wave of the set forming and he paddled into position. With much less grace and more effort, he paddled into the wave and caught its momentum. He pressed the front portion of the board down and hopped up as it picked up speed. The Fort Point waves tended to be somewhat forgiving, even in overhead conditions. The wave launched him down its face and Elliott nearly pitched over the nose. He recovered his balance and turned into the shoulder to his left. It was a nice wave—a foot or so over his head—with about a fifteen-yard wall lined up in front of him. He was careful to not get too far in front for fear of missing the connection to the inside reform. He cut back into the white water to his right and straightened out, allowing the wave to rebuild into a faster closeout just before it reached the small sliver of sand in front of the rocks.

Freddy had taken his wave inside as well. Now he was paddling back out and gave a shout as Elliott kicked out of the breaker.

"Just like riding a bike," Freddy said to him.

"That's the best wave I've ridden in years. I can't believe I don't do this more often." For half a minute, nothing in the world concerned Elliott. He was in the zone, free of anxieties about his career and of the trouble with Task Lyst. He needed another wave to prove it wasn't an anomaly. He paddled with urgency to get another taste. Freddy cheered him on as he got wave after wave, the two of them owning the point until well after sunset.

Elliott exited the surf at the rocks near his car. Freddy was parked nearby and was changing out of his wetsuit. They pressed palms and shared a bro hug. Elliott let out a superlative at high volume. It was nearly dark. Freddy asked Elliott if he wanted to finish their earlier discussion about Task Lyst over a pint at Liverpool Lil's.

CHAPTER 57

TIM SEARCHED THROUGH THE PLATFORM'S BACKEND for information on the homicide that was all over the news. The office was visited by detectives with search warrants for login credentials, usernames, file histories: anything pertaining to the case. Pierre and the other executives were huddling up with the legal team brought in to consult. Tim noticed one task in particular and studied its history. A Taskmaster with the username Wielder101 posted a need for an errand on the day in question. The pay was a very generous five thousand in dollar value. Its vague instructions referenced "requires some muscle." Tim suspected this could be the match. Typically the two parties would continue correspondence offline, using temporary free email handles, like Hotmail or Yahoo. Task Lyst would bring the parties together and take a small cut. The privacy policy stated the transaction would be wiped clean from the servers upon completion, guaranteeing a level of discretion demanded in such categories. Tim had set up a secondary server as a system backup. The intent wasn't to violate this policy, but to preserve the system in the event of a major outage. He had been meaning to cleanse the backup server from these task file histories but just hadn't gotten to it yet. The legal team had mandated Tim and his team to follow through and wouldn't have suspected their failure to abide. Tim was sitting on valuable evidence. He could either alert the information technology and legal teams of his mistake or try to go back and deal with it himself.

Tim thought about Wielder101 and wondered what kind of engagement similar errands could attract. Was the platform enabling bad actors and to what degree? He sent Bulgaria an instant message exchange.

"Zander, we need to set up some test accounts for tasks that "require some muscle." Have your team use those exact words. We're not going to approve any. I just want to watch the traffic."

"What, like tough guy stuff? Break some legs, LOL!"

"Geez, do you ever sleep? I wasn't expecting you to be up at three twenty in the a.m. Keep it vague. No guns!"

"Okie doke. No problem. Let's have some fun."

CHAPTER 58

ELLIOTT AND FREDDY MET INSIDE LIVERPOOL LIL'S and took two spots at the end of the bar by the window. It was a favorite of Elliott's from his early days in the city living in the Cow Hollow neighborhood with hordes of other post-college transplants. It was popular for weekend brunch, casual dinners, and a nice midweek pint. Freddy's damp hair was mostly hidden underneath a knit seafarer's cap, and he wore a navy-blue poncho that exaggerated his linebacker body shape. Elliott placed a wad of crumpled cash on the bar and said, "What you feel like? I'm buying."

They chatted about the last couple of waves at Fort Point before tackling pressing matters. Freddy transitioned into the topic by commenting on the lone stand-up paddler who was dropping into waves the surfers couldn't catch.

"Used to be just us longboarders out there. Then the shortboarders came carving it up on their thrusters, thinking they were Gerry Lopez. That was the seventies. Then it was more yuppie shortboarders in the eighties with their pink and green wetsuits. My gosh, they were awful. Then the nineties came with all those vulture capitalists and their sea kayaks. They'd catch the waves on the outside before any of us could paddle into the waves. I tried it a few times. Wasn't so bad actually. Kind of liked it. And now it's the paddle boarders. I like the idea just not the crowds. Old-school paddle surfing is getting beaten down by progress, just like everything else."

Elliott took a drink of his steam beer and placed the pint glass down on the coaster protecting the dark-stained wood bar. "There's no rules. It's total Darwinism out there. Where's the honor for tradition?"

Freddy continued his rant. "We'll probably see electric surfboards soon. Hell, there's already a perfect manmade wave in the desert."

The apron-clad bartender greeted some new patrons down the bar. A lone television above him was tuned to the local news with the sound turned down. At the far end of the bar a guy with wavy silver hair sat alone eating a hamburger with a knife and fork, napkin draped from inside his shirt collar. A dark-colored sport coat contrasted with crisp stripes on his shirt collar. A streetlight, filtered through yellow- and orange-stained windowpanes, gave it a warm, hazy ambience. Picture frames featuring area luminaries decorated the walls. Mirrors gave the place a more sprawling feel without affecting its intimacy. Light reflected off bottles and glasses, and carefully folded cloth napkins gave Liverpool Lil's the distinction of bar-and-grill status.

"So tell me about your situation, E . . ." Freddy said.

"Man, I'm not really sure what's going on. Like I said, it's gotten a bit sketchy. I'm trying to walk away, but they're not making it easy," Elliott said.

Freddy asked, "They?"

"The people paying me to carry out the deliveries. I think they're blackmailing me. Either to keep working for them or to not open my mouth about it. But I don't know who the hell they are because it's all done online."

"Invisible enemy is a hard foe to fight."

"Dude, exactly! I'm thinking it's a gang or drug cartel."

"Seems pretty slick for a small-time street operation," Freddy said, drawing a swig from his pint.

"And it's not something I'm in a hurry to tell the authorities, for obvious reasons."

"Let me dig into it a bit. I'll ask some artists at the shop and poke around Chinatown. I've got some relatives with ears to the ground. They seem to know everything about everyone."

CHAPTER 59

ALICE CAMPED OUT IN THE BLUE HILL BUILDING'S open-air courtyard trying to make sense of some financial models for Q4. The sun was fighting a winning battle with the marine layer, and it was sixty-eight degrees at 10:15 a.m. She often sat out here to unplug, away from the distractions of her workspace. The layout of Blue Hill Capital was designed to keep pace with the new Silicon Valley workspace dynamic: accessibility, transparency, and no hiding places. This was her vitamin D refuge. Her phone rang, and it annoyed her to have forgotten to silence it completely.

"Alice Seegar."

"Ms. Seegar, this is Stuart McKendrick. Did I catch you at a good time?"

"Hello, yes I got your message from earlier, but I had a lunch. You're with . . . homicide?"

"Nope, district attorney's office. I'd like to ask you a few questions about a company you funded. Just trying to get some context is all. Should only take a few minutes of this beautiful Friday. Can I come by your office in a few minutes?"

"I'm sorry, today? I'm not officially in the office today. And I don't know how much help I can be. How did you get my name?"

"I'm engaged to your old roommate, Robin. We met last year at—"

"Wait, Stuart? Okay, I didn't recognize your name. Sorry about that."

"All good. Look, I know this is out of left field. The mayor's office is frothing at the mouth over a possible Task Lyst connection to the Baxter Morris homicide. I've got to get up to speed on this thing. I'm an old-school, pick-up-the-phone kind of guy—"

She cut him off. "Geez, I'd like to help but—"

He cut her off. "Just give me fifteen minutes. I'm gonna look like an idiot if I don't at least know what the company does. I'm actually pulling up now."

Alice took the meeting out in the courtyard with the intention of escaping after fifteen minutes by scheduling an incoming call. A fake call. Using FakeCall.App. Stuart was pretty green about the company platform but pressed her with savvy questions about venture funding and oversight practices. He asked about her contact with Task Lyst; did she know anyone over there? Stuart's diagonal-striped tie hung un-snug around his collar, which, she speculated, was usually unfastened by the time he arrived to his office. His suit straddled the worlds in which he earned his paycheck: dignified enough to go toe-to-toe with high-dollar defense attorneys without alienating the lunchpail crowd of detectives, beat officers, and average Joes. It was navy blue and contrasted with the white shirt. Stuart had played rugby at Cal, and Alice remembered seeing him at a big game party earlier in the fall. He was known around town as a womanizer, so it raised eyebrows when friends learned of his engagement to Robin. Sure, they dated, but marriage seemed eternally premature for a guy nicknamed Johnny Love. Robin brought old money to the table, and her political connections assured a law grad like Stuart quick ascension of the city hall ranks. Alice hadn't been particularly close to Robin when they were two of five mid-twenty-somethings sharing a house in Pacific Heights. It was through mutual connections that Alice had landed among the San Francisco socialites. And she had a knack for not overstaying her welcome.

Stuart was sitting at the outdoor table on a chair he had flipped around backwards, his legs wrapped around the chair's back in a wide, masculine stance. He didn't take notes. And Alice was amused by his self-confidence. He wasn't arrogant, just cocksure. His salt-and-pepper hair and high, tanned forehead reeked of upward mobility;

Cate School on scholarship, Berkeley, enterprise sales at Oracle, Hastings law school, DA's office . . . and now he was marrying into the Nob Hill elite.

"Alice, this is all off the record. But I personally am not on any witch hunt here. I see a crime committed by a scumbag who needs to go to San Quentin."

Alice talked in circles until her phone rang, and on the second one she glanced at the screen on the table. "I need to take this," she said to Stuart. "Hi, Trish? Let me put you on hold for just a sec while I finish up here."

Stuart got up from his chair and flipped it back around and tucked it back under the table. "Alice, I really appreciate your time. You've been a big help while I try to get my head around this."

"Oh, not at all. Happy to help." She smiled, holding the phone in her left hand while extending her right hand to shake his. He reciprocated and added a left hand pat on her opposite upper arm. "Be in touch," he mouthed, as she feigned returning to her call. Her eyes followed his gait as he strode away at a pace that was neither brisk nor lazy, adjusting his tie and checking his watch, his athletic legs bowed. Alice continued faking the conversation with Trish until well after Stuart disappeared from sight.

CHAPTER 60

TIM FELT THE NOTIFICATION BEFORE HE READ IT. His phone vibrated to alert him of a new email. He was at dinner with Sandra and another couple. It wasn't out of the ordinary to receive an email this late by any stretch. He got a couple hundred a day. But this one came on a Saturday evening when work emails generally tapered off. Weekends saw more texting and phone calls. Usually he would ignore such an alert, as it was likely a newsletter from a clothing company or some product he'd recently purchased. But he'd been transfixed on the Baxter Morris murder and set up an email alert for any news updates on the crime. Earlier there was some activity at city hall; the DA was holding a press conference.

"If you will all please excuse me for a moment, I need to use the lavatory."

"Is that what you call it? It's the head. Or the can. Say it like a man." Steve was a rough-and-tumble kind of guy, brilliant, but no-nonsense, Midwestern upbringing. He wore his Chicago on his sleeve. He was a couple of glasses in, and he ribbed Tim on his pretense.

Tim pushed his chair in, cheeks reddening somewhat. "I'd call it the water closet, but we're not in Amsterdam." His retort fell on deaf ears as the others laughed with Steve's rendition of John Belushi rephrasing the request. Tim headed toward the bar in the adjacent room and pulled up between two empty stools. As he fetched his phone from his jacket pocket he motioned to the bartender. He ordered a glass of Chateau Lafite. Tim didn't like the varietal Steve had uncorked at the table and didn't want to hurt his feelings. Since the Task Lyst checks had started coming in, Tim hadn't drunk a crappy bottle of wine and wasn't about to start now. He checked his email while the wine was poured. Sure enough, a web alert contained updates about the presser. The DA's office would be holding the suspect on suspicion of murder with a bail hearing scheduled for Tuesday. The press asked questions about a Task Lyst affiliation, but the DA's office had no comment other than to say, "An exhaustive investigation would include pursuing all angles, whether they be individuals or organizations, and justice would be served."

Tim swirled the wine and went through the motions of checking the color, the nose, the finish. He looked around at the crowd in the bar of the restaurant and made quick judgments on their line of work, social status, and net worth. Three biz school grads, Stanford for sure, awaited their table at a cocktail high-top. A couple of coders from the latest IPO geeked out over beers, and a private equity whale held court with some younger partners further down the bar. Tim killed the Lafite and made his way back to his table with his party none the wiser.

"Timmer!" A voice he recognized but couldn't assign to a name rattled Tim as he neared his party. Turning, he was met with a handshake as Stuart McKendrick rose from his chair. They were friends from a social circle Tim had ceased to frequent. Still, they exchanged pleasantries.

"Stuart, how you been?" Tim glanced around Stuart's table.

"Everyone, this is Tim, we . . . what, we were pals through Jenny . . . ? It's been a while. You're looking good." Stuart stopped short of introducing the individuals in his dinner party.

"Thanks, man. Feeling good." Both men looked for a next line.

Stuart smiled. "I hear you're back in product work."

"Yeah, consulting. A start-up." Tim wondered how Stuart would have an interest in this. He looked away.

"That so. I'd like to hear about it. Let's get together and grab a beer. Maybe next week?"

"You bet." Tim nodded to Stuart and the rest of his party and continued toward his own table. Next week? Why would Stuart want to grab a beer? Usually when someone says that, they leave it open enough that it doesn't mean anything. But setting a timeline, vague or otherwise, is like violating someone's personal space. There must be an agenda. Tim tried to recall the line of work Stuart was in but blanked on it.

CHAPTER 61

ELLIOTT REGAINED CONSCIOUSNESS AND FELT A STINGING PAIN in his left shoulder. Lights were blurry like stars in a haze above him. Figures were hovering over him making sounds he couldn't make out. He smelled gasoline mixed with rotting organic material, reminiscent of his many shifts taking out the kitchen garbage in restaurant jobs. An older Asian guy wearing a waiter's apron asked him, "How many finger?" He repeated the question several times.

Elliott closed one eye and saw the picture come into focus. "Three."

"You lucky. Garbage save you."

Elliott struggled to get up, first taking a knee and surveying his surroundings. His scooter was submerged under bursting-at-the-seams black garbage bags that hadn't made it into a large dumpster to the right. A soup of fluids flowed under his feet and he checked himself for blood. Vegetable oil drenched a pant leg, but he found no blood there. Disposed rice and what might have been chicken curry stuck to his black motorcycle jacket. He made a futile attempt to brush it off when the pain reemerged.

"Ahhh," he said.

"I call 911."

"No, I'm fine." Elliott stood up, holding his left arm close to his body while he fished for his cell phone with his right. He tried to put the pieces together. Where was he? What was he doing? What did he need to do now? He knew for certain an ambulance was out of the question. Without health insurance, he'd be ruined for years paying the doctors' bills. Plus he wasn't convinced he'd sustained much more than a knock. His phone said 10:34 p.m. He recalled something about going to Last Day Saloon, a music venue in the inner Richmond

District. Yes. Abalone Sunset was going on at eleven, and he was meeting his drummer, Cameron Hightower, there.

"Do you have any ice? Ice pack?" he asked the restaurant guy, who nodded and went inside the back door. It was an alley. Elliott scanned the vicinity for clues. His scooter was in bad shape; salvageable but not convincingly drivable. The dumpster was stenciled Mai Vietnamese Restaurant, alerting him he was just a block and a half from his destination. The ground was littered with cigarette butts, including one that was still smoldering. The guy returned with ice.

"Thanks." Elliott took the small bag of ice and placed it on his collarbone inside his jacket. "What happened—did I lay down my bike going around this corner?"

The waiter shook his head sideways, along with his finger for emphasis. He said something Elliott couldn't understand before finally switching to a hand gesture that showed two things coming together and one ending up near the trash heap. He followed it up with a gesture Elliott took to mean the other thing drove hurriedly away.

"Can I leave my bike here for a bit?" Elliott labored to get the scooter up and against the restaurant's back wall with his right hand and left knee. The waiter helped him. Elliott pointed at his phone and motioned he'd be back in a while to get it. At the corner of 4th Avenue he walked south to Clement Street and then the remaining block to the entrance of the music venue. The doorman recognized Elliott and let him in free of cover charge. It was nice to be treated with respect. He had logged some serious hours on that stage and may have still held the record for the biggest night take at the bar for one of his band's gigs back in the early days. Big Dave, the owner, still mentioned it to Elliott whenever their paths crossed. "Hey, Elliott," he'd say in his gravelly baritone. "You guys still have a Friday night here anytime you want it. Just let me know."

In this instance it was a new, younger band packing them in. Elliott saw Cameron up on stage with Abalone Sunset. He found a barstool at the farthest point from the stage and ordered a beer. He adjusted the ice pack, noticed it was spilling water, and placed it on the bar. He felt along the collarbone for any obvious sign of injury, grimacing as he gingerly touched a bump protruding from bone. When the set ended, Cameron joined Elliott at the bar.

"Saw you limp in here. What the fuck happened to you?"

"I think I got run off the road on my way here. Crashed into a garbage heap behind Mai's and blacked out."

"No shit? That's messed up," Cameron said while looking away to grab the bartender's attention. "A Sierra Nevada and two shots of Patrón." Turning back to Elliott, he asked, "Did you get a license plate?"

"I don't even remember what happened. One of the guys taking a smoke break in back of Mai's tried to tell me what happened in broken English."

"You piss anyone off lately? Maybe one of your old ladies."

It occurred to Elliott that Cameron might be on to something, but not one of his old ladies. All things equal, it would have likely been just a turn taken too tightly. The pantomime business, however, made anything possible. He'd check with Freddy in the morning for any news he might have uncovered.

Elliott swirled the Patrón around in the highball glass and emptied half the shot. "Hey, I hate to ask, but do you happen to have anything to help me sleep? This shoulder might need some attention, but I can't see anyone until tomorrow."

Cameron stroked his reddish beard. "I've got a little smoke. Might have a Tramadol or two in my stick bag."

"Ha, you still taking your doggie's dope?"

"Hey, man, don't knock it until you try it! You need a lift home after the next set?"

"Yeah, I'll come back for my wheels tomorrow. Or I can call an Uber if it's too much hassle."

"No sweat at all. Man, you've been through the ringer lately."

Elliott nodded. "I think I need a vacation."

"I know what you mean. Maybe we should take a break from the out-of-town gigs. I need to catch up on some bills, and these little weekend tours are costing me more than I'm making."

"It's a bitch, isn't it? Colorado was a big time, but we barely make any dough, and I get the shaft from the man." Elliott stretched his arm to test the sore shoulder.

"How's it feel?"

"Still hurts, but I think it's gonna be okay, maybe sore for a week."

"I'll grab you a Trammie, and feel free to stick around if you need a lift home."

Elliott wished Cameron a good second set and finished off the tequila. It did feel like time was up on the band's current trajectory.

CHAPTER 62

TIM DIDN'T RECOGNIZE THE NUMBER of the caller who left a voicemail on his cell phone. He had a hunch who it was though. He'd been thinking about Stuart's cryptic request to grab a beer from the other night. Sure enough, Stuart was following up on just that. Tim found it noteworthy when Stuart suggested they meet at the Red Devil Lounge in Nob Hill, a central location that was inconspicuous and quiet enough to have a chat. The Red Devil played host to many of Tim's gigs back in the day. Stuart would have attended some of these.

Tim parked a block away. He put quarters in the meter to get him through the six o'clock hour and headed north toward the Red Devil. Once inside, he found Stuart making small talk with the female barkeep, who pried the cap off a longneck. The velvety red and black decor stood in contrast to Stuart's athletic build and tan suit, making him look as out of place as a tattooed, pierced musician might in the bars of the Marina District. Yet he appeared comfortable. He'd already started drinking a beer.

"Whattya having?" he asked Tim with a bro shake and half embrace.

"Bulleit Rye, neat."

Stuart nodded his approval. "You heard the man, dirty water, I like it." He placed a couple of twenties on the bar and added, "Keep 'em coming!" With his right hand he loosened the tie around his neck and unbuttoned his top shirt button. "Old lady's out of town tonight and I've had one helluva long day. How you doin', Tim?" He raised his bottle, but Tim's drink was still en route.

"Can't complain. Busy. Rocking."

They sat at the bar on stools facing the bartender as she delivered the rye. Tim raised the glass, swirled it 360 degrees, and sipped. A peppery, bold flavor profile sent a warm signal down his center, and he received it willingly. Stuart ordered a second beer and motioned over to a high-top out of public earshot. They relocated there.

"So tell me about this Task Lyst gig you have. I understand you're making it rain over there." They sat facing each other, leaning in.

Tim moved his glass in small circles on the table, judging the viscosity and processing the question. He had looked into Stuart's recent history searching for a motive for the meeting. "Is this Stuart asking or the DA's office?"

Stuart smiled and nodded. "Fair question. Maybe a little of both?"

"Okay, I'm consulting on some product management initiatives. Nothing too sexy. Why do you ask?"

Stuart smiled, paused, and swayed along with the song "Althea" streamed from the sound system and mouthed a line being sung by Jerry Garcia, "lacking in some direction." He repositioned himself and took another drink.

"Here's the way I see it. And maybe you can help me out? Some scumbag knocks off a guy for a couple bucks using your employer's website service." Stuart brought his hands together and clapped and held up his chin. "Task Lyst is facing some exposure there, dontcha think?"

"And you think I can help . . . how?" It was a power move for Tim, to play naive, deflect the gravity of the situation toward those in a more public leadership role. He took another taste of rye, awaiting Stuart's reply.

"Maybe you know how it works. Maybe you want to clean out the bad apples, get rid of the rotten eggs to keep the platform doing God's work and making investors happy."

"That's a little above my pay grade. My project work is confined to creating efficiencies in the UI." Tim removed his coat and draped it on the backrest of his stool. He wiped some perspiration from his forehead with his cocktail napkin.

Stuart watched. "I get it. You're a low-level foot soldier, carrying out orders."

"Pretty much, yep . . . just focusing on my initiative."

"Happy to be back in the game though?" Stuart kept prodding.

"Back? I've been consulting for years."

"No shit? I thought you'd disappeared down the peninsula amid minivans and soccer practices." Stuart's words stung. They were true, of course, and it irked Tim to hear them spoken out loud.

"Touché, but I've been keeping fairly busy on project work in between juggling the three kids."

"Very noble work. Kids. I don't know how you guys do it. I guess one of these days we all end up with them."

Tim laughed at Stuart's cynicism. "They're actually not that bad. Just expensive."

"Enough to make poor choices, I bet."

"How do you mean?"

"Well, you give up your dreams. Compromise. Run up debt. Start living vicariously through them and their soccer games, piano lessons, college essays. You ever tee up any of those soccer moms in the BMW wagons?"

Shaking his head and smiling, Tim replied, "Tee up, as in screw? Can't say I have."

"But you've thought about it. I mean what kind of guy doesn't, right? You go home and rub one out to the momma llama on the sideline who was yelling at the ref. It's not your fault. It's our genetic code, my friend. The arbitrary moral construct we call matrimony is at constant war with our core fiber, which is all about humping anything that catches our eye. Why is one chick hotter than the next? Because our genes tell us she is. Just walk around downtown during the lunch hour, and you have to fight the urge to make babies. It's a losing battle."

Tim countered, "How does your old lady feel about that?"

"Starting to get the itch, I'm afraid. Thirty-six and counting. I just don't think I can play that game just yet. My old man was forty-eight when they had me." Stuart slugged back the last of his beer and clanked it down on the table. "Do me a favor, Timmy. Sniff around over there and let me know what you come up with. You're just a consultant, right? So you don't have a heavy stake in the game, nothing big to lose. I've got people at city hall wanting heads to roll. Crime is up, city ain't safe, software engineers are moving to Oakland. The mayor thinks we are on the precipice of civil unrest. And that won't look good in the gubernatorial race next year." Stuart stood up from his chair and tightened his tie.

"I'll keep that in mind," Tim said.

"Thanks, pal," Stuart said. "I'll follow up with you if I don't hear sooner." They fist-bumped and Stuart adjusted his junk midstride before turning around.

"Oh, and Timmer . . . "

"Yeah."

Stuart pointed over at the stage. A large mirror served as a backdrop, and brass bannisters framed the performance area. Lights reflected off the mirror and created a state of spatial confusion, as if the stage were the center of the room. It was empty now, a few minutes shy of load-in and sound check for some group arriving for its 10:00 p.m. start. The room attracted a mishmash of regulars who tolerated the disorienting effects of this house of mirrors, whether it be one in the afternoon or early morning.

"Those were some good parties you threw, my man. Always brought in the hotties." He flashed a thumbs-up and vanished as Tim replayed it in his mind.

CHAPTER 63

THE NEWS ABOUT GORDIE HIT THE TECH COMMUNITY HARD and reverberated throughout Silicon Valley, San Francisco, and the broader capital markets. But not surprisingly, the epicenter of shock was Blue Hill Capital.

"Gordie's sudden passing leaves behind an awe-inspiring legacy of fearlessness, business acumen, and personal relationships," read the publicity statement that was trending on social media. He had helicoptered south to Kelly Slater's Surf Ranch with Ned Wolfe and others for a private surf session on the artificial wave.

"The story I got was he was leaving early to get back for a dinner and the bird hit a power line, killing both he and the pilot," Larry said to Alice as she stared out the window of the conference room. "Ned saw it go down. Must have been a horrific sight."

Alice was in a daze. She hadn't slept much after hearing the news. Blue Hill Capital asked for privacy to mourn the loss of their leader but also had to make appearances, send out statements, and plan a transition. Alice contained her emotions as if, on some level, there was an emotional distance that made this more of a professional issue than a human tragedy. "For an adrenaline junkie, you'd think he would have died *on* the wave, not while leaving it," Alice said.

"It's how rich people die: private planes and helicopters." Larry said it and let it marinate. "It's a mess. I don't know what kind of succession plan he had in place, but the timing couldn't be worse," Larry continued. Alice knew it was selfish to think of the firm and her future while Gordie's immediate family was suffering his loss. But she engaged Larry's inference.

"Do you think Cynthia is up to the task?"

"I don't know. At least during the transition. She's got the pedigree, but I just worry about the rest of the sharks in Silicon Valley. They'll see this as a time to pounce."

"Why, because she's a woman?"

Larry waited a second to answer. "Yeah, maybe a little. This is the Valley we're talking about. She'll be tested, both from outside and within." Larry was making a point that Alice was thinking. Blue Hill Capital was run by an old boys' network often called vulture capital. Without Gordie, the firm was at the moment rudderless. Cynthia Varden brought solid intellectual bandwidth, a CV with names like Stanford and Wharton, not to mention being the fourth hire at one of the largest IPOs a decade prior. Alice wondered, though. How much was this business about relationships? About extreme sailing . . . about private dinners at Sean Parker's house . . . about surfing in Tahiti . . . about boarding school reunions . . . about meetings at the Bohemian Grove? Her thoughts circled back to Task Lyst. What did it mean for the firm to lose Gordie just as the shit was hitting the fan about their biggest recent investment? Larry added, "Her being a lesbian could cut two ways, though. There are a lot of closet conservatives in the Valley despite what you read in the press."

Alice made a mental picture of Cynthia and her partner, Kim Cannel, at the recent City of Hope fund-raiser. She admired the courage Cynthia displayed in outing herself, especially with a glamorous icon like Kim Cannel. Maybe it was just what the Valley needed for Task Lyst to stay out of the headlines: a female taking over a corner office and her homegrown rockstar life partner. Then again it might attract unneeded attention in a time better served to keep a low profile. Alice's admiration of Cynthia was informed by her eventual acceptance of her own sister's sexuality. Diane was two years younger and always more of a rebel. Initially, Alice thought her sister was making wrong lifestyle choices, as if trying too hard to pave her own path. It was Alice who always had the boyfriends and Diane who had friends that were boys. If she'd stop wearing flannel shirts and combat boots maybe she'd develop some romantic interests, the thinking went. In college it was clear Diane's "experimentation" had transitioned into what was always her place on the spectrum. After some false-start relationships, Diane and her now partner, Jill, settled into a domestic bliss that couldn't escape being characterized by Alice and Diane's parents as somehow ironic. Alice had gone from protecting her baby sister from poor lifestyle choices to defending her fiercely for who she was.

"Cynthia is gonna need to hit the ground running with the Task Lyst situation," Larry said. "It'll be a test of nerves to see which direction she wants to go."

CHAPTER 64

FREDDY WAS HOLDING COURT IN THE PARKING LOT at VFW's in Ocean Beach with a handful of other surfers. It was cold and inhospitable for any other beach activities short of extremely dedicated surfing. Elliott pulled up on his beat-up scooter and leaned it up against the seawall, having lost the kickstand functionality in his crash the day before.

Freddy, with the upper part of his wetsuit open to expose his chest, worked a towel into his wet hair and greeted Elliott. "What happened to the bike, E-man? It's looking rough."

Elliott placed his helmet on the seat and took off his gloves. "Not really sure. Took a corner too close, maybe a hit and run. Scratched up the bike and was out cold for a second." Elliott nodded to the others and recognized one of the guys as a celebrated big-wave rider who moonlighted as a pediatrician. The guy grimaced a little, disapprovingly. The irony wasn't lost on Elliott: someone who braves bloodthirsty sharks, frigid temps, and monster surf judging another guy for riding a scooter on San Francisco's streets.

"I don't trust city drivers enough to ride on these streets," the doc said.

Freddy added, "Beware the Chinese and our slanted eyes!" The gang liked that one. Freddy whipped one of them with his wet towel, the sound doing more damage than the strike.

Elliott tossed his gloves back to the base of his bike. "Banged up my shoulder a bit, but I think I got lucky."

"Did you get checked out?" said the doc surfer.

"I wasn't in a big hurry to pay for an ER visit, so I slept on it and it feels alright."

"No lingering headache, dizziness, nausea, changes in diet . . ."

"Just from the tequila I had afterwards."

The group dissipated, with only Elliott and Freddy remaining. Freddy chuckled at his friends as they loaded up their vehicles with surfboards and made their exits. He changed out of his wetsuit for sweatpants and a zip-up hoodie. Elliott leaned against the seawall, checking his phone for texts.

"So I did a little digging, and guess what?" Freddy said.

"Haven't the foggiest," Elliott countered.

"You're a preferred 'ma qian zu' of the YB, the Yellow Brotherhood. An errand boy. They distribute, among many things, China White up and down the coast and have been in a turf war with the Chavez Boyz for the Bay Area turf. It's been heating up, and you probably stumbled into it. I bet they're using that website to keep foot soldiers in the dark and expendable. They aren't a very nice group for a guy like you to be messing with."

"How do I get out of their employ?"

Freddy looked away and out to the sea. "That I don't know, Big E. I don't have any mojo with the YB. Maybe take a vacation. Lay low." He pulled Elliott toward him for a parting hug as the latter stared into space. "I gotta run. Niece's birthday party. Keep me in the loop on what's up."

After Freddy drove off, Elliott remained on the boardwalk wall watching the sun go down over the stormy surf at Ocean Beach. It was a troubling predicament if Freddy's intel was true. The whole Task Lyst experience had become an open sore representing everything he despised about what he saw the Bay Area becoming. It was a money grab, a power suck, and he was playing into its hands. He felt like a pawn in someone else's game. He liked the sound of that. Not the "being the pawn" part but the actual phrase: "a pawn in someone else's game." He tried it out as a lyric in a variety of melodies. First, like

Bob Dylan would have framed it, as the tag on a verse. He tried out a series of ideas protesting his Task Lyst situation, capitalism in general, politics, big Pharma, escalating healthcare costs, Middle East wars. He settled on a structure he liked and sang it into his phone's voice memo application. Then he started up his scooter and headed home, repeating his new song idea like a mantra during a kirtan. This was his normal process for writing new material, which he characterized as making one's self available to the creative song energies that float through the air. An artist has to be aware enough to reach up, claim them, and sculpt them into form. Or it might be that the song claims the artist, providing the artist is tuned to the right frequency. He had come up with an elaborate understanding of this during a trip looking at the stars over the ocean in Big Sur. But as the intensity subsided, so did the eloquence. What was left was a vague sense that the muse is fickle and rides alone in the night, like the wind blowing wet in moonlit alleys of last calls and distant foghorns. This was not a day jobber's landscape. It required more commitment. What are you willing to give up at the fulcrum of creative sacrifice? Stay in the comfort of soulless death or claim agency of cathartic rebirth among poets, painters, prostitutes, pimps, pagans, sailors in port, junkies strung out, jazz players loading out with a call to the dealer and a fresh payday to forfeit. *There I go again, resorting to flowery mixed metaphors,* he said to himself.

Elliott had the song written in his head by the time he locked up his bike, climbed the steps to his flat, double-bolted the door, and found a pencil to scribble onto a loose sheet of paper. He laid out several verses, each with the same tag, "a pawn in someone else's game." He realized it was too derivative, obviously *Dylan,* and broke the pencil lead on the paper. The sentiment was stronger than the actual words. Still, he knew to blurt it all out and edit later. Purge the ideas while the purging is good. Alas, he crumpled up the idea into a ball and tossed it at the window. Elliott then studied his surroundings as though he were in a photograph, noting the streetlight shining into his room like a spotlight. A bus passed his building, obvious by the ubiquitous sound of sparks on the electric cable overhead. He inhaled through his nose and found the familiar aroma of Wow Naan Curry wafting through his space from downstairs one building over. He sat perfectly still and focused on the moment. He thought of an older song he'd written with the opening line of, "The back streets of this town I fell, in love with the danger but now you can't tell." It was a tribute to Jerry Garcia and a lament to the changes San Francisco, and society in general, had experienced since his passing. The irony was not lost on him that a new danger had established itself amid the gilded yachts and inflated stock options. But the sentiment was apt nonetheless. He dug the complete song out of his tattered lyric binder, careful not to let the scores of pages become unhinged. He placed a capo on the second fret of his acoustic and started strumming the introduction guitar figure. It had been a while since he'd played this one, but he fell right in.

Upon finishing "Jerome (and the Town He Left Behind)," he noodled around some different combinations of chords and settled into a catchy melody and let his stream of consciousness flow. It came pouring out. He replayed the chord progression time and time again, adding new verses, fixing previous ones. Elliott wrote down words, scribbled them out, added new parts. Eventually he recorded the song as a voice memo into his phone, eager to not forget the original cadence and structure. Five hours went by in a flash while he did nothing but fine-tune his new composition. Rather than feeling exhaustion, Elliott was wired on creativity-fueled adrenaline. The clock said twenty-five minutes to four in the morning. He'd need to title it, but in the meantime he wrote, "Just a prawn in the game (sic)."

It was eleven twenty in the morning when Elliott rolled over and checked the time on his phone. His guitar, an old Gibson parlor model, leaned against the bed, reminding him of the song he had worked on into the tiny hours. He was eager to hear the playback but decided to ease into the day with a couple of breakfast tacos and cup of coffee from the Beanery around the corner. His expectations were high on how it would translate into daylight listening, but the usual apprehension remained. He was a harsh critic of his own work and wanted to give this latest brainstorm a fighting chance. Elliott's new songs went one of two places upon completion. If he liked it, he made sure there was a strong guitar and vocal sketch recorded and saved into his release queue, which was housed in a secure hard drive called "Q Drive." The best of these would be considered for full band recordings and limited quantity self-released demos. Elliott considered this his vault of masterpieces. At some point his genius would resonate for the world, regardless of how under-appreciated he might be in the present. He was his own Theo van Gogh, stockpiling and archiving the unsold work of an artist for some future, ideally not posthumous, unveiling. Elliott would reinforce his own merit by sequencing the collection into prospective release schedules. If he could achieve any modicum of financial success, if he could reach even a modest audience, a river of gold records would flow unimpeded.

The songs that didn't pass muster were sent to his "Pyre of Crap" folder, which he planned to eventually destroy in an incendiary fit of catharsis or, at best, recycle into new ideas. He hadn't decided which ones, hence its tenuous existence. Since none of his creative output had met significant commercial or critical validation, it was possible he wasn't a good judge of his own potential. For this reason, he considered even the worst of his drivel to be worth keeping around, at the very least as a journal entry in his memoir or posthumous biography.

Elliott, refreshed and energized by his writing epiphany, pulled the door shut to his flat as the first heavy rain of the season marked its arrival on the pavement. It was a cold, steady rain that had been forecasted for days. He adjusted his scarf, lowered his chin, and zeroed in on the coffee shop. If the song was as good as it had felt last night, he'd share it with his band members and book some studio time. He had plenty of Bitcoin to foot the bill. Perhaps enough to fund a video. They could release it as a single or shop it to the industry sharks who always said the same thing, "I like it, it's got a retro vibe. It's the kind of stuff I listen to on the way home from work. I just don't know how I'd market it."

The coffee shop windows were more steamed up than normal. A queue of half a dozen waited to order while others stood around waiting for their names to be called. Having worked there briefly as a barista, Elliott caught the attention of a sympathetic employee who snuck him a quick and complimentary cafe au lait. Elliott pulled a weekly from the rack and found a seat by the window near a cluster of students camped out in study mode. He sensed that one of them recognized him, as just another local musician most likely. But it was enough. He thrived on building this brand and knew how to exploit it. He wanted to be the person he thought the students saw him as: a working musician on the way up the scale. It was scalable, after all. Build a small local audience into a larger, regional one. Get some suits to come on board to assist with management, legal, distribution, tour support, better bookings, television and film sync deals, radio promotion. Then he could focus on which songs to pull out of his Q Drive to produce into smash hits. And touring. And his acceptance speech. The funnel was in place. It was time for the infrastructure to come together. For the scaffolding to be erected. Saddle up the palomino and let's ride. Maybe the new number would be the catalyst.

Elliott finished listening to the new song for the fourth time to rest his ears. The rest of the coffee shop was oblivious to the magic in his headphones. It was as good as it felt last night, maybe better. It had everything: melody, structure, a catchy hook, timely yet universal, and a strong lyric. He shot off an email to his band about meeting up later so he could lay it on them.

CHAPTER 65

ALICE LISTENED AS CYNTHIA OUTLINED HER PLAN to transition the firm into its next phase. It had been two weeks since Gordie had been laid to rest. The meeting of partners and major investors was being held in the atrium lobby of Blue Hill's office building. A hundred chairs in six rows were flanked by numerous species of fern, palm, and other greenery soaking in the abundant natural light. A new collection of modern art adorned the lobby walls with the same merlion fountain serving as the centerpiece. Cynthia referenced a slide projected on a screen that detailed the various funds being managed by Blue Hill. Under the words El Dorado Fund was Task Lyst in bold red font. The fund's position in Task Lyst was an anvil of liability with the recent publicity and the pressure from the district attorney. Recent talk centered around what to do with the firm's investment in a company under such duress. The lawyers were starting to squirm about the exposure Blue Hill would have if indictments implicated Task Lyst in deaths, drug dealing, and other clandestine activity. The 10 percent stake invested from the El Dorado Fund loomed on the books like a beached whale. Its valuation fluctuated from $250 million in recent valuations to something below zero if the bottom fell out. Worse, the legal implications scared off the company's talent. Writing down the investment as a total loss was a definite possibility. So was riding it out in hopes of an eventual return on investment.

Ahead of Alice, a couple of rows to her left, sat Ned Wolfe. He wore a casual sport coat with a scarf loosely tied around his neck. Short waves of blonde hair snuck out from underneath a small-rimmed chapeau, and he sported a couple of weeks of facial hair. She imagined him bidding for rare works of art, legs crossed, occasionally whispering to a bespectacled attorney next to him. Alice hadn't seen him since Sausalito but had exchanged a few flirtatious texts, one of which was an invitation to a wine function up at his family's vineyard. She couldn't attend due to a prior social engagement. It wasn't so much second-guessing her prudish behavior that night after the sailing adventure but the manner in which she'd departed Ned's cabin that stuck with her. When he couldn't find the keys to the car in the garage, he made it clear that her spending the night was an option. He'd offered to sleep on the couch and give her the one bedroom, but she wasn't feeling it, preferring to catch a long, expensive ride home. Perhaps it was silly to not stay put and let things play out. But waking up in the North Bay wasn't something she'd signed up for.

"I'm going to turn the floor over to our largest shareholder in the El Dorado Fund, Mr. Ned Wolfe," Cynthia said. Ned rose from his chair and made his way to the podium. He unfolded a cocktail napkin and spread it out in front of him before adjusting the slender microphone arm.

"Good morning. Thank you, Cynthia, for allowing me to say a few words. And thank you for taking on a leadership role in this challenging time," Ned said, gesturing toward her in the front row. He clutched the sides of the podium firmly and scanned the audience, pausing for effect. "John Gordon was a very close friend of mine, and his loss is massive for Blue Hill Capital, Silicon Valley, and, especially, his family and friends." Claps filled the room, and he nodded to the crowd in general and some specific individuals, Alice included.

"It is through El Dorado that this firm is invested in Task Lyst. As the primary source of private equity in El Dorado, I represent a controlling interest in the investment and feel strongly about the best action moving forward. For me, it all comes down to liability. The company is alleged to have aided and abetted nefarious acts through its user platform. An overzealous district attorney facing reelection could make this a populist campaign issue. By the time the courts decide in favor of the first amendment, said DA will have little interest in pursuing the case. Point is, the sides are aligning on this as we speak.

"Look, the safe play for Blue Hill is to get out of this deal. Take the modest profit now, put it in the books, mitigate risk while keeping a small stake in hopes it pays out later. I am submitting a tender offer of two-and-a-half dollars per share of all outstanding initial round holdings and will assume all debts and liabilities. Blue Hill can wash its hands of this and remove the burden to its future balance sheets." Various audience members looked around at others and adjusted their posture. A few mini-dialogues sprouted up.

"In closing, you may be wondering what interest I have in doubling down on Task Lyst. In my due diligence I've found some synergies with other holdings in my portfolio, ones I'm willing to explore on my own. Worst case, it will make a nice tax write-off. Thank you for your time here today."

Tepid applause followed his remarks amid more whispers, grumbling, and a general feeling of disorder. Ned walked back to his seat, smiling at an acquaintance or two and pointing at another with the poise and swagger of someone accepting an athlete of the year award.

Alice processed the dynamics of Ned's offer and its ramifications. She wondered where Cynthia stood on the issue. And Pierre. Larry sat down next to her while Cynthia thanked Ned for speaking.

"I figured this might be the path forward. Ned's the white knight saving Blue Hill's noggin, and he'll make out like a bandit once the dust settles."

Alice replied, "So with the liability, he's taking all the upside. Blue Hill is letting it go for peanuts?"

"Appears that way. No risk, no reward. And there goes our reward."

CHAPTER 66

TIM ARRIVED AT HIS OFFICE EARLY IN THE MORNING after the shareholders' meeting. It had been nuts in the immediate days following John Gordon's tragic passing. Tim had sent flowers and contributed one thousand dollars to the California Land Conservancy nonprofit in Gordie's name. He'd traded messages with Alice but gave her the space he knew she needed to mourn the loss and to deal with the leadership transition. It was weird how Tim had recently mentioned to someone about the dangers of flying drones in flight paths and sooner than later there would be a mishap with some plane or helicopter. Task Lyst assured its employees, respectfully, it was business as usual despite the "tragic loss of one of our beloved board members."

Tim logged into the interface backend and checked the overnight activity. Data indicated another strong twenty-four-hour period. He focused his report on high-volume Taskmasters, including prized pupil Shogun75. Scanning the communications logs, Tim noticed the Taskminder Geronimo69 still had not logged in and had shut off all notifications in his Task Lyst user preferences. It seemed odd to see the user's activity fall off a cliff. Did he migrate to a new competitor to Task Lyst? Did he have a falling-out with the Taskmaster? Tim, in his role as matchmaker—no, kingmaker!—felt responsible and determined to find closure. Against protocol, Tim looked into stored personal details of the user's profile, harvesting contact information that was collected as standard procedure with each user sign-up: name, phone, email, username, password, etc. Tim Googled the user's name, "Elliott Temple," and found pages of links to a modest music career. Tim recognized a few shared acquaintances. It was a small world, this Bay Area. Tim jotted down some of Elliott's info and, as a precaution, scrubbed his browser search history. Next, he logged into the secondary servers he had neglected to destroy. Reaching below the desk, he unzipped a side pocket on his computer bag and pulled out an external hard drive. He plugged it in and began transferring files from the server. Removing the backup and taking it off premises would protect him and the company, he reasoned. While it loaded, he walked to the courtyard and ordered a tall coffee from the kiosk.

Tim's thoughts returned to Baxter Morris. The homicide had precipitated Tim's profile espionage, and Geronimo69 proved an interesting case study. The storage drive he was transferring would include all the details of the user's activity and login credentials. He would delete all traces of it on the local server and smuggle the backed-up copy out of the building. Once destroyed, he could plead ignorance to any knowledge of nefarious conduct. Failure to report such could incriminate him on grounds of aiding and abetting. Tim took his caffeine back to his cubicle. Waiting for him there was an instant message on his office desktop computer. The IT administrator assigned to his team was inquiring about the large file transfers happening under his user account.

"Hey Tim, a bandwidth alert popped up on your profile, and I'm running a diagnostic."

Tim sat down, placed his drink on the desk, and saw the transfer still in progress.

"Sorry, I must have dragged a whole folder when I meant to transfer a report. I'll cancel it now." Tim dragged the cursor to the cancel button where he could stop the file transfer. He spent a half minute assessing his options. Clearly he got flagged for messing with the secondary server, and Tim was concerned how the IT manager would interpret his actions. Plausible deniability came to mind. Plead ignorance. Pull the fire alarm. Ha. Burn the place down. Tim decided it was best to proceed with business as usual and hope the smoke cleared.

CHAPTER 67

ALICE SPENT THE WEEKEND OF HALLOWEEN AT AN ASHRAM. It had seemed like a good idea when her sister Diana had proposed it back in the summer. And even though her interest had waned, she actually found it to be good timing to get away from the uncertainty of Blue Hill Capital's future. For several hours a day she was able to focus on the moment and reinvigorate her body and mind. The vinyasa approach appealed to her in a way the trail running regimen didn't. It was better on her knees, and she loved wearing the flattering yoga attire. There was something about the fit that put her insecurities at peace. She would stock up when she got back.

One of the emails Alice opened while sitting at her desk Monday morning was from Tim's private account. He wanted to get her feedback on the shareholders' meeting that had transpired after Gordie's sudden passing. Word had gotten out that some type of acquisition was in play. According to Tim, the ValleyWag blog had mentioned a possible shakeup at Task Lyst, and user comments hinted at some maneuvering behind the scenes. Alice wrote back about being away over the weekend but, yes, there were talks under way about Blue Hill divesting the fund that held Task Lyst equity.

Another email was a newsletter from a venture capital trade group tying foreign investment to Silicon Valley and relating the dangers inherent therein. It posited that China and Russia had much to gain from strategic investments in technology and in some cases took positions merely to network with big players in the capital markets. *Typical jingoistic banter from conservative, blue-blooded banker types*, she thought. As she read on, she was surprised to see Ned Wolfe's name pop up. He was quoted saying, "The El Dorado Fund has strong ties to the Eastern

Asia market and just recently welcomed an additional investment from our partners in China. Synergies exist that will benefit both sides in a long, fruitful, and cooperative engagement." She searched the rest of the article for more information, but it tailed off into broad, contextual vagaries. She picked up her handset and dialed Larry.

"Hey, girl, how was the ashram?"

"Good, you're here. I'm coming over to see you." She hung up and walked to Larry's workspace. En route, she waved off a few morning greetings with expedient pleasantries. Larry was checking his fantasy football stats as Alice entered. He turned to greet her with a raised eyebrow and a pen twirling in his left hand.

"Jorgensen killed me head-to-head last week, had like five hundred yards passing out of his backup quarterback. I'd fire him if I was his direct report."

"I assume you're talking fantasy football," she said.

"Of course, me and a hundred million other patriotic Americans this Monday morning."

"Right. So catch me up on the Task Lyst deal. What's the latest?"

Larry took his feet off the desk and replied, "Coffee?"

"I've had some, thanks. But I'll walk with you." They walked to the kiosk in the atrium and chatted on the way.

"Well, you witnessed the shocker. Ned's buying us out of the venture. The Valley seems to think he's risking too much, what with all the legal stuff pending. He's taking El Dorado and the bathwater with it. I guess he's got enough play money to not worry too much about it. God, I admire him."

"Task Lyst is my baby, and that doesn't leave me with a feeling of job security."

"Maybe Ned will take you with him. You guys are dating, right?"

Alice mock-punched Larry in the shoulder as he laughed. "You shut the fuck up, nothing happened," she said.

"I know, alone on a deserted island after the shipwreck . . ."

"Do you want to wear your coffee?"

"Ha ha, okay . . . you're just friends. But seriously, I don't know what's happening around here. Cynthia has big hurdles in front of her and agreeing to unload a powder keg like Task Lyst might be the best play for her." Larry stirred some agave sweetener into his cup and looked around before leaning in to Alice. "I've already put some feelers out to several firms and clients. It's lifeboat time; you've got to see that."

"I've been at a meditation retreat, and you already have a new gig lined up?"

"Nope, not yet . . . but I'm working on it. Always know where you are seated relative to the exit row. And never get too far over your skis."

Alice spent the rest of the day fighting off an existential crisis. Maybe Larry was right and she should be thinking about jumping ship too. A complete career pivot wasn't something she had considered in the short term. Yoga instructing at her own studio was a five- to ten-year goal. She stared at a certain text message for the umpteenth time and drafted another belated reply that she doubted she'd send. This time, she did: "Hey, it's me. Your desert island friend." She replied to the last text Ned had sent her following their evening in Sausalito, which was "and, hey . . . nice getting marooned with ya."

Almost immediately, he replied: "thought u forgot about me. drinks?"

She smiled and loosened her shoulders, typing: "aren't you busy hunting unicorns?"

"Always. but I look for balance. come up to the city I'll be at Washbag after 8."

Alice knew the Washington Square Bar & Grill to be an old-school hangout, just Ned's type. She pictured herself being paraded around the place like a Preakness philly for his blue-blooded cronies to place bets. Tempting, but not really. "I'm behind on financials. I was away this weekend. Rain check?"

"Speaking of rain, Squaw Valley Thursday, come with?? Gonna dump snow tomorrow, looks like an early season start!"

"I have to work"

"no y dont, I own the fund now. it IS work. or your fired." He added an emoticon signifying an explosion, presumably her employment status.

"Lol. Okay, boss. I'll let you know tomorrow."

Then she added, "Ciao." He didn't respond. She pictured him having turned his phone off as his happy-hour date returned from the powder room. She looked out the office window into the winter darkness but saw only her reflection, a young, sprightly dressed tech-sector professional headed home alone for a dinner of chicken breast, kale salad, and a glass of white wine. Gone were the days of automatic meet-ups at the Mauna Loa or the Paragon with friends after work. Upon reflection, her mid- to late twenties had seemed like a perpetual happy hour. Those she ran with were now nearly all married or had moved away. Some were even getting divorced. Still, she knew enough to keep some distance from a guy like Ned. But she wasn't sure exactly how much distance. Where was the sweet spot? And her track record in such matters was mostly good.

CHAPTER 68

IT WAS TIM'S BIRTHDAY, and his mother had arranged a surprise lunch delivery for his team at the office. He was incensed. The pomp and circumstance was typical of his overbearing yet loving mother who didn't share Tim's appreciation of taste or nuance. She'd spent decades performing outward acts of love and affection for her cardiologist husband and three children in offices, classrooms, and college dorm rooms. Her Midwestern values and expert homemaker skills simply couldn't be unwired. Tim had trouble accepting that. Doubly annoying was the less-than-stellar choice in catering. Olive Garden betrayed Tim's flyover state family background. They had far more means than refinement. It was always a liability to connect his personal life with that of his folks and siblings, who were less concerned with the hoity-toity details of his West Coast living. Olive Garden was a new low, however, even for her. She was slipping, he told himself while preparing a plate of fettuccine Alfredo and spaghetti and meatballs. One of his coworkers commented about the note from Tim's mother on the birthday card, which read, "Happy Birthday our dear Tim! Your Dad and I wanted to treat you to your usual favorite. Sorry we can't be there! xoxoxo. Mom." Many of Tim's team jumped in and gorged themselves, with a few vegetarians and vegans picking around the edges.

"Tell your mom thanks," one of the junior coders said.

"I'll be sure and do that," Tim replied. "Take some home with you tonight too."

One of his female team members asked, "Should we let some other departments feed on the extra?"

Tim agreed, but under the condition the invite was delivered in person to limit his exposure. The last thing he wanted was to publicize his Olive Garden birthday to the entire company, particularly the executives and directors. Tim saw to it personally that the food containers and bags they were transported in were quickly dispatched to recycling.

But Tim did dish up a heaping plate for himself and took it back to his workspace. He was starving and promised himself he'd burn the carbs later with a ten-kilometer run. While away from his desk he had received an instant message from Legal Affairs requesting his participation in a meeting at 2:00 p.m. in the main conference room. He checked with Raj, the manager overseeing Project Gray DeLorean.

"Raj, is this two o'clock necessary for me? I have another call scheduled with Bulgaria."

"Afraid so."

"What about?"

"Legal update, I imagine."

Tim set aside his feast and called Alice's cell phone.

She answered, "Hey, Tim."

"Yo, got a sec?"

"Sure, what's up?"

Tim said, "Our legal team called a meeting for two today, and I wanted to get the scoop on this El Dorado business people are talking about."

"Yeah, you and me both. I just know Ned Wolfe is buying our majority position in the fund that has a controlling interest in Task Lyst. I'm trying to figure out if I have a job."

"Interesting."

"I may get to chat with Ned later in the week, but until then we're just waiting to see how the dust settles."

Tim pressed on. "So it could be just due diligence regarding the transition."

"Could be. I doubt it will affect contractors, at least initially. You guys still need to hit the numbers."

"Cool. Gotta jump; I'll let you know how it goes," Tim said. He immediately logged into the administration backend of the platform and ran a user report. Separately, he searched for data on Geronimo69. He saved the communication logs of each as PDF files and emailed them to his personal Gmail account. Tim instant messaged his Bulgarian programming team to reschedule their videoconference. They were ready to deliver the rating system for which Tim had contracted them.

"Zander, gotta push our call, something popped up and I can't get out of it. Can you guys wait an hour or so?"

"Tim, it's already late here and I can't keep my guys sober for long," Zander said. He added a crazy face emoticon. He added, "I also fixed that account freeze problem you mentioned about Geronimo69. You'll get an alert when the response time lags beyond 24 hrs and you can interface directly with either party to their personal email."

Tim had forgotten about this feature. "Is it live? This interface button?"

"As soon as you give me the green light it will be."

"Okay, go ahead and go live. I'll play with it on my end and let you know what I think," Tim said. After refreshing his browser, Tim pulled up the user profile and sent a message to the delinquent user account under the auspices of customer service:

"Dear Geronimo69, Your recent lapse in activity has alerted our customer satisfaction team to reach out and (1) answer any questions you have, (2) troubleshoot any issues you have, and (3) solicit feedback on your user experience with Task Lyst."

CHAPTER 69

AN EMAIL HIT ELLIOTT'S INBOX FROM TASK LYST. He opened it and read the customer alert about his latent activity. It was a trivial message, and Elliott considered the delete button. Instead, he reread the email. He clicked on the help desk button and scrolled through the frequently asked questions, looking for information about deleting his account. His profile was temporarily frozen. He submitted a help ticket requesting instruction on how to proceed with the hopes he could bring closure to this chapter and refocus on his music. He thought back to the crowbar and the Porsche and how it had softened him to delivering potentially illicit packages to random addresses while dressed as a mime. It seemed comical now, but at the time he was intoxicated by the dollar signs. Somehow it all felt victimless. The anonymity masked the nature of the tasks. The Baxter Morris situation changed all that. He hadn't heard from the Yellow Brotherhood or whomever he perceived to be the party delivering him threats. It had been over a month and maybe he was in the clear. He could hear Freddy saying, "A squeaky door is better left shut."

CHAPTER 70

ALICE ALLOWED NED TO TALK HER INTO SKIING on Thursday. She feigned a work conflict, but he laughed her off. The midweek ski date was framed as an annual tradition of being the first descent of the season on fresh Sierra Nevada snow. There were seven or eight people going from various corners of Ned's social network. They would fly out of the private jet terminal in San Jose into Tahoe Valley Airport and stay at the PlumpJack resort at Squaw where Ned's family had an interest. From there, a snowcat would take them to the best powder in the greater Lake Tahoe area. He assured Alice that they'd be equipped with the latest avalanche survival gear.

It was an intriguing notion—getting fresh tracks on the first powder dump of the season, flying private, and staying at the PlumpJack. But this was also her ticket to talk business with Ned and get a feel for her job security. To prepare, she'd hit the gym for some squats, her usual pre–ski season training routine. Next, she'd update her alpine fashion game with a visit to the Last Minute Gear store. She'd also need to stock up on Diamox for the rapid altitude change and start hydrating. She didn't want to be the weak link on an extreme skiing expedition.

Alice was greeted by Ned outside the jet. The rain hadn't let up all week, and he was drenched from carting luggage and ski gear to the baggage handler.

"Seegar, glad you could make it. The others are up in the departure lounge. Join 'em while I get your stuff loaded." Holding an umbrella with one hand, she pushed her duffel on wheels toward him.

"This is all of it. I'm renting demo skis up at Squaw. We gonna get out in this?" she said.

"We're definitely getting out. It's the landing I'm more concerned with." Ned took the duffel and placed it on the cart before turning toward her. He added, "Hey, I'm glad you made it."

She smiled back at him and started toward the departure lounge. Inside were some familiar faces that resembled a reunion of the yacht gang. There was Pierre Henry, wearing a white one-piece après-ski jumpsuit. He looked ready to hit the slopes, and his voice was louder and more at ease than she'd remembered it. He was talking to Stuart McKendrick, a mild shock that she had only a split second to process.

They both noticed her arrival and Stuart greeted her. "Alice, what a surprise. Say, do you know Pierre Henry?"

"Yes, of course. Great to see you again, Pierre." She looked back and forth at the two men but couldn't find more words. Finally, she offered, "Which one of you is going to talk me off the ledge and convince me I'm not over my head here?"

Stuart laughed. "Pierre here was just telling me about his exploits in the Alps. Have you done much backcountry skiing?"

Alice answered, "Not really. May have shimmied under the rope a couple times."

Pierre said, "I always tell people to follow their own instincts regarding risk. Write your own narrative. And never trust Ned." Alice laughed, and Stuart went along with it.

She added, "I hope he's a better skier than he is a boat captain."

"Well, wait till you see him fly," Stuart said.

"I hope you're kidding," Alice replied. Stuart looked to Pierre for support. Pierre nodded in agreement. Alice looked for a sign that they were pulling her leg. "Seriously." It was more of a statement than a question. Her mouth stayed open wide for a long pause, as if she was waiting for the punch line before laughing out loud. Pierre reached softly for her shoulder.

"Someone needs a drink," he said. Stuart took the cue and poured a tomato juice concoction from a pitcher into a red solo cup and added a celery stalk, two olives, a prawn, a crab claw, and a lime wedge.

"How about a Bloody Maria?" Stuart handed it to Alice and added, "I don't think we're making turns today."

Alice accepted the offering, peered into it, and asked, "What's in it?"

Stuart winked at her. "The breakfast of champions."

Pierre added, "I hope you like tequila."

Ned entered the departure lounge and announced they'd be leaving shortly, having just got weather clearance. He pointed over to Stuart. "Nice, save me one of those for when we land."

"Of course, Cap'n," was the reply.

"We've got a slim window, so let's move or we'll be rerouted to Reno."

The gang grabbed their carry-ons and braved the rain for the aircraft stairs. Alice sat next to Stuart and took her first sip of her cocktail.

"I'm more of a beer and a shot kind of guy, but Ned insisted. Coats the stomach pretty well though. We may need it with Ned flying this thing," Stuart said.

"That's so reassuring," Alice said. She found the Bloody Mary variation surprisingly tasty, her eyebrows betraying as much.

"Not bad, right? I'm about to pour myself another." Stuart topped himself off. "So, Alice, long time no see. You been doing okay?"

"I've been good. Busy. Interesting seeing you here. How's your investigation going?" she asked.

Stuart finished swallowing an olive while looking into her eyes before responding. "Which one?"

She looked around and lowered her voice. "Um, our meeting, Baxter Morris, Task Lyst?"

"It's looking pretty open and shut as far as I'm concerned." His eyes seemed interested in her reaction.

Alice paused a moment. "How do you know Ned?"

Stuart readjusted himself in the seat. "I saved his life in the war."

"War? Which war?" She half chuckled.

"Cal versus Stanford. He would have killed himself if we'd lost that game senior year. You've heard of the Big Game. Well, football's got nothing on the great rugby rivalry."

"A hooligan's game played by gentlemen," she said.

He nodded slowly. "Right." He kept nodding as he pulled his eyes away from her and leaned his head back and stared into space in front of them.

CHAPTER 71

TIM TAPPED HIS FOOT AT 140 BEATS PER MINUTE under the conference room table while external callers could be heard introducing themselves on the Polycom at the table's center. It was soon his turn. "This is Tim, product manager." He was still technically a contractor, but his title had been formalized with his expanded responsibilities. Raj introduced himself as senior programmer and VP of UI. Also in the room was Clay Crookham, who had just been promoted to chief operating officer.

"Guys, this is Clay. As you all are aware, the Baxter Morris situation has brought more heat on our business model. The district attorney is kicking tires trying to figure out whether to hold us liable for the actions of one of our users. Business continues to grow despite the negative publicity. But we need to tamp down on the ethically questionable tasks on the platform. The new board of directors wants safeguards in place. That means we flag all transactions involving drugs, prostitution, and other nefarious activity. Raj, can you guys deploy an algorithm that identifies key words and places certain tasks under review?"

"We've purposely avoided this so as to protect identities and to maintain plausible deniability. But, yes, of course we can write it into the code," Raj said. "Are we sure we want to go down that road?"

Clay was no longer seated but standing. "That's yet to be decided. I'd like a prototype delivered to at least have the option. We'll test it and then decide whether to go live."

A voice with an Eastern European accent calling in posed a question. "Hey it's me, Taz. I'm stuck in traffic, but let me give you my two cents. I'll play devil's advocate here: We ID a conversation that involves one of the aforementioned transgressions, and then what? Do we report them? Are we KGB now?"

Clay leaned over his chair toward the Polycom. "Nobody said anything about us being cops. Let's not put the cart before the horse's arse. The wisdom is that this adds value to the platform and gives us some bargaining power with investigators in the event of another Baxter Morris."

Taz countered, "I don't know. There are privacy issues here that could undermine our users' trust. I didn't architect this platform to be stool pigeon."

"Like I said, nobody is deciding anything right now. But I want to develop and test it. If legal doesn't green light it, so be it." Clay, shaking his head at the phoned-in comment, turned and made eye contact with Tim. "Raj, can your team get working on this and get me something operable by Monday?"

Raj looked at Clay and then Tim. "I don't see why not. It's just data mining and adding an interface to the backend. Provided we can reverse the encryption that is written into the software." Tim raised his eyebrow to Raj, a quiet acknowledgement of his marching orders.

"Great, let's get on it, then. Oh, and . . . this is for our eyes only. I want discretion used. Taz makes a good point in that this shan't be bandied about among the great unwashed."

Tim and Raj hung behind the others who exited the conference room. Raj opened a bottled water and took a swig, all the while looking at Tim.

"Sounds like a job for your Bulgarians."

Tim nodded. "Right up their alley. I'm going to need a new budget for this. They're already whining about unrealistic deadlines and slow payment. One of them hacked my Facebook page as a joke, posted a silly little meme of me as a slave driver."

Raj nodded. "I'll free up some funds. Make us both look good and get this delivered as soon as possible. I get the feeling Clay is assembling his favorites to take into the new regime. It's starting to make sense: Blue Hill is off-loading us to Ned Wolfe, and he's a real piece of work from what I've heard."

Tim thought of Ned on the boat, nearly capsizing the *Snark II* with one hand on the wheel. His impression of Ned had evolved over time from aloof playboy to cunning Silicon Valley operator. The complexity in Ned both intrigued and annoyed him. He wasn't sure he wanted to be in another vehicle with Ned at the helm. A certain degree of risk-taking and recklessness was a trademark of many captains of industry but so was discipline. Maybe Ned was more levelheaded behind the scenes; it was hard to tell. Perhaps this was a good opportunity for Tim to make his move up the food chain. Raj was right. Eyes would be focused on his team's ability to deliver.

Raj answering his cell phone broke Tim's train of thought. "Hello, this is Raj." He switched his cell phone to his other, dominant hand. "Pierre, what's up? How's the snow up there?"

Tim watched for a moment as Raj listened. Tim made the assumption Pierre was up in Tahoe, where surely the snow was dumping. *Lucky him,* Tim thought to himself. Skiing some early season virgin snow while the troops battle down in the Valley. Tim's upbringing had afforded him regular ski vacations to the likes of Steamboat, Jackson Hole, and Park City. He lamented the fact that kids and real life had cut his yearly ski-day count to single digits. On skis, he could keep up with anyone, and it was good to know there might be time in the future to impress Pierre on the slopes, or at least in conversation. Tim had skied the Alps during his junior year abroad in Strasbourg.

Raj motioned to Tim and mouthed, "I've got to take this," signaling Tim to leave him alone. Tim obliged, collecting his notebook computer and departing the conference room. En route back to his desk, he called Zander with instructions for the tracking tool.

"Hey, man, it's me. A new project just fell on my lap, and I need you guys on it right away."

Zander replied, "What did you think of the . . ."

Tim cut him off. "I haven't had a chance to test it yet. Listen: I'm going to write up a work order here shortly for a tracking tool to identify user tasks associated with various keywords. Can you guys build that?"

"We can build anything, you know this. It's just a question of money."

"Great. It's got to be testable by Monday. Don't worry about the UI graphics, just get it operable. I'll send the work order shortly. Gotta run. Hit me on messenger if you need me."

CHAPTER 72

ON THURSDAY ELLIOTT RECEIVED A TEXT FROM FREDDY that read, "e man, picking up a new board today. u should meet this shaper. 47th and taraval street around noon if you can." It was 9:43 a.m., and Elliott was finishing up at the laundromat, struggling to get a good crease in his shirt folding. He was still hatching a scheme for his new song, which he was humming in his head. He stopped in the coffee shop with his basket of clean clothes. The early morning commuter patrons were now being replaced by artist types and moms in workout attire pushing strollers at a more leisurely pace. He recalled his first visit to this shop and ordering a Keith Richards, tall coffee with a double shot of espresso and sugar. Now the names of the drinks on the chalkboard mimicked those of the giant coffee chains: lattes, macchiatos, and Americanos. Some tech genius flush with new cash had surely acquired the shop from the original mom-and-pop owners, brought in a barista consultant who, in the infinite wisdom of business management school data, aligned the customer experience with that of modern retail. This included balancing its edgy caffeinated legacy with the changes to the neighborhood—namely, gentrification and influx of single-family homebuyers from the technology boom. Elliott's "hood" was now defined as much by its myriad yoga studios as it was by the hip children's boutique selling Scandinavian board games whose shopping bags were the new social currency.

Elliott arrived at the corner of 47th and Taraval by way of the N Judah bus. He heard Freddy's laugh from inside a slightly open door to an aging two-story commercial building. A homemade sign taped to the door identified the business as Tecumseh Surfboards. The toxically pleasing aroma of surfboard resin pulled at Elliott like a siren in rough seas. A mist of sanding dust emanated through the gap in the door and outlined a recent footprint. He gave a courtesy knock and peeked inside. The beautiful clutter of an artisan's workshop welcomed him, and he received a casual, affirming nod from someone inside listening to Freddy describe his early morning surf session. Freddy turned and gestured to Elliott while continuing his tale of epic conditions.

"We went in the water at Sloat and ended up at Noriega two hours later. The current was so strong and the left-handers so good I just gave up. Had to hitch a ride back on the Great Highway." Freddy pulled Elliott over to him with a friendly bro hug and introduced him to the board shaper who had a dust mask dangling from his neck. The guy had a full mane of white hair kept in check by a Balinese headband and appeared to be in healthy, robust middle age. His mustache and chin stinger were vaguely familiar to Elliott.

"E-man! This here's Wayne, better known as Tecumseh," Freddy said.

Elliott reached his hand out. "I'm Elliott, nice to meet you. We may have crossed paths in the water at some point."

Tecumseh reciprocated. "Elliott, welcome."

Freddy added, "E-man, dig the new stick my man just made me." The board lay horizontal in front of them and had just been receiving a final sanding.

"Nice. Big wave gun? You hunting elephants with this?" Elliott rode his palm along the rail of the pristine white plank. He tried to imagine a wave that would require a board this shape. Freddy was a charger, but this looked more like North Shore material.

"Mavs. I'm gonna ride it before I'm too old to make it out alive." He was referring to Mavericks, a legendary big wave twenty miles to the south that attracts the world's top surfers and hundreds of other brave, if sometimes foolish, souls. Mark Foo, among others, had died there, and he was a veteran of giant surf, having plied his trade on Oahu's north shore. Mavs was cold, sharky, and dangerous, particularly if you weren't buoyed by a team of rescue jet skis. Elliott had watched Mavs on some big days but never ventured out. It was either breaking massive or just a splash of ripple against rock upcroppings far out from Pillar Point on the north side of Half Moon Bay. To watch from the cliffs on a day without surf was still eerie, usually chilly, ghost-like. It takes a large west-by-northwest swell to generate the wave heights necessary to wedge through the deep-water canyon onto the rock reef. When it's firing, it is second to very few in terms of intensity. The peak pitches up into a vertical cascade of terror with little margin of error. Foo had drowned after a wipeout on a relatively tame set wave. Who knows exactly why. One theory maintains that his leash got tangled in rocks and held him under. They found him floating in the channel.

Elliott answered, "Better you than me. I'll come watch."

"This board will save your ass. It'll get you outside of the impact zone on sets, and it will get you down the face through to the shoulder before you end up in the jaws of a twenty-five-foot monster," Tecumseh said. One eyebrow stayed perversely scrunched up, nearly vertical, while his eyes stayed fixed on Elliott's for emphasis.

"Wayne-oh, Elliott here's a musician. I didn't tell him about your past as a legendary guitar shredder," Freddy said.

"Yeah? You still playing?" Elliott said.

Tecumseh finally released his eyebrow and grabbed a towel to begin wiping down the board. "Nah, just the occasional ukulele around the campfire. It was a means to an end during the revolution. But the battleground has shifted since those old days."

Freddy egged him on. "Tell him about jamming with the Airplane in Golden Gate Park."

"Really?" Elliott said.

Tecumseh shrugged. "We were city kids. Surfers. And they wanted to send us to Indochina to fight the red tide. I wasn't buying it. We grew our hair, sang about peace and love, and lit the sky on fire. It worked for a few years. And then the walls caved in. We're really not much further along now."

"Tell us how you really feel," Freddy said, looking at Elliott.

Tecumseh continued. "The means of production for the eve of destruction. That's what we used to call our guitars."

"Similar to Woody Guthrie's 'This machine kills fascists,'" Elliott added.

"Good!" Tecumseh answered. "That's good, there's hope for our youth after all. How about you? You making any waves with your music?"

"Trying. I sometimes feel it's a waste of time and money. Music doesn't seem to have the cultural impact it did in your day. Sorry, I meant, you know . . . in the Golden Gate Park Human Be-In Acid Test days. I'm still trudging forward though."

"Hmm. It still does. Always will to a degree. Art has its place in the struggle. 'Art before Arms' is a mantra we used to advocate."

"Used to?" Elliott asked.

"Until push came to shove. We saw six thousand die by '66. Lost my brother in Khe Sanh. Sixty-eight was a total shit-show. Then we crossed into Cambodia, then Kent State happened . . ." Tecumseh kept wiping the surfboard despite it appearing pristine. He knelt low, presumably to inspect the stringer, making sure it was perfectly straight. Elliott broke the pause.

"Something tells me you are still involved in the struggle."

Tecumseh, still kneeling, looked at Elliott. "Who's asking?"

Freddy mediated. "He's cool. I told you about his problem with the Brotherhood."

Tecumseh stood. "Okay, but this is real here. You cross a line into my reality and there's no going back."

Elliott glanced from Tecumseh over to Freddy, looking for measurement. "Am I missing something?"

"E-Man, I told you I'd ask around about your problem. Wayne-oh might be able to help."

"You're having some problems with the Yellow Brotherhood?" Tecumseh said.

"Um, I guess you could say that."

Freddy added, "Tell Wayne-oh about the problem. Task Lyst or whatever it's called."

Elliott narrated the series of events that got him to where he was. Tecumseh listened intently. Freddy answered a call on his cell phone and excused himself to take it outside. Elliott wasn't sure why he was confiding in a cat he'd just met, but he trusted Freddy like a brother.

Tecumseh said, "The YB isn't to be fucked with. You're lucky you're having this conversation, because they don't play. Still, they're reasonable folks and I go back a long way with them. Let me show you something." Elliott followed Tecumseh into a back room through some hanging room dividers meant to keep the sanding dust at bay. Tecumseh opened up a coffin-sized trunk with a key and lifted the top. Inside were metallic pieces that appeared to Elliott as some kind of light artillery, military grade, he presumed, from the green and tan color.

"Whoa."

"Gustaf Bazooka." Tecumseh said. Elliott felt Tecumseh watching his reaction.

"Can I borrow that for the day?" Elliott said, to break the ice. Tecumseh grinned. Then he grabbed a business card out of the corner of the trunk and shut the top. He placed the card on a table.

"This conversation never happened," Tecumseh said, and waited for Elliott's response.

"Of course. I mean, not. Of course not."

"I've checked you out. Freddy says you're a stand-up guy, so I'm gonna lend you a hand. Consider this a get out of jail free card." He pointed to the business card. Elliott moved closer and read it.

"Maynard L. Day, Esq. Attorney at Law," Elliott said aloud and then looked back at Tecumseh. "I need to call him?"

"Yep. Call him and he'll put you on the all-clear list. You see, we're all connected. The freedom fighters, the gang bangers, radical left, radical right. We're all on the fringe of a circle around the corruption of old-world order. Maynard Day acts as a liaison of sorts between the various factions. Think of it as a continuum, but nonlinear. Opposing forces create a stasis. The tide ebbs and flows. Waves bring beauty but also destruction. And reconstruction."

"To live outside the law, you must be honest," Elliott said.

Tecumseh nodded at Elliott and answered, "'Absolutely Sweet Marie.' Bobby Dylan. I like you, Elliott."

"So what's with the artillery? Who's the bogeyman?"

"You own a sidearm, Elliott?"

"Nope, not really a gun guy."

"You're a peace-loving artist, I get it."

"I guess so."

"Ever heard of mutually assured destruction?"

"Ha, yes! From Game Theory 101, in fact."

"Well, it's how the real world operates. Unfortunately or not, a good defense is the best offense. The stronger we are as individual citizens, the stronger we are as a nation."

"Dude, you have a tank killer in here. I mean, no offense, isn't that overkill?"

Tecumseh smiled. "Hopefully. Or hopefully not, to be literal. You ought to come out to the desert next time we have target practice. It's a real hootenanny."

Freddy had finished his call and rejoined the two inside.

"Freddy, Elliott doesn't own a firearm. You need to make him wise to the ways of the wicked world."

"E-man, don't let this old Earth warrior fool you; he's a peacenik."

"Peace through power, I like it . . . I was looking for a new mantra. Elliott doesn't want to dirty his pure, virgin, idealistic blood with a peek into the boiler room. I was like you once, my friend. You'll come around."

Elliott enjoyed the revelry, exchanging barbs with Freddy and Tecumseh like they were old teammates in the locker room. He said, "If I were in the market for a piece, hypothetically, let's say, where would you recommend I look to try and acquire said sidearm?"

"Definitely not Guns R Us," Tecumseh said. "You don't want to register anything with the man. I can hook you up with something when you're ready."

"Something with training wheels," Freddy said.

Elliott played along. "Fuck that, I want something James Bond or Dirty Harry would carry."

"That's the spirit. I think we hooked him, Freddy." Tecumseh fake drew, like a gunslinger in a classic Western. Elliott raised his hands in mock surrender.

Tecumseh said, "Alright boys, gotta get back to work. Three boards to finish today, and with a little luck I'll be able to paddle out for an afternoon session. If the wind holds. Elliott, call that number, tell him Tecumseh sent ya, and stay outta trouble. We'll touch base soon."

They shook hands, and Freddy escorted Elliott out the door into the street. The two decided to walk a few blocks to check the surf before parting.

"Wow, what a trip. Thanks for the intro," Elliott said.

"It's all good. You needed to meet him. You'll learn a lot from him over time," Freddy said.

"It's a little jarring though. He's got to be into some heavy shit what with that artillery and this guy I'm gonna call. I want my innocence back!"

"Yeah, me too, E-man, me too."

They crossed Great Highway and ascended the stairs to the boardwalk. It was mostly cloudy, but the weather had settled into a decent, calm day with a sizable swell hitting the Ocean Beach sandbars. They recognized some surfers far out in the lineup, distinguishable by style. One dropped in on a double overhead left that swallowed him up. Beyond, a distant freighter made its way into the Golden Gate to the north. And just to its left the Farallon Islands' silhouette was visible if you knew where to look.

"Freddy, why does he go by the name Tecumseh?" Elliott said.

"I think it's because he's a connector. Always rallying the troops. He's a little wacky in some of his theories, but he means well. And he's a heck of a board shaper."

"I wouldn't have associated him with such a militant platform."

"He's had many trips around the sun. I would say he's wised up before I'd call him hardened. Most of society sleepwalks through life, paying mortgages, car payments, buried under credit cards, eating shitty food. Living with eyes open isn't always pretty, but it's real, E-man. Wayne-oh did some time upstate for standing up for peace. I think being inside changes a guy. I'm glad I haven't had to experience it. Not much surf on the inside."

"Or sun. So do you believe all the conspiracy stuff? You're not paranoid like that."

Freddy answered, "Naw, but I do respect the syndicate that runs things behind the curtain. It's there. Wayne-oh is connected to the Yellow Brotherhood, the Bohemian Grove, the anarchists . . . I look at it like lipstick on a pig. We're the pig, and the government, bankers, cops . . . they're the lipstick."

"Lipstick on a pig. That's a good one. I'm outta here on that note. I better give this guy a call and finish writing my new song. It's gonna be a hit. My metaphorical firearm." Elliott and Freddy embraced and promised to surf together next week. Elliott walked back to Judah Street along the boardwalk.

CHAPTER 73

THE FLIGHT TO TAHOE WAS THIRTY MINUTES, most of which was spent listening to Stuart and Pierre spout on about avalanche precautions and past close calls. Stuart was sure it was too early in the season to be worrying about avalanches, while Pierre argued that an early substantial dump might not have enough of a base to keep it stable. He'd seen it happen in the French Alps. Alice traded seats so she could view the Sierras blanketed in pillows of soft white during the occasional break in storm clouds. As they neared their destination, visibility made sightseeing futile. Ned announced, in a rare sober tone of voice, that they'd be landing shortly. Touchdown was three short bumps followed by loud braking.

The bar at the PlumpJack hotel in Squaw Valley was as empty as Alice had ever seen it. It was very early for ski season and most people who were on the north shore of Lake Tahoe were wary of driving out in the winter conditions. Alice freshened up before meeting the others downstairs for happy hour. The plan was drinks, dinner, drinks, and lights out to make the early rise for departure for skiing. Pierre greeted her and motioned to an empty barstool next to him. She let him recommend a glass of bordeaux, and they raised their glasses to surviving the earlier flight.

"How are things at Blue Hill with Gordie gone?"

"Emotionally, it's been challenging. He was such an icon of the firm, obviously. Businesswise, I think we'll make it through. Cynthia is working hard to get the confidence of the Valley."

"You think you'll stick around?"

"Me? I haven't made any other plans."

"But you're looking around . . . "

"I . . . you mean with us divesting Task Lyst?"

"Of course; it's your baby. I'm finding a seat for you. You should consider coming over."

"Doing what, exactly? I mean, I appreciate you thinking of me. But I'm pretty vested over there."

"Follow the money. You know the platform, the financials, the people. I need C-level help."

"So what are we talking? By C-level do you mean CFO? CMO?"

"Could be. You've got the pedigree. And Ned likes you. And look, here he comes now."

"Pierre, you making moves on my pal here?" Ned put his arm around Alice in a lighthearted show of entitlement.

Pierre countered, "I was just starting to discuss the offer you and I talked about."

"Yeah, and did she accept?" He looked at Alice for a response.

"We're knee deep in negotiation," she said.

"Well I'm chairing the board now, and I say we keep looking around," Ned said. Alice punched his shoulder.

Pierre added, "Good idea, we can find someone fresh out of Haas School of Business."

"Oh good grief, be my guest," she said.

Ned ordered a bottle of PlumpJack reserve cabernet and took control of the conversation. "No, but seriously, if we're gonna talk shop. You should think about joining Pierre's team. You know the business, and he needs some extra adult supervision, particularly the way we are positioning the company moving forward."

"Oh, and how is that? Positioning, I mean," she said.

Ned checked the nose on the cab and swirled it around in the glass. He tasted a little and nodded to the bartender. "Well, I'll let Pierre frame it for you."

Pierre cleared his throat. "This is all covered by your firm's nondisclosure agreement by the way, but it looks like this. The National

Security Agency has requested help using the broad jurisdiction under the Homeland Security Act to identify any terror-related activity happening on our platform. They are using a private contractor as intermediary to bypass privacy laws. For us, the dilemma is, do we jeopardize the trust of our customers or do we play ball with the feds, to assist as good patriots?"

"And this is all due to Baxter Morris?" she said.

"Somewhat. It has always been part of my research to pursue governmental applications for Task Lyst. In an ironic twist, the Morris tragedy is stimulating the interest."

"I'm a little surprised by this. I would have thought you'd fight tooth and nail to keep your company free of government influence."

"You shouldn't be. The government makes a great enterprise client. It's the technology that is determining the market, not any preconceived idealism I might have harbored as a grad student."

"I thought you were on some grand sociological mission."

"Meh, that was merely my dissertation. A test of humanity. Of which one of the outcomes was always failure. When the sharks started begging to pump money in, I became more interested in the profit potential, a source of irony not lost on either of us."

Alice took a breath and swiveled her barstool toward Ned, who was listening while keeping one eye on the Cal hoops game on the television over the bar. She asked Ned, "And you're okay with this?"

"Okay? More than okay. It's basically legalizing and regulating crime if done properly. The more people outsource and use a platform for nefarious activities, the more we have the ability to regulate, tax, and police. It could be the biggest breakthrough in law enforcement since the hidden microphone. It's really not that far-fetched, using technology to disrupt the crime industry."

"Legalize it. I see."

Ned and Pierre let her process the information. She took a healthy slug of her bordeaux. It was beyond comprehension to her that Task Lyst was turning snitch. Up until now she couldn't understand why Ned was doubling down on a start-up company facing serious legal troubles. But she couldn't have guessed this was the reason. She thought of Gordie and his noticeable mood swings during the final weeks of his life. Blue Hill had become highly stressful as the legal issues at Task Lyst mounted. The Morris murder exacerbated an already dodgy investment atmosphere. She tried to pinpoint the signs she'd missed. She particularly hated being blindsided.

"First, you're monetizing the dark web. And next you're selling the users out to the National Security Agency. It's quite the turn of events."

Pierre tried to diffuse her level of alarm. "We're going to pilot the program locally through SFPD. The feds are sending in some manpower, excuse me, people power, to assist the local jurisdiction."

Ned added, "This is exciting stuff. Probably delays going public, but there'll be enough contract work to make for a highly profitable private enterprise."

"Private . . . no pun intended," she said.

"Good one." Ned smiled.

Pierre said, "Alice, there is nothing new to technology companies partnering with security agencies. It's de rigueur in the post-9/11 world to have some cooperation between private and public sectors."

"You're right. I don't know why I should be surprised. Either way, it's bad optics. Maybe that's the former publicist in me," she said.

Pierre continued, "The revolution won't be televised." He looked over to Ned.

Ned refined the point. "Technically speaking, the privacy change will be buried in the fine print. Nobody reads that stuff when they agree to terms and conditions, and it will be no different than the privacy rights you give away when you speak on a cell phone or transfer files over your internet service provider. This just means the company is growing up, playing with the big boys now. And girls. Big Leagues. The real world. You gotta try this wine." He poured cabernet reserve into Alice's empty bordeaux glass as Stuart sauntered over to join them at the bar.

CHAPTER 74

TIM TESTED THE NEW TRACKING TOOL as soon as Zander alerted him to a working model on Sunday, which they'd turned around in less than a full working weekend. He entered various keywords that provided myriad results, from the thousands to single digits. Results included past and present tasks from the mundane (dog walking, handyman) to the exotic and cryptic (smack, gun, bomb, hurt, kill, escort, secret, discreet). He sorted the results into spreadsheets for more control. In an effort to find something incriminating, Tim focused on keywords with a supporting narrative in the communication threads. One such task involved a truck heist gone bad, which had made the evening news. The keyword he used to find it was "muscle." Another was a thinly disguised cannabis delivery service called Greengrass Messenger—"You deliver our kynd!" was their motto. Seventy-eight Task Lyst users had successfully completed tasks for this customer. The keyword he used to find that one was "herb." Tim made a few notes on a shared Google document for bugs and fixes, but he was pleased with the beta test. He sent Raj a note saying they were on schedule, and the encryption buster was producing positive results.

Tim didn't give the existential nature of his project much bandwidth. He fully immersed himself in the product and thrived in a company dynamic that saw him on the rise. His was an active role in a high-profile firm in a fast-paced business. He couldn't help but visualize the various upsides to his situation. It wasn't out of the realm of possibility for him to benefit from a major liquidity event, an exit valued in the seven, perhaps even eight, digits. It would take some savvy ladder-climbing and best-case-scenario revenue growth with at least five years of commitment. Or, he might use this as a springboard to a new product role somewhere with even more upside. It wasn't yet time to purchase a ski condo at Squaw, but it wouldn't hurt to start looking.

Tim had an idea. To obtain some empirical insight, he'd engage Geronimo69 in a new task using keywords he'd later search for. Based on Geronimo69's user history, Tim created some tasks he thought might serve as a lure. Aware that the user in question had turned off notifications, Tim reset the account so Geronimo69 would be alerted to new opportunities matching his preferences. It stretched the boundaries of protocol, but Tim felt emboldened by his new assignment and wasn't going to let rules get in the way of delivering a working tracking tool to the executive suite. Tim studied his computer screen for any activity from Geronimo69. He'd know immediately if the notification email was opened and whether the links were engaged, along with any corresponding interface action. It wasn't long before the status in question changed to "opened," then "clicked" and "sorted" in relation to the tasks proposed.

CHAPTER 75

ELLIOTT WAS ANNOYED BY THE EMAIL NOTIFICATION from Task Lyst. He was strumming through his new three-minute masterpiece when his phone alerted him of new mail. Like a Pavlovian dog, he was powerless to not answer its call. It was an invitation to accept a task. Elliott stared at the words and processed the intrusion. He was curious and clicked on the task button to receive more information. His search landed on a page inviting him to provide private sleuthing: following a person around the following day and reporting on that person's activity. The payout was a handsome $1,000, or roughly the cost of one day in the studio.

Elliott topped off his coffee cup and paced around his flat. He had quit Task Lyst cold turkey but now was tempted back in. His call to Maynard Day hadn't been returned yet, but he already felt emboldened by association. Tecumseh seemed trustworthy despite being a little off-kilter. Still, Elliott would keep his head on a swivel and take nothing for granted. Just because he wasn't paranoid didn't mean they weren't out to get him. That was a variation on a favorite meme from childhood. It had been on a poster hanging in the laundry room of his grandparents' house, and as a young kid he'd been a little freaked out by it. The animated character looked over his shoulder with a caption that read, "Just because you're paranoid doesn't mean they aren't out to get you." It was a metaphysical dilemma and an existential question that tortured his psyche in ways he couldn't articulate. It supported his gut feeling that there was danger in uncertainty. Would Dad make it back safely from his business trip? Would there be people with missing limbs at the county fair? Did Charles Manson still have some followers on the loose? Elliott laughed about these neuroses now, but remembered the terror he felt as a kid. His sister was little help in squelching such fears. Rather, she would amplify them in her teasing and mockery. Her favorite was reliving Elliott's nightmare about the man with the foot, whose head sat on his lower leg in place of a knee, merely a head on a lower leg. It wasn't clear why or how, it just was. Some degree of reverence was paid to this apparition in his dream. It spoke silently through dream speak and recurred throughout Elliott's sixth and seventh years. Even today, Elliott was reluctant to mention it to a therapist for fear of discovering its potential meaning.

Elliott accepted the task and made plans to execute. If nothing else, it would be a lucrative and quick diversion, and he didn't have any tangible schedule conflicts. The next morning, he set his alarm for five o'clock. He dressed for the task as generically as possible in a plain gray fleece sweater, jeans, running shoes, and sunglasses. He took a small backpack he felt would make him blend in with students and the myriad young professionals out on a workday. Instructions advised him to follow a thirty-something blonde woman from her home address on the peninsula to work and any other activities throughout the day and night, from when she left her house to when she returned. Elliott felt a little creeped out by it but decided not to judge. There was a chance, however small, that the motives behind the task were virtuous.

The woman in question left her house at 6:20 a.m. and spent forty-five minutes running a hilly trail in the area west of the I-280. Fortunately, Elliott had arrived before dawn, keeping a safe distance a half block away. His coffee was still hot by the time he engaged the rented Zipcar's transmission to follow her. He waited at the trailhead and saw her return to her home, where she spent another forty-five minutes, presumably showering and getting ready, before she drove fifteen minutes to her office. Elliott was impressed by the building and also by his attractive subject, who got out of her car, checked herself in the window reflection, made an adjustment to her hair, and walked toward the entrance. He made notes that she was roughly five foot seven and a fit 125–130 pounds. Athletic but feminine with a bust that still defied the tyranny of gravity. She walked with purpose, perhaps to a fault. Her professional outfit was appropriate but not creative or inspiring. Safe, yet expensive. She could stand to loosen up a little, he thought, and she might be fighting her true self. Elliott decided he would make a good life coach.

It wasn't until 11:30 a.m. that Elliott got to move again. The visitor parking lot was discreet enough for him to remain parked while checking email, scribbling some lyric edits, and checking in with a few people by telephone. One conversation with a bandmate ended with the feeling that the group was on its last breath of air going over the falls on a pounding wave at Ocean Beach. Elliott resolved to let the situation play itself out. He lacked the energy anymore to maintain close ties with partners whose artistic and professional goals were no longer aligned with his. His own were coming into focus, and he'd need to be agile to ride the momentum. Breaking up a group was never without complex emotions. It still felt like a loss, regardless of circumstances. This time it felt like the right thing at the perfect time. They'd finish up their current performance commitments, divvy up the inventory of record releases, and break the lease on their rehearsal space. And then, what next? Hit reset. Fly solo. Finish his new tune, record it, rebrand. It had been a good run, but it was time to open a new door down the hallway of possibilities.

CHAPTER 76

ALICE CLOSED HER LAPTOP AND PLACED IT IN HER SHOULDER BAG along with her keys, sunglasses, and cell phone. She took the stairs down to the lobby and out to her car. It was 11:30, and she was running a few minutes late to make her appointment in the city. She made a low, guttural sound as she marveled at how sore she was after the three days of backcountry skiing. She hadn't charged it that hard since . . . maybe ever. Her phone rang as she neared her vehicle.

"Alice, so how was it?"

"Super fun but exhausting. I'll tell you all about it tonight at book club. Are you going?"

"If you are, I will. I haven't read the book, surprise, what else is new?"

Alice answered, "Oh, who cares? We never talk about the book anyway."

"I know, but I always feel bad. Elizabeth will be her usual condescending self about it."

"Yeah, but she'll be that way regardless of whether you read it. I'm always afraid to comment for fear of one of her holier-than-thou diatribes. Okay, we get it, you went to Vassar."

"I hate that bitch sometimes."

Alice added, "She just needs to relax and mellow out a little more. She's probably not getting laid by Mr. Wonderful Dental Surgeon."

"You know he's getting side orders at the office. I get so annoyed by those cute little tart hygienists."

Alice agreed and ended the call as her key fob beeped to unlock the car. She listened to NPR en route to Union Street in San Francisco via the Bayshore Freeway. One of the news stories was covering internet privacy, and a consumer advocate lamented the end of peoples' right to anonymity. She listened to the speaker's argument that "we as a society have passed the point of no return": "Privacy is a nostalgic term and an outdated idea. Anyone participating in a developed economy in Western society should assume he or she is an open book. What you can't find using a quick Google search, you can dig up on the dark web. Most of us have a dossier that's neck-deep just a few keyboard clicks away."

The moderator's voice posed the question, "Are people just signing away their privacy rights without really knowing better? I mean, how many of us are actually reading the terms and conditions we agree to?"

"Very few of us. We're in a hurry to load new software updates, to launch applications we need immediately, and we don't have the attention span to read the fine print."

The moderator added, "In your book you talk about the rush to accumulate consumer data that supersedes the actual product businesses are selling. Has consumer information become more valuable than the tangible products we are buying?"

"Absolutely. First-party data, third-party data, everyone is trading what they know about everyone. We are selling each other out. And the more you participate in this economy, the deeper you get pulled into the vortex. It reads like a dystopian novel for the modern day. Imagine walking down the street and knowing everything about a person within five seconds. Your mobile phone can capture that person's profile data instantaneously and filter it to you in a digestible form in seconds."

"My gosh, it's scary to think about. Makes you want to unplug, tune out, move to a deserted island somewhere."

"Oh, they'll find you. There's really no escaping at this point. You may as well stay where you are. But when you unplug from the internet, and all social media along with it, you're dropping out of society and the economic system as a whole. It's a catch-22, of course."

Alice parked near the corner of Scott and Filbert, put change in the meter, and walked to the Dry Dock. She exchanged hellos with the patrons who were gathered outside welcoming the direct sunlight and smoking cigarettes. Once inside, she took a seat in the main meeting room and raised her water bottle to her mouth, looking around for familiar faces. The interior was pink and its minimal decor served its customers' needs without influence or judgment. Soon the thirty-something chairs were mostly taken and a fit, blonde woman of around forty opened the meeting. "Hi, I'm Ashley, and I'm an alcoholic."

"Hello, Ashley," the room said in unison. One by one the patrons introduced themselves by first name and how long it had been since their last drink. Occasionally someone uncertain of the protocol would pass. Alice felt a surge of anxiety as her turn approached. She glanced toward the door to gauge what her last-second escape might look like. It was too late.

"Hi, I'm Alice. It's been twenty-four hours since my last drink," she said.

"Hi, Alice," the room's chorus echoed. She suddenly felt like a sauna enveloped her as people she didn't know gave flash assessments of her, judging even though there wasn't supposed to be any judgment in the safety of Alcoholics Anonymous.

"Welcome to the Monday lunch meeting, everyone," the leader continued. Alice asked herself why she was there. She thought about her weekend skiing with Ned's crew, what she did and what she didn't do. It was always the second glass of wine that did her in. It led to a third and then whatever. She didn't black out, like in the glory days of her first few years out of college, but she wasn't proud of the way she had let Ned manipulate her. It was clear he'd gotten the upper hand, and now her objectivity was compromised. She continued to play out many of the highlights and lowlights of the weekend. She chanced fate by not leaving the hotel bar earlier after the full day of grueling conditions on the mountain. The fun began with a sparkling wine toast immediately after shedding the skis and boots. And then, after cleaning up for dinner, several bottles of excellent wine over a long, lively dinner. It would have made a lot of sense to retire then. The revelry led her to the hotel bar. She tried to pace herself, but the volume caught up to her. She laughed as Ned used every cheesy pickup line, shooting him down but not leaving. The others fell off one by one, Pierre, Stuart, the rest, until it was the two of them and cleaning staff placing chairs on tables and a bartender resetting the clean glassware. Soon they were on the third-floor hallway landing. She recalled bits of the exchange that included a five-minute session in which they explored each other's mouths with their tongues, taking turns leading and following.

"I'll see you tomorrow," she said, releasing his hands and leaning toward her hallway.

"Come have a nightcap with me. The view from my room is tremendous."

"It's one thirty in the morning; there is no view."

"I'll walk you to your room."

"This ends here," she said barely over a whisper, but neither of them was convinced.

His left hand held her right, with him pinning her back to a table placed below a giant mirror. He kissed her and gently lifted her onto the table in a seated position. "Fine, as good a place as any."

"Ned, get real, we're in the hallway." One of them knocked over the glass of red wine they were sharing, having carried it upstairs from the bar. The foreplay continued. She liked the way he touched her. Her senses intensified. She felt tingly and her breathing quickened and she lost herself in the excitement of the moment. She felt the power to resist leave her. He gently pushed her back against the mirror, and she felt him against her. His hands cupped her breasts as his lips roamed her face and neck, tapping into her sensual weak spots. The fingers of his right hand seemed to know all her secrets. His mouth returned to hers, and their tongues continued their dance. She felt him slide his hands down her lower back, pulling her close to him. She leaned her head back on the glass, arching her back. He squeezed her under her après ski yoga tights, as if getting familiar with the territory. He kissed her lower on the neck, into her cleavage, left hand on her right breast. She bit her lip and looked toward the ceiling through the mirror's reflection. He continued deeper into her chest, one hand under her pullover and the other now holding her left hand again. He moved his right hand down to her lower front and returned to her mouth. He teased her concurrently with his tongue and a wandering right index finger. She was already open to him, straddling his leaning midsection. Her head said it was quitting point for sure, but her body trembled toward ecstasy. She arched her back and he slid her tights down from underneath her. Her pulse begged for what followed, he kneeling down in front of her and pulling her torso toward his head; she slipped toward him, secured by his shoulders. She felt his breath first, and then the softness of his tongue. His right middle finger mimicked the movements on her left nipple. She lost all control as the pace went frantic. She clutched the back of the table with her right hand and knocked off the table lamp with her left just as she felt total release. He ignored the lamp crashing off his right ear and gently brought her back to a soft landing. She lay motionless except for her head swaying, eyes closed. She opened them to see him staring at her as if awaiting evaluation, holding her left hand with his right.

"Wow." She exhaled as if taking inventory from ski wipeout. He gently propped her back up on the table and reached for the fallen lamp. He raised his lips to her forehead and kissed it. She felt his hand move a strand of hair off her shiny, moist face and behind her ear.

"Am I glowing?" she said.

"I hope so, yes," he said with a chuckle, helping her pull up her tights.

Eventually, Ashley, the leader of the meeting, mentioned she was glad to see some returning faces, folks she hadn't seen in a while. "Would anyone like to share?"

Ashley's encouraging eyes stopped at Alice. Alice, startled to be awake from her daydream, felt herself agree through her body language.

"Okay, I'll share," she started. "I haven't been a regular at any meetings for a couple of years. Occasionally I'll drop in on one, but my career has taken me in a direction that has gotten me off track. Same old story: everything is going great until it's not. And I'm back." She saw the faces of many in the audience urging her to continue. "It isn't exactly like I got wasted and slept with my boss. But I feel myself getting further from my core ideals and more willing to put career first. And sometimes that's meant having after-work drinks, wine with a client . . . and then I start stretching my business ethics and social standards. Before long I've signed on to change jobs and put any sense of loyalty at risk. I feel like I just need to anchor myself back with the principals of AA and to accept the things I can't change. Like not having a second glass of wine."

The listeners nodded. They empathized and understood her dilemma intimately. Following the protocol of no cross talk, the body language of a petite and stylish woman named Miriam seemed to be saying, "You're doing great; you can do this, girl."

A handsome, middle-aged man said with his eyes, "Keep going, Alice. You're strong."

A guy with a rock haircut and sunglasses looked at his phone. Alice watched him slip out the door before she concluded, "Thanks for letting me share."

CHAPTER 77

ELLIOTT FIGURED HE SHOULD ESCAPE THE MEETING before everyone started making small talk as it wrapped up. He made that assumption based not on previous attendance but through his perception that this was a social group as much as it was a supportive one. Besides, he was there on a task that required a certain level of discretion. He found the experience enlightening on a few levels. This Alice was a nice gal, a sympathetic character. He wouldn't have made her out to be his type initially. But there was something about her that drew him in. Shame about her weekend. Sounded like a bummer. On his way out Elliott stopped next to the coffee table and took a cup to go. More attendees exited the room and gave him friendly if reserved nods. Elliott returned to the sunshine outside and kept a safe distance from where he imagined Alice would emerge. She chatted with a couple of women outside of the door. They appeared friendly with one another. Elliott decided he might make a habit of hanging out at AA meetings. He could make up some stuff to share. And it might be good to hook up with some musicians who were in recovery and on the straight and narrow. He was sick and tired of babysitting drummers who didn't know the meaning of the word *moderation.* Elliott had been tempted to address the meeting earlier with "I'm Elliott, and I'm on forty-five days." He couldn't imagine what forty-five days sober would be like. Or what it would be like to require forty-five days. So he said nothing. He felt fortunate that his problems didn't include addiction. Booze and cannabis were habits of routine but not monkeys on his back. He abused neither.

His subject said her goodbyes and walked up a block to Union Street, turning left on an eastward trajectory along retail and restaurant shop fronts. He followed her at a distance of roughly three storefronts. She stopped occasionally to peer into boutique windows. Her caramel-colored shoulder bag looked at home among the high-rent shops. She didn't appear to be in a great hurry. Elliott pulled a *Fishwrap* out of a dispenser and faux-read the music listings. He crossed the street and watched her from a spot in front of a real estate office entrance. She checked her phone and appeared to read an email before carrying on down the sidewalk. A bus stopped in front of Elliott and several riders disembarked. He blended in with the mass and crossed the street again to follow her, watching as she stepped inside the popular eatery Perry's. Elliott recalled having a lunch interview there when he'd first moved to town. It was with a financial magazine, and Elliott hadn't yet figured out which path he'd be taking—a day job in advertising with upward mobility into media and technology or the artist route, rock clubs and band rehearsals supported by short-term, part-time jobs bussing tables, parking cars, and following people around for a quick buck.

Elliott loitered out front for a while before taking a seat at the Perry's bar. It was bustling inside. The four-tops were covered in checked blue-and-white tablecloths anchored by condiments in the center. Servers wore white aprons despite its casual burger-joint setting. Memorabilia adorned the walls, and its historical significance to the neighborhood ran starkly counter to the hip new joints popping up around it, places boasting "Asian Fusion," "Extreme Pizza," and "Sweet Hot." The barman landed a coaster square in front of Elliott and asked him what he fancied.

"Arnold Palmer and your chopped salad," Elliott said.

"Coming right up."

Elliott surveyed the room. His subject sat toward the corner of the main dining room well out of earshot. She was with an older gentleman who was very well put together in a tweed sport coat, scarf, and thick-rimmed eyeglasses. His hair was white and cut very neat. He was trim and his movements were composed and deliberate, yet his face was animated. Definitely not a love interest, too old and gay, he convinced himself. Who then? Elliott decided it was above his pay grade to worry about the specifics.

"Elliott," a voice sounded from behind him. As he turned around, he placed the name with the face of Suki, a gal pal he used to run with back in the days of a former band. She was an exotic beauty with whom he'd had a short fling. In fact it was his "tantric affair" he'd often humble-bragged about to friends. They would meet only in semipublic settings like university libraries, museums, and parks. She refused to stay overnight together and insisted on maintaining the last lines of loyalty to a boyfriend who was away at grad school.

"Suki, how have you been? You look great." Elliott rose from his barstool and exchanged a nervous hug.

"I'm here with some coworkers, but I just wanted to say hi."

"Yeah, glad you did. Where are you working now? Still painting?"

"A little, but working at an ad agency, DBA."

"Nice." Elliott checked her finger for a ring and felt a tinge of disappointment.

"Erik and I got married last year."

"Bummer. I'm kidding. No, that's great, happy for you."

"What about you, still playing? How's the band?"

"Okay. I've had a couple nonstarters since the Saul Nitz Ensemble. Working on a new concept."

Suki gave him a sultry smile and waxed nostalgic. "I never heard from you after that crazy afternoon in the Marin Headlands."

Elliott smiled and nodded. "It was fun sneaking around, but I knew you'd end up with Erik. And I kind of liked the guy, so I felt bad. Plus, the whole tantric act was a little too much for me."

"Remember that place with the World War II cannon?"

"Battery Townsley, with the old piano inside. I never did get the story on how a broken piano ended up in a state park bunker. I do recall you were wearing spandex."

Suki shook her head and looked back at her party, who were just sitting down at a four-top. "Well, I better get back. Good to see you, Elliott. I hope we run into each other again soon."

"Me too. Good catching up."

Suki cupped Elliott's jawbone and gave him a peck on his cheek and walked over to her table. Beyond her was his subject still chatting with the older gentleman. Elliott sat back down to his chopped salad.

CHAPTER 78

TIM PRESENTED THE NEW KEYWORD SEARCH TOOL to Raj and Clay in a conference room over a working lunch. They took turns entering words, with delight at the results. The algorithm even flagged combinations of otherwise mundane terms: coupling "target" and "discreet," for example, and "gram" and "deliver."

"It's pretty on point, isn't it?" Tim said, pressing them like a puppy wagging his tail for approval.

"Impressive. It's good work, for sure," said Clay.

Raj added, "This is a treasure trove of third-party data we can market to advertising agencies. Brands will line up to pay big dollars for this."

Tim's first two jabs landed well, but now he delivered the left hook. "Just for kicks, I asked my team about location tracking. They came up with a hack using cell phone GPS to track both parties in a task transaction. Check this out," he said. Tim entered some keys and pressed the return button. The action launched a map application displaying the real time location of the task provider and task requestor. In this case, it was Geronimo69 inside Perry's on Union Street and Tim's own phone at Task Lyst headquarters.

Clay looked at Raj. "This is remarkable stuff. You can imagine what we can do with this application. We're like the C-I-Fucking-A."

"I think legal is going to have some issues with it. At least in terms of us activating it on our own platform," Raj said.

"Tim, this task we are looking at: I assume since it is geolocating a phone in this office, it is a test run?" Clay said.

"Correct. I set this up to monitor and make any tweaks," Tim said.

"So we can watch in real time how the task unfolds. And if we suspected any nefarious activity, we could either report it or not," Clay said.

"Well you could watch the icons move around the map slowly, but it wouldn't be particularly riveting television," Tim said.

Raj saw where Clay was going. "Unless you tapped in to the CCTV network accessing security cameras everywhere."

Clay cut him off. "Which is what the feds are surely doing already. Only they don't have what we have: motive and the ability to predict the future."

"What will happen and where," Tim finished the thought. The three of them sat in silence for several seconds. Clay raised a hand to high-five Tim and Raj and announced he was taking a quick bio-break.

Tim pointed at the screen. "Check it out; he's moving." The icon on the map display was moving along Lombard Street eastbound and went right on Gough. "Twenty bucks says he takes it all the way to the 101 on-ramp. I've done that route from the marina a million times."

"Or he takes a left on Bush toward downtown. You're on," Raj said. He pulled a twenty out of his money clip and smacked it down on the table. They watched as the icon stopped at lights and in traffic, working its way up the hill past California Street on a southward heading. The icon did not stop at Bush and continued down Gough.

"Ah crap. But you only win if he goes onto the 101," Raj announced, adjusting the rules on the fly. "He's definitely going right on Fell, but he's headed to Amoeba Records in the Haight to pick up the new Beck record."

"Ha, no . . . he already has it. He's listening to it now, in fact." Tim said. He had forgotten the nature of the task amid all the tomfoolery. His task provider was following Alice. She'd been presumably up in the city for a lunch appointment and was likely headed back down to the peninsula to Blue Hill Capital. He was going to win the bet with his insider knowledge.

Raj dug in. "Come on now, stay the course. Come on, you mother-fucker . . . fuck!" The icon turned left onto the on-ramp for 101 South and Tim snatched the twenty.

Clay returned from the restroom at a brisk pace, drying his hands with a paper towel, which he tossed into a wastepaper basket from ten feet, and rolling up the sleeves to his button-up shirt. "I've just thought of something."

CHAPTER 79

JEROME AND SIMON ROAMED THE MEDINA *as the golden hour of dusk completely ceded way to an exploding sky of possibilities. Celestial awe reigned down as the two looked out over minarets and blue-washed walls to a horizon westward toward the sea. Not much was spoken, just the requisite communication beyond hand signals and body language. They weren't aware of how long they'd wandered lost around the Byzantine alleys, but they somehow found their way back to the terraced pension. Their English travel mates were fast asleep in the adjoining room. Hunger set in as they realized they hadn't eaten a proper supper. They settled for dried dates and packaged snacks they'd accumulated and attempted to analyze the previous few hours of bliss.*

"I feel like someone's wrapped me in a warm blanket. I'm alert but quite relaxed and in no hurry to change scenery," Simon said.

"Hmm. A blanket and a song. Yes," was all Jerome could muster. He continued his gaze into the stars above and noticed alignments that had been nonexistent to him before.

Simon answered, "A song would be nice—and not another of the prayer hymns. It was wonderful the first ten times, but now it's driving me batty, I'm afraid."

"I know what you mean," Jerome said. "Tomorrow we'll search out the Master Musicians of Joujouka." Jerome plucked at the ukulele and repeated a droning melody that seemed to fit the mood. He tried out some vocal lines that matched the hypnotic trance of calls to prayer. After a while he transitioned into a George Harrison song that Simon was able to help sing, "Beware of Darkness."

The final joint of the evening was passed back and forth and sleep set in. The room's open windows allowed a pleasant breeze to circulate around the balcony. Jerome passed out in the new djellaba he'd purchased that day. Simon had ribbed him numerous times about his adopting the local dress before purchasing his own robe-like garment after lunch. Their two English travel mates did not follow suit.

In fact, the Cambridge duo had had enough of Chefchaouen and Morocco and, presumably, their Christmas holiday. Early the next day they packed up and said their goodbyes to a groggy-eyed Jerome and Simon, who felt obliged to get up and offer a parting hug and words of good luck. The four became two, and the more adventurous duo, with a taste for the unknown, remained to see what else the Rif Mountains had to offer.

Jerome and Simon fueled up on bissara and couscous and several cups of mint tea before haggling a cab for the ninety-minute drive to Joujouka. They communicated with the driver using an amusing combination of English, Spanish, and French with the occasional Arabic thrown in. The driver implied that he appreciated their attempts at Arabic and interest in local customs. He insisted on having them over to his family's riad for tea and supper before their visit to Morocco was complete. Over the course of the drive they spoke of the history of Chefchaouen, with the Jewish WWII refugees allegedly painting the buildings their iconic blue. The driver insisted the blue paint went back centuries and represented happiness and optimism. And they spoke of beatnik writers like William S. Burroughs and acid guru Dr. Timothy Leary arriving in the fifties and sixties before Brian Jones and his Stones entourage and every hippy thereafter. The driver was well versed in how his town fit into Western pop culture. He proudly said the Master Musicians of Joujouka were descendants of the same family dating back four thousand years, before Jesus and Muhammad. Jerome and Simon noted they were merely two in a long list of Westerners making the pilgrimage to follow these magic music makers. Yet it was an exclusive group, willing to cross the Strait of Gibraltar into a more mysterious continent. And a group that felt, in the long run at least, Brian Jones's legacy of introducing the music of Joujouka to the West would stand toe to toe with Mick and Keith's song catalogue. Jerome posited out loud that maybe the "devil horns" hand gesture, especially popular with heavy metal rock fans, originated here. Tough to argue against it with the "goat horn" peaks overlooking the city, he argued. Simon's open-mouthed stare suggested he might be convinced.

The timing of their arrival to Joujouka was fortuitous. The Rites of Pan Festival was in full swing to celebrate the gift of music and fertility Pan had bestowed on the village. Trance-inducing flutes and steady drumbeats welcomed them. The driver explained that Ksar el-Kebir was the indigenous name of the town, and he encouraged Jerome and Simon to pay him to wait and drive the two back to Chefchaouen after the evening's celebrations ended, as formal hospitality was scarce. Jerome lit a joint and walked into the festivities full swing. He was surprised to see other Westerners among the revelers. A Frenchman ran a business bussing in Europeans to experience the Joujouka music. These weren't ecotourists nor were they narcotourists; after learning about the association with the ancient deity Pan, Simon dubbed it "freak tourism." A smattering of Scandinavians, Dutch, and Balkans were also represented.

Jerome commandeered a tabla-like drum and joined the African rhythm making. Chants weaved in and out of the music, and it wasn't entirely clear when one song ended and the next began. A boy dressed as the goat god Pan appeared as the crowd descended into pure delirium of physical abandon. Chefchaouen had provided moments of deep reflection, but here they found in-the-moment presence, where one could lose oneself spiritually, not just geographically. The music lurched forward and pulled back and kept everyone in its dominion. A perma-smile radiated from Simon's face as his limbs followed the cues of the music. The bamboo flutes provided layers of melody, slithering around each other as the beats hit a feverish pitch. The celebrants lost themselves in the trance until the music released them for a brief rest between songs. The next started with a call-and-response chant over a violin-like tune. Jerome had a vision of this sound reverberating through the midway at the Columbian Exposition in Chicago in 1893 and how circular time governed the universe. This was both ancient and the future; it was the now. His mind danced from idea to vision and back while he pounded along at the tribal cadence with increasing urgency. The time signature was foreign to Jerome and the beats per minute unknown. At some point he let his mind get in the way of the action and his focus fizzled as the jam ended.

The music dipped into a percussionless string number, like two instruments having a conversation. Jerome motioned to Simon that he needed a drink. It had been hours since their arrival and hydration was in order. They chatted up a French couple, who offered them bottled water. They were told the music would wind down for the day before a bonfire would be lit later.

"Do you feel healed?" the French woman asked Jerome.

"Oui. Do you feel fertile?" Jerome replied.

She smiled at him. Her boyfriend didn't get the humor and tugged her away. Mental, spiritual, and physical exhaustion combined with hunger for a real meal convinced Jerome and Simon to return with their driver to Chefchaouen for the night.

CHAPTER 80

ALICE STUCK HER HEAD INTO LARRY'S OFFICE and found him on a call.

"Hey, I'll call you later. I've got someone in my office. Okay, ciao." He placed the phone on his desk and motioned for Alice to sit down.

"Alice, so how was the long weekend? The snow must have been terrific."

"It was. I'm exhausted though. What's happening with you?" she said. "I didn't see you in the office this morning."

"I had a little off-site with a potential . . ." He got up and closed the door to his office. " . . . new gig," he continued. "An old B-School pal of mine has a clean energy start-up making some waves in the solar and wind space. I'm gonna take a flyer and go client-side for a while. Huge pay cut but compelling upside."

"Wow, and you've thought it through and everything? When are you telling Cynthia?"

"I've got to dot the i's and cross the t's but probably this week. They're crazy about me, and I'm going to raise a bunch of money for them and go public. Worst-case scenario, I keep the seat warm for six months. And keep my equity."

"Well that's great," Alice said.

"How about you? Did Ned hire you away? Or are you just going to keep house and raise his children?"

Alice pointed at him. "Very funny. I'm not the stay-at-home type."

"Look, the word is you're a favorite to take a seat in their C-level suite. Maybe you're the last to know."

"Wouldn't be the first time."

"And it might not be a bad thing for Blue Hill. Bad thing to lose you but good thing you'll be able to steward their remaining investment and make sure it's not a total loss. They, we, need any ally over there."

"Perhaps. Wouldn't you be worried about stepping onto a ship headed for an iceberg?" she said.

"I'd be more worried about sailing in calm waters with no wind."

"Mmm. Good point."

"Just make sure you have a life raft. In addition to the one Ned is offering."

Alice excused herself from Larry's office and settled into her workspace to take care of busy work—returning calls and catching up on emails. She clicked on a link to a story about the latest craze among teenagers: the sucker punch. Teens were using Task Lyst as a platform to hire "hit men" to "sucker punch" enemies for perceived slights. There were over a hundred reported instances of someone getting decked by a stranger, and speculation mounted that gangs and hoodlums were gladly signing up to offer their services. In some cases it was a rite of initiation. In others it was a gag. Kids were walking around with their heads on a swivel to avoid a surprise attack. There was a meme circulating on social media about it, including one with the president of the United States taking an uppercut while emerging from Air Force One. Besides the sucker-punching gigs, the article reported on other ways that kids were using the service. A fourteen-year-old Pleasanton boy purportedly had saved $13,000 toward his first car in six months by toilet-papering houses, egging cars, and spiking tires. His mother was quoted as saying, "We were thrilled he was making money but were under the assumption it was for washing cars, tutoring math, and babysitting. Those were the code words he was using." The article described a growing pandemic of road-rage vengeance. Users could submit a photograph of a license plate and description of the driver to a retribution specialist, who then performed an act of vengeance.

The going rate for a full-side "keying" was a mere seventy-five dollars as of press time.

Alice copied the link and sent it to Ned via text. "Have we jumped the shark?"

He replied, "Great, isn't it? U can't buy this much pr!"

"So you've read it."

"Naw, but i knw what it says."

"Kids are getting rich doing illegal things."

"What else is new. Goin into meeting, call y latr."

CHAPTER 81

ELLIOTT WAS BACK IN THE PARKING LOT of Blue Hill Capital awaiting his subject's next move. It was nearing 3:00 p.m., he was in need of a trip to the men's room, and the best option was to pop inside and look for one in the reception area. He was also curious about the nature of Blue Hill Capital: Who were they and what did they do?

He entered through a revolving glass door and stepped into an atrium several stories high. The sound of his leather boot heels reverberated, and he wished he had a guitar so he could sit down on a bench and strum songs for an hour. This type of space was terrific for that. Not so much for a full band, but the natural echo could handle just guitar and vocals.

An older gentleman greeted him at a sign-in desk. "Can I help you?"

"Afternoon. Say, I'm waiting to pick someone up. Is there a restroom I can use?"

"Around the elevators to the left."

"Do I need to sign in, or . . ."

"Not unless you are going upstairs. Do you want me to call anyone?"

"Naw, I'm good. They'll be down in a minute. Some pretty good security though." Elliott snuck a peek at some of the names on the sign-in sheet and glanced at a list of company names and suite numbers. Blue Hill took up most of it, but there were some others: Burch Trust and Pacific Union Land Conservancy among them. Elliott wandered toward the restroom and reflected on the sanitized office setting that was so foreign to him. Glass, marble, unused space, clean, paved, newly relined parking lot, art and foliage in the lobby, meant to what, impress? Give employees the sense that they are safe and secure? He disliked coming down to the peninsula, to Silicon Valley, to a suburban malaise of office parks and bland, boxy architecture. He couldn't imagine spending his waking hours inside one of these gilded prison cells, allowed sixty minutes a day of freedom for good behavior. A dreary crawl up the corporate ladder under fluorescent lights and shitty break-room coffee. He'd seen enough of that in several less-than-stellar stints as a temporary worker. Not his cup of meat. And now they were bussing employees down from the city in Wi-Fi-enabled vehicles. Talk about divide and conquer. It was companies like this that probably funded the craziness. Blue Hill Capital C, which rhymes with D that stands for douchebag. He wondered why his subject would get herself wrapped up in this type of livelihood. She was attractive, seemingly smart, and educated, certainly capable of more lofty pursuits. Amazing how the dot-com bullshit economy just sucked everyone in like a black hole. Many a good member of the creative class either buttoned up and joined them or skipped town for greener pastures. Elliott wondered if it was time for him to fly on. North to Portland or down to La La Land. Nashville had potential. Fuck it, why not Berlin?

Elliott was pacing the parking lot for exercise and fresh air when he received a text from his first-call recording engineer, Gideon van Praag, offering kind words for the song sketch Elliott had sent him. It was the new piece, and Gideon suggested they record it over the weekend and get it out on social media directly to listeners. Gideon confessed he didn't always go for the topical song ideas, but in this case "it fit the now as well as carrying a universality that could transcend time and place, like Neil Young's 'Ohio' or any Woody Guthrie tune." Elliott was jazzed and texted back some potential start times.

At 3:45 his subject emerged from the entrance and walked to her vehicle. Elliott followed her out of the parking lot and onto El Camino Real, keeping a comparative distance he recalled from cop shows. Five miles later she pulled into the lot of a coffee shop and parked. Elliott did the same and watched her walk inside and sit down at a table where an early-forties-looking guy greeted her. Elliott zoomed in with his camera and noticed that his subject's coffee date had dark hair and a salt-and-pepper goatee and wore the obligatory Silicon Valley business-casual zip-up fleece vest over a button-up shirt. They appeared friendly to one another, not at all stiff or formal and not romantic. Elliott decided it was safe to enter the establishment and order his own coffee without attracting their attention. It was bustling enough inside that he could remain out of their line of sight while still gathering intel. Without picking up specific conversation, Elliott believed the meeting to be collegial in nature, business and platonic.

CHAPTER 82

ALICE PLACED HER BAG OVER THE BACK OF THE WOODEN BROWN CHAIR and sat down. "Tim, thanks for meeting me here on such short notice. I'm on a time crunch to figure out my next move with Blue Hill and Task Lyst," she said.

"My pleasure. So, how was Tahoe? I saw on social media you were rocking some fresh powder."

"You would have loved it. I was a little over my head but had an amazing time. It was a good group."

"Yeah, you were there with Ned Wolfe's posse? Jet-setting with the beautiful people, nice!"

"Oh please. They're like a bunch of frat brothers. Your boss Pierre was there and, my God, is he a maniac on the mountain."

"Go girl! Moving and shaking."

"Whatever."

"So what's on your mind?" Tim said.

"I'm considering an offer to jump over to Task Lyst and help with the transition. Blue Hill is going to be out of the picture, and I'm not sure there is anything left there for me. It's Duck Duck Goose, and I want to make sure I have a seat."

"Interesting, in what capacity?" Tim sat forward and brought his hands together under his chin.

"I'm not sure yet. They've mentioned something corporate-level management."

"And you have reservations?"

"Well, that's what I wanted to talk to you about. How's everything going on your side?"

Tim relaxed his shoulders and adjusted himself in the chair. “It’s an interesting time over there, what with all the public relations issues and change in overlord-ship. How have they positioned this to you?”

“Ned and Pierre seem rosy as ever about growth trajectory. Unnervingly so.”

“Ha. I’m not surprised. I think there is a general sense that the company can withstand the setbacks covered in the media. There’s more substance than what meets the eye.”

Alice hesitated a little. She wanted to dig deeper but was aware of their potential conflicts of interests; his being the proprietary information with regard to the product pivot and hers represented by an entity soon to be mostly divested of fiduciary responsibility. She took a direct approach. “Do you have any privacy concerns about the platform moving forward? Upper management is getting pretty cozy with the district attorney’s office.”

Tim paused for a second before responding. “In what way do you mean?”

Alice lobbed back, “User privacy.”

“No, not really. I don’t see us doing anything substantially different than most internet service providers or telecom companies. Sure, we have personal data, but we have protections in place, built into the platform.”

“I mean, I get it. I don’t want to sound naive. But I would be concerned if the public was aware my company was bending too much to the demands of law enforcement and homeland security. Wouldn’t people think twice about using the service?”

“Sure, I agree. I don’t think we have to advertise our dutiful cooperation to the point where it’s going to amount to a poison pill. Look at Google, Facebook, Amazon; they’re all collecting and selling consumer data. And people keep signing up and buying their stock. It’s smart business is what it is.”

“I hear ya,” she said. “Yet I feel like we are gradually accepting a new reality despite warnings from our better angels.”

Tim unfolded his arms to check the time on his phone. "Interesting perspective."

Alice checked her phone. "Oh, what time is it? I need to jump." They said goodbye and Alice made her exit.

CHAPTER 83

TIM WATCHED ALICE EXIT THE COFFEE SHOP for her car outside. His eyes followed the rocker-looking dude as he rose from his chair across the cafe in pursuit of Alice. Tim knew if he took this short-notice meeting with Alice that he'd become part of the spy hijinks he'd set up. It was intoxicating to be inserting himself into the drama like something he remembered from studying Cervantes. Metafiction was the term used. Ironic since he didn't retain much from an undergraduate stretch mostly spent skiing and organizing spring break getaways.

Geronimo69, as he was known on the platform, was being far from discreet, Tim decided. He was a decent-looking guy with an air of cool, even annoyingly so. And he wasn't very good at sleuthing if he was hanging out across the room from his subject staring over most of the time. Tim wondered what the recap would look like after the task was complete. The guy looked cool, but could he write a decent report? *We'll see,* he thought. Tim conjectured on how he would be portrayed by this Taskminder.

Alice drove out of the parking lot and her shadow followed by thirty meters. Tim checked his emails and read one from the team regarding feedback for the new tracking tool, which they had now referred to under the codename "Hal (3000)," a tip of the hat to Stanley Kubrick's virtual reality computer villain in *2001: A Space Odyssey.* Clay asked for some revisions and Raj reframed them in more technical speak for Tim. Tim had understood Clay perfectly and took Raj's input as an attempt to maintain his spot in the management flowchart. Raj was an experienced operator, silky smooth from his tenures in the Ivy League and at IBM. He was good at office politics, knowing how to groom loyalists and spot threats to his continued ascension. Tim's rising star couldn't be allowed to shine so bright that Raj's would be eclipsed. Tim understood this and would use it to his advantage like he had at previous stops on his career journey. He replied to Raj directly rather than Clay, but filed away in his head the fact that Clay had opened a door to direct communication that would be available to Tim when the time was necessary to use it. Raj would have sensed this minor detail and would be put at ease, at least somewhat, by Tim's compliance with protocol. Tim was pleased with himself for understanding these nuances of power in the chain of command. The subtext was often thicker than the plot.

Tim called Sandra to check in on their evening plans. She was coordinating with the nanny to get kids home from school and to practices, exam prep classes, and private lessons. He didn't miss being the party responsible for this task. He was back to being the bread-winner. Or a breadwinner. Sandra was still pulling in more with her legacy compensation package, but Tim's contractor gig was closing ground and carrying with it substantially more upside. He'd somehow have to finagle more equity stake or a director title if he was going to really snare the rabbit with Task Lyst. The idea of Alice scoring an office in the executive suite cut two ways. On one hand it would be good to have her as an ally. On the other, why her and not him? He didn't need another layer between him and taking part in a significant liquidity event. Titles would mean the difference between figures on a check, five versus six, six versus seven. Anything below mid-six would be anticlimactic. An exit needed to be at a minimum seven if he wanted to be taken seriously on the sidelines of the soccer game or the school drop-off line as a real player in tech. But it was eight figures that would guarantee a transition into being an angel investor or a seat in a venture capital firm. Tim's fantasy position would be the coveted entrepreneur in residence at one of the Valley's big firms. That was a status on par with being a company founder, and Tim was hot in pursuit of the right to walk with that swagger. Yes, a six-figure exit would be acceptable for twelve months' work. Seven would we worth sticking around for. Eight would catapult him back to a peer level to which he felt entitled.

Tim passed along the "Hal" changes to Zander in Bulgaria. The team there was given a timeline for completion, and Tim went over budget issues with Zander. The problem was Tim's failure to keep the Bulgarian costs below what Raj was allocating. Zander was now demanding back payment while being asked to perform new work. This road bump wouldn't get between Tim and his goals, so he floated the overage with funds from various personal accounts in an effort to stay in the good graces of Task Lyst management, particularly in the heat of the current moment. Zander was being a pain in the ass, but Tim needed him. Deliver now, repay later. There would be enough money to make this action seem like a clever and wise gamble.

CHAPTER 84

ELLIOTT WAS BURNED OUT FROM PLAYING SPY, and he felt pretty sure that his subject was in for the night. It was 9:30 p.m., and the latter half of the day had taken him from the coffee shop in the afternoon back to the office, to an exercise class, then to the subject's home where she hosted a small social gathering; a book club, he figured. The half-dozen guests were mostly business class and new stroller moms parking their imports among the well-appointed bungalows. Several were hotties, Lululemons and shoulder bags presumably weighed down by the latest best-selling beach read. Elliott's subject held her own. Somewhere along the way she had changed into an Adidas tracksuit and Elliott made note of her athletic figure as she greeted guests at the front door.

By now, the guests were long gone, and Elliott briefly considered extending the stakeout to ensure she didn't sneak out—or to witness a love interest arriving later for a booty call. Inside he could see the blue glow of television and was tempted to peek in the window. But that was beyond the scope of his assigned task and a little creepy. Plus Elliott needed to file a report on his findings in order to receive the $1,000 bounty, a sum that would go to Gideon for the upcoming recording session. A figure came to the window and adjusted the blinds. She did it with grace and the slightest look of curiosity at the dark of night outside. Elliott waited half a minute and put the Zipcar in neutral, letting it coast out of earshot before turning on the ignition and driving back to the city.

Later, Elliott wrote a five-hundred-word report on his task. His personal thoughts on his subject softened his approach to the point where he found himself debating whether he'd file the report at all to claim the bounty. He asked himself who would hire out the task of spying on this woman, and why. Was she in danger? Was there a jealous boyfriend? Or girlfriend? It didn't seem like a run-of-the-mill worker's comp case. A helicopter parent? Maybe he'd stay on her tail tomorrow, as awkward as that seemed. He laughed when he thought of hiring another Task provider to follow her around for the day and report to him. It could be a never-ending chain of people spying on one another, replicating itself ad infinitum. On the other hand, it could be someone protecting her. Making sure no harm came to her. A guardian angel.

Elliott jotted down her morning activities, including a vague characterization of the AA meeting and a more detailed description of the lunch appointment with the older gentleman. He included routes taken, as he was instructed. Elliott was careful not to add any speculation and accordingly made several edits. Regarding the afternoon coffee meeting, Elliott simply said "Stopped for coffee at Peet's Coffee Roasters on El Camino Real and left after thirty minutes. Chatted with a nondescript patron." He mentioned the yoga and book club meeting and her turning in at around ten. He sent the report as he'd been instructed and awaited his bounty.

A damp blanket of moisture persisted outside, and he was glad to put his feet up. He thought about his subject and wondered about her identity. Elliott logged onto the internet using his neighbor's Wi-Fi passcode. He searched the web using combinations of terms from the day's adventures: Blue Hill Capital, Perry's, AA, reddish blonde . . . he found her on LinkedIn. Alice Seegar's profile used terms like "hypergrowth," "governance," "early stage investor and mentor," "scale operations," and "metric-based legal strategies." Her titles included "Vice President," "Principal," and member of Blue Hill Capital's "Deal Team," whatever that was. Further down it briefly mentioned some record business experience. Elliott was pretty sure he had no idea what she actually did now but was certain it was soulless and well paying. He pitied her because he questioned the happiness it brought her. It only took a day of observation to reach that conclusion. She was likely wrestling with existential questions more than an artist burdened with student loan debt and two months behind on rent would be. And she was attractive. He admitted that now. She carried herself like she had something to prove to someone. Or to herself. A few more links on social media fleshed out a picture of where she came from, her interests, and things they had in common. He read a statement where she talked about the passing of John Gordon, the managing director of Blue Hill Capital. "Gordie was passionate about early stage growth companies." The statement described him as a man who "pioneered first descents, summited major world peaks, and donated to global causes." There was a photo of Gordie kneeling down next to Sudanese children. The caption quoted him, "It is the responsibility of Silicon Valley to lead positive change in a world tainted by wealth inequality and poverty in developing economies." Another photograph showing the guy speaking in front of several hundred, perhaps thousands, at a conference in Sun Valley was all Elliott could handle, and he felt like punching Gordie through the computer screen for being a publicity-seeking hippo-crate, may you rest in peace.

CHAPTER 85

ALICE SPENT THE NEXT FEW DAYS in a series of meetings with Task Lyst personnel, including Pierre, Clay, and some junior-level managers. Officially she was visiting on behalf of Blue Hill Capital, conducting due diligence as they finalized their divestment. To upper management at Task Lyst it was like a sorority rush, showing off the best attributes of the physical space and the talented people. The mood was upbeat and fast-paced with a lot of clutter, especially compared to the buttoned-up Blue Hill environment. She had missed this type of manic energy, and it reminded her of working in the record business. These were people with deadlines making a tangible product. Pimple-faced software engineers banging out code while lost in their own worlds of headphones and junk food. A six-by-six-foot platform approximately eight inches high was the centerpiece of the main space. On it stood a stainless steel rolling table with a turntable and box of vinyl records. A couple of large black speakers on stands flanked it. An 8½" × 11" sign read "DJ Raj, spinning today at 4."

Alice was ushered into a glass-walled conference room visible to all. She was offered a bottled water and asked her thoughts on her office tour so far.

"It looks like an inspiring place to work. I haven't been inside since our initial seed investment, and the intensity is palpable," she said.

"We've scaled up quite a bit and are outgrowing our space. I've got a couple of satellite offices too. We're definitely in need of a new home," Clay said.

Pierre rolled his eyes. "We've got a long way to go before we start designing our own campus. But I appreciate your ambition."

"Would be good to have a park nearby. Get my little minions out for some much-needed sunshine," Clay added.

"You're up to, what, two hundred employees?" Alice said.

"Including contractors, some part-timers, and interns. And a few teams of outsourced help. Headcount needs to be three-fifty, and five hundred by FQ2," Clay said.

"How's your EBITDA?" Alice said.

"Strong. Up 29 percent and rising. We're onboarding some institutional clients who will offset the smaller margins we have with individual accounts," Clay said. He slid a report over to Alice and added, "Let's have a seat and I'll walk you through it."

The three of them waded through the financials of Task Lyst and discussed various accounting methods they were using to forecast their projections. Alice's strengths were less in day-to-day numbers and more in projection modeling, but she held her own in the sea of spreadsheets.

"It all looks remarkably healthy," she said.

Clay grinned. "We are sailing with a steady wind at our backs."

"What's the latest on the legal front?"

Pierre said, "We are well represented, and our insurance underwriters are confident they'll be able to cover us. We're in good shape."

Alice watched the activity outside the four walls of the conference room. A soccer ball rolled by and bounced off a bicycle being pushed by an entry-level analyst. The analyst removed her helmet and parked her bike against her cubicle. A guy roughly the same age popped his head over the cubicle wall like a prairie dog and engaged the cyclist in dialogue. Alice watched the flirtation as Clay reiterated what Pierre said about their legal standing. She wondered what it would be like working in this atmosphere. Might take some getting used to; the close quarters and the trend toward workplace transparency would mean she'd give up some personal freedoms a venture capital office affords.

A cherub-faced sales type knocked on the glass and entered carrying a football, which he tossed between his hands.

"Yes, Ryan, whatchu got?" Clay asked him.

"Marketing asked me to make a beer run for Raj's DJ happy hour today. Can I get a keg of that Mt. Tam Dunkel Bock? It's a little more dough, but they just released it."

Pierre said nothing. Clay took a breath and answered. "You're asking me because . . ."

"Well, last time you mentioned the beer we got was crap."

"Fine, yes. Thank you, Ryan."

Pierre chuckled. "Clay leaves no detail to chance."

"I see that," Alice said. "I miss the days where that would be a critical part of my workday."

"No you don't. It's all body odor and ill-fated office romances. They are really no better than middle-school teens," Clay said.

"Smart though. These millennial kids we are hiring are all off-the-chart sharp," Pierre said.

"Demanding as all hell, though," Clay said.

Alice added, "That's for sure. The young analysts and summer hires at Blue Hill are incredibly entitled. It wasn't like that when we were young."

Pierre said, "Our hiring rubric has changed a good deal. Our mantra originally was 'hire the best and the brightest.' Now it's 'hire competent talent that fits in, likes to work, and doesn't bitch and moan.'"

"Scaling up as rapidly as we are now, it's become a numbers game. We just need cheap labor to grow the existing business model," Clay said. "And an experienced M and A venture capitalist to help guide us through the next stage."

"Which is where you come in, Alice," Pierre said. "Clay will handle operations, and you would be our external face, dealing with bankers, communications, looking for deals." They discussed organizational charts, day-to-day responsibilities, company culture, and job expectations. Pierre asked her if she had a number in mind.

"Number? I would be looking for medium to high on the range for a senior management role. Generous stock award, options, PTO, executive-level medical benefits, mental health days . . . car and fashion allowance. What am I forgetting?" she said.

"Housing allowance, first-class travel?" Clay said.

Pierre laughed. "Don't listen to him. We won't make you fly commercial: jet-share or charter only." The three of them went on to discuss sacrifices necessary to make a bootstrapped start-up succeed. Alice convinced them, more than herself, that she was no prima donna. She'd be able to roll up her sleeves and work the hours in the trenches to get the job done. Venture capital hadn't ruined her for an honest day's work. Still, she wrestled with the opportunity in her head. Was she willing to give up the lifestyle to which she'd grown accustomed?

Another visitor knocked on the glass door. A late-twenties brunette with a scarf around her neck motioned to Clay and Pierre. She wanted to have a private word. The two of them excused the intrusion and stepped outside, where they conducted a two-minute conversation. Alice noticed a more serious context to the spontaneous huddle than the one earlier. Body language suggested this was of more significance than the type of beer needed for happy hour. Soon the woman hurried off and the guys slipped back into the conference room.

"Well now I've seen it all," Clay said. "You might as well know since it will be in the press shortly; an alleged assassination attempt took place today at SFO, and the assailant is telling investigators she thought it was a prank. She used a squirt gun that was loaded with something deadlier than water. The victim, a Russian political dissident, is being transported to the hospital with symptoms consistent with poisoning."

"Oh my God. And, what, they think there is a connection to Task Lyst?"

Clay nodded his head. "We got tipped off that it might be one of ours. I'm having our team look into it, and I'll know something shortly. Welcome to our world, Alice."

CHAPTER 86

TIM READ THE ONLINE NEWS ALERT about the assassination attempt with a personal interest. He cross-checked it with his database using his new tool. Within a minute he had confirmation it was conducted using the Task Lyst platform. It appeared to Tim the alleged assailant had conducted a string of similar acts in the weeks leading up to this. Each one entailed a prankish surprise attack using water balloons, a pie, or squirt guns. The acts were directed to take place in the financial district, Ghirardelli Square, and, in this case, the baggage claim carousel at SFO's domestic flights terminal. The net pay for each act was one hundred dollars. A quick search online revealed no reported cases of these assaults in the media. Tim made the assumption these were trial runs for the real thing.

Tim dialed Raj's extension, but he got no answer. He dialed Clay's and got him on the phone.

"Yes, it's one of ours," Tim said.

"Interesting. Were you able to ID the two parties?"

"The requester used encryption but the provider didn't. I'm assuming they didn't know they'd be trying to kill anyone."

"Before we do or say anything, let me run it up the chain of command. There's a right and wrong way to do everything," Clay said.

"I'll hang tight."

Tim logged into the Task Lyst platform using his test account. He opened the document detailing the report of Geronimo69's sleuthing a few days before. He read through the description of "the subject's" morning run and was impressed with Alice's fortitude; up bright and early on a Tuesday, charging the trails before he'd turned on the coffee machine. He speed-read through the boring bits about returning home and parking in the lot at Blue Hill. Yet he appreciated the detail. This task provider was on the job. Tim was excited about her "determined pace" on leaving the office at 11:30, eager to know where she was heading. Tim liked this. It wasn't what he would consider dignified, per se, but having eyes on the ground was something that could prove useful for additional applications. Who was it that touted "the value of information and how to get it"?

The visit to the Dry Dock was a bombshell. He wasn't aware of her being in Alcoholics Anonymous. There wasn't much detail about her time there, and Tim couldn't assess whether her tail followed her in or stayed outside. He wished there were more and was annoyed; next time he'd insist on having an insider report. The report continued on to the subject's lunch appointment. Tim imagined who the mysterious older man might be based on the descriptions. Alice was having an eventful lunch break on a day usually dedicated to catching up from the weekend. Tim read on, anxious about his own costarring role in the report, which spontaneously came about thanks to Alice's surprise invitation. It delighted Tim to find himself in the plot.

It was with great dismay to read of being reduced to a role of a "random patron." Merely a footnote! Hardly a casting extra! Tim was given little description and no significance to her afternoon coffee break at Peet's. They had talked for half an hour, and it had made zero impression on this jackass. Or worse, the jackass deliberately left him out. Tim read back through again, making sure he didn't miss any subtext. The report mentioned, in a good bit of detail, the post-work book club meeting and her 9:30 curtain call, but Tim struggled to not dwell on his exclusion from the narrative. He convinced himself there must be some intent by which the author of the report edited him out of the picture. It was clear to Tim that this should have warranted an equal or greater amount of focus. He would need to investigate the reason.

A second "follow-up" task was set up and offered to Geronimo69 to, again, tail Alice. Tim planned to monitor this with his own reconnaissance as well as "Hal's" cell phone tracking hack. He'd insert himself in the theatrics again to see if Geronimo69 would dare omit him a second time. While Tim awaited a response from him, he fielded calls from Raj and Clay regarding the assassination incident. It was decided to bring in Pierre and Ned for a huddle-up to discuss strategy. A conference call was set for the top of the hour so Tim hydrated himself, used the restroom, and did ten minutes of meditation. He was being pulled into the inner sanctum, and it was his golden opportunity to advance his own cause.

"Talk to me, team, what are we looking at?" Ned's tone was assertive but not urgent. Tim pictured Ned with his bare feet up on a desk, looking out over the bay, eager for the next weekend adventure but enjoying his new pet company.

Pierre led off for Task Lyst. "Hi, Ned, it looks like the incident at SFO was carried out on our platform. Our contractor lead, Tim, is here, and he's confirmed this using our new keyword and geotracking tool."

Tim listened while Clay and Raj took turns detailing what Tim's team had created and how it worked. In broad terms they took pride in delivering what Ned and Pierre had requested. Tim jumped in. "If I may, I think I can offer some context here. The backend tool was in beta mode and passing all the stress tests we were throwing at it. Within minutes of reading about SFO, I was able to run a search and identify possible matches for the task involved. I zeroed in on one in particular that involved a series of similar, if not deadly, tasks, which I feel may have been dry runs. You create repetition and eventually the culprit becomes a robot, delivering results with little consideration of what they are carrying out. My theory is this was a setup, and the poor woman had no knowledge she'd be attempting to kill anyone today."

"It's also a convenient defense to hide behind the wall of ignorance," Ned said. "Either way, nice job, team."

"This is Clay again. I'll bring legal into it. We need to decide how, and if, we share this data with the authorities."

Pierre added, "No question they'll be knocking on our door within hours, if not minutes."

"Call Stuart at the district attorney's office. You have his cell number, don't you, Pierre?" Ned said.

"Of course."

Ned added, "He might be a little wiped out from last weekend, poor guy."

CHAPTER 87

ELLIOTT ACCEPTED THE FOLLOW-UP TASK, reasoning that another $750 would pay for an extra day, if needed, in the upcoming weekend's recording session. Plus, he'd already decided to tail his subject regardless. She had occupied his mind all morning, so he planned to begin recon at her office, in hopes of catching up with her between arrival and lunch. Elliott found her vehicle in the same spot as it had been on Monday. It was almost 11:00 a.m. and the sun peeked through clouds, with temps expected to hover in the low sixties. He stood outside his car in the sunlight, enjoying the warming rays. He checked the surf report on his phone and saw that clean, double overhead waves were forecasted for the next couple of days. He wasn't sure he'd find time to join in on the fun. He thought about Tecumseh and how he'd order a new board if he stayed flush. Tecumseh had really hooked him up with the lawyer contact, who had finally gotten back to him with instructions on how to make things right with Yellow Brotherhood. It was simple, really. Keep his mouth shut and stay low profile. They'd probably keep an eye on him but would otherwise give him a pass. Freddy had come through again for his haole friend.

Elliott was starving when he checked his watch at half past one. He should have brought a snack for his stakeout. His subject, whom he'd dubbed "Dallas Alice" after the great Lowell George song "Willing," finally emerged from the lobby, walking with another woman to a different car. They got into a late series, cashmere-white Mercedes S-Class and led Elliott to a sushi restaurant a mile away. *Quick lunch,* Elliott told himself. *With a coworker, too busy to overthink it.* With one eye on the restaurant, Elliott ordered a sandwich at a deli nearby. It was barely thirty minutes before they were headed back to the Blue Hill office parking lot. Elliott spent the next hour stretching his legs, careful to not attract attention and also to not miss Dallas Alice's departure. Using his earbuds, he checked in with some bandmates and a former love interest, an artist nicknamed Girl from the North Country. Her little studio apartment in heavily wooded Mill Valley was the site of many mornings spent listening to music, drinking herbal tea, while the steady rain pocketed them in. Theirs was a mutually well-timed affair, but he felt it lacked a future. Why? Something instinctual, in his unconscious being, he thought. Perhaps it was a genetic decision on procreation. Reproducing had been the furthest thing from his mind, but how else could he explain a waning interest in an attractive, intellectually stimulating partner? Ultimately it was one he'd had to walk away from. And he did so quietly, without the courtesy of mature communication, which she certainly deserved. It was one of those breakups without drama but which still had a sense of sadness. Subtle sadness, sans closure. At least she'd gotten his vintage red-label Levi's she coveted. It was okay though; she wore them well and he had nothing but fond memories of the tryst. In return, Elliott had, quite possibly, the best mixed cassette tape in his collection. Her eclectic tastes had introduced him to Laura Nyro, Harry Nilsson, and Tom Waits, for which his musical taste was eternally indebted.

In front of and above Elliott, about a hundred meters away, something flying caught his eye. It hovered, took off, and then came crashing to the ground in the grass next to the parking lot. He continued walking in its direction and saw a guy jog over to it, scoop it up, and jump in a BMW sedan. Elliott guessed it was a drone, perhaps someone flying it around for leisure or maybe surveying the area on official business. Drones, in a short time, had become ubiquitous: a fixture in sporting events, heavy industry, surfing coverage, and they'd seem to have replaced kites as the classic father-son activity on a windy beach or at a park. The guy was gone before he got too close, but Elliott noticed a piece of the drone on the grass near its crash-landing spot. On closer inspection it was a GoPro camera that must have separated on impact. Elliott saw the BMW leave the parking lot, too late to be flagged down.

Another hour went by with Elliott twiddling his thumbs. It was a slow day in the sleuthing business, so he decided to see his new friend at the security desk inside the lobby. He carried the GoPro inside with the intention of leaving it at the desk in case its owner returned for it. He hit the head first, listening for elevator chimes alerting him to someone like Dallas Alice leaving the building. It was quiet. He washed his hands and checked himself in the mirror, striking a few poses to be sure he was still looking like a wannabe rock star disguised stealthily as a regular schmuck. The GoPro sat on the sink counter while Elliott dried his hands. He didn't have a GoPro of his own and wondered if there was a way to report it to the front desk while keeping possession of it. If unclaimed, he would make it his own. Seemed like a win-win.

Still in the lobby, Elliott caught a glance of Dallas Alice walking down the stairs toward him from the second floor. She was looking at her mobile phone screen and carrying her bag. Elliott didn't have time to move out of view so he reached down into the magazine rack for a tabloid to hide behind. The two of them exchanged non-verbal greetings, with Alice doing a slight double take. She continued through the lobby's revolving front door and into the sunlight. Elliott opened the periodical to the music section and followed her out. Taking extra care to not blow his cover, he lost sight of her turning left out of the lot.

CHAPTER 88

ALICE NEGOTIATED HER EXIT on amicable terms with Cynthia. Gordie's death had precipitated talks with other Silicon firms about mergers and acquisitions. Cynthia had much more on her plate than to worry about Alice's junior partner role at Blue Hill Capital. She admitted that it was a good opportunity for Alice and that she'd probably do the same were she in Alice's shoes. A staff lunch was hastily organized where she'd receive some well-wishing cards and a spa gift certificate in addition to her vested equity in the profit sharing plan. Larry, who hadn't yet announced his own departure, regretted that he couldn't make it due to taking some accrued paid time off to cycle down the coast. They'd grab drinks soon.

Drinks sounded good to Alice, but she'd vowed to take a break and dry out after the very wet weekend in Tahoe. It was a miracle she'd escaped the trip with her dignity intact. Ned was making it difficult for her with his innuendos and charm. She was flattered but wary of his playboy reputation. Someone might make an honest partner of Ned, but Alice doubted if it would be anytime soon. There was too much at stake in the small-world town of Bay Area tech circles to risk being one of Ned Wolfe's castoffs. The strategy seemed to work to her advantage, as Ned validated with his recommendation for Alice to assume the chief marketing officer role at Task Lyst. She called her de facto AA sponsor with the news of the job offer. They'd had lunch last week at Perry's, and he was delighted to hear of how things had transpired.

"Alice, this is just terrific news. Thank God you are extracting yourself from that humdrum peninsula. Welcome back. Now we just need to find you a man." Roderick spoke with a distinctive upper-market enthusiasm, slightly cynical but always entertaining. He was one of the old-school queens from the Harvey Milk days. He'd survived the AIDS crisis with only a positive HIV diagnosis but no symptoms and enjoyed a lucrative career, first as a wedding planner and more recently as one of San Francisco's most in-demand corporate event designers. Roderick was not Alice's official sponsor—males didn't typically sponsor females and vice versa. But Roderick delighted in bending genders. He told her how proud he was of her for getting back in the program. She had gone eighteen months sober almost a decade ago. Secretly, they shared a tendency to fall off the wagon and had a mantra that "what happens on the weekend doesn't necessarily count against chip meetings."

"I know; I seem to be attracted to the ones I should probably avoid."

"Honey, that makes two of us."

"I was with Playboy Ned last weekend and then almost drooled on a rocker guy I passed today."

"Frying pan to the fire."

"Exactly."

"Can I have the one you don't choose?"

Alice laughed. "I don't think they're your type, actually."

"As long as they don't look like Grizzly Adams. I don't do beards. Anymore."

"I'm a little nonplussed about running marketing instead of operations or finance, but it'll do for now. May be a blessing in disguise."

"Honey, that's a little over my head, but I know you'll do a fabulous job."

CHAPTER 89

TIM LOOKED IN THE TRUNK OF HIS BMW AGAIN. It had to be in there. Then he looked under the seats and in his duffel bag he used for the drone but found no trace of the GoPro camera. On the garage workbench, the drone sat wounded from its crash landing. It still functioned but it would need to be serviced to fix the damaged rotor. Tim had been out of practice flying his drone and blamed the accident on pilot error. The bigger worry was the missing camera. He'd been back to the site of the crash and failed to locate it in the grass and adjacent parking lot. Either it was somewhere here or that damned Geronimo69 had picked it up. If the guy downloaded the pictures, he'd figure things out and the jig would be up. There was video footage of the guy along with footage of Alice's car and of her entering the Blue Hill Capital offices. It'd be relatively easy to make the connection to Task Lyst but impossible to link the camera to Tim directly. Only from the inside could you identify the two parties involved in a task. Tim would await the report from the Taskminder and decide his next move. Meanwhile he looked under each seat again and once more in the bag.

Tim cursed himself for taking unnecessary chances. It was of little consequence to be concerned with what Alice was up to let alone some errand boy who'd disrespected him. Guessing that Geronimo69 would be following Alice back to her office, Tim's hubris had gotten the better of him. Now he realized he'd been dumb to insert himself in the picture. Yet he'd rationalized it as being crucial to understanding his product better. It was this empirical knowledge that made Tim a Machiavellian badass. He thought about the footage he'd collected and may have lost. It was a sight to see. Hovering over the Blue Hill Capital building at a hundred feet as Alice and the Taskminder went about their idling below, unaware of the eyes in the sky. Through his monitor Tim was able to view in real time what his drone camera was seeing. At one point it looked like someone was in a window observing the flying nuisance. Tim was careful not to get too close for fear of security being alerted and bringing charges of trespassing. Drones had become commonplace to the point where seeing one was hardly a curiosity. Still, having one humming by your office window would surely cross a line of what a powerful venture capital firm would see as a safety breach. Tim had turned away from the viewfinder when the drone malfunctioned, but he was fairly sure errand boy had seen the plummeting spy craft ditch. It was Tim's quick thinking to pull his car around for an emergency escape.

Tim stayed up until one in the morning, hoping the task report would hit his inbox. But by dawn it still hadn't come. Tim woke to Sandra asking him why he'd fallen asleep on the couch. "Binge watching Star Trek reruns" he explained, entering the password to his notebook computer. Still nothing. Tim helped with the morning ritual of kids and dodged as many assignments as possible being heaved at him from Sandra.

"I need you to come to dinner with my mother and her new boyfriend tonight."

"Ah, tonight? Can't, I've got a late call with Bulgaria."

"They won't even be up yet."

Tim's backpedaling was no use, and he was roped into an evening commitment. This irked Tim, as he emphasized again and again his need for "total flexibility on the home front if I want to maximize the opportunity at work during this critical, transitional time." It was what he was paying a nanny for, to handle domestic duties. Sandra reminded him that he had responsibilities as a husband and father that perhaps he was taking for granted. A war of wills was brewing, and Tim knew better than to fuel the fire, particularly in front of the Swedish au pair.

CHAPTER 90

ELLIOTT DROPPED A HALF DOSE OF TINCTURE into a full Gatorade bottle and swirled it around. The waves sucked, and he wasn't going to paddle out into frigid, blown-out slop surf. Rather, he would put his ears on and spend the afternoon listening to the rough mixes of his song demo. The tincture would provide a subtle change in perspective and open him up to hearing new sounds, melodies, and lyrical edits to further shape the tune. Then he'd be ready to record a full production version. He played the song on the car stereo while leaning against the hood studying the unsurfable breakers. He warmed his hands inside the front pouch of his track top, and his headband kept the hair from whipping into his eyes. Inside of twenty minutes he could feel the warm onslaught of the medicine transporting him to an elevated plane. The song was good: melodic, lyrically rich, of palatable construction, providing a narrative arc. Elliott took mental notes on dynamics he wanted to implement. There would be a bridge section to provide a denouement before the extended chorus outro. He thought about a string section to pad the sonic layers. Or maybe pedal steel.

His trip was hijacked by a vision of Dallas Alice. What would she think of his song? She had no idea who he was, but he'd sensed something during their flash encounter. Was it a genetic attraction? Something stronger than words, telepathic. No. Physical, or magnetic. The magnetism of sexual attraction, a profound dimension deeper than words. Elliott fantasized about her in vivid, lusty detail. Perhaps they would never speak to one another. It would be a purely physical affair with strict rules against cerebral communication. Animalistic and visceral. Natural and organic.

Elliott sensed hunger. The other hunger. The one that made him decide to pack in the mating vision and walk over to La Cotija for a chicken burrito dragged through the garden. It was a "horse cock" of a meal, wrapped in wax paper and tin foil. The tortilla was steamed to perfection with tomato-based pulled chicken packed among beans, rice, sour cream, and avocados. Elliott didn't do "guac"; he always requested fresh-sliced avocado and cilantro. He ate a little more than half before resealing the foil over the leftover portion to save for later. Epic horse cock.

Back at his flat, Elliott fidgeted around with the GoPro camera. It was still technically unclaimed, though he hadn't returned it to the security desk at Blue Hill Capital like he had intended. It seemed natural to view the content on the camera for any identifiable clues needed to match it to its owner. He hooked the camera to his computer using a universal cable and opened it to access the most recent folder. He scrolled through still photos and video of Blue Hill Capital's office building on a partly cloudy day. Nothing stood out except for the fact that Elliott was in some of the shots. One in particular caught him leaning against the back of his vehicle. And then there was a series of progressively zoomed-in pictures. It was fairly obvious Elliott was a key subject. The final pictures were blurry, culminating in one on the ground of the drone's owner reaching down for it. He looked through more folders and found mostly coastline shots and a few of what could have been hills above Silicon Valley.

It wasn't a shock to Elliott that he'd been on the receiving end of surveillance. He assumed it to be a continuation of his hassles with the Yellow Brotherhood. There didn't seem to be another explanation. He wondered if Maynard Day had his back after all. Another possibility occurred to Elliott. The drone operator might be the same person who had hired him to spy on Dallas Alice. Meta-sleuthing. He was being spied on while spying on another. Elliott remembered that he hadn't sent a report on the previous day's task. It was a conscious decision on his part. He was fed up with the Task Lyst platform and didn't feel like rehashing his failure to find her after she'd left the Blue Hill Capital office. What did it matter; he probably would get a poor rating and might not get paid. He was through. And there was the matter of reporting anything further on Dallas Alice to an unknown entity. In fact, he was worried about her. He should probably alert her, get her out of harm's way.

CHAPTER 91

RATHER THAN TAKE TIME OFF BETWEEN JOBS, Alice jumped right in and spent her first week acclimating to the fast pace of Task Lyst. It was important to keep the growth trajectory despite the negative publicity generated from the assassination attempt and other incidents. Clay handled day-to-day operations while Pierre, with Alice in tow, met with analysts and journalists and oversaw marketing and publicity campaigns. The message they wanted to spread was Task Lyst was serious about privacy rights but also cooperative with law enforcement. It was a tough sell, pitching both.

Alice found herself on a Saturday morning participating in the post-Thanksgiving Turkey Trot, a new "Bay to Breakers" type road race covering the coast from the Golden Gate down to the zoo. The company entered a team to represent the brand. Eighteen staffers wore matching Task Lyst T-shirts with the tagline "Get it done while you're on the run." The race was known for its ridiculous costumes and other eclecticism. Alice argued against using a pedicycle flatbed equipped with a Bloody Mary bar but was outvoted. At the finish-line party, the team celebrated among the thousands of revelers to live music from local bands. One act on the main stage caught her eye. The lead singer looked familiar. She couldn't quite place him, but she liked the music, which was also popular with her team. As the music concluded Alice continued socializing with other team members in the sponsor tent, where Task Lyst and other corporate sponsors enjoyed free food and drinks. The singer from the band walked in and ordered a beer from the bar. Alice interrupted her conversation partner and tossed a compliment to the singer.

"Hey, great job up there."

The singer thanked her without looking up from receiving his draft beer in a red solo cup.

She pressed him. "You guys look familiar. What's the name of your group?"

He made eye contact with her and gave his complete attention. "We're the Golden Mean. Or were, at least."

"Not sure where I've seen you guys." She studied his face. "Maybe it's because you look like Rod Stewart and Ron Wood's love child. Without the pointy nose."

He smiled, perhaps surprised by Alice's classic rock 'n' roll knowledge, she thought. "Well, you've read my file. So which corporate giant are you with?"

She pulled her zip-up fleece apart to reveal the Task Lyst logo on her T-shirt.

He looked down and back at her. "Ha. Speak of the devil."

She furrowed her brow. "Do tell."

"I was just telling my drummer about, oh forget it, not important."

Alice watched him take a swig of beer while maintaining eye contact with her. He shrugged a partial laugh and had another sip.

"What? You're laughing at me." She was playfully curious at what appeared to be his inside joke.

"Nothing. I'm Elliott.

"Alice. Nice to meet you."

"So you work with Task Lyst?"

"Yes, well, I just started. I'd been working with them indirectly, but now I'm wearing the uniform."

"It is sort of like a cult, isn't it. You guys have your own commuter busses yet?"

"Ha. Not yet. We're scaling up though. You looking for work?"

The singer leaned in. "I've messed around on your site a bit. Done some little things here and there."

"Really? I'd like to hear your user feedback."

The race event coordinator and remaining band members butted in to settle up on the performance fee. He signed a tax document and held up a check for a thousand dollars. "Let's go to Vegas and put it all on red." He fist-bumped and bro-shaked with his fellow musicians.

"You can tell me your feedback on the way."

Elliott smiled at Alice and paused, looking at the others. "We're gonna go grab a drink up the street if you care to join us."

Alice laughed off the invitation but was prompted again by the others. She agreed to join them for "one." It was an opportunity to hear empirical insight on Task Lyst from someone with whom she was finding herself intrigued. He was kind of a bad-boy type, aloof, distant, with a certain intensity. The sort who probably didn't make first moves, preferring to let the action come to him. Yet he seemed to be a strong leader among his musician pals and carried himself with confidence. Alice told herself she'd have a virgin Bloody Mary and get out before compromising decisions could domino.

CHAPTER 92

AT THE AFTER-GIG HANG, ELLIOTT ASKED FOR A PINT OF GUINNESS from the bartender and indulged in a postmortem with his bandmates. All agreed they'd played well under the circumstances. It was a gig they'd had on the books for a while and, to a member, it was feeling like their swan song. But it had gone well, and they were suddenly energized and toasting a good time. Being hired for outdoor festivals meant you had to have broad appeal, playing mostly upbeat numbers with some covers mixed in. There wasn't time to play new songs as much as Elliott would have preferred. Several numbers were received like covers, having been played at numerous street fairs around the city, including Union Street, Haight Street, and Fillmore Street, not to mention nearly every club and restaurant stage in town. They enjoyed a small degree of celebrity, homegrown and homeknown, while struggling to expand regionally and beyond. Their classic California rock sound paid homage to both the Marin County and Laurel Canyon sounds of the early 1970s. But it languished there and had trouble convincing record executives and listeners outside of the West Coast that it was relevant beyond nostalgia. Elliott recognized this but had faith that a breakout song or two could change minds in a heartbeat. He wasn't about to start over with a sound he didn't believe in, nor did he think it was possible. While he had great self-confidence in what the band was creating, he'd been considering testing the waters as a solo performer, and the new recordings he did without the band felt like new momentum and worth a fresh start, all while being cynical that it would be accepted organically by a mainstream audience. He also believed that one well-placed song on a film or television program could be a game changer. He visualized this transformation daily if not hourly. The dream was always fueled by new material to reinsert into the funnel: write, record, release, tour. It was the cycle Elliott wanted to scale into a legitimate career, gradually expanding the circle from the Bay Area to Southern California to the western US to the greater US and then overseas. Plug and play, scale it up.

Dallas Alice walked through the entrance with two colleagues rocking the same Task Lyst spirit wear. Elliott played it cool, pretending not to see her, making her find him. While continuing his gig recap, Elliott kept tabs on her progress from ordering drinks at the bar to approaching his group. The noontime sun kept the late November temperature at bay as they stood around a bistro table outside the patio doors. Elliott's drummer, Cameron, mixed some organic tobacco with some hashish and passed it around. Elliott declined, preferring to keep his wits about him, for the time being at least. Dallas Alice maneuvered her entourage out to the patio and greeted the band. Elliott let her introduce herself and her friends while he resumed a passive-aggressive posture. He laid low behind his wraparound sunglasses and allowed the others to fill the space with idle chatter. Cameron explained how he'd earned some side money playing gigs via Task Lyst.

"I went down to LA to play the Viper Room, and we hooked up with this pedal steel player on Task Lyst who turned out to be a total disaster. Nice enough fellow but not a great fit musically."

"Oh, I'm sorry about that," Alice said.

"Ah, no biggie. He got paid. I think that group ended up with a record deal."

Dallas Alice turned to Elliott. "So what's your story with Task Lyst?"

Cameron butted in. "E has some great Task Lyst stories. He should write a book about them."

"What happens on Task Lyst stays on Task Lyst," said Elliott. "I don't kiss and tell."

Alice laughed. "Is that your title? It could be our new marketing campaign. I like it."

"Or how about, 'Spiral down the vortex of misadventure with Task Lyst,'" Elliott countered.

"Easy; we're not that bad, are we?"

"*Bad* is a relative term. *Evil* is a little more poignant."

"Seriously?"

"Okay, that might be a generalization. I just don't trust it anymore. I've had some creepy experiences and I think everyone, you included, should be careful."

"Well, thank you. I appreciate your caring."

"I aim to please." Elliott enjoyed the sparring as he expected Dallas Alice did too. She was no pushover. Her physical dimensions revealed themselves through a tight-fitting Task Lyst T-shirt and yoga tights. She was athletic and attractive up close. Her face was framed by subtle cheekbones and an occasional faraway smile. She was animated, going from furrowed brow to wide-eyed laughs. She seemed happier than when he'd followed her around for two days. Perhaps the job change had put her in a better place. Ironic, to be sure. Elliott debated disclosing his espionage to her but decided against it. There were certain parts of his Task Lyst tenure that he should take to the grave, stalking an attractive female being one of them.

The group spent the better part of an hour bantering collegially about friends who worked at Task Lyst and other start-ups, where they'd attended college, and other local bands they enjoyed. Eventually the Task Lysters announced they were heading out, and Alice asked one of them to drop her off. Elliott traded social media contacts with Alice and made a vague promise to follow up with her. It seemed within boundaries, aided by a couple of rounds of drinks, to hug out the departure. Elliott hugged two at once to avoid the awkwardness of his and Dallas Alice's mutual attraction. He would have enjoyed continuing the conversation, but he wasn't one to chase, and the party split.

Cameron prepared another spliff, and this time Elliott partook.

"Well that was interesting, running into a bunch of Task Lysters," Cameron said.

Elliott held in the tobacco-hash vapor and then released it. "That chick Alice. I tailed her on a task recently. Crazy coincidence running into her. I think, subliminally at least, she recognized me but couldn't place me. I spent two days following her around for some tech guy stalker."

"I thought you were kicking the Task Lyst habit."

"Yeah, I relapsed."

"Well I think she was digging you, bro," Salami, the bassist, said.

Elliott turned to him. "She is pretty hot, huh? I mean, in an uptown kind of way. I wouldn't normally be into the bitch-on-the-go type."

"Definitely not your typical groupie but more like a label rep. I bet she could get us some corporate gigs playing on yachts and shit. Or wine country. Remember those vineyard gigs we used to do?" Cameron said.

"I'd rather hit the road and build our fan base than fuck around with corporate gigs. They pay but never lead anywhere. Get back on the Colorado circuit and try to make the jump to Austin, Chicago, Nashville . . ." Elliott continued.

Cameron shook his head. "I've done those long van rides across the flyover states and you spend all your money on gas and hotels. It's not sustainable without tour support money from a record company."

Elliott pressed him. "Dude, nice attitude. Are you packing in the life for a spec house in Walnut Creek?" Salami laughed.

"Never," said Cameron. "But I know the economics of touring, and it's very difficult to get further than Colorado and still make money. You need to build your local and regional following before you go national. And you need some help from the man. I say we keep it local for a while, gigs like today . . . ten minutes from home!"

"Fuck that noise. I want to go international. I don't give a shit about local, regional, national. I want to be in Holland playing festivals by the end of next year. They'll love us in the Benelux countries."

"Who's gonna front the airline tickets?" Cameron said.

"Dallas Alice, that's who." Elliott smiled and finished his pint.

CHAPTER 93

TIM, MIRACULOUSLY, WAS REUNITED WITH HIS GOPRO CAMERA when he rechecked the front desk in the lobby at Blue Hill Capital after more than a week of searching. They said, "Some delivery guy found it in the parking lot a couple days ago." There wasn't a note, and minimal damage on first inspection. Tim thanked them and walked back out to his BMW, which he'd left double-parked with the engine running. With Alice no longer working at Blue Hill, he had no additional business there and returned to his office.

Upon inspection, it was clear the footage on the camera was unmolested, but the time signatures indicated it had been viewed. Tim assumed that someone had looked through the content before turning it in to the front desk. Initially he had no way of knowing who that might be, and their identity was probably inconsequential. What irked him more, though, was the errand boy's failure to recap his task and, in turn, claim his bounty. Who walks away from $750? Tim noticed from the surviving drone footage that Geronimo69 was using a rental Zipcar. He wondered if this made errand boy the "delivery guy" who'd turned in the drone to the Blue Hill Capital building's front desk. Taking his theory a step further, could errand boy then link Tim to the drone, and, through association, the surveillance task? Tim was all but certain the Task Lyst platform couldn't connect him as the Taskmaster, but the radio silence from Geronimo69 continued to eat at Tim and affected his disposition at home and at work. At night he was hearing an heirloom grandfather clock ticking from the first-floor foyer, something he'd ceased noticing at least ten years prior. He took large doses of indica tincture as a sleep aid and wore studio headphones over his ears to drown out the noise. All in vain.

The next day, still concerned about his own exposure, Tim used the Task Lyst backend to dig deeper into Geronimo69's user history and personal data. He saved screenshots of personal data like address, phone, and password info. Tim searched again through the task histories and flagged the damned errand boy's involvement with the mime deliveries and a previous job bashing the window of a Porsche. These would come in handy, Tim said to himself, if errand boy, aka Geronimo69, got out of line.

Later, at a 2:00 p.m. meeting at Task Lyst, Tim joined Pierre, Taz, Clay, and Alice in the conference room to discuss next steps for the keyword geotracking tool.

"Tim, good work on this. Ned is bringing in someone from the district attorney's office in a few minutes to get an overview of the application. Do you want to give the demo?" Clay sprang this on Tim without warning, and Tim noticed Raj was not in attendance. Clay added, "Raj is off-site, so why don't you just walk us through some examples and highlight the features."

"Of course, no problem. Glad to," Tim said. He talked with the others about the context of the meeting for a matter of minutes before Ned strolled in with Stuart behind him. The others rose to greet them.

"Hey, guys, thanks for huddling up on such quick notice. Most of you know Stuart with the DA's office. I want to show him our new capabilities. His office is a potential partner of ours, as you know." Stuart backslapped Ned, glad-handed with Clay, smiled at Alice, and winked at Tim.

"Nice to see your familiar faces," Stuart said. "And thanks, like Ned said, for the quick meeting."

Tim had never seen Ned and Stuart in the same room together, but he quickly drew comparisons between the two. They were roughly the same height with similar athletic builds. Ned was dressed more casually, in a retro fifties button-up shirt, untucked, with jeans and sandals. Stuart was in coat and tie with top collar unbuttoned. His suit was a conservative blue but not banker stiff. They seemed to be cut from the same cloth and straight out of central casting for active California white male. Pierre asked Tim to run through a demonstration of the technology using his laptop and the conference room projector screen.

"Okay, so starting with a ten-thousand-foot view, you have the option of being a 'Taskminder' or 'Taskmaster' on the home page. You register and log in as either one. We'll log in as a 'Taskminder,' or someone looking to fulfill a task in exchange for money. We can search by category or by keyword or by latest offers. The keyword is important, as that's what we'll be looking at in a moment. So let's say we want to search for something related to 'housecleaning': we enter 'housecleaning' and we get the following results. Not bad, 237 people looking to hire housecleaning help." Tim scanned the eyeballs for approval. Everyone was nodding along.

He continued. "That's the Task Lyst business model, right? Matching providers with minders, supply and demand." Tim paused and deferred to Pierre, who spoke.

"This is where it gets interesting. And herein lies the intrinsic value of Task Lyst to the capital markets," Pierre said, instructing Tim to continue.

"Each one of these tasks, and the communication between the parties back and forth, creates a database of keywords used to describe the task and frame the context for which they are conversing. When you consider the number of users on the platform plus the task frequency coefficient, you get the idea of just how big the database is getting."

Tim paused the slideshow and sat at the edge of the table. "This is where Task Lyst cashes in. By mining this database of keywords, we can identify what people want and what they are willing to do to get it. Under the instruction of Pierre and Clay, our team developed a backend search tool where we can collate the data and pinpoint conversations and tasks. Take this example for instance." On a separate tab Tim entered the keyword "deliver" and hit "go." Over a million results came from the query. Tim added "mime" and came up with less than a thousand. "You may recall some allegations made in the *Fishwrap* about a mime delivering drugs." He looked around at his audience.

Alice said, "Of course, the article that Gordie about had a heart attack over."

Tim continued. "With this tracking tool, we can zero in on the conversations that led to that action: the perpetrators, the recipients, the victims." He zoomed in on dialogue between parties about the alleged "mime smuggler." He nodded at Pierre and Clay.

Pierre stood up and paced the floor. "There are obvious law enforcement applications to having access to this data. We can deliver the bad guys to city hall."

Stuart said, "We'd have to get a warrant for it to be permissible in court." After a pause he added, "But it's still useful information."

Tim watched Alice fidget with a pen against her chin, as if she were uncertain about something. She spoke up. "The minute people suspect this they'll stop using the platform."

"We'll send in a Trojan horse," Pierre said. "A little display of its power. An isolated security breach, which we will promptly fix, calming all fears."

Ned followed. "What is it you called it, Pierre, a little 'tit for tat'? We'll give law enforcement some unofficial assistance from time to time in exchange for freedom to operate without regulators looking over our shoulder. Alice, this is where you come in. You'll manage the marketing and public relations to keep Task Lyst squeaky-clean in the eyes of the media and general public."

"And we got the all clear from legal?" Clay said.

"Of course." Ned smiled. "Stuart's got access all the way up the chain of command, don't you, old buddy?"

"Access yes, guarantee, no. I will say, though, we've got a law and order candidate gearing up for a gubernatorial run who's very interested in this conversation."

Tim listened with great interest, beaming with pride at being in such close proximity to the inner workings of the power elite. He felt comfortable, at home amid backroom dealings like this. It wasn't a cigar-smoke-filled room, but Tim felt the tingling delight of this new power broker threshold he'd crossed, not unlike any historic meeting between private enterprise and civic leaders in pre-independence Philadelphia or Gilded Age Windy City. He was witnessing Faustian bargains being struck at the crossroads of good and evil.

Alice jumped in. "So my job is to spin any poor publicity and keep the bad guys using the platform."

"Pretty much. It won't do us any good, the DA either, if there's an exodus of users. They'll find a new platform to fill the void." Ned explained.

Pierre added, "Parasites always find a new host."

"Don't private enterprise and government agencies make strange bedfellows?" Alice said.

"Not really. Stuart is gonna keep city hall off our backs, and we'll supply the occasional intel. We're halves of the same whole. That's the real world at work, for better or worse," Ned said.

CHAPTER 94

ALICE'S ROLE AS COMPANY MOUTHPIECE HEATED UP IMMEDIATELY. Alice was familiar with stories of Homeland Security and the National Security Agency subpoenaing phone and email records from suspected terrorists. She also was aware of internet service providers reporting file-sharing abusers. She tried to reconcile what Task Lyst was undertaking with any precedent in her memory banks. It would be her responsibility to control the narrative on how Task Lyst was perceived in the public eye. She felt the weight of that pressure and understood now what her unique qualifications and skill set brought to the job. Ned was no dummy. He had groomed Alice for the role; getting to know her, reeling her into the fold. She was now an executive in a pivotal moment at a potential "next big thing." And she thought her last job was pressure-filled.

She found herself presiding over a press briefing regarding developments in the Baxter Morris case and drafted a letter to Task Lyst users about legal and security concerns. She oversaw a customer service initiative focusing on the company's heavy volume users, throwing an event at a warehouse in the South of Market district. Her image became familiar to San Francisco Bay Area residents, appearing on television, radio programs, events, and briefings. She also became a lightning rod for cynical commentary on the company's whitewashing of public criticism. The complaints included the continued gentrification of San Francisco housing by the tech boom, further widening of the "us versus them" mentality, the wealth disparity signified by firms such as Task Lyst positioning themselves for public offerings, and the existential question of whether a platform like Task Lyst was good or bad for society. It was apparent to pundits that money and power were snuffing out opposition to an obvious breach of ethics.

Alice spoke at a visitors bureau breakfast meeting attended by a couple hundred area business leaders. "Task Lyst is in the business of providing liquidity and efficiency to daily life. The new share economy and the concept of 'the power of *and*' is defining a younger generation with new rules and a recalibrated compass. San Francisco and Silicon Valley have always been thrust forward by the unbridled power of dreams. Next to love, there is no force more powerful. The Task Lyst platform brings parties together to get things done, to increase productivity, to grease the wheels of labor, and to act as the wind beneath the wings of capital. I want to thank the San Francisco Visitors Bureau for giving us the opportunity to speak at this meeting and for naming Task Lyst Ambassador Company of the Year."

Applause overpowered the jeers in the room as Alice sat back down in a chair flanking the other individuals near the podium. As the meeting adjourned, Alice was approached by audience members.

"Alice, I'm a reporter with the *Fishwrap*, and I'd like to get your comment on rumors that Task Lyst is striking a deal with the district attorney to cooperate on criminal investigations, like in the Baxter Morris murder." The reporter was Quint O'Rourke, and he wore a tweed sport coat with a wool scarf draped around his neck. He held a small reporter's notebook in his hand and a pen in the other.

"I can't comment on that other than to say I am sure we are doing whatever is necessary to bring the victim's family the justice they deserve."

"Will Task Lyst be cooperating in other criminal cases involving drugs and prostitution?"

Before she could reply, another question was fired at her by an African American woman around forty years old.

"Ms. Seegar, my husband has been out of work since your company has sprouted up and stole all his landscaping help. He can't keep employees happy on account of them all leaving to go make tax-free wages."

Another audience member, an elderly Chinese gentleman, held a picture of a young family member and said, "Task Lyst killed my grandson."

One of Alice's team members rescued her from the growing crowd of people wishing to speak with her and shepherded her into a secluded staging area.

"It was starting to get scary in there," Alice said.

"Sorry about that. We'll know for next time to anticipate the crowds," the staffer said.

Alice opened a bottled water and rehydrated. A friendly face came toward her. It was Elliott, the band guy.

"Nice job on stage. You had us all eating out of your hand," he said.

"It was terrifying. I'm not great with crowds, and I don't know how I'll survive another."

"Did you write that stuff yourself? You'd make a good cult leader."

"I had some help. What are you doing here?" she asked him.

Elliott explained how he'd read about her appearance in the paper and thought he'd drop by to offer moral support. Alice thought that was nice. Elliott wore an army fatigue with a Netherlands flag patch on one sleeve and an orange patch on the other that said KNVB. He placed his saddlebag and his black helmet on a table. She could see his eyes behind the light-green tint of his wraparound sunglasses.

"You a motorcycle rider?"

"Scooter."

"Ha, cool."

"You guys wrapping up here? Heading back to the office or . . ."

Alice thought about her schedule and regretted having committed to a ten o'clock meeting that would immediately follow her appearance at the breakfast engagement. "We have another meeting right after this."

Elliott nodded. "Right on. Well, maybe another time I can give you more user feedback on my adventures with Task Lyst."

"Yes, absolutely. I've got a crazy work week, but Thursday I'll be back up in the city after a lunch meeting," she said.

"Thursday, Thursday . . . I'm mastering. Finishing up a new song. You should come by the studio. I'll hit you up with an address."

CHAPTER 95

TIM MET WITH CLAY AND RAJ TO DEVISE A PLAN to implement the company's cooperation with city hall. The heat was on from the law-abiding public for Task Lyst to come under some semblance of control. The company would have to provide sacrificial lambs in order to steam through the turbulent waters and pursue its long-term plan for a public offering. It was a fine line to negotiate but necessary. Tim was charged with flagging users who were violating terms and conditions of the user agreement, one of whom would surely be his errand boy customer, Geronimo69. Tim took pleasure in throwing him under the bus and believed that his own complicity couldn't be linked. Tim entered keywords into the system and produced a list of profiles to turn over to Stuart for investigation.

Raj praised Tim for his work, looking over his shoulder at the computer screen displaying the results. "Okay, great. Stuart will get some collars from the worst of these and we'll win back the hearts and minds of San Francisco."

"And the banks," said Clay. "The analysts will see this as an improvement on liability concerns and help our credit rating."

Tim clicked the down arrow and viewed the scores of profiles that now were in imminent danger of prosecution. Among them were suspected drug dealers, violent thugs providing muscle on demand, and loads of pimps, whores, and massage therapists, a wet dream of leads for any vice division. Included in the list was Geronimo69, flagged for delivering drugs, vandalism, stalking, and harassment. Included in the profiles were contact and billing information. The latter could be used to pursue tax evasion for failure to claim income from the Task Lyst platform. Tim printed out a report and sent a digital copy to Clay.

• • •

Tim took advantage of his rising star status to campaign for a senior management role in the company. He viewed Raj as friendly competition for a higher spot up the organization ladder but was transparent with his intentions. Raj was younger and more interested in managing product, while Tim's focus was on titles and status. There was room for both at the top, particularly with Tim's priority on being viewed as genius programmer and less so corporate manager. Clay promised to meet with Tim as soon as Q3 financials were approved and they'd "formalize a more senior spot for him." Tim began thinking of his near future as being anchored by an imminent liquidity event. He'd have the title he longed for and the disposable income that comes with it. He'd be in line for a big payday when the firm finally went public. Then, he'd be assured of a substantial exit, the kind that defines careers and births fortunes. He'd roll some of his gains into a managing director position at a venture capital firm and live out his sunset years as an angel investor. He'd sit on some boards, mentor young highfliers, and be an adjunct professor at one of the MBA programs around the Bay. He'd become a unicorn hunter, an investor in ideas, and an oracle for youthful brilliance. He'd get the choice tables at the top restaurants and access to the private wine lists.

Tim had set up a midweek overnight in Napa for Sandra's birthday, promising to leave work behind. He splurged on a new wristwatch for the occasion, one that connected to his email and instant messenger program to stay abreast of happenings at Task Lyst. He'd try to give the impression of limiting his screen time and still be wired in while receiving spa treatments. Tim even curtailed his wine tasting to "stay sharp." It wasn't lost on Sandra. She encouraged him to relax, so Tim ingested a fifteen-milligram gummy bear, which he regretted when a work-related email came through on his new gadget.

The message concerned Task Lyst cyber security with an alert that their database had been compromised overnight. The information systems were assessing the damage and alerting department heads of the trouble. Tim assumed it was a hack, or attempted hack. He thought of potential adversaries who might be responsible: Russians, Chinese, domestic. Perhaps cyber pirates looking for a bounty or someone in cahoots with Wikileaks. He considered his own liability; was there anything incriminating or loose ends that might leave him exposed? Apart from downloading the copy of the transaction database, he couldn't think of anything that raised concerns. He had of course finally destroyed the original, per protocol. The initial Task Lyst business plan called for total anonymity on behalf of users on either side of the transactions. There was to be zero chance of connecting real life people to the tasks on the platform. It was touted as new and proprietary technology to maintain discretion and encourage activity. Sure, many viewed this as enabling nefarious activity. But it was hyped in the spirit of the great American tradition of individual freedom. Citizens were entitled to privacy. Fences make great neighbors, and Task Lyst offered an impenetrable libertarian barrier to maintain this pursuit of life, liberty, and happiness.

When Tim started contracting at Task Lyst his team was developing new products and features for a thriving platform. Overlooked was a procedure to safeguard against the company retaining incriminating data that would create liability for its members and itself. Tim was trusted to destroy the shadow database, which he had done, but a downloaded copy remained in his possession. He was pretty sure the external hard drive with the shadow database was in his home office next to his camera equipment. It might be smart to keep that under lock and key, he decided.

CHAPTER 96

ELLIOTT AND HIS RECORDING ENGINEER, GIDEON, OR GUP as he was sometimes known, were in the studio editing vocal tracks when a text alert sounded on his phone. Dallas Alice was in the neighborhood.

"I've got a friend stopping by," he announced. "Let's queue up a playback and listen to the mix." Elliott walked out to the studio entrance on Mission Street and greeted Alice. They exchanged an awkward cheek kiss, and he escorted her through the dark, musty studio that smelled of decades-old smoke permeating from the redwood walls and carpeted sound baffles. Patchouli oil and jasmine incense added to the exotic ambience. Amber lighting in the control room created a dreamy atmosphere, and a groovy melodic hook came through the speakers. The music creaked to a halt and the sound of tape reversing replaced the melody.

"Okay, Elliott, fixed the pedal steel edit and I think it works well. You ready for a listen?" Gideon nodded politely at Alice and rolled his chair a couple of feet to his right and engaged the tape machine controller. He slid back in front of the monitor with one hand on a mouse and the other adjusting knobs and faders.

"Yep, fire away," Elliott said. He motioned to his guest to sit on a black leather couch facing the monitors behind the producer chair. He joined her there. "Hope you like it."

The song began to play, filling the room with a mid-tempo jangle of guitars, harmony vocals, and a steady backbeat. The sound paid homage to a variety of Elliott's musical influences yet avoided being pigeonholed in one genre or vintage. There was a newness to it and an urgency that felt both polished and ragged. Lyrically, it was a call to arms through effective use of metaphor, topical but universal. *All alone in the city at night, it's the priorities of the folks that ain't right. I miss the colorful sights and sounds, it'll take a good shaking to bring 'em back around.* Alice listened to the playback with total focus. At one point, she nudged him with her elbow as if to say, "I'm impressed." They all listened to the end through three verse-choruses, a middle-eight section, some soloing, and a vamp outro. The rough mix came to a crashing conclusion and the producer spun around with arms folded.

"Well, we've just waxed a hot one," Gideon said in a faux-Cockney accent.

"I quite like it." Elliott reciprocated the Anglophilic diction, saying the words in a trancelike cadence. He was looking past the producer into a reflection of the three of them in the tilted glass window that oversaw the tracking room. The back of the producer's head was flanked by Dallas Alice and him. He gazed at the image for several seconds until Gideon, returning to his normal voice, broke the spell.

"Well, let's live with this mix for a few days and meet back here to make any minor tweaks we deem necessary," he said. "Not that it's not perfect already, if I don't mind saying so my damn self."

Elliott stood up to stretch and studied Dallas Alice's reaction.

"Wow, that's some powerful stuff. I really like it," she said. "I'd like to hear it again, but it looks like you guys are wrapping up."

Gideon responded, "Now's when we give it the car stereo test. My old studio had the front half of a 1975 Fiat 124 Spider sticking out of a wall for the car speaker perspective. You lovebirds will have to settle for your own hi-fi outside."

Elliott felt a rush of blood to his face from Gideon's comment. He looked at Alice, who displayed similar discomfort. They chuckled to each other. Gideon, sensing their awkwardness, verbalized a disclaimer: "Well, whatever, you guys make a nice couple, just throwing it out there."

"Dig it, so you think there's a sort of Keith and Anita vibe between us?" Elliott played along, pulling Alice toward him in a playful side embrace.

"Yeah, more so than John and Yoko," Gideon replied.

Alice joined the gag. "Hey, I always felt Yoko got the shaft. She's a powerful symbol for women, you know. An artist in her own right."

Elliott and Alice exited the studio and walked toward her car, which was parked at a meter along Mission Street near 11th. It was nearing rush hour and the parking lane would be opening to traffic soon. Elliott invited her to join him in the car stereo test but suggested they rendezvous to another location, perhaps one with a more inspiring view. It was agreed they would drop his scooter off and drive together somewhere yet to be determined. En route, Elliott, careful not to lose her, decided on the Marin Headlands as his first choice for listening. There was a perfect spot up high with a view looking over the Golden Gate Bridge to the city. It was panoramic, too, offering perspectives down the coast and out to sea toward the Farallon Islands. There were old cannon bunkers left over from WWII, including the one with an old piano inside. They could get out and walk around, take in the surroundings.

After dropping off the scooter, Alice drove while Elliott navigated them around traffic snarls, taking side roads off of Van Ness and Lombard, winding their way to the bridge. In the headlands, they parked in the precise vantage point Elliott had in mind and listened to several playbacks of the new song. Alice offered her perspective on what she liked and loved. She truly seemed moved by the recording and Elliott enjoyed the accolades. He was aware of her former music industry stint, having sleuthed her LinkedIn profile, and was impressed by her insightful feedback.

"So, what inspired the lyrics? How would you sum it up to a music journalist?"

"It's whatever you want it to be. I don't like to, you know, muddy the waters with too much heavy-handed back story."

She pressed him. "Would you say it's social commentary, more than a love song, though?"

Elliott shrugged. "I could get behind that. I think there's a little protest in there somewhere. Sort of a 'wake the fuck up, people' theme."

"It's a little . . . sentimental."

Elliott waited before responding. "Is that a question or a statement?"

"Let's call it a question."

"Sure, I guess. It's me, the old guy, through the song, yelling 'get off my lawn.'"

Alice laughed. "Something we can all relate to."

"There is a divisiveness that occurred, and is occurring, in this age. The world is getting smaller while the universe is expanding. Technology is bringing us closer yet causing incredible wealth disparity and loss of individual identity. The developed world is eating up resources and telling the third world not to pollute." Elliott was on a roll and caught himself before continuing.

"Modernity's a bitch."

"And technology's a motherfucker."

Dallas Alice laughed. "Hey, I resent that. Technology has been paying my bills lately."

"It's dirty money."

She pulled her head back with mouth agape. "Okay, holier than thou!"

"No, I'm guilty, too. I've been sucking on the devil's nipple like the best of them. Excuse the crude metaphor."

"What do you suggest, go off the grid, farm organic vegetables, and make barefoot, towheaded babies?"

"Meh, at some point maybe. That takes some money. Like trust fund money. In a perfect world I'm singing songs or doing something creative to make a stand, not to run away and hide."

"That's noble. How about the argument that technology can advance this cause? Medicine, communication, new energy resources."

"Yeah, I'm down with that. There's good with the bad."

The sparring was in her favor now. He backpedaled a bit toward the corner.

She said, "And to go a little deeper. Have you read Voltaire's *Candide*?"

"Which one was that?"

"We have to tend our garden. I take it to mean we must act individually, at the end of the day. Take care of what's ours, nurture our own existence, and the world will follow."

"Yeah, existential but a little defeatist. I believe in using a little force when push comes to shove. Darwinism is real. Stamp out fascism. Write a song and shout it from the mountaintop."

"True." She thought about that.

He continued. "Have you ever seen Woody Guthrie's guitar?"

"Probably."

"He painted on it, 'This machine kills fascists.'"

"Oh, right."

"The power of protest verse."

"So can't technology help get that word out to the world? His guitar was a tech weapon of sorts."

"I wonder. I'm hopeful, but the digitization of music, for all its democratic benefits, has seen the power consolidate behind fewer and more powerful gatekeepers. The song is at the mercy of who owns the distribution system, whether it's a music tech company or the owner of the fiber-optic lines. I'm beginning to think we're better off in the ownership model." He grabbed a CD from her car console and held it up. "Here's a tangible product. You can play it without your internet going out. It cannot be banned, or if it is, you already have your own copy for safekeeping. That's the trouble with music tech; they're destroying the tangible aspect and making it virtual." He leaned back. "I mean, as an artist, I'd be able to go out and perform live in front of a paying audience. Songwriters, arrangers, and session players are losers in this sea change."

She nodded and smiled. "I'm sold. Seriously though, I agree but not absolutely. I think some of the tech companies are bringing positive advancement to society and can't all be lumped together as villains just because one sector is experiencing hardship."

"You are more complicit than you think," he said.

"Harsh. You don't think Task Lyst is helping people by putting extra money in their pockets and fulfilling basic needs of everyday people?"

"I think you're drinking the Kool-Aid."

Dallas Alice searched his expression for a level of sincerity on which she could base his claim. "Oh, really. How do you know what I'm drinking?"

Elliott looked down and smiled. They paused, and he looked at her looking at him. "I know more than you think. I've been a Task Lyst user since it launched. I've financed this recording doing tasks ranging from parking cars to, let's just say, things I'm not going to repeat for fear of legal repercussions. It's the dark web legalized, you've got to know that. It's removed the conscience from the soul and that's dangerous territory."

"We're working on cleaning that up." Her chipper mood soured.

"Look, I know, empirically even, that the intentions might be good. If Granny needs some groceries delivered, and little Johnny can mow a few lawns for some extra bucks. But for every one of those there is a drug deal, an underage girl pulling a trick, and a homicide hit. I'm all for scoring a little of what you need for what ails ya, but . . . and then there's the bigger picture."

"Which is . . . "

"Which is the consolidation of control and wealth by fewer entities. Mainstream and social media, distributors of goods and services, music . . . these companies get obscenely rich and form their own little universes with their own code of ethics and morality. They have their own busses to get the workers from the city down to their Valley campuses where everything is provided for them. They use their power for more privilege and exacerbate this 'us and them' mentality. Their special interests take priority over others and the little guy is fucked. Artists can't afford to live among the techies who make ten times more dough and buy up all the real estate, ruining neighborhoods with their remodels, and pretty soon, here come the strollers. Now they'll need their own schools, so they lobby to channel public school funds to these charter schools that lack any diversity. So, you have tech companies bringing the world together but dividing it at the same time."

"Should I be writing this down? This is really good stuff." Alice smirked and Elliott laughed.

"And don't get me started on all the old music clubs that are shuttering. Sometimes I feel like moving to LA."

CHAPTER 97

ALICE SAT AT HER DESK ON MONDAY struggling to wade through scores of emails flooding in on topics ranging from human resources to senior management updates to reminders on office policy regarding recycling. From a professional perspective, a cloud of malaise had followed her from Thursday's encounter with Elliott. He'd made some strong points, and she was realizing that the trajectory for Task Lyst was less sparkly than she had anticipated. This was offset, though, by a warm, fuzzy feeling of puppy love. She was, as her grandmother might say, smitten. He was irreverent, idealistic, flawed, thoughtful, precocious, and a maybe a little pretentious all at once. He was attractive to her in a way that she felt rather than thought. There was no logic to them taking a relationship anywhere, yet it was a collision of passions she could feel building. She began to view her job as merely a break from moving things along too quickly with Elliott. It had only been a few interactions, but they were meaningful and hinted at some kind of growing, spinning light pulling them in.

She had an impromptu afternoon coffee with Tim in the courtyard at the Task Lyst office building. They sat at one of the new communal picnic tables built to accommodate the increasing numbers of employees.

"How are you liking it so far?" Tim said. "Pretty crazy pace, huh?"

"I forgot what it's like to work on this side of the business. I'm fine with it though, just keep reminding myself to keep a healthy balance, you know?"

"That's critical. You can't let it take over your life. It happened to me when I realized I no longer knew the names of the parents on the sidelines of soccer games."

"How are things going on your end?" she said.

Tim slurped some of his latte. "Operation Big Sting is under way at the DA."

"I see. And how's it looking?"

"They are pretty much going down the list and either assigning investigative teams or issuing warrants. The hope is to round 'em up like cattle with a press junket and some 'hang 'em high' chants."

"I'm sure. Well I'm meeting in the morning with High Seas Public Relations to spin it to our advantage," she said. "Not sure how exactly."

Tim hesitated but continued. "We're going to call it a hack. Our database was breached and turned over to authorities. We'll have fixed the problem, but scores of bad guys will be off the streets. Everybody wins." Tim flashed his raised eyebrows for punctuation and finished his coffee. "I've got to jump and catch Bulgaria before they close up shop for the night."

Tim's explanation and body language made the situation very real. It was happening, this collusion, and she hadn't made peace with her role in it. She thought about the bad guys who would be off the streets because of this operation. She imagined Baxter Morris's loved ones and the mourners of the Russian dissident feeling some relief at the justice being served. Then she wondered if enough safeguards were in place to keep checks and balances on due process. And was she being asked to lie, to spin this as something it wasn't. Nevertheless, she gathered her things from the table and headed for the conference room for the Monday morning update.

Later, after lunch, Alice looked at her watch and thought about Elliott's afternoon meeting with the programming director at KHIP radio. He had told her of his plan to finish the mix and take it straight over to the popular listener-supported radio station and conduct his own radio promotion. He wouldn't leave until they agreed to air it live. Alice escaped the office to her car in the parking lot to tune in just in case.

It was the beginning of a drive-time show and Elliott was reasonably confident of his chances.

"You're listening to KHIP afternoon drive show, and we've got a guest in the studio today. Elliott Temple, from the group the Golden Mean, and now also a solo artist, has written and recorded a new song. Elliott, thanks for dropping by and welcome to the show."

"Thanks for having me on."

"Tell us about your new song and what you've been up to."

"I've just been trying to get by, you know, survive in the digital age of ubiquity. This track is a cry for help, I'm told."

"Interesting. 'Digital age of ubiquity.' Wanna tell us more about that?"

"Everything is everywhere. There's no mystery anymore. That's the way I see it," Elliott said.

"What are your plans with this new material?"

"Plans? I'll probably print a bunch of copies and sell twenty-five out of the trunk of my car, and then the rest will sit in the corner of my closet with my other releases. If I'm lucky, I'll get a band together and play some gigs. If anyone out there is interested, I'm hiring."

The radio host laughed. "Copy that. What kind of benefit package should our listeners expect from your offer?"

"I've got a generous stock options package with full health and 401k, sick days, detox treatment, should things go sideways on the road. And they likely will."

"No dental or vision?"

"Leave the vision to me; dental starts on the second record."

"What are your thoughts about streaming? Will you make the record available on Spotify and Pandora-type platforms?"

"I'm not sure about that. I have nothing against giving something away for free as long as someone else isn't monetizing it. If I post a new record and make it streamable, it doesn't incentivize anyone into buying it from me directly at a gig or out of the back of a Caprice Classic. The dollars and cents won't trickle down fast enough to me to make it sustainable. Meanwhile, those tech companies are paying their own salaries with advertising dollars, and shareholders are cashing out stockpiles of equity. They get paid every two weeks but I get paid, what, quarterly?" There was a pause.

"Are you asking me? I don't know."

"It's a joke, right? They'll advance the Beatles and Led Zeppelin millions, but I'll never meet the minimum to warrant them sending a check. No, it's not a good strategy for someone like me, especially with a new record. Not until blockchain currencies like Ethereum and Bitcoin can ensure 100 percent transparency and value transfer."

The radio host cut Elliott off. "Sounds like a terrific plan. Well, what do you say we give it a listen? This is a new one from Elliott Temple. Give us a call and tell us what you think, 877-KHIP or @KHIP on the Twitter."

Alice listened to a minute of the song before texting Elliott, "Sounding good, Rockstar!"

In return she received a shaka brah emoticon and then another of a smiley face behind sunglasses. And then "call ya later."

She wrote back, "k."

The song finished and the radio host congratulated Elliott. "Elliott, strong effort, my man. That is a catchy number. It's got a little more punch than your Golden Mean material. And it looks like we've got some callers too. Hello, welcome to KHIP. You're on the air with Elliott."

"Hi, I just wanted to say that's a killer tune, and I'm a guitar player looking for a band."

"You sound young; how old are you?" the host said.

"I'm seventeen."

Elliott answered, "Do you rock? The blues don't discriminate by age."

"Does a shoe stink?"

The host cracked up, and Elliott answered, "Right on, my brother. Tell you what, hit me up at @Elliott76 and I'll follow up with ya."

The host added, "You're gonna have a ton of new followers. Here's another caller. Welcome to KHIP."

"Hi there. Really great tune, Elliott. Is that about Jerry Garcia? I'd have to hear it again, but lyrically I was inferring a Jer vibe."

"It might have some Jerry in it somewhere."

The host said, "Are you or were you a big Deadhead?"

"I've always been aware of the Dead and, you know, liked them. Saw some shows . . . I wore out the Cornell '77 cassette before I'd heard any of their records. But I'm also into all kinds of other music, from Jamaican rocksteady to Chet Baker, Elizabeth Cotten, KISS . . . you name it. Jerry was a fan of disparate musical forms."

The host said, "Did you ever see KISS?"

Elliott replied, "Once. On their unmasked acoustic tour, which is really like not ever having seen them."

"Yeah, you take away the pyro and makeup and you're left with a really bad Long Island garage band. Oops, sorry Gene."

"I think they were better looking with the makeup, definitely." The host continued, "We used to write the KISS logo all over our school notebooks."

"Right, and before that fans were spray painting 'Clapton is God' on London walls."

"And peace symbols."

"And then anarchy signs!"

"What would be your preferred call sign, say, if fans took to the streets on your behalf?"

"Ha! How about just peace and rock?"

"Ooh, I like it. There's balance there in the disparate solutes. Two fingers tempered by Devil's

Horns"

"Reality I suppose, the way of the world."

"Okay, let's read a couple of tweets: Christina in Pleasanton says, 'Do you need a tambourine player? I can't sing but I look good.'"

Elliott said, "Yes, like Brian Jonestown Massacre, I want a dedicated jingle-jangler."

“Here’s another. ‘Do guys mind shutting the eff up and play the song again?’”

Elliott said, “Sage advice, always a good idea to shut the eff up.”

“And another. ‘@Elliott76 what happened to #TheGoldenMean did u breakup?’”

Elliott said, “Nope, just taking a hiatus, sorting it all out.”

“Last one, from @Tbone, it’s the (holding up his hands) ‘peace and rock. And so it begins.

Well, thanks, Elliott, great having you in the studio here today. Wishing you the best with yournew recording, a very compelling one at that. Good luck!”

“Thanks again for having me on your program.”

CHAPTER 98

TIM SLAMMED THE RECEIVER BACK ON THE HANDSET. The Bulgarians were being unruly about getting paid what they believed they were worth. Zander claimed his hands were tied—"What can I do?" Tim threatened to cancel their contract, but both parties knew he couldn't afford to at present. Tim would have to revise his budgets and get approval from Raj. He had carried the overage for too long and had run out of his own cash reserves. Despite his rising salary, bonuses, and stock grants, he was hand to mouth, paycheck to paycheck, covering tuitions, travel soccer, ballet, spa weekends, and normal indulgences.

He called Raj. "Raj, Tim here. Whaaaaaat's happening?"

"Oh, hey, Tim, what's up?"

"Bulgaria is being a pain in my ass."

"Better yours than mine."

"Yeah, right. I think I'm going to have to revise their budget a bit. They, well, they want market rate for what they are delivering."

"I thought you had them under your thumb. Why the new hassles?"

"It's been a growing concern. Slow growing."

"Kind of a brutal time to be revising your overhead. We're going to be reporting numbers to the board in a couple of weeks."

"Yeah, I know. I'm not happy about it."

"On another note, Stuart's task force is starting to bring in people from your list for questioning. They leaked it to the press, and it's all over the six o'clock news."

Tim pulled up the internet feed of the local television news and watched as they brought suspects into the main police booking station. It was a motley crew of young gangbangers, streetwalkers, a high school football coach, a soccer mom. Tim was able to guess at which individuals matched up with the profiles he had become familiar with. He didn't see his errand boy but saw several others through whom he'd lived vicariously all these weeks. Some of them hid their faces as they exited squad cars. Others stood brazenly, like they'd been down this road before. A few wept.

"Holy crap," Tim said.

Raj answered, "It's nuts. Poor fuckers had no idea, I bet. Wonder what the football coach is in for."

"You don't want to know."

"Really? Fuck."

"The soccer mom is like, 'I want to talk to my lawyer.'"

"She's probably been very naughty."

CHAPTER 99

ELLIOTT WAS ANXIOUS TO FINISH UP THE RADIO SHOW. He was thrilled with how it went, getting a spot on the show and broadcasting the song on air, and listener response seemed positive. However, he was getting text messages from his neighbor alluding to police knocking on his apartment door. Elliott left the station studio and loitered in the lobby to catch up on his messages. He answered his neighbor's text.

"Yo, so what's up?"

"Fuzz came round asking for you, left a few minutes ago."

"wtf?"

"Dunno, peeked through windows, checked around back on your fire escape. Landlord was with them. Sorry bro."

"Oh good it's the . . . police. LOL" Elliott decided against supporting his gallows humor with an emoji. "Thx, lemme know if they come back or anything. Laying low for now."

Elliott wasn't sure what to make of the news, but he knew the radio appearance had made his whereabouts public information. Not that the cops were listening to KHIP. But still. He relocated to the coffee shop on the corner for a couple of minutes to further suss out the situation. And maybe the cops weren't there for him or to incriminate him. Could be something else. Better to figure that out first, though. Nobody had called or contacted him. He ordered a small coffee and sat at a high-top table at the window. He kept one eye on the lobby of the radio station building and the other scrolling through social media looking for clues. Social media channels were buzzing, with the *Fishwrap* editorial staffers tracking a coordinated police operation involving some prominent individuals. None of his close friends seemed to know anything.

Elliott made it home by dark and staked out his entrance for the five-oh. After fifteen minutes he decided to chance it. Everything inside was the same as he'd left it. He knocked on his neighbor's door, but there was no answer. Once settled, he went online and caught up with the local news, including footage and updates of a large-scale sting operation involving drugs, sex trafficking, and racketeering. It was being described as a major coup by San Francisco law enforcement. Elliott didn't like the coincidence of the media coverage timed with a visit from police. A direct message hit his Twitter handle. This one provided a link to the subject of blockchain-based ecosystems which he had referenced on the radio earlier. Elliott spent half an hour getting sucked into a wiki-hole, reading the origins of blockchain and theories behind its benefits. There was a philosophical framework on which it operated that interested Elliott. The democratization of commerce: to eliminate the middlemen—the filters, the banks, the brokers, the filthy handlers of cash, the counterfeiters—was to purify the transaction of goods and services. This was a good idea. Profiting off the productivity of society was the game of parasites. Suits calling the shots on who gets played and what they get paid. Elliott had seen enough of the music business to know the game was rigged. Amplify that to all industries and it was clear the status quo was ripe for disruption. Banking was surely another sector about to get fed its lunch.

It was just before eight when his phone alerted him of Alice's text. She offered to pick up some takeout if he was interested in a late bite. Elliott was mixing a drink and agreed a couple of tacos couldn't hurt. She was parking and would grab some around the corner. Elliott decided against straightening up. She hadn't been to his place before, and it was what it was: a bachelor musician pad with a bed on the floor and more guitars than furnishings. There had been roommates along the way too. So many, in fact, that Elliott couldn't trace the lineage without forgetting a short-termer or two. There was Max and Ronnie and Carolina Slim. His favorite was Reggie, who had left in a huff after someone had used a couple of ounces of his treasured balsamic vinaigrette. Reggie was a practicing vegan who held the club a little too tight. Decent piano player though.

The doorbell rang and Elliott buzzed Alice in. She climbed the stairs to his flat and he greeted her outside his door. There was an awkward moment when the two didn't know whether to nod at each other or produce some kind of casual embrace. They chose the former.

"Any trouble finding a spot?" he asked her.

"No, I parked in front of the launderette. So this is where the magic happens, huh? Where you lure innocent women back and then write songs about them."

Elliott laughed. "They usually jump out the window when they see what a shithole it is. But hey, it's rent controlled!"

"What are you drinking?"

"I call it a Delray Demise. Here, try it and I'll mix another." Elliott's offer was received with apprehension by both hands.

"Wow, it's cold. Is this a mint julep cup?"

"Indeed. I found a set of them at a flea market and, well, there's really no substitute for real silver." She followed him over to his kitchen counter as he conducted the mixology lesson: two ounces of wheated bourbon over crushed ice followed by enough water to barely float the ice. Then, shaved lemon zest around the rim and into the cup. "I'll occasionally add some sugar, maybe a teaspoon, but you have to mix that in water first. Don't forget that, it's critical."

Alice hesitated, thinking about her recent desire to recommit to sobriety, "Sounds very Southern and refreshing."

"William Faulkner liked variations of this. It prolongs the drinking into an all-day affair suitable for climates such as Mississippi and New Orleans. Works just fine in foggy old San Francisco too." He raised his glass to hers and they clinked.

Elliott studied Alice as she glanced around the apartment, taking inventory of his personal space. He liked the way she looked tonight. She was dressing for the occasion with her faded jeans, vintage sneakers, and flattering casual T-shirt under a lightweight parka, which she took off upon arrival. She was old enough to be a hot young mom but showed no signs of motherhood or childbearing. They hadn't discussed if she'd ever been married, or even had kids, for that matter. Regardless, she was mature, confident, and independent.

Alice brushed off the couch and sat down with one leg folded under the other. Her left arm bent as her hand supported her head under her hair. She held her cocktail in the other, nursing it in between awkward moments. Elliott removed a record from its sleeve and, using both pinkies, finessed it on to the turntable. He dropped the arm onto the spinning vinyl. The gentle white noise gave way to a simple piano figure followed by two horns chiming in, not unlike the sound of ships passing in the San Francisco night. It was repetitive and hypnotic, and it opened up into a menagerie of walking bass, ride cymbal quarter notes, and solo saxophone. The piano stayed true to the original melody with minor variations resembling a chirping bird. The six instruments carried on a conversation that centered around the same voicing, with each taking a turn to stretch out.

"Nice," Alice said.

"You like Miles Davis?"

"I like this record. My uncle used to play it for me. I haven't listened to it in a while. Reminds me of him."

Elliott, who had been seated on the floor next to the stereo system, rose to check the activity out on the street. He peeked through the tapestry that hung over the window. All seemed normal. He retrieved the tacos from the white bag and brought them back to the couch where he joined Alice. A stray bottle of hot sauce awaited the tacos on the glass-top coffee table.

"Thanks for picking these up. Best in town when convenience is factored in," he said. "Here, aren't you joining me?"

She agreed to have one but claimed to be not particularly hungry. "I'll take a chicken taco, but keep that tongue or whatever it is away from me."

"You don't like lengua? How about some tripe? Really good stuff."

She smiled. "I'll take your word for it."

Elliott scarfed down a couple of tacos before deciding he was satisfied. He adjusted the pillows on the couch and reclined as John Coltrane blew his saxophone.

"How's your drink, ready for another?"

Alice answered, "Not yet, still working on this one."

Elliott swirled the ice around in his cup in time with drummer Jimmy Cobb's tempo. He got up again and peered through the tapestry. "Yeah, maybe I'll hold off too. The heat came looking for me tonight. Cops. My neighbor downstairs texted me."

"Whoa. What for?"

"I have a hunch it's related to Task Lyst. There's some shit going down all across town." He could see Alice processing the information. Maybe she was connecting dots. She repositioned herself on the couch.

"And what makes you think they'd be interested in you?"

"I don't want to get into specifics, but I think I'm part of the shakedown, guilty by association."

"What do you plan to do?"

"I'm going to throw a couple of things in a backpack, and get lost for a stretch."

"Go on the run? Is that the smartest course of action?"

"I'm not on the run if I don't know they're after me."

"Clever. How can I help?"

"Got a spare cottage up in the mountains?"

"I wish. You're welcome to stay at my place down the peninsula if you're in a pinch."

"I don't want to put you out. I'm a liability."

"Well why don't you let me put you up tonight at least? You'll be out of the city limits."

CHAPTER 100

ALICE TOOK 19TH AVENUE SOUTH HEADING FOR INTERSTATE 280. Elliott was on his phone. He mentioned heading up to the Sierras "to wait it out." The person on the other end of his conversation was trying to get him access to a ski house. Alice, too, racked her brain for a way to help Elliott. She could ask Ned for the use of his PlumpJack spread. Oh the irony, on so many levels. Or he could hide out at her place, but that seemed too weird and risky. She was anxious about the insider knowledge she had of Elliott's predicament and how she would proceed. Come clean? Deny? Avoid the topic? None of which seemed easy. The phone discussion transitioned to excitement about his radio appearance, which apparently was attracting attention from industry types. Alice overheard Elliott say he'd get down to Los Angeles if a meeting was arranged.

A steady rain was coming down and the wiper blades created a rhythmic white noise that ticked like an urgent clock. The tension of Elliott's legal drama had tempered whatever sexual awkwardness existed between them. She was bringing a guy into her house for the night. However, under the auspices of a helping hand, she felt safe from moral ambiguity. True, they hadn't known each other long, but there was mutual attraction and a shared willingness to explore the synergy. Being with Elliott took her back to her music industry days: the tours, the artist liaisons, the expense account perks along with the shitty pay. She had gotten out while the business was at its peak. Albums were going five times platinum; money was thrown around at every whim. The profits were lining the pockets of record label presidents, artist managers, and the lawyers who wrote up the deals. And if she slept her way to the top, she'd have a shot at an elusive female executive office in New York or LA. Good advice and better angels had steered her away to business school and Silicon Valley. The money was better, but the glass ceiling still hovered. The ignorance of not knowing how dirty it could get toward the top was the bliss that maybe she now coveted. She admired Elliott's dogged pursuit of the artist's path. Foolish on one hand but pure, still, in its intention. Her years of experience told her he was talented enough and possessed an interesting look, but he had aged out of signability. Nobody was looking for a thirty-something new solo act with artistic integrity. His would have to be the independent route, and that window was closing fast.

Yet there was creative energy and a sense of purpose that intrigued her. Elliott was committed to his cause and willing to lead. Silicon Valley was welcoming to these types, idea people hell-bent on a concept with blinders on from the naysayers. They either succeeded, some beyond their highest expectations, or crashed and burned. They weren't corporate ladder material. She wondered if business school had sapped her creative potential. Spreadsheets and risk analysis trumped wild-eyed, spontaneous ideation. In her predatory role as a VC, she could smooth out the rough edges of an innovator like Elliott and take him on a dog and pony show to raise more money. She was aware of the label some placed on people in her position. Back in the day, she would be called a "suit." Now, ironically, she was more schooled, more refined, had more access to capital, but definitely didn't wear more suits. Silicon Valley was becoming as rock 'n' roll as the music business had been back in the nineties. Hoodies, sneakers, and T-shirts among the tech founder class kept the "suits" honest. Still, the telltale signs of designer outdoor wear ruled the wardrobe closets of most in the venture capital world. The Canada Goose vest button-up shirts with sleeves rolled up twice were the new suits.

Elliott finished up his conversation. "Catch up with you later, Freddy. Love you, man."

He turned to Alice. "Sorry about that. Phone is burning up tonight."

Alice replied, "Don't be. You've got a lot of balls in the air."

“I think my plan is to get up to Tahoe tomorrow and hole up in a friend’s ski house for a few days. I might need to get down to LA if a meeting comes through with a subsidiary of Universal.”

Alice turned to him. “That’s great! For the new song?”

“We’ll see. It might be a one-off Netflix series placement deal through a music supervisor who is a friend of a friend.”

“That would be nice residual income.”

“Right, that I can spend while in jail.”

“Stop,” she said.

“But yeah, movies and TV: the gift that keeps on giving. I still get occasional checks for a few songs I had in an indie film that plays on cable. If only it were McKinleys instead of Jacksons.”

CHAPTER 101

TIM VIDEO CHATTED ALICE ON HIS SMARTPHONE. It was a little after 9:00 p.m. and amid all the law enforcement excitement, he was checking in for her perspective. She answered.

"Hey, Tim, I'm driving, so I have you on speakerphone. A friend is with me, so don't reveal any incriminating details of your and Sandra's exotic sex life." Her delivery was followed by a chuckle.

"Ha, funny. If only I had some to share," Tim said.

"What's up?"

Tim answered, "Nothing urgent, just hit me later. Work stuff."

"Okay, I'm headed home, so give me a bit."

The call ended and Tim thought for a moment. His overactive analytical mind processed the fine details of the conversation, and he entertained the possibilities. A friend was with her and she was headed home. After nine in the evening. Maybe it was a girlfriend who lived nearby. Or some guy. Although it was none of his business, he did the math: fifteen-minute drive to her house with another five to get out the door with his drone. He'd be back in forty-five, or roughly the equivalent of a leisurely trip to the store for emergency coffee or school lunch supplies.

He called to Sandra in the other room, "Hey, babe, I'm gonna run out for some coffee, need anything from the store?"

"Do we need coffee? I thought we had plenty?" she said.

"I only see a little, hardly enough for the morning. I want to grab a *Fishwrap,* too. Back in twenty." Which he knew she knew meant forty. Regardless, Sandra was busy editing a pitch deck for the next day while binging her latest Netflix series.

• • •

Tim coasted around the first corner of his Los Altos Hills residential street before thrusting it into second gear for stupid acceleration down the hill toward the interstate. He cranked the car audio system to a song from a Radiohead album he couldn't name but enjoyed occasionally. It was one of the ones after *OK Computer*. He lowered the two front side windows enough to defog the windows from the rain. He kept the RPMs high enough to maintain traction on the slick surface.

It took him slightly less time that he'd anticipated to make it to his destination, and he killed the headlights as he approached Alice's address. The sight of her and her friend at the front door meant he'd arrived a minute or two after them. Good, he thought. He parked and set his drone camera to the night vision setting. The rain had mellowed a little, allowing for some white noise to mask the sound of a drone flying around someone's dwelling. Tim was positioned across the street with a clear view of two sides of the one-story bungalow. He had a good idea of the floor plan, having picked up Sandra there once after a book club meeting. Using all his tactical know-how, he exited his vehicle with minimal danger of detection and placed the drone on the hood. Tim piloted the drone straight up fifteen feet and directed it across the street to the corner of Alice's bungalow. This new stealth model drone was hard to track by naked eye, making it crucial for Tim's virtual reality goggles to function properly. Through the onboard camera he was able to make out activity inside the two windows flanking the corner of the house. To the left was the front picture window and what appeared to be a comfortable, well-appointed media room with a sofa and book shelves. In the window to the right, facing the side lot, Tim could see Alice and her male guest in the kitchen area.

Tim's heart rate increased. He wasn't sure which emotion was governing him at present, admiration or jealousy. He'd been married nineteen faithful years and had come to realize that his visits with Alice meant more to him than networking. She was attractive and would have been attainable for Tim in his younger years as a high-flying tech professional on the ascent. A blur of domestic bliss had changed his reality and rendered him neutered. Guilt, shame, and fear regularly intercepted flirtations with women he encountered socially and professionally. Alice represented this, a potential fling, a flirtation unresolved, a lustful image in his secret mental scrapbook. His coffee meetings with her always reenergized his sex drive, which occasionally benefited Sandra. The optics weren't great for a married guy to be repeatedly drinking lattes with an attractive single woman, but it was always business. And now here she was "cheating" on him, if you looked at it in a certain way. A single woman pursuing happiness in the privacy of her own life. Tim maneuvered the drone for a better peek inside. It flew deeper into the lot only to find a curtain distorting the contents inside. It hovered higher for perspective and angled to the back for a new vantage point. Tim was being reckless and he knew it. Too much margin for error with hidden branches and other obstructions blocking the camera's night vision. He flew back to the original spot in time to catch a glimpse of the two figures inside moving to the front room. He retreated for safety and a wider lens shot. The rain was diffusing the purr of the drone but limiting visibility. Still, he was able to make out the identity of the male guest as the two entered the front room carrying glasses of red wine. Tim moved the drone in closer to confirm his first impression. It was clear. He looked away from the image to process his discovery. It stung.

Tim zoomed in on the errand boy like a rifle target. The thought entered his mind of being equipped to send a bullet through the picture window into the perpetrator's shaggy mop. For what? For crimes against domesticity. For crimes against maturing with dignity. For not having a goddamned minivan. For not having a high six-figure savings portfolio weighed down by a comically relentless river of family expenses and future liabilities.

"Click," Tim whispered aloud. The tactical weapon in his mind was lowered as he instructed the drone to return to base. Further curiosity was trumped by self-preservation. He needed to get back home, and nothing that would happen here was of any consequence, especially at the potential cost of mission failure. Tim removed his goggles and scooped up the drone as it landed softly on the hood. He slipped out of the neighborhood and bought a bag of crap coffee from the convenience store.

CHAPTER 102

UPON ARRIVAL TO ALICE'S HOUSE ON THE PENINSULA, Elliott made a series of phone calls sorting out his options. Alice turned some lights on, opened the mail, and turned on the television for an update. The ten o'clock news wasn't on yet, so she muted the sound. Elliott's eyes took in the decor of the bungalow as they made small talk about how Alice had come to be living on the peninsula. Her home seemed to be in transition from shabby chic to higher end contemporary. Framed watercolor prints competed for wall space with bolder, mixed media art and a notable abstract still life.

"What's the story with this one?" He pointed to it.

"A gift from my father. I saw it in a gallery in San Miguel, Mexico. He retired down there among the other reinvented expat painters and sculptors."

"It's nice. Definitely rules the room, doesn't it?" Elliott took a closer look, admiring the rich color palette and textural complexities. He made out the objects to be a paring knife, some kind of fruit or nut next to a cylindrical glass on a table, and a hilly landscape in the background. "Very pastoral." Elliott imagined himself in such a place, far away and free of the uncertainty looming over his head at the moment, living simply, listening to the wind and taking time to study the landscape for its beauty.

"I think so. It's my happy place. I meditate to it in my mind. Simple, quiet, tranquil."

Elliott added, "All it needs for me is a coast behind those hills. Put a board in the truck and go surf unmolested waves until my legs quit. And then I'll be back to help you finish that bottle of wine."

"You think it's wine? I always wonder. It could be water or tea. The color is noncommittal. And the lighting seems too early in the day."

"It's never too early in the day for an artist to imbibe. This is good, by the way. What is it?" Elliott swirled the wine around in the glass to see its color and body.

"Nothing special, Trader Joe's coastal pinot or something. Not the super cheapo but a good drinkable table wine."

"I thought all you tech superstars drank 1990 Petrus like orange juice."

"Hardly, although I know some who fit that profile. Is that what you require on your tour rider, thousand-dollar bottles of bordeaux?"

Elliott looked at her and winked. "Touché."

"I actually go on and off the wagon, if truth be told. I insert occasional mental health breaks in my drinking as a check and balance," she said.

"Smart," he replied.

Alice sat down on one end of the couch with both legs underneath her, a bare foot dangling over the edge of the cushion. She was at a forty-five degree angle facing Elliott, who remained standing on the area rug nearly under the arc that separated them from the other front room, which was dominated by a dining table. He struggled to decide on a seating option—join Alice on the sofa or sit opposite on a fluffy chair symbolic of a formality they both were fighting. Instead, he punted, buying precious minutes by feigning interest in one of her watercolors.

"How about this one?"

"Ha, a sentimental favorite at best. I think it's a remnant from my first apartment out of undergrad. Please don't judge."

Elliott passed it for a view of framed photographs on the fireplace mantel. He paused on the second one, making out a little girl getting on a yellow school bus as an attractive woman with feathered hair dragged on a cigarette.

"Mom, ever glamorous even while smoking."

"Smoking hot, if you don't mind me saying." The next photo was from the same era and featured what Elliott inferred to be a news broadcaster. "Your old man?" he asked. His eyes shifted to the television, having been reminded of the imminent news updates.

"Yes, he was with ABC for a long time. On their short list for the network news."

Elliott didn't press her for info. Having run out of mantel photos, he made his move to the sofa, joining her with glass in hand. "Well, you have a nice place here. Do you enjoy living alone?"

"I do." She sipped her wine before adding, "I mean, it's served me well. I'm not ruling out a different arrangement at some point, but I like my alone time and privacy. I get more than enough people time at work."

"I feel like some cats are going to come out of the woodwork any second now."

"Funny. Old cat lady I'm not. Definitely more of a dog kind of gal."

Elliott started to reply as Alice shifted her position to be closer to him. Elliott watched her while still muttering something about golden retrievers. She put her arm along the back of the sofa and took another drink of wine. Her body moved in a way that showed off her cleavage. She was bustier than he'd noticed before. A nice size that she could flaunt when necessary, which was now, he determined. Her body was speaking to him. He hated himself for thinking that she was of good stock, like something one of his family members would say at a Thanksgiving dinner. Elliott wasn't used to initiating contact. His modus operandi was to lure them into the shallow water and drown them in his own brand of aloof charm, which could sometimes be mistaken for disinterest. He was sensing that the move was his to make, but he struggled to find the right tool in the box.

Alice broke the moment with a sudden and final swig of her glass. "I'm going to rinse off; it's been a gross day. I've got an extra bedroom down the hall or there's this couch if you prefer. Whatever makes you comfortable. There's a television controller there and help yourself to anything in the fridge." She got up and checked the front door lock and switched off the outside lights.

"Hey," Elliott interrupted her. She stopped and studied him. "Thank you. For putting me up and everything."

She smiled and turned, continuing around a corner to part of the bungalow Elliott hadn't yet seen.

Elliott cringed at his inaction. She was testing him and he'd failed. Or in his mind he had. She wanted him to show some initiative, and instead he was following her lead. Women her age, their age, were aware of the running clock. Time wasn't as much a luxury in their mid- to late thirties as it was in their late twenties. A maturity gap was evident. Elliott didn't like to be reminded of his proclivity for boyishness. His armor of keen intellect and wry humor masked a vulnerable, damaged human, which he took pains to abandon. That layer of protection always grew back, quick to shed but slow to return. It was too late in this instance to make a move. He had to stew in his inaction and hope for redemption. A text message alert ended that thought, and he got up to investigate the sleeping options and to brush his teeth.

The sound of the shower running aroused him. Only a wall and a door lay between a mutual attraction that he had let linger. In a film the protagonist might claim his bounty through a purposefully unlocked door. Passion would prevail. But in real life dignity and tact would hold firm. It was another test. One of trust and patience. And subtle teasing. Meanwhile Elliott's heart sped up. He pictured her nude proportions in the steamy washroom and imagined her thinking of him, wishing for his initiative to engage. It was a siren song, that damn shower. His lustful trance was interrupted by another, this time unfamiliar, notification chime. He followed its sound to the kitchen counter where Alice's phone lay faceup. The lingering text read "Hey, gimme a shout asap," and it was from a Larry Chang.

Elliott, nonplussed at the intrusion, particularly from a "Larry," jettisoned the passion play for his own phone to check in on the real world. It wasn't good. The DA's office had published a list of arrest warrants with instructions for each to turn themselves in to any police precinct within twenty-four hours to avoid extra charges of obstruction of justice. Elliott was among the two hundred. His call with Freddy earlier had foreshadowed the news so, along with the visit to his apartment, it came as little surprise. A friend had arranged a loaner vehicle to get him up to the Sierras, but legal help was the next pressing need Elliott faced. Elliott decided against involving any more friends in order to protect them from conspiring with a fugitive. He would go dark and wait it out.

Alice emerged from her chambers with a towel around her head, wearing a bathrobe. She carried her empty glass toward Elliott, who was sitting on a stool at the counter. She reached for the open bottle of red.

"Catching up on emails. It's not looking good. City hall has me on their list of most wanted. Fuck me," Elliott said.

Alice raised an eyebrow at his comment and shrugged. "Well, we knew that was coming. Might as well roll with it. Your plan still to go up to the mountains tomorrow? Are you still against turning yourself in?"

"I want to see how it plays out, see what I'm charged with. They haven't tried calling or emailing, and I'm sure they can figure out my contact info. This whole thing sounds like a witch hunt."

"That's because it is," Alice said. Elliott sensed she was making a loaded pronouncement, one that would have a punch line if it were a joke. He processed the idea of a witch hunt and the fact that he was sharing a bottle of wine with an insider responsible, indirectly notwithstanding, to his predicament.

She continued. "Look, to a fairly large degree I'm party to this. They're throwing Task Lyst customers under the bus to placate the district attorney and survive a legal crisis. I got the company funded and now I'm totally embedded in a publicity stunt that's gonna ruin peoples' lives."

"You think the company is working with the DA? What makes you so sure?"

"The Baxter Morris murder and the recent airport thing have forced our hand. We have to cooperate." She finished her glass and poured another, topping off Elliott's too. "I hate that you and others are being caught up in it."

Elliott was quiet. The news didn't rattle him like he thought it should. He wasn't sure it mattered. He wasn't lily white regardless of a greater conspiracy and was at peace with his predicament. His intent had never been evil, but he knew that his darker nature had won out in agreeing to several of the Task Lyst operations. The taste of the fruit had been too seductive. The means were serving a greater end for him, one manifested in his creative pursuits. His crypto-proceeds were merely of value to him in their ability to feed the insatiable drive to write, record, and perform. The cycle of need and validation was to blame. What did it accomplish and where would it lead? Was it justifiable and worthy of his compromised values?

Elliott took another long, satisfying drink of wine and stared at an image on the wall of Alice's sitting room. It was a framed painting on which his eyes fixated. A coastal landscape done in a postimpressionist style. His focus was on what he presumed to be a white sail beyond the waves off a rocky point. It seemed more East Coast than West. The invisible sun and reflected clouds suggested the same. A lone vessel at sea. He spoke.

"The first task I did was to bash the windshield of some poor fucker's nine eleven. I might not have done it if it had been any other make or model. Something about it just seemed to justify the deed. The creative class getting priced out of the market by these hot-shot hedge fund managers and biz school douchebags. The dot-commers and their stock options. I bought the rhetoric hook, line, and BAM! I figured nobody got hurt, and it was a drop in the bucket for someone like that to get it repaired. And that was the worst thing I did." He looked over at Alice who was listening. She let him continue.

"After that it was just odds and ends, nothing inherently criminal that I was aware of. But the thing is, you don't know. You fulfill a task, an errand, a delivery . . . you don't ask questions . . ."

"But you cash the check," Alice finished his thought for him.

He nodded, "Yeah, you take the money."

Alice ran her free hand through her hair and placed the wine glass on the end table. She pulled her knees close to her chest. "It's no different than me guiding the company through a round of funding and to eventually go public, all the while knowing about the detritus building up in its wake. I took the money, the accolades, the personal satisfaction of a job well done, the power. I'm the Porsche driver who deserved to get a windshield bashed in."

Elliott looked over at her again. He forced a chuckle. "Geez, take it easy. Don't be so hard on yourself. Did I tell you about the mime outfit I wore for several weeks? Pathetic if not criminal." He continued with a complete history of his time in the employ as a mime.

"Did you report their threats to the police?"

"Yeah, right. I was going to admit to the authorities dressing as a mime and delivering unknown product."

Alice considered his sarcastic response for a moment and then laughed, spewing a mouthful of pinot. He joined her. They regained composure and then lost it again. Elliott made his way to the counter, tossed her a towel, and opened a second bottle of wine while she struggled to pull herself together. She held her side as if she'd broken a rib.

"Okay, don't look at me. I'm fine."

Elliott enacted the classic mime pose of being stuck behind glass, and the cycle of hysterics continued.

CHAPTER 103

TIM FOUND HIMSELF SITTING ALONE in the small glass conference room near the executive work cubicles. His phone clock said 9:15 a.m., Tuesday, December 8. It had been an eventful morning with all the overnight arrests and the publicity whirlwind. He noticed Alice arriving in a tan raincoat carrying an umbrella and her purse/computer tote over her shoulder. He wanted to ask how her evening went with the damn errand boy. His sardonic tone was called out by his rational self, who posited that it was none of his beeswax and he should stop spying on his friends and acting like a creep. Tim was connecting the dots, though, on this odd triangle taking shape.

His presence had been requested for an unscheduled meeting as soon as he'd arrived. Now he waited for the others. The coffee he'd brought in was less than appealing. It was cold and his internal hearth was already ablaze. It was annoying to wait and irked him even more not knowing the purpose of the meeting. He contemplated going back to his cubbyhole.

The posse arrived, led by Clay and Pierre. The company's newest hire, a human resources vice president, followed. They entered and Clay shut the door.

"Tim, I believe you've met Ms. Edgeworth," said Clay.

Tim feigned a smile and extended his hand to her. "Of course. Good morning, Monica."

"Hi, Tim," she said, shaking his hand.

Tim observed that Monica was anything but relaxed, displaying formal body language and unremarkable officewear. Her demeanor lacked any emotion, and Tim figured she'd make a decent-looking undertaker if things here went south. Tim shifted around in his seat.

Clay continued. "Tim, we've got a problem with the data breach. Forensic contractors reviewing our electronic records indicate that you downloaded a hard drive that may contain the data in question. You don't have authorization for this, and it raises a huge security question for your project and the company in general." Clay kept his eyes fixed on Tim's. Nothing was said for several seconds.

Tim answered. "Must have been inadvertent. I routinely download files."

"Mate, this one requires a password, and you're one of the few with access."

"I see." Tim remained still and studied the faces of his interrogators. "The inquisition, is that it? I'm the fall guy for the breach that saves the company? The roundup will be blamed on a manufactured security lapse caused by a contract hire. Remove the tumor and Task Lyst gets a clean bill of health. How much?"

Pierre jumped in. "Tim, you've given us little choice here. Your digital fingerprints are all over this. Unfortunately we can't unwind this without letting you go."

"How much?" Tim repeated.

Clay piped in. "Ms. Edgeworth has prepared an exit package for you. You'll agree to a noncompete clause and a comprehensive nondisclosure, and you'll receive full value of your vested shares, an enviable bounty by anyone of your station's standards."

Monica passed Tim his exit folder. Tim finally lowered his gaze and thumbed through the documents. He took five minutes reading the fine print, most of which he pondered existentially: Was his professional career over? Was there an escape pod he hadn't yet considered? He'd been here before but in less contentious circumstances. And what did Clay mean by "station"? Was that an underhanded slight at his being on the wrong side of forty-five? Either way, Tim knew he was in a bind. By violating an inconsequential security protocol, he had served himself up to be their scapegoat, a "get out of jail free card" that was, in reality, unconnected to any "data breach."

Tim could almost hear Clay saying, in that accent of his, "checkmate, mate."

"I'm going to need my lawyer to look at this." Tim closed the folder and leaned back.

Clay inhaled and tapped his pen on the table. "Tim, this is pretty cut and dry. You're being let go, not brought up on theft charges. We don't have to go down that road."

"Clay, I'm not an idiot. And I'm trying not to take this personally. I understand it's business. But I'm not going to go quietly if you're not showing me the respect and dignity I deserve. This is an exit package for a meddling sales associate. I'm director level and you know it. I'd rather drag this through the press—"

Clay stood up and leaned forward, interrupting Tim. "You'll be dragged through the courts is more like it."

Pierre pulled Clay back by his shoulder. "Tim, I think Clay is right. Nobody wins if this ends up on the ValleyWag blog or Page Six. What do you have in mind?"

Tim took a breath. "I want a mid-six-figure exit. I want a sterling reference. I want six months' severance with benefits. And you get my acknowledgement of a minor security lapse. I will valiantly fall on the sword, ensuring the public's faith in Task Lyst is restored."

Monica cleared her throat. "Tim, we're not in a position to negotiate that in this conference room." She looked at the others. "We'll need to take it to the board and make a decision. In the meantime, we'll need your identification card, your security code, and all logins. You'll be on leave effective immediately, but publicly you'll be taking some PTO days. We'll aim to resolve this in seventy-two hours."

CHAPTER 104

ALICE FOLLOWED TIM AND HIS SECURITY ESCORT down the stairs. He carried a box of items and lugged a saddlebag over his shoulder.

"Hey, Tim." She repeated it until she caught up to him at the turnstiles.

He stopped and turned to her. "I'm out."

She read his face. "Out?"

"Out. Done. Shit-canned."

"I'm calling you later. We need to talk." She hugged him.

Alice headed for the executive wing. She walked with purpose, ignoring the usual exchange of office pleasantries with coworkers. A voice called out from an office midstride.

"Alice, in here. Join us." It was Ned. He was chewing gum and sitting against the corner of a desk with arms crossed. Inside, Alice found Clay and Pierre at either end of a sofa.

"So your pal Tim crashed and burned, huh?" Ned continued.

"I have no idea. I saw him walking out."

Clay said, "He got a little careless on database security, and we had to let him go."

"Careless?"

"He caused the breach that released the names—"

"I'm not sure I follow," she said.

Clay sat forward and responded, "He violated security protocol. Look—"

Pierre spoke over Clay, "Our outside counsel feels we need to separate from him, and the board agrees. He's not taking it well."

Clay sat back and crossed his legs. "You're friendly with him. Maybe you can talk some sense and get him to sign his exit papers."

"Well, I don't know why you think I'd want to get involved in a human resources issue."

Ned answered, "Nobody wants to see him get dragged down by a criminal complaint that will be costly to his career and wallet."

Alice let the words settle before replying. "Criminal?"

"At best, he grossly mishandled some proprietary data. A full investigation, however, could find malicious intent," Clay said.

Ned checked his watch and cracked his knuckles before adding, "I'm sure it was just an oversight. A mistake. Which is why he needs to accept the consequences and move on. We'll make sure he has a soft landing. I need to jump into a call."

Ned exited while Alice processed the conversation, thinking back to meetings with Tim, searching for clues that might predicate something resembling nefarious practices.

"Alice, you up to this, or do we need to go to plan B?"

She studied Clay's body language. He was suddenly a bigger asshole than she'd initially feared. The condescension was palpable. His arms were crossed and his use of "we" indicated she was either for or against the inner circle of trust. She was being tested—for loyalty, competence, combativeness, it wasn't clear. But if it was bait, she took it. Or at least she wanted them to assume as much.

"Yeah, no problem. I'll talk to him. I'm sure he's just in shock mode and needs a couple of hours to clear his head. I'll get something set up for later today."

The meeting adjourned and Alice returned to her workspace. She ran several different scenarios in her head. In business school she'd learned everything but real-life decision-making. There was no accounting for the dilemma in which she now found herself. There wasn't a case study she could refer to. Minutes went by as she did the math, lost in thought. A calendar alert brought her back to reality. It was a reminder to touch base with Larry Chang about having lunch soon. The fortuity of the alert was a clear sign. Larry was the perfect sounding board for the drama that was playing out in front of her.

CHAPTER 105

ELLIOTT WAS DRIVING THE LOANER CAR UP TOWARD TRUCKEE on Interstate 80. A small contingent was working to see to it that he could avoid the heat as long as possible while his options were sorted. The older model Jeep Cherokee had a cassette player, so he drove to the soundtrack of a classic 1968 debut record, *Fantastic Expedition of Dillard & Clark.* It was a tape one of his musician pals gave him.

Elliott was in fair spirits given the circumstances of running from the law. It was a departure from a clichéd liberal-arts college-graduate life of rising debt and urban cynicism. And there was the irony of him potentially gaining some traction as a recording artist while in the midst of a legal conundrum. Something seismic was afoot. Not just for him but for San Francisco and Silicon Valley. The arts community was in lockstep with the technology sector in this publicity rinse cycle. A microcosm of greater unrest.

While the legal issue weighed on his mind, there was something that taxed more of his mental faculties. It was Alice. The evening before had been marked by the most elemental of human emotional drama. It was so in the moment that his criminal concerns had felt secondary. There was enough romantic tension at Alice's house the night before that Elliott was still radiating a natural rush of adrenaline. He replayed the scene again and again. Laughing hysterically at his mime role-play. The ease with which they interacted, patiently awaiting how the attraction would resolve itself. They were in no hurry. Eternity awaited and the immediate crisis only bonded them more. Somehow, and it wasn't just the legal drama, they avoided making rash advancements in their courtship. A second bottle of wine had rendered them both unable to take a romantic lead. They settled for light spooning and a gentle embrace, fully clothed, to be continued.

He remembered then that he had let slip his recent task of spying on her. She was alarmed by it, he recalled. She pressed Elliott for details, a little of which he provided, some he kept tucked away under the pretense of self-preservation. It was pretty clear there was another element to the narrative that would reveal itself. For Elliott, it was a question of who was this other party. He believed Alice to be preoccupied with this revelation as well. Driving east from Sacramento up the climb to the Sierras, Elliott mined his memory banks to connect the dots.

His phone rang.

"Freddy, my brother, what's the latest?"

"E-man, this shakedown is the talk of the town. You figure out a game plan?"

"I'm taking your original advice and going on a vacation."

"Can't blame ya. Let the dust settle. There's another thing."

"What's that?"

"You mentioned dressing up as a mime."

"Uh huh, not one of my prouder moments."

"What do mimes do?"

"What do they do? Well, they don't talk, they gesture."

"Right. I was thinking about that. It seems a little funny, don't ya think?"

"Freddy, help me out here."

"Well, besides being a white boy in white face, did you ever talk while you were miming and making deliveries?"

"Not me, man, I take my miming seriously."

"I bet you do, E. Well, think about that."

"I get it, a miming bird doesn't sing."

"I dunno, something like that. Well, I gotta jump. Got to get back to the ink. Be safe, E-man."

Elliott finished the call with Freddy and kept the car stereo off to decompress from his conversation. It was an odd exchange. Freddy wasn't an abstract conversationalist. The talk of mimes got him thinking. Maybe there was something symbolic to consider, and why hadn't he thought of it? What drove Freddy to bring it up now? Pantomime was an ancient form. A lost art. Elliott was sympathetic to its history and tradition without knowing much about it. In a hyperactive world of self-promotion and social media, mimes kept their mouths shut. It reminded him of the concept "show, don't tell." Stoic in their commitment, dignified in their discipline. Mimes represented something he could get behind. Perhaps he wasn't ashamed of his miming after all. It might even make a good future band project. Name it "Mime's Eye" or "Mime Vice."

Elliott tuned the FM radio dial and The Rolling Stones' "She's a Rainbow" bled from the speakers. The song took his mind away from Task Lyst and the Bay Area. It was Nicky Hopkins playing the intricate piano figure in 1967. Elliott was obsessed with that era of rock 'n' roll, particularly the British scene in '66 and '67. Swinging London was in the process of passing the torch to California's West Coast as the epicenter of cool. Brian Jones and Jimi Hendrix carried their androgynous fashion sense from Carnaby Street to the Monterey Pop Festival in June of that year, just as the Grateful Dead and Moby Grape were turning on. The Stones were in the midst of losing their grip temporarily. Drug busts and a struggle for the soul of the band were in full swing. Brian, the group's founder, had by now been rendered ambassador of decadence, partially by choice but also exacerbated by the sequence of events on a holiday road trip to Marrakesh. The essence of their music had gotten lost in a shroud of lysergic experimentation, country estate purchases, and the unholy trinity of Jagger-Richards-Oldham wrestling for control of the band's artistic and management direction. The mythology of Brian's demise could be traced on a map through Spain and across the Strait of Gibraltar into a mountain town where a mystical band of musicians performed as the Pipes of Joujouka. It had been Brian's intention to record these players and introduce their ancient music to the West. Accompanied by his main squeeze, Anita Pallenberg, and joined by fellow Stone Keith Richards, Brian directed the chauffeured Bentley south on a heading for Morocco. Brian's declining physical and mental health, coupled with a propensity for domestic violence, opened the door for Keith and Anita to abandon him and explore their growing mutual attraction. Another unholy trinity was cemented in lore.

Elliott hit the Call Back button on his phone's display. Freddy picked up right away.

"E-man, what's up?"

"You got me thinking. Let's say I decided to take a little more of a vacation, say, to somewhere harder to get to using my own passport."

"You bouncing to Brazil, my man?"

"It just occurred to me, there's a place I've always wanted to go, and, well, there's never been a better time to do it. You got anyone who can create fake papers? I obviously don't want to use the Task Lyst site for this right now."

"Man, you're serious. Let me think a little. Maybe Tecumseh would know better," Freddy said. There was a pause. " . . . you know, I might have a contact for you. Another one of my Chinatown cousins . . ."

CHAPTER 106

IT WASN'T LONG INTO TIM'S MOUNTAIN BIKE RIDE when the message appeared on his wristwatch. Alice wanted him to meet her for coffee before close of business, hinting at "developments." When Tim had left the office earlier, he'd decided to immediately head out for some exercise. Tim was tempted to keep with tradition by drowning the job loss in a bottle, telling the barkeep, "keep 'em coming." But he needed a clear head, and a long pedal up Skyline Boulevard would bring him the clarity he required. He didn't even mention his bummer morning to Sandra when they exchanged a drab text about a domestic issue. He did, however, solicit some legal advice from a friend. As for Alice, he wasn't sure how much he could trust her. She was gallivanting around with his rival, the errand boy. Maybe she deserved the benefit of Tim's doubt. A mile into his slow climb, he started to find the clarity he was looking for.

Tim played through different scenarios in his mind: take the insulting exit package or gamble for more. Potential legal issues rubbed at him like a new pair of shoes forming a blister. It made the most sense to cut and run, take the loss and the smaller windfall versus letting ego hold out for all or nothing. Cocktail napkin calculations had him currently walking with half a year's pay at $90,000 and vested stock options worth a hundred grand. If he doubled down, he could get shares that would net a million or two once the company completed a public offering. Had he stayed and prospered with the company, his long-term stake could have exceeded fifty million. Conversely, if the company tanked, he could be left holding a bag of funny money not worth the paper the shares were written on, not to mention the thousands he'd fronted the Bulgarians.

He recalled hearing his soccer-dad nemesis Trip Lerner describe a seven-figure exit as a requisite for Silicon Valley success. The dialogue was branded in his memory, Trip saying, "I don't take calls from anyone who hasn't either had an eight-figure exit or just finished undergrad at one of the HYPS: Harvard, Yale, Princeton, Stanford. Those theoretical guys coming out of Wharton and University of Chicago don't add up to dog meat. They should stay in academia. And I honestly don't know how you could escape the nineties in San Francisco without accruing a nest egg of at least twenty-five mill. Go back to Cleveland, Sparky; it's time for adult swim."

Tim's net worth, combined with his wife's stable income and 401k, was hardly the stuff of paupers. Not counting any family trusts or estate planning on either side of their family, Tim figured he was gaining on the three-million range once you added up all liquid investments and retirement accounts, home equity, school funds, hard assets, and an optimistic assessment of some family property in a flyover state. It was chump change in the professional circles in which he ran. Sure, there were plenty who had less, coworkers whom he truly respected, friends back home who never left, fraternity brothers who taught high school and coached lacrosse. But it was the paper billionaires who haunted Tim in his sleep. The ones who had "fuck you" money. Buy a yacht money. Retired at forty money. Jet-set around with your son and grease his way into the perfect college soccer program money. And there were the blue-blooded scions of the Upper East Side who multiplied their birthright fortunes despite never breaking a sweat. Tim was at the precipice of making his career. Losing this gig was going to make him either a mediocre success or an also-ran.

Tim felt his head twitch recounting Trip's monologue as he passed under a eucalyptus grove at around a thousand feet elevation. Pillar Point was visible off on the horizon, whitewater encroaching on the lighthouse above the cliff. Tim wasn't a surfer, but he was aware of the break and wanted to test out his new drone against the largest waves on the West Coast. Another day. Today he'd need to decide his Task Lyst fate, and Alice seemed to be holding the next piece of that puzzle.

CHAPTER 107

ALICE MET TIM WITH AN EXTENDED HUG and a sincere, "How you holding up? What did Sandra say?"

Tim wore a ball cap and fleece pullover and answered a defiant, "I'm fine. I went for an intense ride to clear my head and, you know, it's gonna work out. I'll be good. It's good."

Alice acted convinced and asked again about Sandra's reaction.

"I haven't told her. She's in meetings today, and I want to decompress a little. So, did they send you here to talk sense into me?"

Alice swallowed a sip of latte. "Of course. They asked me to convince you to settle before the whole thing gets too far. But I've got my own reasons to reach out. We've been friends a while, and I feel like I got you into this racket."

"Racket?"

She nodded. "Yes, I'm not proud of where this has gone. It's like my baby has become a monster, and I'm the helpless mom."

"Well, yesterday I would have argued that point. Today, maybe I concur."

Alice continued. "Look, this criminal shakedown doesn't pass the smell test. People are being brought in on trumped-up charges that will ruin careers and break up families. I'm not proud of this, and I didn't see it coming. But you've got to consider the likelihood of winning a pissing match against an entity as well funded as Task Lyst."

Tim listened and then answered. "Why are you so bent out of shape all of a sudden, why the change of heart?"

Alice sat back and looked out the window through the parking lot and watched the speeding freeway cars flash behind trees like ghosts one after another. It was a constant stream of colorful images. If she didn't know they were vehicles, they might represent some kind of abstract art installation or a picture show. It occurred to her they were going against commuter traffic, and the opposite lanes were stuck in gridlock. Such was life on the peninsula.

She answered, "I've got a friend who's facing an arrest warrant. I'm not sure which team I'm on anymore. It definitely has me reevaluating my professional goals."

"You're in a good position to make a ton of money if things progress according to plan," Tim said. "I would assume so at least, providing you negotiated a good piece of equity."

"I'd do well. But I'm not sure I'd walk away with my conscience intact."

"Do you doubt the company's ability to shed the dark shadow following it right now? Asking for a friend."

Alice replied, "Not really. The people, the resources, the ties to city hall and Sacramento. That's why I think you should consider taking the exit package and starting fresh. Just walk away. But know that I'm telling you this not because it's what they want, but because I think it's better for you and your family."

Alice heard herself say the words, letting them sit for a minute, hoping they would penetrate Tim's deserved stubbornness. She imagined what Elliott was up to and fought the impulse to check her phone for some kind of update from him. The pace at which things were progressing between them along with the external drama was exceeding her adrenaline comfort factor. She was tempted to go for a massage or put a mask on with some aromatherapy and herbal tea.

Tim interrupted her meditation. "So what is your friend charged with?"

Alice turned her focus back to Tim. "Oh, he's a . . . a musician, Elliott Temple. He did a bunch of different tasks and thinks some of them may have been illegal. Unbeknownst to him. Now he's holed up in the mountains weighing his options. He's pretty freaked out." Alice's answer trailed off as she thought about Elliott. She'd drop everything and drive up to meet him if circumstances allowed. But the publicity at Task Lyst meant she'd be taking no early weekends anytime soon.

Tim sighed. "Let me think about this all, and I'll give you a heads-up before I formally reply. I just need a few hours to process it all."

CHAPTER 108

ELLIOTT ASSIGNED HIMSELF THE NEW NAME of Jerome E. Garcia. He liked the cultural reference and the way it masked his Anglo heritage, figuring where he was headed it would help him blend in and avoid attention. Using the fake passport he received after a two-day turnaround, Elliott ordered supporting documents in the way of a permit to operate motor vehicles and a bank card. Online he bought a coach ticket to Barcelona by way of Amsterdam. The rest he'd do on the fly: itinerary, hotels, trains, currency exchange.

Elliott was antsy to remain under the radar, even in his hideaway cabin. He made some final tweaks to his cryptocurrency holdings and communicated some details to friends and family on where he'd be and how to reach him. Officially, he was heading out on a solo motorcycle ride from California to Austin, Texas. He framed it as a birthday present to himself. He'd be out of touch and only checking email sporadically. To his de facto manager and Alice, whom he felt he could trust, he revealed the true timeline and his ultimate destination, from where he'd be able to sort out his affairs.

He'd packed light when departing his apartment in San Francisco and opted against taking a six string guitar. Instead, he'd get by with a 1959 Martin ukulele his mom had passed down to him. It was a sentimental choice but also one that would keep him light on his feet and free of baggage carousels, cabbie trunks, and the obvious sign of an itinerant traveling musician. He had his laptop, phone, and a few changes of clothes all bundled into a duffel bag he could carry as a backpack. A pal would be picking up the borrowed car at the cottage, so Elliott stepped out onto the front porch of his temporary safe house and pulled the locked door shut. He looked out over Lake Tahoe as the sun peeked through the snow clouds, and he set out in search of the kind soul who would take him to Reno. He hadn't hitchhiked in ages and wondered if it was still a thing. Like, who would risk picking up a stranger anymore? Hitchhiking and riding freight trains pulled at his heartstrings as relics from a more innocent time. A time when uncles and aunts were fleeing the Vietnam draft and confounded by a domestic America in flames. Kerouac had spoiled the supposed post-war bliss for a new generation of mop-top hipsters and earth mothers who saw the Red Scare as no threat to their utopian ideas of grass, psychedelics, and outdoor music festivals. Elliott had bought in at an early age. It was those stories that moved him: the Stones and New Riders of the Purple Sage concerts, skiing Vail in blue jeans, bringing a trunk-load of Coors back to Chicago for thirsty mouths who wondered what Rocky Mountain spring water tasted like. In the seventies everyone was cashing checks that they couldn't cover by the time the eighties came around. Divorce, bankruptcies, and deaths reared their ugly truths. Elliott knew this fallout intimately, and it informed his worldview. He also knew that his chosen path, or the one chosen for him, wasn't as easy as alternatives that he'd sidestepped, like pursuing a graduate degree or jettisoning his artistic pursuits altogether. He'd been seized by the music bug, and it had never let go. Occasionally he'd escape into a straight job, but the pink slip always came.

It pissed Elliott off how easily he found his ride to Reno. He lugged his pack less than a mile into Tahoe City and fashioned a "Reno or bust" sign out of a cardboard box using a borrowed Sharpie from the gas station clerk. He hadn't yet staked out a prime spot to shake down the patrons when a couple pulled over who had just filled up their black Mercedes sedan.

"We are headed as far as Truckee and then west to the coast. Happy to help you get at least that far."

Elliott figured the interstate would be further toward his destination and a place where eighteen-wheelers might take sympathy on him. He climbed in. The middle-aged couple had been visiting their daughter, an aspiring ski racer turned "ski bum," and were making their way back to Marin County. The conversation was easy, and soon they offered to drive him out of their way to meet his plane. It was all Elliott could do to decline their generosity, but they insisted. He was careful to not reveal too much about his personal life but was amazed at the small-world connections the twenty-minute car ride produced. Mr. Bob was a lawyer in Corte Madera who had spent his early career working in the music business and now mainly handled outsourced contract work for Los Angeles and New York clients. Prompted by his wife, Brooke, he was adamant that Elliott hit him up with any legal questions whatsoever about his music and he'd be happy to negotiate any licensing or distribution deals on a pro bono basis. Elliott felt so at home with his chauffeur tandem that he was tempted to ask to see a picture of their daughter, Ashton, just in case.

CHAPTER 109

TIM PLAYED THE DIFFERENT SCENARIOS IN HIS MIND driving back from his meeting with Alice. It was a position of power in which he found himself. The company needed him to be the fall guy. Perhaps it was their master plan. Set him up to be the source of the leak and assign him blame for the security breach. This gave them a means for displaying cooperation with law enforcement and a way to negotiate public scrutiny over privacy concerns. Further, it was a demonstration of the power of the weapon. Like a nuclear bomb test, Task Lyst's mushroom cloud would include a few casualties while serving notice to prospective enterprise customers the potential of its platform.

Tim also lorded over the future of Alice's friend, the errand boy, Elliott. Tim held a grudge against the guy for not fulfilling his task report and for fraternizing with Alice. Put in this new context, however, Tim realized he didn't need to hold a grudge. In fact, he started to admire his former rival. An online search revealed a side to Elliott that shared much in common with Tim's own interests and path through adulthood. Tim appreciated his commitment to music and even found a few song clips rather enjoyable. And while Tim might have harbored some midlife-crisis-fueled romantic fantasies involving Alice, he accepted that her interest in Elliott need not be taken personally. She had helped him, there was no question. Tim's tenure with Task Lyst had been a resurgence, one that rebuilt his self-confidence. For this he should be thankful. He could parlay the experience, along with any financial proceeds, into something new. Why risk destroying that possibility? Take the losses with the gains and move on, build on it.

When Tim returned to his home office he put his thoughts to paper, combining his own predicament with Alice's and Elliott's. Each had their own personal interests to consider and all three, he found, were connected. He dialed Alice's mobile phone number, and she answered after the first ring.

"Tim, what's up?"

"I think I have a solution. It's a way for all of us to get what we want. I don't want to email it, but I'll tell you over the phone. You have a second?"

"Of course, let me just get some privacy." There was a short lag. "Okay, shoot."

"Our friend, Elliott . . . known around here as Geronimo69. I can get him off the hook. I know everything about his task history and even aided and abetted some of his activity. I have his file, which includes proof of Task Lyst's complicity in whatever criminal acts city hall is charging him with."

"Wait, so . . . are you thinking of threatening the company with taking the information public? Doesn't that jeopardize your own—"

"No, they won't call my bluff. Here's why: you'll broker the proposal and suggest that I'm concerned with some of my digital fingerprints that can be easily cleansed from the record. I'm willing to accept their terms if Geronimo69's involvement gets erased or reversed. We all walk with our hands clean."

"What about your deal? Are you content with their terms?"

"I am. As long as I get some expenses reimbursed. I floated our overseas developers fifty-six large to get the latest system-tracking tools online."

Alice answered, "Wait, you went out of pocket?"

"I had to. The budget Raj earmarked through year end was miniscule. I figured I'd make it back tenfold once—"

"I hope they'll cover it."

"You and me both. I'd take it in shares if it comes down to it."

"Okay, this sounds like a wise path forward, not to mention a great escape for Elliott."

Tim replied, "And are you cool with it? This should make you look good, having brokered a settlement. And your friend walks free."

"Sure, but I am so jaded and cynical, I'll need to be planning my own extraction from this nightmare."

"Doesn't have to be a nightmare for you. You'll have a nice exit if you can stick it out long enough."

"I'd settle for a physical exit. I'm over it."

CHAPTER 110

MONDAY MORNING ALICE MET WITH PIERRE, CLAY, AND MONICA Edgeworth and laid out Tim's proposal. She had scheduled the meeting close of business Friday and used the two days to prepare her pitch. There was more on the line than brokering someone's departure package. The nuance of her presentation could mean the difference between her being viewed as a competent new executive or betraying Judas. It would have been easier to sidestep the whole issue and let things fall as they would.

Her conversations with Elliott ended with him getting on a plane headed east out of Reno. He listened to her vague exit strategy about a coworker Tim getting fired and possibly having a way to get Elliott's charges dropped. Elliott warned her not to trust anyone associated with the company but gave his blessing to negotiate on his behalf. He offered little optimism that she'd be able to broker the deal she wanted, but he encouraged her nonetheless. Otherwise he was prepared to see where the chips fell and deal with them then. He invited Alice to meet him abroad, saying "Deal or no deal, come have an adventure. I'm buying." On the topic of his music, he had no news other than he might be working with the lawyer who'd picked him up while hitchhiking. Elliott said he believed in serendipity. He said goodbye as the boarding announcement was made.

The meeting took place in the same conference room where they'd fired Tim. Clay was anxious to cut to the chase.

"So you met with Tim. What'd he have to say?"

"He's bitter but philosophical about it all. Wants to put it behind him and move on."

Clay looked at Pierre to his left. "Okay, good. The terms?" He folded his arms across his chest.

"He's willing to accept our terms." A pause filled the air, as if they all knew another shoe would drop. "But he's nervous about legality issues around him and a certain task provider and he'd like to receive a, for lack of a better word, form of immunity."

"Meaning . . ."

"Meaning he wants to clean up his digital handprints vis-à-vis a specific case where he may have aided and abetted criminal behavior, however arbitrary. I assume during the process of developing the platform, he facilitated some activity with a user named Geronimo69."

"What exactly did he do, I wonder?" Clay looked over at Pierre, who entered the conversation.

"Did Tim indicate we'd be vulnerable as well? I imagine he'd only ask us to commit fraud if this was the case."

Alice shook her head. "I don't know for sure. I think he's concerned, what with all the legal brouhaha, there could be more collateral damage."

Clay piped back in. "So let me get this straight. Tim wants us to fix this file, and then he's good to sign on?"

"That and he has some expenses he wants reimbursed."

Clay looked at Pierre and back to Alice. "Right, have him fill out an expense report for Raj."

"It might be over Raj's pay grade. Tim fronted fifty-six thousand dollars to the Bulgarians to get the product tools prioritized."

"He did fucking what?" Clay was no longer seated and rubbed the back of his neck as if he'd just pulled a muscle.

Alice raised her palms in the air chest high. "Hey, I'm just the messenger."

Pierre intervened. "Can we call him?"

"Sure, he said he'd be available today."

They dialed up Tim to discuss the Elliott and expense matters and he answered.

"Hello, Tim, it's Pierre. Thanks for taking the time here. So about this case you were handling. What is it you are suggesting we do with this Geronimo69?"

"It was an error of judgment by me to manipulate his account. He was my default test account. I encouraged him to accept some tasks that he eventually got popped for. I worry that Task Lyst will get implicated in aiding and abetting a felony."

A pause ensued while they exchanged looks and whispers, briefly putting him on mute. Then Pierre spoke. "What's your suggested course of action?"

Tim's voice reassured over the speaker. "It's simple. We delete his file and notify city hall of the mistake. Your database won't have a record of specific tasks he was involved in. Only my backup, which I have in a very safe place, will. He'll walk. I'll walk. Nobody talks."

Alice sweated out the silence that followed. As much as possible, she manufactured empathy for her coworkers to show that she felt cornered, like a rabbit under the same snare. It was all she could do to keep from gloating like Tim surely was on the other end of the line. Clay gave her a stern, furrowed look, the kind that a teacher gives a student when they suspect cheating but can't prove it. She was careful not to counter with anything that would betray her lack of innocence.

She said, "I don't suppose we want legal involved."

Pierre was looking out the conference room glass but not at anything in particular. He cleared his throat and shifted his body in the chair. "No need for that, since this is a simple workflow issue. We need to expedite this and move on to matters of higher import. Tim, I trust Raj knows how to make the adjustment? Obviously your security clearance has expired."

"I can walk him through. We have an exit meeting already scheduled for today to reassign coders and UI team members. I can shoot over a signed copy of the termination agreement. When can I expect a countersignature?"

"Now what about this expense with the Bulgarians. I'm afraid you're on your own on that one. Nobody authorized fifty-six thousand extra funds."

Tim replied as if he'd anticipated the question. "Look, guys. I put everything I had into building those tools and scaling up the Task Lyst brand. I was even willing to put my own cash equity in to get the results we needed to be first to market. What's that worth? Fifty-six thousand? Five hundred sixty thousand? Fifty-six million? Fair's fair, and I'm not asking a lot here."

Pierre was silent for ten seconds. "Fine, have the paperwork to me by lunch, and we'll countersign and close the books on this. Best of luck to you."

They disconnected the call with Tim and processed the conversation before departing. Clay spoke first.

"Fifty-six fucking K my arse. Other than that, I've got no problem with it. This Geronimo69 guy doesn't know how lucky he is. He ought to buy a lottery ticket. But how can we be sure he doesn't talk?"

Pierre sighed. "Not sure it matters. What's he going to say: 'I should be in jail, too'?"

Alice jumped in. "If he hasn't been implicated yet—I mean, if he hasn't been brought in and charged with anything—it will be like he'd never been fingered at all."

"And what if he has? How do we get the DA to drop charges?" Clay said.

"I'm sure a conversation between Ned and Stuart can clear that up in a heartbeat," Pierre said. "Let's move forward. I want this deal done and a publicity campaign launched clarifying the breach and the measures taken to regain status quo."

Alice volunteered to see the agreement through and reached out to Raj about confirming his meeting with Tim that day to expedite the Geronimo69 file. Raj, with Tim's help, would see to it that the file would be removed from the database and showed little interest in asking why. Task Lyst was in the middle of both a legal hurdle and the excitement of high growth and high-profile market penetration, the likes that rivaled the highest flyers of recent Silicon Valley success stories. There were rumors of secret meetings with the largest tech giants, acquisition talks, and mergers, to go along with the imminent IPO plans. Pierre was flying to Dubai later that week for an international conference on blockchain issues. He'd be meeting with representatives from the largest players in banking and tech and flying private with several other Valley founders. As Alice exited the meeting Clay grabbed her arm, holding her behind as Pierre walked toward his next commitment.

"Something doesn't sit right with me about all this. I trust you have the interests of the company exclusively at heart." His eyes searched hers for any sign of truth or deceit. Alice wasn't used to being manhandled and was shocked by the way Clay was imposing his physicality into the conversation. After locking eyes with him in a battle of wills, she slowly looked down to where his hand clutched her arm and then raised her gaze again to meet his. Clay released his grip and Alice continued out of the conference room toward her workspace. She didn't stop but kept walking on by.

CHAPTER 111

IT WAS MONDAY MORNING *after the winter Rites of Pan Festival, and Jerome and Simon woke to the morning call to prayer. Simon stretched and groaned, commenting that it sounded like dogs wailing, "but not in a bad way." Jerome found it peaceful, an opportunity to be mindful and present. He lay supine, very still, and blinked away the sleep from his eyes to find pink and purple hues in the turquoise sky over the balcony. He was in the moment and that moment was somewhere new, far from where he'd come from, like he had aged beyond the mere days of his travels. But he didn't feel older, he felt energized. He thought of Dylan's line, "I was so much older then, I'm younger than that now."*

After their own morning rituals of cleaning up and having some tea, Jerome and Simon made their way to Fez for the midday arrival of some San Francisco friends. Simon would be starting his journey back to graduate school in England as the others arrived with a brief one-day overlap for day-tripping in Fez's legendary souk market and hiking the two peaks overlooking Chefchaouen on New Year's Eve day. Jerome and Simon would make the journey in indigenous clothing despite the challenging terrain. It had become a point of pride for them to assimilate to their surroundings and traverse the trail like Jesus and Muhammad had.

Simon was more than a curiosity for Jerome. They seemed to connect on levels that included sense of humor, a muted but distinct ambition, and a jaded worldview with hints at Western optimism. They made plans to stay connected whether it be Down Under, in the UK, the US, or elsewhere. Simon told Jerome he'd like him to be best man at his wedding if he ever married. Yet Jerome shared little detail about his past. He had begun experimenting with a new identity. Since Barcelona he'd been Jerome, or Jerry, and was elusive about how he'd ended up on the backpacking trail in Europe and Northern Africa. The continental divide afforded him an elastic application of fiction in his personal narrative. Simon likely granted him the benefit of the doubt since it seemed that Jerome's background wasn't too far from his own, based on education and conversation.

It was in the bazaar, or souk, of Fez where Jerome and Simon snuck up on Alice as she haggled with a rug vendor. Neither Jerome nor Simon had shaved since arriving, and their djellabas helped them further mesh into the surroundings. There had been sporadic updates from Alice when connectivity allowed. She seemed to have made great progress extricating Jerome from the legal web of Task Lyst, which paralleled the success Jerome was having getting his new music shopped to the Los Angeles music community. He encouraged her to take a week off and meet him in North Africa, telling her that she needed a vacation from the "Babylon of technology." He even paid for her flight with stockpiled cryptocurrency he dubbed "funny money." Jerome promised he wouldn't return to the Western world until he'd shed his Task Lyst past, winnings and all. She said she wouldn't travel alone to Morocco and hinted at bringing a friend, which Jerome agreed was a wise idea. Jerome insisted Simon stay the extra day in case Alice's friend was an attractive fit. Together they'd vanquish the Brian Jones ghost of unholy trinity past by traveling as a foursome and settling in a far-off land. They'd raise chickens and harvest artichokes and smoke their own kif. Jerome, jokingly, offered Simon first pick but warned of a recent history of sexual tension with Alice that might be tough to overcome.

Jerome pointed Alice out to Simon as they approached the vendor stall."

"Hallo, do you need guide? Or sleeping place? Americans? You like hashish?" He feigned smoking a joint.

At first Alice was startled. Undoubtedly she had spent her first hours in Morocco warding off advances of men offering to be her guide for hire. It was de rigueur for foreigners to have a local representative usher you through your travels to help translate, haggle, and simply to keep an endless assault of offers coming.

"Oh my god, Elliott, you've totally crossed over!" Alice said.

"Method tourism, we call it," Elliott said as they embraced. He twirled her around, laughing, as she marveled at his attire and facial growth. He introduced Simon. The three migrated to a mint tea vendor where they caught up on

the adventures of intercontinental travel. There was upgraded seating on the SFO to Madrid leg and delays getting to Marrakech. A lost bag was found and the train to Fez included livestock, which Tim had not prepared for. Elliott and Simon laughed along with Tim's self-deprecating discomfort with Moroccan overland transportation standards.

"I think you need a joint, my man. How about some hashish to help acclimatize." Elliott handed Tim some local kif and a match.

"Thought you'd never ask. What are we working with here, ten percent, twelve percent THC?" He sparked one up and held it in.

"Haven't the slightest. It's homegrown Rif Mountain north slope trip resin as far as I know. Mixed with a little tobacco." Elliott accepted the spliff back from Tim and forwarded it to Simon. Alice opted out, saying she was going to wait until she was feeling more settled in her surroundings.

"So Simon here, my brutha from a down undah mutha, is in grad school at, where'd you say, University of Kent in England? Studying something or other—"

"Early English literature, to teach—"

"Yeah, that." Elliott turned to Alice, "So, you came solo after all. What happened to bringing a travel companion?"

"Oh, Tim. He didn't make it"

Elliott raised an eyebrow, "Who's Tim?"

Alice answered for him. "He's your white knight. It's Tim who is unwinding you from the Task Lyst mess."

"Brilliant! So much intrigue here," Simon said.

"Not so fast, pal, we're not selling the book rights," Elliott said, pointing at his new friend.

Alice told the story of Tim's brainstorm and the negotiated deal. There had been some back and forth and a few moments of drama, but the public relations tempest left the company little time to get bogged down in a human resources entanglement. Some protests had turned violent, and accusations had surfaced of collusion between company brass and legal authorities. This pleased the law and order minority but royally ticked off the free speech and privacy advocates. Once Task Lyst had formally accepted Tim's terms and deleted Elliott's account from the database, Tim considered the Morocco trip as a quick getaway with his wife's approval. He needed a mental health vacation and offered to accompany Alice there before rerouting to Iceland on his own two-week drone photography sojourn.

"Well thanks, Tim in Iceland, I owe you one," Elliott said to the absent stranger.

Tim nodded. "It's the least I could do." He made eye contact with Elliott before pulling away. Alice continued, "Your song has made a real impact while this has all been going on. KHIP has been spinning it and people are treating it like an anthem for the times. You've really got something there." She fidgeted for a second and pulled up a photo on her phone which she handed to Elliott. It was her in front of a spray painted wall with the image of a peace sign and the devil's horns.

Elliott looked up at her.

"I know, right?" Alice said. "It's a thing!"

Simon was completely drawn into the story. "This is bonkers! You Yanks are a real-life Bonnie and Clyde!" Simon then pointed to his friend. "But I'm confused, you keep calling him Elliott?"

Elliott pulled his passport out of a pocket and tossed it on the table. They took turns checking it out as he explained his double identity. He said he'd been taking "precautions."

Simon shook his head and replied, "Fascinating. And are you still with this Task Lyst company, Alice?"

"At the moment, yes. I need to help them get into the new year or my professional reputation will suffer a lethal blow. I've got three and a half days to forget about all of it. But hey, we are looking to staff a London office." She turned the focus on Elliott, nudging his arm. "So have you made any plans?"

"I'm gonna have some tea and then show you guys around Fez before we return to Chefchaouen for a hike into the clouds. It's my new high."

"And what about after? Any word from Los Angeles?"

"Couple of offers brewing but still some doors to open. I'm enjoying my anonymity and will head east until my ill-begotten spoils run out: Santorini, Istanbul, Kathmandu, Phuket, and hopefully some waves on the North Shore.

Try to find some inspiration along the way, and some penance. I'm going to give away every cent of my Task Lyst money to orphanages, women's shelters and peace organizations, return penniless for a clean start. Maybe I'll pursue a new creative outlet, something dignified for a geezer my age. I have an idea I'm working through about how digitization is our generation's atomic power, a discovery with potential for good that devolves into a mortal threat to the very existence of life and the pursuit of happiness. Maybe you can help sell it. But first, here's to Brian, Keith, and Anita. And Task Lyst." They clinked teacups, and Elliott looked over at Simon. "Now that you know everything, we may have to kill ya." Elliott, still holding Alice's phone, looked back at the photo and laughed silently at the image of her standing in front of the graffiti mural, a populist shrine to his on-air earnestness. A spray-painted peace symbol behind to her right flanked by the rock "devil horns" one to her left. "Peace and rock," he said to himself. He imagined the queue of tourists awaiting their turn for a selfie. Then something caught his eye in the lower-left corner of the frame. He zeroed in closer, enlarging the photo using his thumbs. "Fuck," he mumbled, through clenched teeth. It was the stenciled mark of the Yellow Brotherhood, the same symbol from the hundreds of deliveries he carried out under the banner of not knowing.

JEROME (and the town he left behind)

The backstreets of this town I fell
in love with the danger but now you can't tell
and in the gold rush of ninety-nine
they speak of his ghost but there's nary a sound

Ooh ooh ooh, he probably saw it coming
Ooh ooh ooh, he knew it was time
falling asleep in a lazy boy chair
dreaming in technicolor, of love
where did it go?

The danger's gone not the billboard signs
Uncle Sam's been eating steak again, nobody
seems to mind you saw him once in a
convenience store
he winked at you on his way out the door

Ooh ooh ooh, he probably saw it coming
Ooh ooh ooh, he knew it was time
alone in the can, backed it up again
and freedom is what you wanted, and love
where did it go?

Since you've been away, it's been real hard
to keep it all together, to keep it all in tune
and since you've been away, it's been real hard
we got to keep it all together, we got to keep it all
in tune

All alone in the city at night
it's the priorities of the folks that ain't right
i miss the colorful sights and sounds
it'll take a good shaking to bring 'em back around

Ooh ooh ooh, he probably saw it coming
Ooh ooh ooh, he knew it was time
back in ninety-five, you took one last dive
and the markets rallied, for some
and why i don't know

KATHLEEN

Kathleen, I'm only making minimum
wage and this scene, has barely got me
making the grade

I'm only one break away
No more time for waiting around
to you it's only a dream
I know I'm gonna make it somehow

It's been a lonely lonely lonely lonely
long time

Kathleen, I know it's been hard on you
I've been gone and you've been carrying the weight of two

We'll take it on up the charts
Only time can arrest me now
and this is only the start
of something bigger than both of us

It's been a lonely lonely lonely lonely long time

Please stick around for my acceptance speech, yeah

Kathleen, I know you said that you are late
I got a song that's gonna make it all work out great

It's been a lonely lonely lonely lonely long time

Please stick around for my acceptance speech

Lonely long time
It's been a lonely lonely lonely lonely long time

ACKNOWLEDGEMENTS

	To	Task
✓	Family	Grateful for an immediate and extended family that supports my creative pursuits
✓	Wife	Ashley, my first A to Z proofreader and de facto agent who believed enough to pick up the phone and get me a pub deal. All this after not knowing I was writing a book
✓	Workshoppers	Humbled by the encouragement and invaluable critique from Miriam Mimms, Hunter Moore, Tarp Jones, Kim Bundy, KK Fox, James Kerr, Janet Karns, Matt Kimball, Loring Curry, Vivian Carmichael
✓	Vanderbilt MLAS	Life altering experience learning from Cecelia Tichi, Edward Friedman, Lorraine Lopez, Kate Daniels, Wade Ostrowski, John McCarthy, Leonard Folgarait, Holly Tucker and wonderful classmates
✓	(see above)	Dean Martin Rapisarda and letters of reference from "Coach" Richard Klausner and Alistair Millar.
✓	(also re: above)	Joe Henry (lyrics) and Roger Moutenot (music) for advising my Jack London capstone project which dovetailed into writing Task Lyst. And Tom Wagenbrenner for research assistance.
✓	Bands	Thank you Rolling Stones and Grateful Dead for inspiring parts of this novel and the author's life
✓	Bands, cont.	Blues x 5, Janitors of Anarchy, Illustrious Dreaded Burn Monkeys, August West, Emma Jean Psalm, Buckeye, Peat Roses, ik ben, Sin City, Scott 76, Upper Middle, Getdown Band, Stolen Faces, Elliott's The Golden Mean, some of my best times have been making noise with you.
✓	Book Team	Thanks Turner Publishing Company for rolling the dice on this: Todd Bottorff, Stephanie Beard, Heather Howell, Kathleen Timberlake, Kelley Blewster, Elizabeth Thorlton, and Carey Burch. Also, Phil Ollila at Ingram Content, huge thanks!

	To	Task
✓	Alt-weeklies	Hat tip to former colleagues at *SF Weekly, Village Voice, City Search, In Pgh, Nashville Scene* for doing important work. "Fishwrap" is a term of endearment.
✓	Friends	Glass raised to friends who informed the novel, proofread galleys, offered expertise, guidance, tea and sympathy, blurbs, withheld mockery, inspired me with your books and songs and life pursuits, accommodated my oranje mist on the pitch. Much gratitude. Peace and Rock!
✓	Mom and Dad	Thanks Mom, Dad, Katharine, Bob, Eileen, Joe
✓	Please	Support live music, local record & book stores, read newspapers and magazines

ABOUT THE AUTHOR

SCOTT HYLBERT identifies with each of the three main characters in Task Lyst having been a struggling musician, an aspiring media entrepreneur and a sideline dad looking for a career pivot. Born in Saginaw, Michigan, Scott spent most of his youth surfing in San Diego, before attending Denison University in Ohio to play soccer. He toiled in the alternative newsweekly and music businesses for over a decade before enrolling in a creative writing program at Vanderbilt University. In 2015, with his photographer wife Ashley, he opened a creative content studio and boutique event space in Nashville called White Avenue Studio. This is his first book although he's released several records as a recording artist and producer.

www.scotthylbert.net www.tasklystbook.com
Facebook: /TaskLystNovel
Twitter: @TaskLyst
Insta: @scotstoffersen
Linkedin: https://www.linkedin.com/in/alice-seegar-04b421184/

CPSIA information can be obtained
at www.ICGtesting.com
Printed in the USA
BVHW031600210719
554009BV00004B/10/P

9 781684 423170